ALSO BY BRIANNA WHITROCK

Never, Never
How To Make Out
The Art of French Kissing
Kissing Ezra Holtz (And Other Things I Did For Science)
The Liar's Guide to the Night Sky
Rebel Boys and Rescue Dogs -or- Things That Kiss With Teeth

With Sara Waxelbaum:
Margo Zimmerman Gets the Girl
Don't Forget To Breathe

A FROZEN THRONE

Brianna R. Whitrock

CORVUS HOUSE

For Tabitha.

Who loved Reyan and Kasia first. And whose story has been written in the
same ink as mine from the beginning.

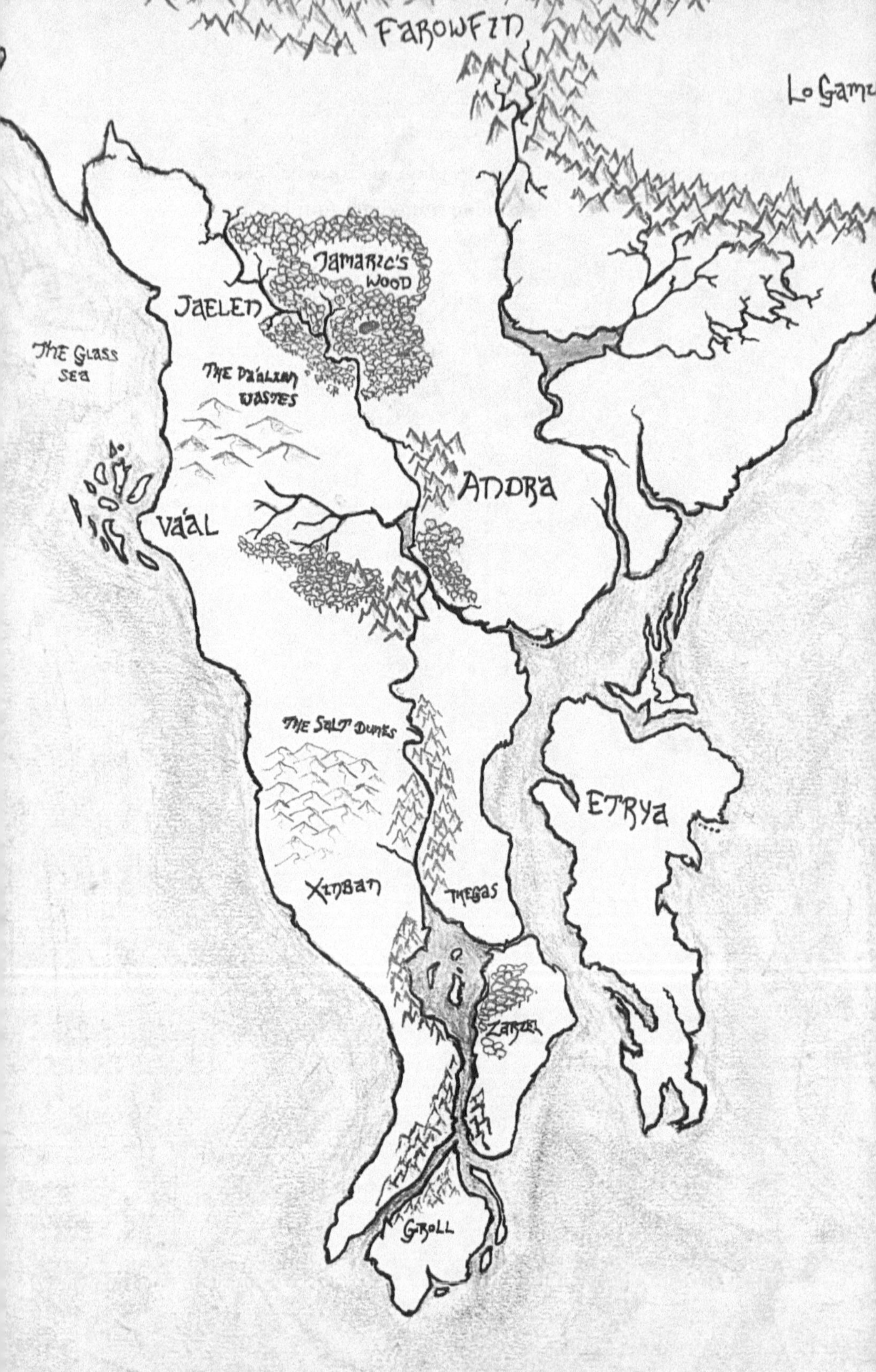

FAROWFIN
LO GAME
THE GLASS SEA
JAELEN
Jamaric's WOOD
THE DA'ALIAN WASTES
ANDRA
VA'AL
THE SALT DUNES
XINBAN
THEGAS
ETRYA
ZARZEI
GROLL

CONTENTS

PART ONE

The trouble was that none of the gods were worth Death's time.

Not anymore.

He'd wondered for ages—in the truest sense of the word—when they would get bored with the game, or at the very least, with one another. There was no one to wager with as to when, but if there had been, Death would have lost it all.

So, at one point or another, he'd simply receded. Stopped speaking, stopped paying attention to them altogether, and started paying attention to the world they loved to ruin. As it turned out, that was interesting.

When a person fought, they did it with teeth. When they bled, they did it with intention. And from this vantage point, the world was less of a messy bramble than it was a tapestry, with all the threads fitting together just a little wrong. There was no way to know whose fault the innate wrongness was. But it was there, pulsing and bleeding underneath the surface, purpling the earth as it spread. Beautiful, in the way of a bruise.

It had begun as fun, but now the world throbbed and changed and threatened to break at the whim of children. Jaelen, arguably the strongest power in the world—Thakros's player—stood at the edge of ruin, with a king who was too noble and afraid to truly rule. Farowfin stood cold and alone, cut off from many of its allies and liking it that way. And Etrya was poised to be the next to fall to the shadow in the south, the one Death had flicked off his fingers and allowed to begin eating the earth. It had been a god's fault; he'd broken the rules.

It had become messy. A hassle.

Death wondered if it wasn't time for all of this to end.

He'd wondered for years.

And so, Death had chosen a player. And he'd entered the game.

CHAPTER ONE

THE FIRST THING ANYONE ever asked Kasia was the name of the god who'd gifted her.

They used to ask after her:

Aren't you the girl who blinded the bowyer's boy?

They tell me the Webers—

—The beggars?

Yes. They tell me they ran the town before they met you.

Did you really burn down the temple with a priestess inside?

She hadn't. Not with the priestess inside.

Kasia had never had any use for death.

Aren't you

they had so often asked

a Vane?

Of course, that had all been when she was a girl—no one.

At twenty-two, she'd had for years what she'd clawed for all her life: the unmatchable power of a god's gift. And everyone had forgotten her name entirely.

They wouldn't soon. People would stop asking because they would all *know*. In hours, she would be queen.

That didn't mean it wasn't grating in the meantime.

That every minute she waited in this humid dressing room that was not *quite yet* hers, didn't scratch at her skin.

A servant girl worked on every strand of her hair, either attending her or keeping an eye on her, she couldn't say. The girl was Farowfin, one of her own, and that much, Kasia did appreciate.

She kept opening her mouth as though she wanted to speak, then closing it again, until Kasia said, "What?"

"Oh," said the girl. "Nothing. It's nothing."

"Say it."

"It's just—" The servant blew out a breath through her nose. "You're Kasia Vane."

The rush at her name being spoken like that nearly made her shudder.

"Did you really behead the Farowfin king?"

Kasia snorted. "Well, he was dead already."

The servant grinned and kept working. It wasn't long until the ceremony.

Kasia ran her fingernails down her dress, lightly enough not to fray it. Here, when they wedded, they wore the colors of their elements—air for her and frost for Reyan. The dress had been made when they'd gotten engaged, bright white and shimmering and close-fitting. She would wear Reyan's color. It dipped very low in the neck, held up by little threads that looked like ribbons of snowfall on the wind. Out of place in the wet heat—perhaps that was how Reyan felt all the time.

Her dark curls were piled everywhere, in a way that was utterly unfamiliar to her, several shiny strands spiraling out around her face, to her collarbone. They had painted her eyelids with silver that stood out against her light skin, lined them heavily with kohl. Her lips were pale. That was all wrong. It was...here. This place. And seeing it painted on her only made her more anxious for the binding to start. Only then would she be able to begin to relax.

At least they'd given her oil—the kind that made her skin smell of boronia petals; she would smell like home, and that was something. They'd also dusted her shoulders so they shimmered when they caught the light and wound dark silver around her in a pattern meant to mimic the wind, to recall the memory of snowfall. In this climate, she imagined they never saw snow apart from when Reyan summoned it. But in Farowfin, they knew it well. Bits of her home sprinkled into this ceremony that was entirely Jaelen.

Not that she had much of an attachment to home. But it was familiar, and she had an attachment to who she was, where she'd come from. So, she clung to the tiniest shreds of familiarity that made her who she was and ground her teeth waiting for what she would become.

She had been dying, begging, doing everything she could for this since she was a girl. Then she'd heard of Reyan.

Reyan, the king of Jaelen, was known across the realms for a good many things; hardly the least of those was power. He held more of it than perhaps any other royal on earth—at the moment. He sank into it quietly, like a slow storm, from his throne. And he wielded it like a weapon when he walked into a room. The first time she'd met him, she'd nearly felt it slice into her. *Here,* her heart had pumped through her chest, *in this country, with this man, you will change the world.*

She could hardly breathe past it. Her veins quickened, anticipation thrumming beneath her skin. This was it, was all that mattered. All that had mattered since she was a girl being ignored as her oaf of a father swept arrogantly through the room, gathering up her brothers.

She was moments away from having everything.

Somehow, just the sheer proximity of it made her nerves spike higher, like being this close was begging for it all to be taken away. She would hesitate a moment too long, slip down the stairs in front of them all, forget a word in the blessing, and Jaelen would crumble beneath her feet.

And she would wake up in Farowfin.

No one.

Alone.

Ignored.

She squared her shoulders, dusting of glitter winking in the beam of light that shone in through her window, and the first lonely trill of a violin wafted up the stairs and under her door. Her fingers tapped against her thighs. She wished she were the one playing it. It would soothe her nerves, perhaps, to grab hold of a violin's neck.

But that was not possible.

The servant girl smoothed the final errant strand of hair away from her face and smiled. Kasia felt a quick wave of affection for her—not just for being one of her own, but for knowing her name. So she asked, "What did you say your name was?"

The girl bowed at the neck. "Nagonia, my lady."

Kasia made a note to remember it, then rose. She crossed the threshold of the dressing room, and the violin sounded louder in her ears, and louder still when she descended the stairs. The rich fabric glided behind her, rippling like water and weighted like it. She was in bare feet—that was tradition in Farowfin. Bare feet so the earth of your home or family would stick to your toes and mingle with that of wherever it was you were going.

Kasia's feet were clean, but she could feel Farowfin clinging to them.

She stopped behind two large, arched doors that came to a point at the top. They were engraved with designs nearly as intricate as those in the silver paint that wound up her arms and legs.

The violin quieted.

"Lady," said a man beside her, bowing.

She didn't acknowledge him.

Then the doors groaned open, and Kasia's breath caught. This was nothing more than ceremony, not romantic like the stories she'd read as a child; this was politics.

But what was romance, really, if not something desperate?

Kasia was desperate.

The lights were dimmed, room lit only by candles that flickered on the walls and tables and hung from the ceiling. Everything bathed in candlelight and shadow. Five hundred people had come, at the very least. Dignitaries, royals, military. The captain of the guard bowed low to her, grey eyes that matched his hair twinkling when he did. They were all dressed in finery, staring intently at her as they spoke below their breath. She did not flinch back from the gazes that studied her. She paid them no mind; none of them expected a future queen to look them in the eye.

She did, however, meet Reyan's eyes. They were cold and quiet and locked on hers. His garments were black, from the buttoned silk at his throat to the shine at his shoes. But when he shifted, hands clasped in front of him, Kasia could see the little threads of a thousand colors woven into his simlah, into the soft fabric beneath that fell to his knees, shadowing the pants that covered his long legs. Everywhere, everything that touched him, each flicker illuminated another color—it was all of them, like the air, like the wind. Kasia's colors.

The violin started again, high and desolate, every note longing and beautiful. At this, the whispers of the crowd fell to nothing. Kasia watched Reyan watch her as she walked on silent feet to meet him under the bare olive wood archway. Other than half an instant in which his gaze flicked down to her naked feet, then snagged on her chest on the way back up, he didn't waver. His face was impassive, ice.

When she reached him, the music bled into silence, and he took her hand.

Kasia glanced down at their intertwined fingers—hers pale as starlight, his golden brown and powerful. Even the veins in his hands, the grip of his long fingers on hers, spoke of strength. She looked up and took a step so that she stood level with him. The king was tall, but so was she. Even in bare feet, he only had four inches on her.

She blinked slowly, holding his gaze. His jaw was locked. The few times she'd met him, he'd been polite, cordial. She'd flirted, and he'd laughed and agreed to a marriage, and that had been that.

But now, standing inches from his chest, this close to his eyes, touching his hands, she wondered for the first time if this hadn't been a mistake.

If only the gods of Farowfin were the sort that talked back, perhaps she would have asked.

She felt the eyes of five hundred important people on her, people who raised countries and crippled them, who formed the very world she lived in. All breathless. Over her.

Perhaps she wouldn't have asked after all.

It was far easier to leap at what you wanted and only beg answers and forgiveness if you slipped.

Reyan dropped her hands and backed to the other side of the arch, and she did the same. They'd rehearsed this twenty times.

Reyan would begin.

"For you," he said, eyes fixed on her. The recitation was rote and cold.

His hands remained by his sides, power in the nothing of it, and gentle ice crystals appeared on the ceiling. They glittered quietly and grew from the walls, reflecting the candlelight and cooling the room by degrees.

Appreciative murmurs from the crowd, the tiniest noises of delight from the few children there.

Kasia watched. She watched her future husband look right through her. She watched him bathe the hall in cold without any exertion to speak of. And she watched the people gathered react to a parlor trick.

The eyes of the gathered turned to her.

Kasia felt the breeze form in her fingertips, felt it sweetly blow outward, felt it do exactly as she was supposed to do: cause a perfect snowfall in the hall. It was to be beautiful. It was to be enchanting. *Charming.*

She gritted her teeth.

No. She had not come to charm them.

She had come to *dazzle* them.

Kasia grinned and said, "For you, king."

Something flickered in Reyan's eyes.

Kasia swept her hands in an arc, and the gentle snowfall that had elicited *oohs* and *aahs* from the so thoroughly charmed nobility spun into a rushing wave.

It spiraled up into the ceiling, bits of ice and snow collecting in a swirling chaos of weather.

A muscle in Reyan's jaw jerked, and a woman shouted as the frosted wind kicked up, and the fire blinked in and out.

She could turn this entire room into a wonder. Into a devastation.

She wanted them to know it.

Kasia clenched her hand into a fist and pulled the ice in a spiral around the archway, sent it to caress the king's throat and melt into his clothes, then let the frost wind die just a little. Moment by moment.

Until Reyan's ice, shattered into miniscule pieces, began to melt, and what fell was a rain.

The crowd was shining and wet.

The shimmer and silver paint dripped down Kasia's skin.

When she and the king met again beneath the arch, they were drenched in the water. Drenched in her.

Kasia smiled.

If Reyan was furious at the display, it did not show on his face.

To his credit, the priest hardly stuttered when he said, "Welcome, all gathered," and began speaking, words about alliance and loyalty and love, words she hardly heard. They didn't matter, really. Much of this didn't, and she suspected Reyan felt the same way. He never once flinched at a word, never showed a glimmer of feeling in those dark brown eyes. She mirrored him.

"*Shask'viernes.*"

Reyan lifted his fingers at the priest's command; this was tradition everywhere. Kasia followed.

The arch above them seemed to breathe, waiting.

"*Shask'vien.*"

Silently, little flecks of snow clouded out from Reyan's fingertips, crystallizing into ice when they bit into the air, and Kasia felt the wind shudder through her. It flowed from her hand, not nearly as quiet as Reyan's frost, and swirled with his, whipping the freckles of ice into ribbons around the naked archway.

A low rumble of murmurs went up from the gathered crowd, a delighted gasp here, an appreciative noise there. They made quite a sight, she figured, particularly after the stunt she'd just pulled—wind and frost, a pair not seen united in decades. Beautiful and cold and terribly dangerous.

Kasia had to fight not to choke on it.

As the snow and wind twisted above them, the priest said, "*Trist n'vell,*" and in that moment, something in the young king's eyes flickered. It was there and gone in a flash, so quickly Kasia could hardly puzzle it out. It wasn't warmth, wasn't kindness, desire. There was something...terribly sad about it. Frightening, almost.

A frown flitted across Kasia's face, and just like that, he was stone again. His fingers cooled around hers.

He blinked several times, too quickly, mouth a hard line, and brushed a single curl back from Kasia's face. Then, as the priest had told them to do, he bent down and kissed her.

His lips were cold, which was not unexpected. He tasted like snowfall. She wondered if the wind she'd summoned had her lips tasting of the spring or the autumn.

Reyan stood to his full height and turned toward the crowd when they were presented, allowing himself one small smile, and Kasia turned the raw force of hers on them. She would not show them her fear. Let them see power. Let them see crushing beauty. Let them see a queen.

Kasia had no crown yet, but she didn't need one.

As they passed, every person knelt.

CHAPTER TWO

Ri kept his head bowed, counting the divots in the stone floor. He had fallen to his knees, along with several others here—foreign dignitaries, princes, queens.

But Ri did not do it as a sign of respect. Ri was on his knees to better count the blades at the guests' hips. The king of Jaelen passed close enough to him that he felt the chill curl in his jacket. Close enough that he could make out exactly where the king's four blades lay beneath his clothes. He kept his eyes averted, straight black hair falling into them, and held his muscles tense as the king and queen passed out of the hall.

Ri's fingers itched to find his dagger; it was uncomfortable to go longer than a few minutes without touching it. But tonight was not about death, and Tallel willing, it would not be about defense. Tonight was simply about scouting. About familiarizing himself with the court and the major players in it. Even a tick toward the dagger strapped beneath his coat could have been a warning bell, given away an advantage. So he bowed. And when everyone rose, he rose.

He followed the throng into the banquet hall, moved smoothly and quickly, and sat where he saw his name. The one he'd been given, at least: Haru, ambassador of Etrya. He was seated next to Gwin of Jaelen, a woman whose name alone made him groan in annoyance. He'd met her once or twice in his dealings with nobility and gone away exhausted every time.

"You're from…" She furrowed her brow.

"Etrya. I have very few dealings at court."

"Oh." She said it dismissively, with a wave of her jewelry-laden fingers. "Yes, I'd wager that's true, what with the skirmishes going on there."

Ri smiled tightly and raised his glass of wine toward the older woman. "To peace, then," he said.

She smiled. The crow's feet around her eyes deepened. "To peace."

Ri did not plan to bring peace.

Ri would bring war.

Perhaps it showed on his face. At any rate, the woman suddenly seemed to find herself in a hurry and left him alone to observe. To wait. To drink.

People murmured and shifted and laughed—ten minutes seated and many of the guests were well on their way to getting drunk. Ri laughed to himself. It would take a lot more than this to affect him. At home, they drank wine and mead from childhood. It took a great deal of alcohol to make an Etryan sway on his feet.

The doors to the massive dining hall opened again, and everyone rose. The king and new queen walked in arm in arm, and Ri swore he could feel the ice and wind on his skin. The room may very well have dropped several degrees, just from their presence in it. Often, when fire and water united, the wedding and reception were a passionate affair. It was a stereotype but an earned one. Ri had never seen water and wind. But everyone saw it now, and what they saw was stillness.

The room sat and quieted simply to hear their footsteps. They cut a sharp line through the aisle, passing all the tables (of which there were a great many) and coming to rest in the middle of the grand, empty dance floor that the dining hall opened up into. It transformed there from the polished grey stone of the dining hall into glittering windows—windows that opened up to show the black night and sparkling stars over the grasses. The floor itself shone as though it were made of glass. It gave the whimsical illusion that the young king and younger queen stood solid on top of a lake.

The king, Reyan, was purported to be a fan of the violin, and this ceremony had proven it—every phase of the wedding had been led by the high, whining vibrato of the strings.

But Jaelenian tradition dictated that, when a man and woman married, it was the bride who commanded the reception. She had chosen the wine—rich, velvet red that dried in the throat and snaked slowly through the veins like chocolate—had chosen the colors in the hall—blue so pale it looked almost white, and another so dark some might have thought it black—and she had chosen what they would dance.

Ri found himself watching more closely than he intended as a cello and a quiet Farowfin drum began to lilt a song he did not recognize. The king slid his hand down the queen's back—delicately, as if she were made of frost and the slightest touch would crumble her away.

The cello and the drum combined in such an odd way that Ri could not pry his ears from listening, and the king and queen combined into something even stranger. Their dance was careful and calculated, punctuated with moments of emotion—a tap of his finger against her lower back, the slightest tightening of hers around his neck.

Ri jumped when he heard a whisper in his ear: "Ambassador Haru, you haven't finished your wine."

And he turned as the last strains of the music died, and the king and queen bowed to one another—he at the waist, she at the neck.

He turned to find what looked like a servant girl—six or seven years younger than he, he wagered. Twenty-one? Twenty-two? She had pale skin, like the new queen's, and wide brown eyes that shone with knowledge.

"Dance with me, ambassador?"

Ri narrowed his eyes. She wasn't in finery like everyone else here; her dress was short and simple, hair loose and light. "You aren't serving?"

"Not at the moment. Dance with me," she said.

He stood and held out his hand as the full band began to play—something lively, Jaelenian. Jaelen hardly had sad songs at all; it had rarely had reason to write them.

The girl took his hand, and they walked together to the dance floor. The surety with which she caught his eye when she slid her small hand up to his neck and the solid grip of her fingers in his made him wonder.

He spun her, and they fell into line with everyone else on the floor, colors flashing, bodies whirling. Ri simply looked.

"No reason to hold me at arm's length just because the dance is quick, ambassador," said the girl, and Ri pulled her immediately closer.

"What is your name?" he whispered in her ear as they moved.

"Nagonia."

"And who are you, Nagonia?"

She was close enough that her lips brushed the shell of his ear when she said, "Handmaiden to the queen."

Ri's pulse spiked, and he waited a breath before he spoke. His next words needed to be chosen very, very carefully. "And? How do you find your position?"

The girl could answer the question, "To my liking," or "I've worked under better conditions," and nothing would matter. They would finish the dance, and he would bow to her and stalk through the halls.

As it was, she whispered so softly he could hardly hear it, "Up the stairs to the right. You need clearance to get past the doorway that winds you down into the queen's room."

"And you have it?" said Ri.

Nagonia pulled back and smiled.

The dance ended.

Ri felt, for an instant, the assessing gaze of the queen caressing his cheek. And he glanced her way before slipping his hand down Nagonia's back.

"I'm sorry," he whispered.

Nagonia laughed and stood on her tiptoes, sliding her fingers up his throat and letting them rest at his ear. "Don't be. Disappear with me somewhere private. And leave like you mean it."

He dipped his hand low enough that perhaps the queen would look away. Perhaps she would be embarrassed. Everyone else was certainly giving them a wide berth. Not that they were behaving entirely inappropriately; it was a revel, after all. But that didn't mean everyone would be comfortable with it. He pulled Nagonia closer and glanced up. The queen had not averted her eyes and didn't, even when he locked his gaze with her.

Nagonia was the only bit of familiarity to her in the room—the only Farowfin girl in miles. And she was her handmaiden; she would draw attention.

Ri caught Nagonia's ear between his teeth, eyes on the queen's, and she finally blinked away, fixing her attention on her husband.

Ri and Nagonia disappeared.

He followed her into a closet, and her hands linked in his pants for the benefit of passersby. She laughed high and loud at nothing, then shut the door behind them and shoved the lock in place.

"Are you not Farowfin?" he said the moment the door was shut behind them. She removed her hand.

"My father is Farowfin. My mother, however, is Etryan. I've never set foot in the north."

Ri blinked. "So you're…you're Etryan. Like me." Just saying it relaxed Ri's mind in a way he knew was dangerous. But a breath of home whispered in his ear, and gods, he'd never been able to ignore it.

Nagonia raised an eyebrow and spread her arms. "Do I not look it? Best not to assume."

Heat flooded Ri's face at the mistake, and several mumbled voices floated through the door. There was a light thump as someone leaned against it, and Ri rolled his eyes, then hit his fist on the door.

Nagonia responded by knocking over a mop and making a high noise from the back of her throat that was clear enough in its meaning to make even Ri blush.

There was an immediate shuffling in the hall and the sound of very quick footsteps as they all left.

Nagonia laughed. Ri grinned.

"Tell me your name," said Nagonia.

"Haru."

She pursed her lips. "I've given you my name. You give me yours."

His nostrils flared lightly, in nervousness. But he said, after a beat of hesitance, "Ri."

"Mm. I was told you would come."

"Were you?"

"Were you not told about me?"

Ri leaned against the wall and folded his arms across his chest. "I was told I would have a contact."

"Well. Here I am."

He ran his tongue over his teeth. "You know what it is I am here to do."

"Yes."

"Is your mistress so cruel?" he said.

Nagonia laughed. "My mistress, I hardly know. But no, I wouldn't call her cruel. I would call her Farowfin. And I would call her entirely unconcerned about *my* country. About yours. She and Reyan will side with Andra in the conflict. Andra is too large and too rich and too valuable an ally for him not to, what with all the money he's bleeding on trade and the displaced refugees coming in from the south. He will ally with them, and Etrya will fall. We have no choice, you and I."

"Even if she dies, Jaelen will never see the widowed king united with our country."

Nagonia laughed. "I'm not a fool. Etrya will never wield the power to change the landscape of the world. But I want them safe. I want them not *annihilated.* And if we do as Va'al has paid us, they've promised—"

"An alliance." He'd been testing her, and she knew it. But she had passed. She knew everything, and no amount of sentiment for a queen or loyalty to her Farowfin blood would deter her. No. He could see it now—Etryan fire burning behind her eyes. There was a specific kind of loyalty, a particular fierce want that he'd never known in anyone but his own. And the way Nagonia looked at him now, he could feel those flames licking at his bones.

"With Va'al our allies," she said, "Etrya cannot fall."

Ri reached out, and gripped the back of Nagonia's neck, forehead touched to hers. She mimicked him. It was a vow in Etrya, one it would be a terrible disgrace to break.

"When I return, you will help me," he said.

"When you return, I will help Etrya."

Ri shut his eyes.

They released each other, and Nagonia said, "I only wish you could do this now."

Ri shook his head. "I need time if I'm to set this up to look like an Andran assassination. And anyway, it's their wedding night. In hours, they'll be so tangled in one another, I couldn't hope to find her alone."

Nagonia snorted and ruffled her hair, bit her lips so they'd look kissed, then left the closet. Ri rumpled his clothes and followed behind her.

CHAPTER THREE

REYAN COULD NOT REMEMBER the last time he'd hated someone so thoroughly. It was a struggle to recall if he *ever* had. Kasia shut the door behind them, and they were alone in the suite. He wanted to take off everything above the waist that choked him, so he wouldn't strangle here in the closeness of the room, but he didn't want to give his new wife any ideas. So he brushed his fingers over the silk at his neck and leaned against the dresser, and said nothing.

Kasia had situated herself against the bed, which put her a decent distance from him. Every curve on her body was so readily apparent in the damn dress—the press of her breasts against the silver, the smooth arcs of her hips and stomach. He could practically feel himself sweating. The room had always felt too massive to Reyan, the four-poster bed absurdly large, the bathroom, a cavern. But with Kasia leaning there against the post, dark hair curling against too much bared alabaster skin, he suddenly felt that everything in here was too small.

She watched him quietly, eyes sharp and assessing. He could smell the coldness on her, the desperate desire for power she suppressed, folded neatly and tucked behind her ribcage. The girl was dismissive and arrogant and manipulative; it had taken a single meeting to see that. And yet, he'd agreed to marry her. Because Jaelen was large enough a city-state that peace with anyone was constantly teetering on a knife's edge, and an alliance with Farowfin made far and away the most political sense. They were the farthest from the growing shadow in the south, wealthy, and boasted the most lauded military by a large margin, apart from his own country's.

That, and he wanted his queen to be able to work the wind. His father had begged him on his deathbed to join with fire when the time came. It was safe, it was tradition.

It was shit.

Reyan would not control anyone. And he refused to be controlled.

So he'd married her, and now when he looked at her, it took everything in him not to let his lip curl at the sight of her. She was beautiful, almost devastatingly so—when he'd seen her parting the crowd and walking toward him covered in his colors, in bare feet and silver like lace on her skin, coy smile on her lips, his knees had nearly buckled. But that was nothing next to the hundred things about her that he hated.

"I don't expect anything." His voice sliced into the quiet when it shifted from uncomfortable to intolerable.

"What?" she asked, blinking.

"From you. Tonight. I don't...I don't expect...anything."

The girl threw her head back and laughed. Loudly. "Oh, how chivalrous of you."

Reyan blinked.

"Did you think I was scared of you? Did you wonder if I was *nervous*?" She smiled a predator's smile. "There is very little that makes me nervous."

He ground his teeth together and shook his head. "I only meant—"

"I know what you meant, boy king."

A muscle twitched in Reyan's jaw. Most people, he knew, only called him that when they thought he couldn't hear. Remnants of being given a throne at fifteen. The title had been whispered when he had ascended to rule, and it had never quite died. People had called him many things, but none he hated more than that.

"Do not call me 'boy king'," he said.

"Why? Is that not what you are?"

Reyan nearly choked on the swift anger that flared up in him. "I'm twenty-seven, Kasia. Older than you."

"Oh. That's the first time I've heard you use my name. Careful, King, your tongue is slipping already."

"It will not be slipping elsewhere."

She laughed again, long, dark hair sliding over her collarbone, and said, "All right."

Reyan couldn't decide whether the skepticism he heard came from her mouth or his head.

Kasia leaned harder against the bed, sinking down into it. She flicked her fingers, and a little gust of wind blew up from her hand, wind that smelled like springtime. She'd tasted like spring when he'd kissed her.

"Don't," he snapped.

"Don't what?" The wind curled higher from her fingertips.

"I'm exhausted. Please, could you not—"

"*You're* exhausted, so *I* should have to stop—"

A little burst of cold and ice let loose from Reyan's chest and caught on the wind. Then, it fell to the ground and shattered.

"Oh," said Kasia, amused lilt to her voice. Her dark eyebrow rose mockingly.

"Gods. Please." He didn't want to sound desperate, but he was beyond weary. At all of this. At this arrogant poisoned dart of a girl and the weight of a kingdom that sometimes threatened to crush his bones into dust. At the looming threat they all kept whispering from the south, and the vulnerability of Jaelen to damn near everyone in the realm that required a political alliance with a country he'd hated for years. Since his mother's death had introduced him to the concept of hate.

He suspected the murder of his mother had something to do with his father's desperate insistence that he ally with Andra over Farowfin. But the shadow in the south only grew, and at some point, it had grown large enough that Reyan had been forced to take steps to contend with it, if the time came. And it would.

And history or no, hatred or no, Farowfin was by far the superior choice. Everyone, his father included, knew it. Even then. So he had waited until he was old enough to marry and far enough from his grief, until the southern threat had grown large enough that it was impossible to ignore, and then he'd pursued Kasia. He'd made several visits to the Farowfin palace, flirted, whispered to her in dark little alcoves. He hadn't fooled her, certainly, into believing it was entirely apolitical, but it had been enough. Her family was extremely receptive—of course they were. They had nothing, had come from nothing. Her family had built a name based on lies and cheats and things that had pulled them out of poverty but hadn't exactly given them a sterling reputation. They had been on the outside of nobility and always would be.

And then a god had given Kasia a gift.

And suddenly, kings were coming around.

And Reyan was not just a king. He was a King, and he knew it.

It had been easy.

Visits had always been timed perfectly, everything had been so simple about it. Simpler than politics were supposed to be. And now, she was here.

He was beginning to regret it already. She wasn't just a Farowfin girl; she was the whole damn country personified.

"Are you all right?" said Kasia, tilting her head.

Reyan leaned his head back and shut his eyes, dark waves of hair spreading over the wall. "I am tired," he said.

"And angry, it seems." He looked down at her through hooded eyes, and she knelt. Her gown slipped from her shoulders. "I apologize for my existence, boy king."

Reyan slammed his hand down on the dresser he leaned against, and Kasia jumped, but he could see the grin digging into her cheeks, even though her face was turned toward the ground.

"I am your king," he said.

She looked up at him from the ground, eyes suddenly fierce. "And I am your *queen*. Perhaps it is you who should be afraid of me."

A muscle jerked in his jaw. "I fear no one," he said, and Kasia's light laughter followed him into the bathroom.

He wished he had a door to slam.

He didn't. So, he drew a bath so hot it would almost scald him and stripped down to nothing, hoping like hells his wife wouldn't take it upon herself to follow him in here, then sank into it. It was a bath big enough for four people—six, if no one minded being a bit uncomfortable. Carved into the floor and painted with fifty little scenes—some sensual, some violent. Sometimes the two went together. His great-great-grandfather had had it made when his family had taken the throne, because he said he rather missed the odd comfort of being able to enter a public bath house. He hadn't wanted to use the rest of the palace baths; he'd wanted his own private rooms modeled after one instead. They were always hot, always felt like power.

Reyan ducked under the water, letting the heat sting his eyelids and water drench his hair. He needed this. Needed this moment to think of nothing. Nothing but the steaming water lapping over him.

"King?" he heard. He stayed under for a moment longer than he should have, then forced his face up out of the water. "Would you prefer I call you Reyan?" she purred.

"Call me almost whatever you wish."

Kasia grinned at the "almost".

Water streamed down Reyan's face and chest. Kasia had changed out of her wedding gown. Now, she wore a little silver slip of a thing—hardly worth taking note of, it had so little fabric. It was obvious what she was trying to do. Heat flared below his hips. He snarled, and amusement tugged at the corners of her lips.

She lay on the cold bathroom floor so that he couldn't really see her unless he chose to look. He did not.

"Tell me why you chose to marry me," she said, and whatever he had expected her to say, it had not been that.

"You first."

"I'm unused to being commanded."

"So am I."

Silence hung there for a while, a silence Reyan was not inclined to break. He would have been perfectly happy if she didn't speak at all for the rest of the night. The rest of the week.

"I chose to marry you because it made political sense, Reyan. And because when I met you, it turned out that not only was your country the most sensible to ally with, but that you yourself were the kind of handsome that injures people if they look at you for too long."

Reyan smiled a bit, despite himself.

"Shall I stroke your ego more?"

The smile thinned.

"The moment I heard your name, I knew this was what I wanted. Because you and I both stood to gain spectacular things from it. I would have never been anyone in Farowfin because of my idiot brother, and the incompetent rest of my family, and you cannot defend your borders against your enemies and against the shadow in the south, both. You'd have to choose." She paused, then said, "Without me."

Reyan leaned back and stared at the ceiling. It was unfinished—wooden beams and rafters that had eventually been coated in such a way that they would not rot.

"I chose you," he said, "because of war. And borders. And politics. And because the Andran girl was fire. I chose you because I did not wish to have my frost melted by flame."

"And I do not wish for my wind to be tamped down by earth."

Water and wind, after all, did not balance one another. They did not soften each other into something manageable, sensible.

No, water and wind could choose to be a hurricane.

He wondered for a moment what her options might have been—who they might have been. And it struck him that they had done this for the same reasons.

It didn't cool the hatred in his veins. She was still Farowfin, when it came down to it. Would always be one of them. Still moved with such arrogance he marveled that no one could taste it when she walked past. He could feel the ruthlessness, the calculation, behind every damn word she said, every move she made. It didn't make him hate her, or any of this, any less. But it made him wonder. The realization that if she was telling the truth—and he wagered she was—they wanted the same things. And neither of them would do a thing to dampen the other.

Suddenly, the bath water shifted, and Reyan scrambled back. He didn't lay eyes on Kasia until she was already chest-deep in water across from him, shimmer from her shoulders floating in the water like snowfall.

"What are you doing?" he said.

"Is this not allowed? We *are* married. I don't think any of the gods frown upon bathing together when you're husband and wife."

Reyan's jaw locked, and his throat bobbed. Kasia laughed. "Unless there's some stigma up here in Jaelen about things like this, and you're struggling to move past it."

Reyan rolled his eyes, and Kasia brought her elbows up out of the bath, hair floating on the water, covering most of her in shadow. Her leg brushed against his, and he forced himself to remain still. To remain ice. Instinct compelled him to look down. His skin was so dark compared to hers.

"No," he said, little laugh riding the word. "None of our gods care what we do with our bodies, married or not. And I can assure you, I've never struggled with it."

"Then this shouldn't be a problem."

Reyan locked his jaw and let the water around them go cold.

Kasia narrowed her eyes, and Reyan turned away from her and rose from the bath, wrapping a towel around his waist as quickly as he could find one.

"You know, our marriage isn't even valid until we—"

"I know," he said, voice harsh. And he'd intended it. "I'm tired."

Kasia snorted. "Did you not feel it back there under the arch? How electric we could be if we gave ourselves over to it, Reyan?"

His body responded frustratingly to the way her tongue wrapped around his name. "Kasia."

"We are blessed, King. Blessed by the gods in more ways than one. This union is blessed, or will be, when it's…when we bind together. When it's validated. And you and I could be a force the realms have never seen."

Reyan stalked out of the bathroom without another word. He got dressed before Kasia had the chance to follow him, and descended the steep stone stairs that led from their rooms. He spent the rest of the night in his shrine, wrestling with unchecked rage over his Farowfin wife and begging the gods for sign that he'd made a mistake.

CHAPTER FOUR

THE DOCKS WERE NEXT to empty today. Gallien wagered it had something to do with the sky. Really, it had everything to do with the sea and the promises the sky made for it. It was a dark purplish at the moment, striped through with black, as though the gods had taken a razor to the heavens.

The superstitious among them might say that was a bad sign for the weather. Gallien was superstitious. But she was also getting paid.

She leaned against a high post at the docks—one that was empty now, in the morning, but that lit up the night with fire—and waited. The boy was late. Gallien hated it when boys made her wait.

The smell of the ocean wound its way into her nose like it was a tangible thing, and Gallien wrapped her arms across her chest, itching to be back on board.

"Heading out today?" said a man with an unwashed beard as he passed by her.

"Thinking on it."

He glanced up at the sky, then raised an eyebrow at her. "Y'know what they say about the sky, don't you? Bad sign to—"

"I know what they say about the sky, and I know all the things they say about the sea."

He laughed. "And you're still planning to head out? In this?"

Gallien's eyes narrowed. "What I plan to do with my ship is none of your concern." She wasn't sure what it was that caused people to do this—talk to her like she wasn't the captain of a ship. Perhaps it was that she was a woman (that would certainly be the case back home, in Va'al), and perhaps it was that she was younger than most of the silver-bearded captains on the water. No matter which it was, she hated it. She stood to her full height, which was considerable. She had three inches on the man, and he was over six feet tall. That sometimes made them shrink a bit.

"Gods. You Va'alians. Foolish," he said, and he shook his head and walked off.

Gallien locked her jaw. But she didn't have the energy to follow him. Her dark brown skin and accent when she spoke Jall always marked her as Va'alian, and she was used to it when she came to this damned country. Fuck it. And all of them—where was Ri? He should have been here a half hour ago, and Gallien was now in a fouler mood than she'd been in before.

"Captain?"

"Not yet," said Gallien, glancing back over her shoulder. The girl at the bow of the ship glanced up at the sky and bit her lip. "It'll be fine, Leylya," Gallien said with a sigh. "You trust me?"

Leylya straightened immediately and said, "Of course, Captain. I didn't mean to question you."

"I'm not angry." It was very difficult to be angry with Leylya. For anything.

"Of course. My apologies," she said again, disappearing back onto the ship.

Gallien tried very hard not to watch her leave.

"I'm sorry, I'm sorry," she heard to her left, and she spun around.

"Are you Ri?"

"Yes," he said. He was wearing a cloak meant to hide his face, she was sure, but it made him stick out like the lamppost she leaned against.

"What in all hells took you so long? Do you not see the sky, boy?"

Ri pursed his lips. "I'm sorry."

Gallien snorted and waved a hand back to her ship. "Get on." Ri nodded, and she said, "For the future, I don't like to be kept waiting."

Ri said nothing, just stalked on board. Gallien followed him and nodded quickly at Leylya. "Let's get going. Gods aren't going to be kind today."

They weren't. The gods never blessed anyone with lightning, which Gallien thought was because they liked keeping that particular power for themselves. Pour it from the sky when they were bored.

The sea had been quiet when they'd left port, quiet until they'd gotten far enough into the water that they couldn't see land on either side. And now, the clouds were roaring, and Gallien was slipping on the deck as the ocean rocked and roiled beneath them, black as the sky.

The *Horizon's Promise* itself threatened to topple, but it had never toppled. If Gallien had anything to say about it, it never would. Not while she was captain. "Trim the sails! Leylya, what are you doing? The sails!"

When the wind kicked up, the ship had begun moving everywhere, flung to and fro by it, and it was difficult enough to stand without the damn sails catching the wind from every direction. Water fell in sheets, coating Gallien, the ship, the crew. She stood, and each time she rose, a fresh downpour held her down, or splashed across the floor, so slick she could hardly even sit without sliding.

She snarled and tried to force herself up, slipping on the water again and knocking her shin into who the fuck knew what.

It only served to boil more rage in her veins; she let out a slew of swears that were swallowed by the storm.

Leylya and several other girls rushed to the sails to try quieting the ship even a modicum, and after a minute, Gallien could stand, at the very least. She staggered across to the helm, fresh bruise on her shin bone shrieking at her. Nazalie struggled to remain upright, blinking and choking out water into the rain.

"Turn it!" Gallien screamed over the roar. "We need to move with the wind, I don't care if it's the wrong direction. Go!"

The ship groaned as it moved, and water splashed over the sides.

"Gallien—"

"Shut up," she said, whirling viciously around to find Ri.

"What can I—"

"Shut the hell up and get below deck. If I need someone killed, I'll call you. Right now, you're in the way."

Every third word disappeared into the churning black.

But Ri left, and it didn't *fucking* matter either way. Gallien didn't have a thought to waste on the man.

The ship was turned quickly, but it felt too slow. Felt like everything was too slow. Damn the Va'alian king and his money.

Well.

Damn the Va'alian king, anyway.

When the ship faced the way of the wind (the wrong way), the whole structure took a breath. It rode, for the moment, on that momentum, and for a second, Gallien didn't feel like her ship was going to be torn in half. Didn't feel like *she* would be torn in half. The rain continued, hard, and the waves tossed the ship—*her* ship—so violently that Gallien felt an irrational anger blaze up in her. As though she had any right to be angry at the sea.

She stayed out in the hard, freezing rain until the winds died a bit, enough that Nazalie could reroute the ship toward Va'al again. Then she scowled at the sky and stalked back toward her cabin. This damned assassin was more trouble than he was worth. Stupid man back in Jaelen had been right. That was more irritating than whatever damage the ship had undoubtedly sustained this trip.

Gallien wrapped her arms around herself and felt the cold and wet begin to sink into her bones. What she needed was dry clothes. Dry clothes, any kind of alcohol, and a sea that consented to let her finish out this short excursion. Then she could meet the king of Va'al, demand payment, and set out on her own, with her girls—breathe in the sky until she was called back to earn her pay in another damn war.

Maybe this time, she would leave.

Maybe this time, when the king called her name, she wouldn't listen.

Maybe. Maybe.

Leylya passed by her in a hurry, and Gallien couldn't stop herself calling the girl's name.

Leylya turned, hand clutched to her chest.

"Are you all right?"

"Yes, Captain," said Leylya. Her cheeks were slightly drained of color. Or perhaps it was just the dark and the frigid water dripping down her face.

A dark spot bloomed on her shirt where she pressed her hand to her breast.

"Let me see it."

"You don't need to—"

"Come into my cabin." Her voice came out harsher than she intended. "And let me see it."

Leylya nodded once, then crossed in front of Gallien to the captain's cabin.

Gallien let the wind blow the door shut behind them.

"Show me your hand," she said. Dammit; every word she ever said to anyone came out like a command. She was so used to it, she sometimes forgot how to talk to anyone in a way that ended in a question mark.

Leylya complied.

"You're slit down to the bone, Leylya."

The girl shrugged. "I've had worse."

She had. Gallien had led her into combat for the king of the Va'alian isles more times than she could count. Men had always scoffed at her and hers before they fought with them. But she'd been fighting for him since she was sixteen, and in the past fifteen years, she'd made a name in too many battles. Now, her ship was the first to land on an enemy shore when war knocked at Va'al's door. They were the first vicious force to land and the last to leave. Now, her name was whispered, and people trembled beneath it. Leylya was one of hers. And that meant that the girl had bled.

She had warm brown skin and a shy smile that made Gallien want to brace herself on something sturdy on the rare occasions it was turned on her. A wicked scar that split her delicately pretty face in half. It had been from a blade—started at her hairline on the left side of her face and ended at her chin on the other.

Gallien would never forget when it had happened. They'd sailed their ships to an island off the coast for the old, conquering Va'alian king, one that was supposed to have offered little resistance. And the second they'd left their ship, the hordes flooded in on them. Soldiers were coming with the *Horizon's Promise*, of course, but who knew how far behind?

While Gallien hacked and slashed somewhere in the throng, a girl had caught Leylya off-guard and sliced her across the face.

There had been so much blood, and something in that moment had turned to ice inside Gallien. She'd never known that a person's heart could squeeze so tight without bursting. She'd roared across the battlefield and stabbed the other soldier right in the lung. It gave sickeningly, and she would die slowly. But good. Gallien wanted her to.

Thank the gods, or luck, that Leylya had survived. Face wounds bled much worse than they reasonably should have.

"Captain?"

"I'm sorry. Sorry," said Gallien, rummaging in her desk for a disinfectant herb and a wrap.

A frown flickered across Leylya's face, at the apology, probably.

Gallien brought forth the herb—paste, really. It was green and gritty and would not feel good going in. But it would disinfect the wound if there was anything terribly nasty in it, and it would help the skin around it to mend back together.

"Your hand," Gallien said.

Leylya held it out, refusing to acknowledge the way it shook. Violently. Blood dripped everywhere, staining the cabin floor.

"I'm s—sorry," Leylya gritted out, and Gallien handed her a bottle of spiced wine.

"Just drink right from the bottle. Should dull it a bit, all right?"

Leylya drank.

Gallien found a glass of water she'd kept at her bedside, and poured a little into the wound, washing away the blood, though more bubbled up the instant it was clean. She shoved the paste into the wound, and Leylya hissed and jerked back. Then she attached herself to the bottle.

At that point, Gallien willed her hands to be gentle. She could be gentle, dammit. She wrapped the cloth around the girl's hand and watched as the wine began to work—clouding Leylya's eyes, relaxing her shoulders. Her hand stopped shaking.

"There," she said. "You'll be fine."

"Of course I will," said Leylya with a scar-broken smile. "Like I said, I've had worse."

"Yes, you have."

Leylya's mouth was still drawn, face still oddly pale.

"Does it still hurt?" said Gallien.

"No." Her eyes shuttered, and she moved to stand.

"What in hells in wrong with you today?"

"Nothing, Captain. Nothing that concerns you."

Gallien's eyes flashed. "I'm captain, and if I say it concerns me, it concerns me. Now keep your ass in that chair and talk to me."

Leylya's nostrils flared lightly, and when she met Gallien's eyes, Gallien could see the tears shining in them. She shrank back almost imperceptibly.

"What is it?" she said, and her voice was gentler this time.

Gentle, gentle, gentle. This is a thing you can be.

"I received news," Leylya whispered. "Just before we left. My mother, my littlest brother..."

"I remember them," said Gallien.

"They were too far south, and—and when the grey surged, do you remember? Anyway, the grey surged, and they were too...None of my family could afford to leave, even though half the village had. But moving is—it's expensive, and...anyway. It surged. Seven people died." Leylya's eyes went hollow. "They were among them."

It hit Gallien like a bronze pipe. The sudden memory of her own mother, her sisters. Existing, and then, simply...not. She ground her teeth together and blinked everything away. "Gods, why didn't you tell me? I wouldn't have made you sail."

Leylya sucked in a breath. "Not like being on land would have brought them back."

The sorrow settled in the room like fog. And the guilt was so thick Gallien thought she might choke on it.

"I'd meant to send some of my pay back to them. Get them out of there; that was the plan. Maybe after this job. But, you know...and I should have...gods, I should have—"

"You can't blame yourself for the breaking of the world."

The girl blinked, and just like that, her eyes were hard as steel again. "Yes, Captain. Of course."

Leylya stood to leave, still utterly drenched from the storm, still haunted, and Gallien opened her mouth to say, "Stay with me. You could stay here. With me. If you wished it." But then Leylya turned toward her, eyebrow raised, mouth flat, in what looked like a grin because of the scar, and Gallien couldn't say it. Instead, she said, "When you get below deck, tell that fucker Ri he'll be cleaning up my ship from sunrise to sunset tomorrow. Makin' me set out in this."

Leylya stared into Gallien's eyes just a beat too long, but Gallien couldn't decide what her eyes were saying. She was good at reading the sky, a wonder at reading the sea. But she never had figured how to read people. And Leylya said, "Yes, Captain," and left.

When Leylya had gone, Gallien could still feel the pain, the guilt, creeping over her skin. Couldn't stop seeing the shriveling skin of her own family, couldn't stop smelling the pungent scent of sea and earth when she'd watched all their bodies float out to the vast, empty nothing. It had been years. This didn't matter anymore. Gods.

She stripped out of her clothes and didn't bother changing into new ones before she fell asleep.

CHAPTER FIVE

C LEANING THE FUCKING DECK. Ri had thought the girl was joking when she'd told him. Trying to bait him into causing trouble and getting thrown in the brig—if a pirate vessel had such a thing. But the girl, whose name was Yaloi, Ri had learned, had been entirely serious. As though he had called down the storm from the skies and begged Tallel to sink them.

He scowled when he came above deck, and the girl handed him a mop, a sponge, and a bucket.

"Are you serious? This is real."

The girl shrugged, wicked twinkle in her eye. "Something about this seem unfair to you, cabin boy?"

Ri's nostrils flared. "I'm not a damned cabin boy. I'm a passenger. A *client*."

"I don't care what you are. Captain says you're to clean the decks, you clean the decks. She tells me to get you the supplies, I'll shove them up your ass if I need to. Now, get on your knees, and *clean the deck*."

His jaw locked, and his fingers brushed the dagger at his back. Not that he was going to use it, only that he very much wanted to. But all that would do would be to give him something more to clean.

The girl flashed her teeth at him and pranced away. Nearly skipped. He'd never pictured the members of the *Horizon's Promise* skipping anywhere when he'd heard stories about them. Had thought of them as warriors down to their souls. But they were human as well, and Yaloi was the sort who wielded a sword on her back that was almost as tall as her, but also managed to paint her face as flawlessly as a woman of the court every morning they awoke at sea.

That massive blade shone in the light as she walked off, and Ri couldn't rip his eyes away from it. It looked gods damned wicked. He stared down at the bucket.

"If you're thinking about mutinying, I'd rethink it," said someone behind him. Judging by the absurd height of her shadow, Ri wagered the voice came from the captain, Gallien.

Ri pursed his lips and turned to glare up at her. "I'm a mercenary. I kill for a living."

Gallien cocked her head. "Is that a threat?"

"It's a fact."

"Clean the damned deck, Ri."

He grabbed the mop, fingers tight around the handle. "I've paid for my passage aboard this ship."

"Have you?" said Gallien. "Or has the Va'alian king?"

Ri clamped his mouth shut.

"I don't much care who you are and how many men you've killed. As though that should intimidate *me*." She appeared even taller, somehow, when she said it. As though the world lived in her shadow. Ri did not often find himself intimidated.

He was intimidated.

"You've probably told stories about me to your brothers to scare them into sleep," Gallien continued. "What I care about is that you made me late, and my ship had to pay for it. So you'll pay me back, and sit on your pretty ass when I tell you to. And scrub my deck."

Ri swallowed, vein popping out in his throat. He dipped the mop in the dirty water. Gallien smiled. And he cleaned.

It went that way for two days. Two days of working and being humiliated for being a little late to an appointment.

Va'al could not come up soon enough.

Ri was drenched and stinking when they docked. He'd had nothing to change into that hadn't gotten destroyed in the storms—hadn't had much time even to get his things settled before the winds and the rains started. Spending forty-eight hours on his hands and knees with dirty mop water hadn't helped. He twisted and stretched his arms as he made his way to the palace, wincing at the salt that had crystallized inside the sleeves and now scratched at his skin.

This was not how he'd planned to greet the man who controlled a nation, but his plans often didn't go as he intended. So he brushed back his black hair, fully coated in seawater and sticking together in clumps, straightened his jacket, and headed to the palace.

They'd met enough times by now that Ri supposed it didn't matter.

He gritted his teeth and entered the throne room, which, no matter how many times he went inside, would always feel astonishingly vast to him. Perhaps it was the five-man-tall ceiling. The echo when you spoke. The frescoes that were splashed with expensive inks, gems glittering in the stone floor.

This palace had been constructed in a bygone age, one in which Va'al had *mattered.*

They clung to the history of opulence like lifewater.

"Well," said the king as Ri and Gallien bowed together before him.

The king of Va'al was absolutely ancient. Ri sometimes feared that if the man moved too quickly, his dark brown skin would crack and crumble into dust. Even his voice felt on the ragged edge of being used up entirely. He was old. But Ri knew him well enough to know that old did not mean weak. The king was a razor of a man, vicious and sharp no matter which way you came at him. He was ruthless, toward every human Ri had ever seen him come into contact with. Only a fool would drop his guard in this court.

"Seems you had a bit of trouble," the old king said. "My Etryan assassin, and the young privateer—scourge of war, defeated by a storm." He laughed.

Ri would not bother asking why. He was too busy bowing. Ri was always bowing.

"Gallien, my privateer, you will find your payment with my treasurer. He is waiting for you. You will return before three weeks are out."

"Yes, my lord," Gallien said, also to the floor. She was uncharacteristically stiff, quiet.

"You are dismissed."

Gallien rose and slid a quick glance at Ri, no doubt wondering who in hells he was and what business he had with her king that she could not hear.

"Approach," said the king, and Ri rose. Finally. He was getting very sick of floors.

He took long steps toward the throne, and stopped when he was close enough that the king could whisper. "Your horse and supplies are being readied, assassin. You leave at first light."

"Yes, my lord," said Ri.

"You will have three weeks from the day you set out."

Ri did a quick calculation in his head. Subtracting travel time to Andra and back, that left him six days. Fine. He could set something up by then, broker a tenuous (and false) peace with the Andran nation.

"My horse," said Ri. "Is it Va'alian?"

The king laughed—so dry it sounded like a cough. "Of course not," he snapped. "Do you think us fools? Your horse is Etryan. Thin and short and black as night."

"Of course, King," said Ri, now averting his eyes out of respect.

"Gather your things, and sleep well. You will depart when the morning is grey."

Ri bowed again, very low, and left the throne room, passing by a very suspicious Gallien, and the treasurer, on his way out.

Ri would not be getting paid the other half of his (sizeable) sum until his job was done.

He headed across the palace grounds, skin scratching red underneath his salt-hardened clothes, and ducked into his little room. His muscles tightened when he felt the other man in here. His presence was something any person would feel—powerful, mischievous, nearly suffocating.

"Prince," Ri said under his breath.

The prince of Va'al leaned against Ri's doorframe. Ri had been given temporary accommodations in a small building attached to the palace—servants' quarters, he thought. The prince seemed to be visiting them frequently as of late.

"Ri," said the prince. His voice was like rocks, being rolled smooth in a river.

Ri looked up at him. "What do you need?"

The prince shrugged, full lips turning up at one corner. "I dunno," he said. "I was bored."

"I don't have time for games, Prince. I leave out tomorrow."

"Just a drink, then."

Ri avoided the prince's eyes. It was easier if he didn't look at them.

"Look at me, Ri."

Ri couldn't disobey. And as he'd expected, Adè's eyes were dark and glittering, and clouding Ri's judgement already.

"You will be fine," Adè said, folding his arms across the wide expanse of his chest. He looked very much like the king, if the king hadn't been so old he was falling apart at the seams of his skin. If the king had no glimmer of cruelty in his aging eyes.

"I don't like it."

"You can say my name."

Ri felt a sharp pang in his chest when he said, "Adè, I do not like it."

"What don't you like, assassin?"

Ri's mouth twisted up. "You can say my name."

Adè laughed, and Ri's entire body wanted to move with the sound.

Ri said, "If this plan goes as it is supposed to, if I live through it all somehow"—Adè snorted at the notion; he figured Ri for immortal—"then you will, in all likelihood, be joined with King Reyan in Jaelen, and I will go back to Etrya. Is that what you want?"

Adè's jaw had locked at some point while Ri was speaking, and the way he looked at him now was...very sad. Something more than sad. "Of course," said Adè.

It was ideal for a man and woman to be paired when it came to royalty—the gods had a slight tendency to bless those in a royal bloodline with powers. (Though that was certainly not always the case. And Ri privately held the opinion that this was due, more than anything, to abject laziness on the gods' part.) But if a time came that a royal needed to marry and no one of the opposite sex was available or suitable, same sex pairings were not unheard of. The joining of two powers into a force that could possibly contend with the growing shadow meant more than children. And if Reyan's queen was out of the way, then there would be nothing stopping this prince joining the

Jaelenian king. Adè and Reyan would be pawns. Pawns who would save the world and be bound forever.

And Ri would go back to Etrya.

"Good, then. I'm happy for you," said Ri.

"Ri—"

"With all due respect, *Prince*, I am exhausted. My skin is crawling from salt water and rain and sweat and no baths for two days. And tomorrow, I have to infiltrate a country so I can get you set up on a throne with a man I've never met, whom I'm rapidly beginning to hate. Please, your highness, leave."

Adè stood straight and blinked down at the ground. Guilt flared in Ri's stomach; he was being an ass. He had no right to feel even a tick of jealousy. And he certainly had no right to take it out on Adè. Adè was just as much a plaything in this game as he was.

But rational arguments didn't matter to Ri. What mattered was that he wanted to be alone. More than anything, he wanted to be away from Adè.

So the prince nodded and left, and Ri stripped angrily out of his clothes and had a bath.

CHAPTER SIX

R EYAN WONDERED IF, DURING the hours between waking and this very moment, his head had split in two. If it was a slow sort of thing, perhaps he wouldn't have noticed. Perhaps little by little, a seam in his skull had separated, until now, he would look up any second and find blood pouring down his face and dripping into his eyes.

"Are you all right?" said his captain of the guard. The man's eyes did not bely warmth, but they never had. They showed concern and aptitude and loyalty, and those things were all that mattered.

"Yes, Cariq. I just—gods, my head feels like someone has taken a sword to it."

"Interesting how frequently coming into this room seems to trigger such things."

"Yes," said Reyan, small smirk on his lips. He did hate this room. It was small and a ridiculous shade of green and felt smaller and more ridiculous because of the utterly *boring* business he had to attend in it. "Well, I was always one for horses and magic and war. Never did have much of a head for the minutiae."

Cariq shifted, feet planted firmly on the ground, hands clasped behind him in parade rest. He was always so excessively formal. As though he hadn't known Reyan since before he could walk. As though Cariq hadn't sat awake on a chair in silent comfort a hundred nights when Reyan was too small to lead and too old to cry in public, after his father had died and Reyan had been left with a country weighing down on his neck. The captain's grey hair gleamed in the light, and he waited.

"Report," said Reyan.

"Of course, sir. We expect an influx of refugees to head this way."

"From where?"

"Thegas and Xinban, mostly. Some from neighboring villages. Shadow's moving."

Reyan flicked his hand dismissively. The shadow was always growing, and refugees were always coming. Which meant endless meetings with the guard, and the treasury, and everyone else worth a title in this damn palace. And with the shadow decimating crops in every region it touched, it meant food was going to become a worry. It wasn't immediate, but it bit at the back of his mind. "We'll have no room soon."

Cariq shrugged. "The world itself will have no room soon. Not if the grey keeps spreading like ink in water."

Reyan groaned. "Hells. Just—send an envoy down to Andra and see if you can convince them to accept the half from Xinban. Gods know they've done little in all of this."

"They have open borders, sir."

"If we don't ask them, there will be no encouragement for anyone to go there, and every refugee wants to come straight here." Jaelen had, during the rule of Reyan's father, earned itself a reputation as some glittering bastion of freedom and wealth and beauty. It was both maddening and a point of pride.

"As you wish. And the Thegans?"

"Have them put up in the same place we made for everyone else."

"Everyone else still lives there from the last village we took in, highness."

"They linger? In *that* corner of the city? Fine, then scare the people still there into working, and moving."

"They're already working, sir. They've been contributing since they got here, to the person."

"Cariq," said Reyan. "Find a place."

Cariq bowed at the waist. "Yes, sir."

"Send Varien in."

Cariq nodded and left the small room, shutting the door behind him. He would follow the treasurer in, and stand with them for the length of the meeting, unmoving, unspeaking. Simply listening. When rule had passed to Reyan after his father had fallen ill, Cariq had been the one who'd stood beside him. While everyone else had snickered and whispered and called him "boy king," Cariq had treated him like a ruler. Had advised him, bowed to him, done a hundred things that Reyan was old enough now to be grateful for.

He'd made more decisions than Reyan had those first couple of years. But when Reyan had turned nineteen and finally settled into authority, it hadn't been a struggle to untangle his own power from the man who'd quietly been wielding it since he'd taken the throne. Cariq had simply moved from a place beside him to a place behind him and said nothing of it. As though since the man had served his father, he believed that aiding Reyan was simply a continuation of his duties. He'd treated him like a man when he'd been a boy, and for that, Reyan never said a thing when Cariq deigned to sit in on meetings or suggest things too strongly. He'd earned his position. And truthfully, Reyan enjoyed the solidity of the man's presence beside him.

Cariq calmed him in a way that no one else could.

There was such astounding comfort in being *known*.

Reyan waited, straight-backed in his chair, fingertips drumming on the table before him. The stone floors in here made each tap echo, though the soft olive fabric on the walls absorbed much of the sound. The door opened, and the treasurer walked in, dark purple gown trailing her and Cariq following behind.

"What news, Varien?"

"The refugees, highness."

Gods. It seemed the entirety of his rule was comprised of refugees and dealing with them.

"Tell me."

Varien sat when Reyan nodded at her, running a long fingernail over her dark red lips. "Our funds are lower than they've been, King. The last influx has been contributing, and well, and should earn back their keep and more soon. But they haven't yet, and with the new crop of people fleeing the south, as well as grain and fish stores being ruined, and the cost of imports that share crops with those that were destroyed being driven up, I am concerned we may need to raise tax—"

"Absolutely not."

Varien's dark eyebrows shot up. "Highness?"

That had been his father's way of doing things—bleeding the poor and middle class. But it had been a decade since he had slipped away from the crown, and Reyan would be damned if his own rule was governed by the ghost of his father. "I refuse to believe that in a city-state as prosperous as this, the only way to care *temporarily* for several small villages of people is to suck it from the citizens."

"Highness, I mean no disrespect, but the Fire Festival is being held in Farowfin at the end of this year, and—"

"Fine. Cut it."

Varien blinked, and even Cariq shot Reyan a look of surprise.

"The—the support for Farowfin's festival, highness?"

"Yes."

"All of it?"

Reyan blew out a breath through his nose. "Yes."

"Highness, you realize what an offense that will be when you've only just formed an alliance with them."

The yearly elemental celebrations were massive, global in scale. Reyan knew exactly what sort of message a withdrawal of funds would send.

"Yes, Varien. I am well aware. But Farowfin does not need my kingdom's money like I need it to keep a country running. If they've a large problem with it because of my marriage, then they can take my wife back."

He stood, and Varien jumped to stand with him. Then he bowed slowly, eyes cold and locked on hers. Varien took the message as it was intended, bowed, and scurried from the room.

"Snubbing Farowfin. You're playing with fire, King."

"On the contrary."

Cariq's flat-lined mouth ticked upward at the pun, and then he took his leave of the king.

Reyan waited several minutes to leave the council room, then left for his stables, trailed by guards.

These were the things he'd dreaded when he'd learned, as a boy, that his father was to die. The loneliness, the grief, of course, the danger of ruling. But what he'd worried over most had been the day-to-day things that had seemed to suck out his father's very spirit. A thousand decisions that would offend a thousand people.

All of this, when the world was being eaten alive by a furious threat, and no one seemed to care. It took up nearly all his time, handling the small problems in the kingdom, when what he should have been doing was riding down to the grey himself, amassing an army of godsblessed to do it with him.

But it didn't matter. However much time he spent in his temple, or in his room, poring over strategies and theories on how to push it back, there was nothing whatever that he could do to save the world without cooperation.

Perhaps sending envoys wasn't enough. Perhaps he needed to go himself. For gods' sake, he didn't have the *time*.

Neither did your father. And look how much difference he made in the world before he died.

Reyan flexed his hand. He was on track to fuck up the handling of the greatest threat the world had ever known because he couldn't get out of the throne room for long enough to deal with it. And couldn't get an aging royalty to care.

Panic set in, like it always did, wrapping around his heart like a living snake.

He needed to be outside, where he could breathe.

There were two stables on the grounds—one everyone knew, and one that was only accessible to a select, trusted few. Reyan had three horses in the latter—horses he loved deeply and that had cost him enough money that it likely would have hurt less if he'd pulled payment from his own arteries.

"Vii," he whispered when he neared his favorite horse's stall. "Run with me today?"

The horse's eyes smiled, he swore. So he led her out from her stall and rode her bareback along the edge of the woods outside the grounds, until the sun fell and he could no longer justify his absence. Until the palace tugged at him. *You are the king*, it said. And let the command hang.

Reyan complied.

CHAPTER SEVEN

K ASIA WANTED TO WALK smoothly enough that people would call it gliding. That when they saw her move, they would say, "That woman does not control the wind; she *is* the wind." It was how Reyan moved anywhere. She'd watched him flowing like liquid from one room to another, in a carved path. All he had to do was shift forward, and the whole world moved around him. Everywhere the man went.

Even sitting next to her on his throne, unmoving apart from the occasional tap of his fingers, he was smooth like that. It was evening, and they'd been here an hour, taking complaints, questions, a hundred petitions from peasants and nobles—complaints big enough to go to the king and queen themselves.

But Kasia said nothing, as she had said nothing for the past hour. No one looked at her when they spoke. They looked at Reyan, and they waited for *him* to answer. Kasia very deeply wished to squeeze her fingers around the throne's armrest and watch it crumble into dust.

"My lord," said a woman, bowing before Reyan.

Reyan said nothing; he so rarely said anything in this room, Kasia had noticed.

The woman stood, smoothed her ratty dress. "I come on behalf of my village. It's small, quite a way south of here. And I know—we know..." The woman drew in a deep breath, and Reyan just looked down at her. His mouth wasn't overly harsh, face wasn't particularly hard today. It was just that there was something—something about a man who *relaxed* into a throne—that was intimidating. "We know we owe a good deal of tax. But many of the refugees from Zariel were relocated to us, and we can barely afford to care for them all. We're working on everything, but—"

"Your debts are still required to be paid. Surely you know this."

Kasia pursed her lips then opened her mouth to speak, and Reyan slid a look over to her. Lazy, challenging, tens of things that made Kasia's blood run hot.

"Of course, my lord," said the woman, falling to a knee. "But none of us can eat and pay at the same time. Does it not—"

"Surely the housing of refugees counts for some sort of payment. *Surely*," said Kasia.

The woman looked up at her, eyes wide and dark—the first time anyone had ever looked at her that way. Like perhaps she had the power to help them. Perhaps she was worth paying attention to. Kasia let her shoulders drop and her head lean back into the hard throne. These people would not make her nervous. Reyan would not intimidate her. No one would.

Reyan blinked over at her, face still impassive. Then he ran his hand over his chin and blew out a breath. "My queen speaks the truth."

Kasia fought the instinct to audibly snort at the possessive, for more reasons than one.

"Your contributions to the country have been noted," he said. He was quiet for a minute, eyes focused on some invisible point over the woman's head. Then he said, "Your housing of the refugees will grant your township taxes reduced by half this term. But I expect these people working; you will be required to pay the full amount next term. Is that clear?"

"Yes, my lord," said the woman, bowing so low that her hair scraped the floor. Then she left. She didn't spare another look for Kasia, though Kasia was certain it was her voice that had spared the town the money it needed to eat.

Her eyes burned right along with her face.

Reyan said, "What?" under his breath in the lull between someone going and someone coming.

Kasia's nostrils flared lightly.

"They won't listen to you," he said, voice still low and even, "because you are new. And because you are Farowfin."

Something she refused to hide. The women here liked to darken their lips, but she darkened her eyes. They bowed at the waist in greeting, but Kasia bowed her head, as she'd always done. She was Farowfin, and to hells with anyone who thought less of her for it.

"I am queen. I have the same authority as you," said Kasia.

"On paper."

Kasia looked at his eyes, then, and was met, once again, with that striking *nothing*. She had no idea how to read him, and if there was one thing Kasia had always been good at, it was reading people. But with Reyan? A wall. He hid his emotions behind such a shield that it would take something massive to crack it, she was certain. So she let her eyes search his face. His beautiful, sharp, cold face.

"You're angry," he said.

"Yes."

"I'm sorry." He turned from her to look straight ahead as the next person came in with their complaint. And Kasia counted down the seconds until she could leave.

Most of her things had been unpacked and set in her rooms, and most were easily accessible. But her violin, she'd tucked up into the top back corner of her closet, hidden enough in the shadows and high enough that someone would had to have been looking for it to find it. She had to get on her tiptoes to reach it, despite her height, and the old, ratty case tumbled into her arms. She knelt right there on the floor, dress pooling and wrinkling around her, and slid her fingers over it. The coating on the outside was worn through, so it was black in some places, and light and bare in others—frayed around the edges. Kasia had spent her entire childhood with this case and its contents.

When she opened the case, it coughed out dust. She grimaced, on the verge of apologizing to the thing. She hadn't had much time for music as of late. Then, she pulled the violin from the velvet where it rested and set it beside her. Ran dark rosin down the bow over and over, until the closet smelled like rosin dust. She fiddled with the knobs, plucked the tinny strings, then set it under her chin and shut her eyes.

Having the instrument here, cradled against her chest, it felt like...home.

It was a shock to her that she missed it.

She drew the bow across a string, just listening, even though an open string meant no vibrato and a thinner sound. Still, it vibrated in her chest, skipped across her arms, wound over her fingers. Until she was playing.

Her fingers found their places on the neck before she needed to think about it, and she found herself, sitting there right in the middle of this tiny, dark place, playing something slow. Something high. Something sad that she'd known since she was a girl. It was one of those simple songs that anyone could learn to play technically. But it took an artist to make it sing. Kasia hadn't been able to pull a smile from her teacher with it until she was seventeen, and even then, it had taken another year at least to perfect it.

It had been years, but her fingers knew exactly where to go without her consciously commanding them.

Kasia let her fingers glide over the strings, swaying with the music. She always moved when she played, enough that her teachers back in Farowfin when she was a girl had found it almost improper. Inappropriate, somehow, to interact so physically with sound. But she was alone in here. And she could do what she wanted.

The music filled her ears and her chest until she was lost entirely to it, feeling nothing but the low vibration of the bottom strings, then the high, mournful cry of the top. She wished she'd been paying attention to this instrument since she'd come here. With this in her hands, she wasn't concerned about power. She was concerned about the music.

Kasia floated away on the air for several minutes in the dark, utterly gone in the sound. And when she opened her eyes, she was still sitting in the closet, still in Jaelen, still next to powerless because of a nation that didn't care to know who she was. But she didn't feel it like a cavern in her chest.

She left the closet, instrument still clutched in her hand, and stopped short.

Reyan was sitting on the bed, lost in thought, thumbnail caught between his teeth. He seemed unaware she was even there. But he had to have heard her playing.

Kasia stepped back into the closet and tucked the violin into its old case, then hid it up in the top back of the little room against the wall.

For reasons she couldn't quite nail down, she was shaking.

She slipped back out into the room, intending to just leave. It was one sort of uncomfortable to be married to someone who wanted nothing to do with you, and who you were rapidly beginning to agree with on that front, but it was quite another to voluntarily force yourself into such a small space with them. It felt empty and suffocating all at the same time.

"Kasia," he said quietly as she moved to leave.

Kasia stopped, hand on the door.

Reyan turned his face toward her, hard eyes thoughtful, wondering. "I didn't know you played."

"Well. I do."

"I love the violin," he said.

"I know. You chose it for our ceremony," said Kasia.

He smiled lightly, then really looked at her. His eyes darkened with something that looked to Kasia like affection—desire, even—for half a second, and then he was as closed off as always. More, perhaps. The room's temperature dropped several degrees, and Kasia blew out a breath, then left without asking to be dismissed from his presence. Why should she have to ask?

She was the damned queen.

CHAPTER EIGHT

THE QUIET WAS SO sharp that Ri couldn't sleep.

Adè had left his room hours ago, but his nerves were still so tightly wound that he had to force each muscle to relax into his bed, and all the effort he put into commanding one seemed to bleed that tension right back into another. He listened to the utter stillness and drummed his fingers on the bed. Again, again, again, until the rhythm of it pulled him so far out of the realm of the possibility of sleep that he sat up.

It was velvet dark outside. He could hardly see outside the window of his little guest villa at all, because the moon was barely a sliver, and the stars were hiding.

And the cover of nightfall was very, very tempting.

He ran his nails over his chest absently and looked out into that vast nothingness, listened to the quiet. But every time his mind began to trend toward oblivion, the guilt behind his ribs stabbed up into his throat. He couldn't ignore it.

Why did it matter that he'd been rude to the prince? He hadn't even been particularly terrible; it *shouldn't* have mattered.

It was dangerous for it to matter.

Ri, however, had no sense for avoiding danger.

So he pulled on some loose black pants and a looser grey shirt that hung over his shoulders and collarbone and pushed his door open. The way to Adè's rooms was so familiar to him now that he didn't even think about where he was going. His body naturally found the shadows, and his feet found the winding paths that led from his villa to the palace. The guards were used to him coming and going for the king at odd hours of the night now, so he had no issue getting inside. And once he was in, it was simple to be silent enough that no one saw him making his way to the prince's bedroom. He was something of a professional at getting into people's spaces without being seen.

He knocked, once. Adè took his time coming to the door.

"I'm sorry; the prince is sleeping. You'll have to come back tomorrow," he said when he cracked it open.

"Well," said Ri, "forgive me for disturbing you." He bowed very low. "Your highness."

Adè's lips turned up, and he opened the door into his room. Ri slipped inside.

As it always did, the room felt too close and too warm.

"I'm sorry," said Ri. He sat on the hard floor.

"You should be."

Ri growled and lay back on the shiny wood, hand tucked under his head. "Wine?"

"Not tonight. I ride in the morning."

Adè's footsteps sounded softly on the floor, circling away from Ri, and then back. "How responsible of you," said the prince, and when Ri turned his face, he could see that Adè was currently draining a glass of something bright red, and probably potent, very quickly.

Ri turned back so that he faced the ceiling, and Adè lay on the floor next to him, head at Ri's hips, feet brushing against his bed. "What's got you drinking?" said Ri. "I'm the one committing espionage tomorrow."

Adè laughed once at that, without humor, and when he stretched his arms behind his head, his wrist brushed Ri's ribs. Ri blinked, visibly ignoring the contact. Had Adè not been drunk, perhaps he would have felt the sudden tension under Ri's skin. As it was, there was the wine.

"Did you know that the Jaelenian king once bathed his entire throne room in ice? On accident. Froze his attendants to the bone, I heard. Back when he was a boy."

Ri's mood instantly darkened. "I doubt very much that that is true."

"Well. I'm drunk. Everything feels true."

Ri was a step away from asking if he had any more liquor in the cabinet beside his bed when Adè said, "They say he prefers women."

"So? A lot of people prefer women."

"Exclusively, I've heard."

Ri's eyebrow did rise at that. "Has your father bothered to ask him about the grand royal plans he has for you?"

Adè laughed again. "My father never asks anyone anything."

That was most certainly true.

"Has he bothered to ask you?"

Adè rolled his eyes.

"You're an adult, Prince."

It was dangerous to be asking the prince questions like this. Dangerous for Etrya if a single thread of this tapestry unraveled. But sometimes…sometimes a man's loyalties got crossed.

"You know as well as I that I could be fifty years old, and it wouldn't matter. Not in this case. Not when it comes to a 'blessing from the gods'."

Ri blew out a breath. It wasn't fair to be angry with Adè. He had to remind himself of that every time he saw him.

"It's political, Ri." Adè was looking up at the ceiling now, and he sounded so young. He was twenty-seven, but drunk, everyone sounded young. "She dies. We marry and complete the binding and combine our powers into something that will give people hope that we can save the whole damn world, and then what? We…fight it? How does a person do such a thing?"

"I don't know," said Ri, honestly.

"We'll have sex, a single time to bind our powers, and then never again if the rumors are true, and then there we are, shackled to one another."

Ri slid his teeth over his lip. He was very much regretting that he had to work tomorrow. It was uncomfortable being the only sober person in a room. "That's politics."

"I suppose." He looked up at the ceiling, eyes hooded, biceps shifting as he stretched. "Why will you do it, Ri?"

Ri's stomach muscles tightened. "For my country. I have no choice in this."

"For your country."

"Etrya is my blood, Adè. You've no idea what it was like before. It was rich and wild and…free. A thousand things I could never describe to you. Gods, I miss it. What it was. What it could be again if the damned Andrans weren't razing it in their bloody war. There is—there is very little I would not do for it."

"I can hear it," said Adè.

"Hear what?"

"In your voice. I've never loved any—anything like that."

"As I said, I have no choice in this."

Adè blinked, slowly. Whether that was the wine or the subject, it was difficult to tell. "Neither do I."

"What a blessing, your gift." The words came out more bitter than Ri had intended, and they tasted like acid in his mouth.

Adè flicked his fingers against one another, and a flame jumped out from them.

"Careful," said Ri. "If your skin catches fire, it'll all go up. And I'll go up with you. You're soaked in alcohol." Ri could smell the sweetness on the air.

"You're not," said Adè, making the flame disappear into his hand then flare again. "You'll be all right."

"Are you performing this year?"

Adè waited a moment, in silence that felt tangible. Stretched tight. He shifted up from his back, not careful at all to avoid brushing Ri's skin when he sat up. He turned to look at Ri, fire casting small shadows on his face. "Where?"

"It's fire's year. Festival in Farowfin."

"Gods," said Adè, groaning. "Every damn year. I'm sick of traveling to celebrate something every one of us sees every day."

"Host years are worse. When I was small, Etrya had the honors on a water year. Some Andran boy fucked his performance all up and flooded the palace."

"I'll probably perform."

"Of course you will."

He didn't say what they were both thinking. That the massive fire festival was in Farowfin this year. If he didn't kill the Jaelenian queen, she would probably have been excited to go home for it. But that didn't matter. Because no matter the cost, Ri was *going* to kill the king's wife.

His nose wrinkled, jaw clenched. Somehow everything kept coming back to Reyan.

"Should be odd," said Ri, to distract himself from any number of things he needed distracted from. "Dances and contests and bold displays of fire in a land of ice," said Ri.

"That's the metaphor of it. Heat and cold. Balance."

Ri swallowed hard again and flicked his gaze over to Adè's fire. If only he hadn't been "blessed," none of this would be happening in the first place—this wicked business with Jaelenian royalty. Gods, it always came back to the damned Jaelenian king.

"What will you do for it?"

Adè said, "Burn the place down."

Ri laughed. It was strangely easy to laugh with the prince, and he'd never had a very easy time with laughter.

"I haven't practiced. Been hoping I wouldn't be asked. Of course I will."

Ri shrugged.

"I'll show you what I'll do, if I have to."

He sounded so tired, from all of it. For a prince, Adè had a deep hatred for crowds.

"Show me," said Ri, because they were swiftly running out of comfortable things to talk about, and he wished for an excuse to stay in the man's rooms a little longer.

Adè breathed out a long, low sigh that vibrated through the floor. Then he pulled himself up, and Ri with him, and Ri thought about the space between their chests, not the lack between their hands.

He moved back immediately and leaned against the dark bedpost that jutted up in a whorl of wood from the prince's bed to the ceiling.

Adè reached his hands out to steady himself.

"Are you sure this is wise?" said Ri.

Adè grinned, a cocksure thing, and said, "I've practiced this since I was a boy." Then he whipped his arm toward the fire in his hearth, and the flame vanished from its box and flowed over to Adè, winding over his arm like a snake. He tossed it into the air, and it rocketed up, then disappeared again, only to make a reappearance behind Adè's other hand and dance atop it.

Wielding flame was one thing, but *that* level of control…it was breathtaking.

The room would have smelled like smoke and Adè, if Ri could breathe.

Adè drew in a deep breath, hard chest expanding, brow furrowed, then sliced through the air with his hands, and the fire went out completely.

The entire room was drenched in the dark. Ri moved his fingers in front of his eyes and could not see them.

Then a shower of sparks rained down from the ceiling, flowed around Adè's body, and winked out before they could hit the ground and erupt into smoke and flame.

It was black.

The only sound in the room, at least the only one Ri was trained to, was Adè breathing like he'd just run the length of the palace grounds.

"If only a person with magic could be a *magician*," Ri breathed into the dark.

Adè's voice was much closer than he expected it to be when the prince said, "No. They wish us all to be liars. Street magicians without magic and magicians who play at politics."

Gods, he could feel Adè's breath on his cheek.

He couldn't breathe.

"It's late," said Ri, and suddenly the fire was crackling in the hearth again.

"Are you leaving?"

"I should."

The knot in Adè's throat bobbed when he swallowed. "You could stay," he said, looking down at Ri. "Play cards."

Ri grinned over his deafening heartbeat. "That's hardly fair. You're drunk, and we've nothing to wager."

"My shirt? My honor?"

Ri backed for the door. "Don't give me those things," he said, and he left.

CHAPTER NINE

REYAN WORE WHITE ON the days he had to use his knife. His father hadn't used it at all, said it was a nasty business—executions. Reyan agreed, and that was why he insisted. Anyone the king personally condemned to die, he would personally carry out their sentence. If he couldn't look them in the eye as he ended their life, they hadn't earned death.

Only twice had he ever faltered when the golden blade was pressed to a criminal's throat. And those two women, both killers but with good enough reason that he couldn't slit their necks, he'd allowed to live. They would be severely punished, but they would live.

Reyan didn't believe in shutting his eyes to anything.

That was why he wore white. Black disguised the blood. White, and he had to live with it. He'd made plans, after yesterday's airing of grievances by the populace, to travel to Andra. See if he could drum up an ally to begin work on the southern threat before it became too wild. But he'd worn this, not only because he always wore it—because it did not allow him to be distracted from the task at hand. If he was to take a life, whomever's it was, he owed them his full attention, at the very least.

There were three young men today. Too young, really. Too young to have committed treason, too young to be disillusioned enough to conspire against the crown. But they had done it, and they would die for it. Never had a person who'd plotted Reyan's death been caught and lived to tell about it.

Reyan unsheathed his blade and stood with the men in the grove. All of them were hard-faced. No one cried, no one begged; they simply knelt, heads held back by guards, and Reyan approached. He used to shake when he did it.

He didn't shake anymore.

"Do you wish to name your god?" he asked the first man as he knelt before him.

"Favros." God of passion. A common god to traitors.

"Sast k'asyanall Favros," Reyan whispered in the man's ear. *May Favros welcome you to his halls.* And he slashed the golden blade across the man's throat.

The man coughed and choked, red bubbling and spraying, and fell to the wet ground. Crimson drenched the neck of Reyan's shirt.

"Do you wish to name your god?" he asked the second man.

"Favros," said the man. He was shaking.

The same god as the last. Perhaps Favros hated him. He hoped not.

Reyan held the man by the back of his neck and whispered in his ear, "Sast k'asyanall Favros," and slipped the blade over his neck.

There was enough blood on his shirt now that he could feel it soaking into his skin.

He knelt before the third. "Do you wish to name your god?"

"Not to you," he said.

"Very well." The man resisted when Reyan fisted his hand in his hair and moved his mouth to his ear. But Reyan was strong. "Sast k'asyanall lofyi." *May you be welcomed on the other side.*

The blade did as it was made to do, and this man left his mark splashed across Reyan's face.

He stood, shut his eyes, and faced the sky. His face was wet; his chest was wetter. There was no smell but salt and iron in the air. The guards waited in silence. They would dispose of the men; that was their duty. An unpleasant one, but Reyan thought that his was considerably worse.

He opened his eyes, took a final glance at the men in the orange grove, and strode across the palace grounds, in a back entrance to his room. There was a little hall inside, one he used to get to his shrine.

Kasia stood there in the hall, nearly startling him visibly. But she didn't say anything. She just glanced over him—over his hands and wrists, covered in blood, freckled up to his biceps, at his face and hair and throat, at his shirt. Parts of it remained white. They were the minority.

She bowed her head silently and left.

Reyan entered the shrine before he'd washed the blood off. He wanted the gods to see him like this—to *see* what he paid penance for. The room was big enough for two, and two only. Lest he ever had the opportunity to pray in here with his wife. He snorted. That was unlikely.

Reyan fell to his knees, and slid his arms out in front of him, bloody hands smearing on the wooden ground. The candles were already lit—he kept them that way. Always burning. He wished his gods to know that they would always be honored in his home.

"I beg forgiveness," he said to the god of ice—Thakros. Thakros had always been his favorite, would be the god he would give if he were asked before he died. He was wickedly pale, large and cruel-mouthed if the renditions were to be believed—the god of control, of cold, of steady, solid things.

The good thing, and the frightening thing in equal measure, was that unlike the gods who ruled Farowfin, the Jaelenian gods sometimes deigned to talk back.

Take up your knife, boy king, and I will forgive you.

Reyan tried not to bristle at "boy king." After all, to a god, that was what he would always be. But his thoughts flitted back to Kasia, that title, and he wondered, then, just how much the gods watched of him.

Oh, a good deal. Did you not find my joke amusing?

Reyan took up his blade—the same one he'd used to execute the men—and doused it in holy water that sat in a bowl at the front of the shrine. The water went pink for a moment, then faded back to clear.

He held the knife to his chest and shuddered, hoping that Thakros did not notice. Of course he noticed.

Two at the collarbones, one at the heart, boy king.

Reyan grit his teeth and complied, thin slashes that bled like monsters, mingling with the drying red on his shirt. One under each collarbone. He hissed when the gold pushed through his skin. One vertical slice between them, at his heart. Reyan's breathing quickened. This was nothing. It was *nothing.* It was what his god required, and compared to the prices asked by a hundred other gods of their subjects, begging a little blood was laughable. More importantly, penitence ensured that his house had favor from the god of ice. Favor his father had not earned.

His father had not been particularly spiritual. And even if he had been, he never would have had to make amends for the executions of men. He'd never given these a second thought and never done it himself. But Reyan was better than his father.

Reyan shut his eyes, leaning into the pain of it, the lighting on his nerves, the repetition in his head of something just short of a prayer: *Do you see? Do you see what I do for you?*

He resented it and craved the immediate release all at once.

Very well. You are forgiven.

Reyan rose, the slightest bit dizzy from loss of blood, and wondered again if the god of passion hated him.

Why do you ask?

"The men I killed. I did so because they tried to kill me."

I know.

"Two of them claimed the god of passion."

The third was Favros' as well.

"I wonder at the similar motivation." Reyan kept his head bowed as he spoke. "And I wonder…"

You wonder…

"I wonder if it was not Favros who cursed me with Kasia Vane for a wife."

There was silence in the shrine. Long enough that Reyan began to wonder if his god had left. He waited. Then he knelt; perhaps he had said too much, asked too many questions. Perhaps he had presumed himself too worthy of the time of a god.

He was still bleeding, wanted to lie down, but had half a mind to slice himself again, lest he'd committed some offense.

And then, in a voice as cold and sharp as iron: *Your wife is a gift from me.*

Reyan blinked, and fell lower. Frigid worry pierced his chest.

And you call it a curse. You give the blessing to Favros. Kasia Vane does not even know of Favros, boy.

He dared not even breathe too loudly.

I gave her to you. I blessed you with the water and the cold and I blessed you with the woman who will drive you mad with power and tear down the world.

Ungrateful boy.

Slice the back of your neck.

Reyan did not hesitate, didn't even flinch when he sliced himself and the blood flowed over his neck, down his back.

"I am sorry," he whispered, mouth muffled against the ground.

A moment of quiet bleeding. Then, Thakros said, *You are forgiven.*

He said nothing else.

"Did you come from a battle?" said Kasia as Reyan entered the room. The shirt stuck to his self-inflicted wounds already. Reyan glared at his wife for a thousand reasons, not the least of which was the haughty air in her words. She said it with her eyebrow raised. As though coming from a battle was something to be laughed at.

"No," was all he said.

"Is that your blood?"

"Some of it."

Kasia furrowed her brow. "Far be it from me to question what you do in your own time."

Reyan gritted his teeth and yanked his shirt over his head. He was in no mood to spar with his wife. He was leaving within the hour. He glanced at her before he headed into the bathroom to wash out the wounds Thakros had demanded.

"Hells," said Kasia, gaze raking over him. Her voice suggested concern, but when Reyan met her eyes, they were sparking with something far outside the realm of worry.

He ran some hot water into the sink and splashed it over himself, until light, hazy pink covered his body in a river. Everything stung, but it didn't matter. If this was his penance, enough to win him favor with his god, then fine. It was worth it.

A soft fabric touched his back and he jumped.

"Let me help you."

"I didn't ask for your help," said Reyan.

"Gods, you men are ridiculous creatures. You're bleeding everywhere, hissing like a cat, and you won't let me touch you with a towel."

Every muscle in Reyan's body tensed, and he leaned against the marble counter, glaring in the mirror. It was fogged already so he could hardly see anything but the slashes of red and Kasia's dark hair behind him as she wiped the towel across his cuts.

"What happened?" said Kasia.

"Executions."

Kasia's hand stilled. "You...carry them out yourself?"

"If I sentence a person to death, I will take their life myself or I will let them keep it."

"A twisted sort of honor."

"And what would you know of honor, Farowfin girl?"

Kasia pressed a hand into his shoulder, spinning him around. Her eyes were narrowed, scarlet mouth set. "My country is known for the arts, and for its lovers, and for its passion. That reputation says nothing of dishonor."

Reyan stared down at her coldly. "How can a country that runs red with blood, and 'passion', and the blush of whores ever call itself noble?"

Kasia laughed, and the ice in it outdid even Reyan's. "There's red drying on your face, king," she said, and she dropped the towel, and left the bathroom. "We're wanted in the throne room," she called over her shoulder—dismissive, conceited, Farowfin.

"What?"

"Oh, you wish to speak with me now? Though I'm red with the blush of a whore?"

Reyan growled and followed her into his room. "Why are we wanted?"

"How would I know?" she said, and her eyes were not playful. They silently said, *No one trusts the Farowfin girl. The Farowfin queen.* She left the room, presumably heading toward the throne room, and Reyan quickly wrapped his wound and donned a shirt and long, black coat, then followed her.

When he reached the massive room, Kasia was already sitting in her place. She looked very tall from here, he thought. He sat beside her on his throne, and glanced over at her.

"Your red is showing," she said, nodding at his collarbone, and he quickly moved to cover it, raising a little smile on her lips.

Minutes later, an advisor came scurrying in and bowed low, almost tripping, he was in such a flustered hurry. He was trailed by Proch, Reyan's cousin, whom Reyan trusted almost as implicitly as he trusted Cariq. Proch's face was grave.

"Your—your majesties, there is word. Word from the south—no. I'm sorry, I don't—"

"Slow down," said Reyan.

"The shadow in the south," he said, and Kasia's hand tensed on the arm of her chair. "It grows. Slowly."

"And this is news?" Reyan drawled.

"Only because a new village was evacuated, and they've been sent all the way up here. But the guards aren't allowing them in, and there are weapons being drawn—"

"Hells," said Reyan. "I know all of this; I discussed it with Cariq days ago. I'm not the damn captain of the guard; I'm the king. I shouldn't be bothered with matters like this. They're villagers—"

"Villagers and soldiers, King," said Proch.

Reyan frowned at his cousin. "Soldiers?"

He looked at Kasia, who was deep in thought.

"Yes," said the nervous advisor—Barlo. Or Barone. Something like that. "It was a military-occupied territory—where much of Groll's army evacuated after the first wave of the curse. Or, whatever it is. It isn't pretty."

As the man talked, Reyan could feel the power in the air crackling between his hand and Kasia's. He wondered, for a moment, if they were fully bound, how high it would reach. If he could snap his fingers and end the border conflict all the way from here.

It didn't matter. Not right now, it didn't.

"Well," said Kasia, and Reyan's head shot up at her voice—it was the first time he'd ever heard someone speak in authority beside him, "that sounds terrible, certainly. Very stressful. For a *guard*. And yet you dare ask the king and queen to handle this squabble for you?"

"As I said," said Reyan, "call the captain of the guard. That's the sole reason he exists."

Where in hells *was* Cariq?

The man fidgeted, and looked at the ground. He shifted his weight, mouth shut.

It was Reyan's cousin who spoke. His voice was alarmingly gentle. Proch met Reyan's eyes when he said, "Cousin, Cariq is dead."

CHAPTER TEN

R I FOUND HIMSELF, FOR much of the ride to Andra, wondering about Adè's hands. There was nothing particularly special about them. They were strong, but so were his. Veins that stood out under his skin, but so did his. Ri's were more extraordinary, really, between them; after all, Ri was left-handed. Adè's were more common. But that didn't stop his mind wandering as he traveled.

It slipped between Adè and tactics most of the way there. Between the prince, and planning something he had no real way to plan. He needed some-thing—*something* that would mark Andra as the assassins. Not just a typical item he could purchase in a market, either. It needed to be something marked as royal, high enough in status that it would bait Jaelen, and something that would reasonably be given to an assassin. A particular poison, perhaps? A bit of armor? An enchanted weapon?

His mind turned the possibilities over and over. He would find something in the palace when he got there.

Ri had never been one for intricate forethought, had certainly never been gifted with patience. So the king had entrusted him with the task, and he'd set out as quickly as he could. There wasn't time to delay for setup, for elaborate plans, for gathering a guard to follow him. Etrya came closer to falling to Andra by the day, and he would be damned if he let it happen because he'd been busy *waiting.*

He rode. There were two days of travel to ponder, after all.

It was a long and quiet ride—nothing but dirt and soil and the slightly shifting colors of the trees. The closer he got to Andra, the closer the land-scape changed from something wild and unfamiliar and vast to something resembling Etrya.

Etrya was an island, and very humid. Lush, so green it looked almost painted. The flowers were the same—bright. Brightness and life everywhere. Andra didn't have the sea breeze or the salt on the air, the smooth, white sand as you approached its edges. But Andra was green enough. It was arid, but farmers worked the land to coax it into sprouting plants and the air was fresher for it. The entire country of Va'al was dirty with fish and trade.

Not Andra.

He had no love for this country, but he had a great love for home—a longing in his chest. For the rivers and the ocean and the smell of his stepfather's garlic noodles and iolle fish. Ri swallowed back the thought of them. His stepfather, who knew how ill now, lying in a bed somewhere, and his blood-father and decade-younger siblings waking up without Ri. His father had begged him years ago not to get involved in work like this. But by then, he'd been involved for too long, and now there was no getting out of it. Not with his father's husband sick and the rest of them just waiting for him to die. Without more gold lining his pockets, he would. Tallel, Ri wanted home.

If this cheap imitation was the closest he could get, then so be it.

Ri slept under the stars, body bruised and aching from being jostled for days. He hadn't brought quite enough water to be comfortable; that had been a mistake. But he'd brought a tarp for the night it rained, and torches to keep away any little creatures of magic that haunted the night. Most tiny spirits were afraid of fire. At least, that was what the legends said. And he met no barrowelliqs or naviers, so he could only conclude that they had been true.

He passed very few travelers, which was good, as by the time the journey neared its end, he hardly had the energy to smile. He would have scowled at the wrong person and wound up in a fight that would have been messy and complicated, and he had no time for either.

The journey still took a day longer than it would have otherwise, because Ri needed to fool Andra into believing he was coming from the east—from the direction of Etrya. He was coming under the pretense of being an Etryan ambassador, not a spy sent by Va'al. So he overshot the country and circled back around, and by the time he saw the city gates, his thighs were so bruised he was worried he wouldn't be able to stand. He thanked Tallel once again that he'd been able to ride an Etryan horse. On a broader back, the extra time would have wrecked his thighs further, and probably his groin as well.

The former, he liked well enough.

The latter, he was *particularly* invested in keeping unscathed.

The gates were open today—Andra had enough allies that it rarely worried about attack or any matters of national security. Ri rode right through with hardly a second look. Unexpected, given that Andra was embroiled in a brutal war with his people, and he looked Etryan to the bone.

The palace gleamed in the distance, sparkling in the bright daylight. It wasn't entirely extravagant, but it stood there like a member of royalty itself—surrounded in the green that peppered the city, shining with silver and jewel tones. And the city around it, through which Ri was slowly riding, was a labyrinth of dust roads and chaos and activity. Andra was a wonder; it always had been. Ri had only been here once as a child, and when he was, he vividly remembered the awe that sunk into his very marrow. It roared to life under his skin now.

This place was a gleaming behemoth.

Even the buildings here were as bright as any flowers in Etrya. Shopkeepers shouted, selling wares from a thousand places, and the spicy smells of the food at every corner made Ri's stomach twist with hunger.

Ri shook his head hard and forced himself to focus. He was sure he would be fed well when he reached his destination. And he had no need whatsoever for foreign perfumes or wooden shoes, though everything looked enticing. No. He had a job. He looked straight ahead, and rode toward the palace.

He stopped outside it, and a guard stood at a tall, gleaming silver gate.

"What business have you?" the man said.

Ri did not dismount. "I have business with the king. My name is Haru, ambassador from Etrya." Ri reached into his jacket pocket to procure a forged document and hand it to the guard as proof.

The guard gave it a cursory glance. "Yes," he said with a sniff. "I can smell Etrya on you. Proceed."

Ri refused to allow the insult to land. He would ride into their palace, and later, he would tear it down. Let them laugh.

Ri was struck again when he made his way inside. The palace was huge. Brown and grey rock that sprawled out everywhere, in a perfect square, amid a spray of greenery. This place was an oasis. Beautiful enough he felt a moment of regret for coming here to set the place up to be burned down by Jaelen.

Not bad enough to turn back, however. Fuck them for what they were doing—what they'd already *done*—to a place he loved more than his own life.

At the stables, Ri dismounted, and allowed his horse to be taken. He was met by a woman just a few inches shy of Gallien, with bright blonde hair that fell over her eyes.

"Ambassador Haru?" she said. Her steps were long and confident.

Ri straightened. "Indeed."

"The king has been expecting you."

"Yes," said Ri. "I would prefer to meet him under cleaner circumstances, if possible—"

"Curious," said the guard, stepping too close to him. "Curious that you would come here, while your nation and ours are embroiled in a conflict you cannot hope to end with ink and voice and papers alone."

Ri stiffened immediately. "I am an ambassador. This is what I do."

The woman smiled, posture relaxed. "Oh, absolutely, of course. But what a time for words." Her hand drifted to the sword sheathed at her side.

Ri's face hardened, eyes darting from her fingers back to her face.

"Unless you've come to negotiate the terms of a surrender," the woman said, "which would be strange indeed for a low-ranking ambassador. Most rulers would not entrust such a task even to their children."

Ri felt the shadows on his back when three more guards emerged from several points around the stable. "What are you doing?" he growled.

The woman continued smiling. "Perhaps you are here to discuss politics. And perhaps you are here on behalf of Etrya in order to spot our weaknesses and destroy us from the inside."

Ri rolled his eyes. "Is this how Andra treats its—"

"Take him below," she said, waving dismissively as three guards wrested control of his arms.

"Like hells!" Ri said, and the world went black.

CHAPTER ELEVEN

R EYAN'S DISAPPROVAL OF KASIA'S plan to accompany him to the city gates had not been quiet.

But Kasia didn't care.

Reyan did not command her; as of now, he wasn't even bound to her, except by a contract, a cold kiss, and half a spell. So when he said, "I'll go," she said, "So will I." And when he'd confronted her in their rooms as he'd donned his armor, insisting that it was foolish, that he could take care of this on his own, she'd stripped out of her dress and into cured Farowfin leather.

"Kasia, I forbid you to come," he'd said.

Kasia had smiled with her teeth.

She rode beside him now, on a grey horse, speckled on his rump, little spots dotting their way almost up to where Kasia sat. Some women chose to ride side-saddle; Kasia did, when she was out in a dress. But today, Kasia was dressed for battle.

Reyan kept his jaw tensed, his eyes stone cold and straight ahead, for the length of the ride. They had come with a team of guards surrounding them; no use getting the rulers of the country killed in an argument over immigration. But Kasia had the sense, looking at the set of his shoulders, his face, the veins that stood out in his hands though he gripped the reins loosely, that they would have managed with or without the guards.

When they approached the city gates, Kasia's stomach dropped. The area was a wonder of dust and steel and blood; how had things escalated this quickly? Damn brutes. And they called Farowfin base and run by passions.

The guards stationed at the massive gates raised them slowly, and no one seemed to notice. No one in the fray seemed to care at all. They rode through, and Kasia choked on the dirt and smell of blood in the air.

"Halt!" Reyan called as they approached, but even his voice was drowned out in the squabble. Guards lay dead outside the gates, foreign soldiers too. Somewhere in there was the captain of the guard, the older man who'd attended Kasia's wedding. She hadn't known him at all, but the memory of a face that had looked friendly twisted something inside her.

"In the name of the king!" Reyan called again, and yet again, nothing. No one could hear to kneel before them. Kasia didn't even bother to raise her voice; it would do nothing but give her a sore throat.

They rode closer to the violence, and Kasia's ears rang with the metallic sounds of the fight. She backed her horse up several paces, then held on with one hand to the reins. She raised the other in the air and focused on that feeling of unfettered energy inside her. She let it swirl in her stomach and wind around her arm, then release from her fingers in a blast of wind that tore through the group.

Immediately, several weapons were torn from men's hands, and there was a breath of hesitation. The wind kept coming.

Reyan glanced at her, and his eyes caught fire—or the closest she'd ever seen from him. He shook his head once, then summoned the frost, and shot it toward the group. When the elements combined, they blasted out with such force it rocked most of the fighters to their knees. Kasia's horse reared up on its legs, and she frantically gripped its neck, eyes wide.

"ENOUGH," Reyan roared into the icy wind, and Kasia let the air recede as Reyan did the frost. The sudden stillness in the air felt loud—the quick absence of noise filling Kasia's ears as thoroughly as the clamor of battle had moments before. She felt it like a velvet weight sinking into her skin.

Reyan's lip ticked up, and the rest of his face returned to stone. He rode his horse into the middle of the group, muscles flexing with his horse's as he wound his way across fallen bodies and bowing men. Kasia followed carefully, delicately maneuvering the dapple's steps. It felt wrong to tread on men, no matter how dead they were.

"What in all hells has happened here?" said Reyan. His voice was low as thunder, chin tipped down so his brow shaded his eyes.

Kasia did not speak. Though she was queen, her word meant little to most of the people here. They didn't respect a Farowfin. Not yet.

No one answered but the leftover breeze.

Reyan's next demand was quieter—so quiet Kasia could see several of the men on the ground leaning in, straining to hear. It was quieter than death.

"What," he said, "happened here?"

Still, no one spoke. Kasia could almost feel the anticipation of *something* on her skin. She shivered under the soft-spoken power of it.

"I will start using this knife in ten seconds if no one speaks."

Several people began at once.

"You," said Reyan, pointing to a younger man—a soldier from a southern village—whose knees dug into the soft, bloody ground, but whose eyes were raised to his.

"My lord," he started.

"You will bow when you speak to your king," Reyan hissed.

The man's pale face drained paler and he averted his eyes instantly, bright blond hair hanging over his ears and forehead. "Sincerest apologies, lord."

Reyan said nothing.

The man continued, voice shaking now, "The shadow came to us. It came and there was death and terror and we all fled, all of us who could." Kasia glanced up past the battlefield where armored men and women knelt, to see a massive group of peasants—men, women, boys, girls, young, old, all standing in the lilacs and grasses of the fields and watching. Terrified. "We fled here," he said, "because our village was equidistant from both city-states' borders. Andra and Jaelen. We had to go to one of you."

"And what compelled you to come to my walls and begin slaughtering my people rather than go to Andra's ever-open gates?"

The man was quiet for a moment. Then he said, "Jaelen is cautious, and larger than Andra, more fortified. You, lord, are a better king than Andra's. And many of our ancestors migrated all the way from northern Farowfin to settle down in our village. Those of us with Farowfin blood wished to swear allegiance to you and your queen, not Andra."

Apart from another tick of his lip, a hardening in his jawline at the mention of Farowfin ancestry in them, Reyan's face betrayed nothing.

"What was it like?" said Kasia, and Reyan glanced over at her, eyebrow raised. The mention of Farowfin, that at least some of them had come here for *her*, had her feeling bold.

"M—my lady?" said the man.

"The shadow. No detailed accounts of it have reached Farowfin; we're too far north for the people to be terribly concerned about it yet." Reyan's eyes flickered momentarily, and Kasia ignored it in favor of the man at her feet. "But I wish to know. What was it like?"

The man glanced up at Reyan—for what?

Kasia moved so that her horse stood between the man and his king.

"No," she said. "Don't talk to him, talk to me." She could hear Reyan's snort behind her and wondered if he was amused or angry. She didn't care.

The man lowered his eyes again and said, "Of—of course, my lady. It was...I've seen it twice."

"Look me in the eye when you speak," she said. "I'm giving you permission. I want to see it."

He locked eyes with her—his pale brown, pretty, shining with fear and sadness. "Both times, it felt the same. Creeping and slow, but sudden somehow. We all think it will stop before it hits us, you know? But it doesn't. We all go to sleep, and wake up and it should be dawn, but it's empty outside. Grey like ash. The kind of hollow that snakes into your soul and leaves bruises on your bones. We wake up, and outside, the leaves on the trees are curling inward, blackened, the grasses melting away like soot under our feet. And suddenly it's difficult to breathe. And everyone is outside, and no one can yell, because we're too afraid to waste breath on it until the shadow stops, until we can get past its edges. It feels malevolent, like a living thing. Like something ancient and angry, something sent from the making of the world. Pulsing through your veins when you're in it. Seducing you and tearing your lungs to shreds all at once.

We didn't save enough of us the first time and we didn't save enough the second, but we got out. Again. And the bones in the village are dust."

"Which village are you from?"

"Groll, originally," he said. "Xinban, more recently."

Groll had been utterly devastated. To experience that level of destruction twice in a lifetime…Kasia blinked down at the ground, and let her horse back a few paces away. In Farowfin, they knew of the shadow, of course. Knew that it was deadly, that it was spreading, that it had been caused by the gods' meddling in the world. No one had hard evidence as to how to dispel it, though magic was theorized as the likeliest possibility. But they didn't fear it so much. They told it as a bedtime story—a fantasy to frighten children. Because the shadow was far, far away. But she had married Reyan because he had wished to defeat it, or at least to fight back, and because of the dizzying hold on the world that would come with being the ones to do it. Which meant that here, she was much closer to it. Here, she was standing with a man who had faced the nightmares that had whispered her into scared sleep only a few years ago. And it was growing, and coming fast.

Kasia backed far enough away that she was no longer in the king's way, and considered.

Reyan dismounted his horse, handing the reins off to the guards. "Who did this?" he said, voice like steel, kneeling before a silvered head of hair, attached to a body Kasia recognized. A body soaked in blood, faced crusted over in dust and crimson. "Who killed *my* captain of the guard?"

No one spoke.

Reyan's voice was like fraying silk—smooth, but rough around the edges. "Who did this? What happened here?"

A different man, light-skinned, probably of some amount of Farowfin blood, stood, eyes averted. "When we came to the gates, your guards refused to let us in. We were afraid, king. We had come from a nameless horror, a withering, and we were desperate to be let in."

Reyan narrowed his eyes and Kasia waited, as he looked out over the fields. "Afraid? Of the darkness on the horizon?"

The man said nothing.

"The darkness leeching up past our grasses?"

Silence.

Reyan grabbed the man's face and turned it toward the fields beyond the gate. "Do you see darkness here, soldier?" he said.

"No."

"Then your fear is no excuse."

The man's nostrils flared slightly, and he pursed his lips—not out of aggression. He was decidedly larger than Reyan. But he was afraid.

"You all decided to slash your way into the city, then?"

"No, king," said the man, face still caught in Reyan's iron grip. "After your captain lay dead, the other guards attacked, and we had to defend ourselves."

"You are soldiers," said Reyan. "You expected my guard to allow you inside without so much as a security check?"

"That wasn't how he presented—"

"Who did it?" said Reyan. Gods, his voice was dangerous.

The man blinked, ice blue eyes glinting in the sun. "I did," he said.

Before Kasia could react, the king had slid his sword from its sheath and shoved it into the man's heart. The man made a noise that wasn't a grunt, wasn't a gasp—it was right in between, and terrible.

The man who'd been speaking with Kasia choked watching it, blood draining from his face, his torso crumpling in on himself. Shock crushed at Kasia's windpipe and her horse stumbled backward.

"Those of you unarmed may enter the city escorted by my guard. They have a place for you. Soldiers, you will follow the other half. And I will decide what to do with you." Reyan glanced down at the ground, hard gaze flickering when it landed on his captain, then pulled his sword out of the blond soldier's chest and sheathed it, still bloody. He mounted his horse and headed slowly back into town, and Kasia followed him.

Just outside the palace, they dismounted, and Reyan made for the gardens, and a back entrance to their rooms. Kasia grabbed his arm when they were close enough that she could see the door, and none of the guards. "Was that necessary?" she hissed.

"Was what necessary?" He glanced down at her fingers digging bruises into his arm, and a muscle twitched in his jaw.

"Those people are frightened, Reyan. They have witnessed *horrors*, and you murdered one of them for—"

"For murder. That man"—his voice cracked—"has captained the guard since before my father died. That man was noble and good and absolutely irreplaceable. Should I have slapped him for it, Kasia?" He jerked back from her grip and she let her fingers fall. Then he walked two paces toward her, until they were breathing the same air. "Should I have lectured him? Should I have given him a night in jail to think about what he'd done?"

Kasia blinked. Then said, "You were very quick with that blade. Was it because the man killed your friend? Or was it because somewhere down deep, part of him was Farowfin?"

Reyan's lip curled and he stepped so close, Kasia was surprised their chests didn't touch when either of them breathed. "You know little to be a queen," he bit out.

Kasia's eyes thinned to slits and she laughed. "And you *do* little to be a king."

She did not have to say what he already knew: that he was foolish. That perhaps if he would lower himself enough to bind himself to her, they would be powerful enough together to push back the darkness altogether and if they'd done it already, perhaps his captain of the guard would still be breathing.

They would be more powerful than the world had seen in decades; she could feel it crackling in the minimal space between their chests. They would be something that the forces of the world would bow to.

And Reyan was a fool.

He breathed hard, face twisted in a mask of hate and resentment.

Kasia held his stare, until he shook his head hard and spun away from her with a frustrated noise, probably heading to his damned shrine. And she stayed in the gardens until night fell.

CHAPTER TWELVE

DAWN BROKE IN VA'AL. And this morning, the sky was pink and pale yellow. So light and rich that Gallien thought perhaps she could run her fingers through it and they would come away smeared in color. She lay on the hard deck of her ship—a ship she had fought for, had given blood and sweat and years for, the ship that was freedom and a shackle to the king at once, and gazed up at it. She wanted to walk in those clouds and dive into the sea. She wanted everything. Wanted to feel it all on her fingers and taste it on her tongue.

A shadow passed over her torso, and Leylya smirked down at her. "What are you doing down there? You can't even see the horizon."

Yes. She wanted everything.

"No," said Gallien, "but what a view I have of the sky."

Leylya glanced up. "It looks real enough to eat."

Gallien blinked away from Leylya and back at the clouds.

"Are we spending the night at sea, then?" said Leylya.

"Yes."

They'd left port hours ago, and by now, nothing but sparkling water surrounded them.

Leylya frowned, then sank onto the worn wood beside Gallien. She lay next to her, and Gallien's heart leapt in her chest. "Where are we going, Captain? The women need to prepare if we're to form a raiding party. And we need to—well, we need to know where to steer to."

Gallien smiled, through the twist of guilt in her stomach when she heard the residual heaviness of mourning in Leylya's voice. How long did that particular timbre last in a person? It had been over a decade for her, and she wasn't sure hers had left. "Yes I imagine that would be important."

Leylya shifted, and her shirt fell down just below her shoulder.

"We're not raiding," Gallien said. She refused to explain herself further. Gallien didn't explain herself, not to anyone. This ship was hers. The sea was hers. Her girls could trust her or not.

But they didn't need the risk, given the climate. She knew she needed to be back at Va'al so soon. Things went wrong with the king's assassin or thief or whatever that boy was, they need to be ready for war, not limping home because they attacked the wrong ship.

It burned in her veins, the desire for it. To find a ship marked with the flesh trade or the seal of one of tens of governments she didn't give a flying fuck for. To take what she pleased and sail off on the waves into the horizon.

Free.

But there was a time for freedom. And that time, for her, was not now.

It wasn't *yet*. That rankled under her skin, scraping at her muscles.

But. It wasn't yet.

"Where are we going?" said Leylya, as though she had the right to know.

"If I told you, you would turn us around."

"Far be it from me to defy an order."

Leylya smelled like salt and open air, on the sea or off it. She smelled like everything Gallien loved. Gallien locked eyes with her. "I can't tell you," she said. "I am your captain, and this is reason enough for you to follow."

"You don't trust me, Captain?"

"I trust you to follow me," said Gallien. "I don't trust you not to be afraid."

Leylya's eyes shuttered for a moment, then she took Gallien's fingers in her hand. Gallien's eyebrows shot up, and Leylya brushed Gallien's hand over the scar that split her face in two. "You don't?" she said.

"A scar proves nothing, not in this case," said Gallien, but she did not move her fingers away.

"It proves that I am unafraid."

"It proves that you are brave." Gallien allowed her hand to drop to the deck with a thud.

"Are they not the same?"

"They are different."

Leylya furrowed her brow and sat, arms draped across her knees. "You don't need to trust me, Captain. I presume too much."

Gallien was silent for a moment. "We are on a route south, are we not?"

"We are."

"All that matters is that we follow that route," she said.

"All right." Leylya stood and bowed, leather laces in her linen shirt just the slightest bit too loose.

Gallien nodded at her and she left, and Gallien continued her dreaming of the sky. She prayed that the sky would be so forgiving as they made their way down, down, south, where only the careless would dare venture now.

Hopefully, the gods would not punish her for her foolishness.

And fuck every last one of them if they did.

The further south they sailed, the colder it got. This would have been strange, if not for the darkness that bled out down here. Gallien walked the deck, fully clothed in leather armor, blade now swinging at her side. One would think she and her warriors were headed into battle, not the ocean.

The stars were out now, and away from people, they sparkled so brightly they nearly stole Gallien's breath. And still, they sailed south with the wind, and the darkness felt clean. She breathed it in.

"Captain," said a woman in her crew. She was small for a warrior, short hair, medium brown skin, dark eyes. Lovely girl, and one built for fighting down to her bones. Gallien noticed that the longer they sailed, the more women were decked out for battle. One by one, they'd all changed from sailing clothes into those meant for self-defense. This woman, Yaloi, was no exception.

"What do you need?"

Yaloi clasped her hands behind her back and stared out over the dark water. "You know what I need."

"I would prefer if you spoke plainly."

"Honesty," said Yaloi. "We sail with you and fight alongside you, and I do not believe that requesting honesty is too much."

Gallien clenched her teeth.

Yaloi said, "We sail for the south. Toward an enemy none of us can touch."

"Watch yourself," said Gallien, eyes turning on Yaloi, blazing. Gallien could feel the heat floating up inside her.

"Not questioning you. We all just want to know what we're getting into, Captain."

"And you drew the short straw."

Yaloi smirked. "I did."

Gallien nodded. "There is something I must do," she said. "And it concerns us all. It's—it's bigger than you and me and this crew and this ship. Bigger than the sky and the sea itself. You ask for honesty; I need to ask you for trust. You can tell the crew I said so."

Yaloi nodded and left, and Gallien urged the helmsman to steer on, though it only grew colder and dimmer as they went. They sailed through the night and into morning, Gallien was sure of it, though the light outside could not speak to that.

When it was so dark in midday that it looked like twilight was falling, and so cold that no one could stomach being outside without a jacket, Gallien ordered them to put down anchor.

She made her way for a little skiff that hung from the side of her ship and stopped when she felt a small hand on her shoulder. "Where are you going?"

"Nowhere you need to follow, Leylya."

Leylya pursed her lips. "Let me."

"It's dangerous."

Leylya said nothing to that, only accompanied Gallien to the little boat, and silently got in with her when the crew lowered it to the dark water below.

The sea was quiet, freezing water lapping at the little boat's side. Gallien could feel the fear and the heaviness licking over her skin. Wordlessly, Leylya took up a paddle, and Gallien took the other.

"Why?" said Leylya. "When others flee the south, why are we venturing here?"

Gallien said, "I have my reasons."

"One surge of the grey and you've doomed the crew."

Gallien's eyes flashed to her. "Why did you accompany me if you don't trust me?"

"I do."

"Can I trust you?" said Gallien as the light spray of the salt water against their tiny boat prickled her face.

"Yes," said Leylya. "With anything."

"Do you mean that?"

Leylya shifted forward in the boat until her knees touched Gallien's. "Anything, Captain," she said.

She felt it like a tangible thing—the desire to confide one thing about her life in someone. Anyone.

As it was, she was so deeply, fathomlessly alone. A ship floating along in the black sea with no hold on the weather, no port in which to dock.

It was her, silent in the water.

Always.

Gallien bade Leylya stop rowing and the boat sat mostly still, bobbing on the sea. The darkness was so close. Gallien worried that if she gasped in a breath, she would breathe the grey right into her lungs.

She reached out into the air, grasping for nothing, and let smoke wind through her veins. No one knew; no one had ever known. Because she had never wanted what this blessing of power signified. Hadn't spoken to the gods in eleven years, since one of them had chosen to gift this to her on the worst day of her life. If she spoke to anyone, she feared they would respond with a command. She didn't want this. Gallien had never wanted anything more than a ship, and the thrill of laying claim to a life of freedom, of adventure.

And perhaps vengeance.

So she'd never had reason to show a soul. In fact, if anything, she'd had a thousand reasons not to.

But now, the darkness had reached her crew. Had reached *her*. She'd barely been able to breathe for days when she'd had to watch Leylya walking around the ship like a ghost, utterly lost to grief. Maybe...maybe if she'd done something about this before, if she'd tried this months ago or years ago, maybe Leylya would not be splintering with sadness over the loss of half her family.

Maybe then, Gallien would have been able to walk straight without shame crushing her.

Maybe if she'd been *brave*, she could have been *free*.

She shuddered past the fear of everything, the wretched vulnerability of Leylya watching, and let her hand be wrapped in shadow. She shut her eyes as flames burst forth from her fingertips, showering the water around them in sparks. Leylya gasped, and the high noise from her throat made Gallien's stomach flip-flop. But she shut it out, and focused.

Magic had been speculated as a solution to the shadow. It had been debated and theorized and wondered about for years. But no one had tried it. No one in these realms was truly *brave*. So many blessed were royal, and so many royals were *weak*. Weak, and old. But Gallien needed to know.

"Gallien," said Leylya, in a voice hardly above a whisper. It was the first time she'd called her anything other than *Captain* in recent memory. "Look."

Gallien opened her eyes. And where her fire had shot, the milky dark had begun to recede.

Even after it disappeared, the shadow did not return.

They waited, floating in the dark silence. And Gallien, for a moment, could do nothing but breathe. Think.

When they had been bobbing long enough that perhaps the crew would begin to worry, they turned the skiff around, air thick with silence and questions, boat nearly sinking with secrets.

CHAPTER THIRTEEN

WHEN IT CAME TIME to bury the dead, Reyan always found himself wishing that he lived in the north. In the cities built into the frost, tradition said that the deceased were to be entombed in ice—frozen in clear-as-air water and left in the mountains of the dead. If time wore away the memories of your uncle's face or the particular color of your child's hair, you could make the journey and find them there, perfectly preserved until the world ended.

Reyan had wished this for the first time when he'd seen his mother's body, wrapped in linen, ready to be laid atop a pyre. It was too warm in Jaelen to do anything but let the bodies burn. He'd been eleven, and her dress and linen covered the scars from the daggers that had killed her so perfectly, and her mouth had been smiling so gently—she'd been one of those people who wore a smile at all times, even when she was sleeping. He'd wanted to keep her like this.

Reyan had been allowed a moment alone with her in the stone shrine, and he'd used it to cover her in ice.

She'd melted in minutes, and his father had been furious when he'd come in and found Reyan kneeling in a puddle, his mother soaked and freezing. It would take longer for her to burn now, he'd said.

And Reyan had thought, *Good.* He couldn't keep the panic away when he thought of fire burning her body away into ash, and then into nothing at all.

He hadn't bothered trying with the ice when his father had died.

Now, sitting before Cariq in his little shrine, he could feel the cold at the tips of his fingers. Cariq looked strong, even in death. Like Reyan would order the servants to light the wood where his body rested, and the man would sit up and walk straight out of it.

"It's only fire, King," he would say. "You didn't hire me to be kindling."

Reyan fisted his fingers, and uncurled them, over and over. Breathing. He shouldn't be dead. It was senseless.

And Reyan was hollow.

"Cousin?" came a soft voice from the shrine's door.

"Come in."

Proch was silent when he slipped in and sat next to the king. Reyan had always been particularly fond of his cousin, an advisor of his as well as family, and so he did not mind his presence now. He would have gutted anyone else for daring to come close.

"I am sorry," Proch said simply.

"I know."

Reyan could hardly bring himself to blink. Something felt so very bone-achingly lonely about having no one left to ask questions. No one who was older than him anyway. The pressure of it crushed in around his throat.

"I have to tell you, I'm surprised."

Reyan raised an eyebrow. "About what?"

Proch's face was quite serious when he said, "I half-expected to find you in here with the place flooded."

Reyan's mouth twitched up in something like a smile and he said, "Gods, Proch. Have some respect for the dead."

Proch breathed out a single laugh. Then he flattened his mouth into a line and rested his arm on his knee. "I have the utmost respect for *this* dead, Reyan."

Reyan shut his eyes for a beat too long. And when he opened them again, he'd frozen himself in a way that would not melt, even in the Jaelenian heat.

"He knew the risks of his position."

"Yes," said Proch, sliding a glance at Reyan from the corner of his eye.

Reyan took one final look at the dead man before him and stood, then exited the shrine. When the sun sank below the horizon, he would give the command to light the pyre, and Cariq would fade into oblivion.

"Where is your wife?" said Proch, following him out into the suffocating heat.

"I don't know."

Proch caught up with him, matching him stride for stride. "She isn't here to comfort you in your time of need?"

"I don't trust her, Proch," said Reyan, and he stopped before a deep pool in the middle of his gardens and stared down into it. It was so clear, a person could see right to the bottom of it, to the bright, glittering stones underneath. He could see every fish that split the water with its pink, blue, yellow scales. Reyan often came out here, just to think. To watch something so very simple live its simple, little, pretty life, and die.

"Why not?"

"She's…gods, I don't know. An adder."

"Ah yes. I forgot how much you fear snakes."

"I'm not afraid of her," he snarled.

"Thought you said you'd met her before you decided to marry her."

Reyan ran his hand through his hair, and decided immediately that he needed to bathe. His hand got caught too easily in the curls. He would wait, probably until after the funeral, when he would have the smoke smell of a burning body to scrub out of his skin.

"I did. More than once. She was beautiful, which hasn't changed. But…quiet. Easy."

Proch choked on nothing.

"Yes," said Reyan, flatly.

"She got her fame by decapitating a dead king, Reyan."

"Well. Nevertheless."

"Is that what you wanted?"

Reyan ran his teeth over his bottom lip and sighed. "Not really. No. It's just the…it's the change that has me worried. How can someone transform from a rabbit to a snake so quickly, unless one version of them is a lie?"

Proch laughed, high cheekbones making themselves very apparent against his pale skin, and straight black hair brushing the edges of his jaw. "I wager you weren't such an ass courting her either. Don't tell me you've never charmed a person, then changed who you were the minute you'd left their bed."

Reyan's lips thinned.

"It's not a good enough reason to delay the binding, cousin," said Proch.

Reyan said, "The power we will have when we do…Proch, I can feel it underneath my skin. It rattles my bones. The very gods…"

Proch furrowed his brow. "The very gods what?"

It was as though something had sewed his lips shut. He didn't want to tell Proch about Thakros and their conversation in the shrine. Feared something dark, something too large. It felt…dreadfully secret. "Nothing," he said.

Proch was quiet.

"It's not only that."

"Not only prejudice, you mean?"

Reyan's nostrils flared. "Excuse me?"

Proch looked at him like he was foolish. "You and I both know why something as simple as a change in demeanor has you bothered. That girl is Farowfin and you cannot stand it."

"Don't accuse me of irrational prejudice."

"I didn't say it was irrational. Those are your words."

Reyan locked his jaw and tapped his fingers against his leg. "She said, just days ago, that in Farowfin, they're not even concerned about the shadow eating the world. Did you know that?"

Proch finally fell silent. Not the quiet he usually wore, where it felt as though he had a smart comment waiting on his tongue.

"She said it's nothing but a story. That they're too far from it for any of them to really be concerned." He brushed his thumb absently over his chin. "If she wasn't even worried over it, if none of them are, then why would she join with me in the first place?"

"Because you're powerful, Reyan."

"That's what worries me."

"Because your reasons for having chosen a wind-gifted woman so powerful you can 'feel it under your skin' are entirely altruistic?"

Reyan shook his head. "I wanted to drive back this thing to save the world as much as anyone else does."

Proch laughed.

"What?" said Reyan, and his voice came out vicious.

"Then why not call a council and assemble the most powerful royals in the realm together to drive it back?"

A frown flickered over his face. "Because they're all *old*. They're cowardly and don't want to leave their gilded palaces. They don't want to risk anything for the safety of those who would outlive them. No one would listen to me if I were to ask."

And because I was going to. I was finally going to do it—to ride with envoys and stop all this on my own. I haven't been ignoring it. I wouldn't. But perhaps if I had done it sooner, if I had gathered up the courage, then Cariq—Cariq wouldn't...

"No," said Proch.

"No?"

Proch shifted his weight. Reyan was sure he could hear the venom in the word. The quiet warning.

"You may be right, cousin. Perhaps that is the way of it. I'm inclined to believe the assessment, if we're being honest. But you haven't even tried, and you know that your word as the king of Jaelen would hold more sway over the rulers of the world than any of the rest of them. You haven't tried because you want to save the world *yourself*. And you want to do it in such a way that the entire earth knows that you are not weak."

Reyan was quiet for so long that the sun began to set.

Shadows fell over both their faces, and he could no longer see the bottom of the pond.

"What if I bind with that girl, and my suspicions prove true? And I cannot trust her, and she only wanted all of this for the addictive power of it. Then I've given her this thing and I cannot take it back."

"Well, she will have given something to you as well."

"Perhaps I was wrong to marry her at all. Perhaps I made a mistake." A reversible mistake, as long as he didn't complete the binding.

"Well," said Proch, patting Reyan on the back, and turning to leave for the beach, "world's going to hell either way. Might as well risk having a good time while you're at it."

When a person died before their god could be named, the priestess named their god for them.

"Sast k'asyanall Narro," said the priestess, who was clothed in the color of the sky.

Narro was a rare god to choose in Jaelen. But he was the god of honor, and if anyone had the right to claim the god of honor, it was Cariq. Reyan felt a sudden stab of sadness that he'd never known. Could never discuss it with the man, though it wasn't as though they would ever have chosen to discuss religion no matter how many more years the man had lived.

People did not wax poetic here, did not drone on and on about the lives of the dead when they were not here to hear it. Jaelen did not have the long speeches of Va'al or the songs of Etrya. They named their god, and then the dead left the world in smoke and silence.

"Light the pyre," said Reyan.

Kasia stood beside him, quiet and still and tall. Like a pillar.

The servants lit the massive structure on fire.

He burned.

CHAPTER FOURTEEN

RI SPIT OUT A colorful stream of Etryan swears. Everyone spoke the common tongue, but blood poured out of a man in his own language.

"I am *nothing*. I am an ambassador, I swear it. How many things do I need to swear on before you—"

A fist smashed into his face, rattling his bones. Ri snarled, anger coursing through him almost more potent than pain.

"If you are an ambassador," said the pale ghost of a muscled man before him, "then your country is stupid. Why send a man into a den of vultures without a guard?"

"Nest," said Ri.

"What?"

"Vultures *nest*, you idiot."

That earned him a not-unexpected crack across his shins. Ri could hardly even feel it anymore, his senses were so deadened. He had forgotten how it tasted to swallow without thick salt and iron choking him, what it was to breathe without shards of rib needling his lungs. He'd forgotten why any of this meant anything at all.

His lips were dry and cracking, and that shouldn't have mattered in the face of his skin being ripped apart, but it did. He tried to swallow—blood again, thick saliva coating his throat and refusing to move—and shifted, wrists rubbing raw against shackles that held him chained in a dingy cell. Old iron holding him to stone walls—wet with who knew what. By now, Ri presumed much of the damp was his own sweat, probably some of his blood as well. His body was certainly slick with it. The iron bit into his wrists when he moved. He wanted to stand, if only to give them some relief, to let himself be supported by his feet, let his arms hang at his sides instead of over his head. But his legs were weak, and in enough dull pain from being hit again and again, he feared he would fall if he stood.

He had no idea how long he'd been down here. It could have been two days or it could have been five. Judging by how little food and water he'd consumed in recent memory, he hoped it was the former. For hydration's sake.

Not that hydration mattered. He would die down here, most likely. No one wounded a man like this only to let him walk free. Sooner or later, they would kill him. He hoped it would be sooner. He hoped it would be later.

The man stood in front of him, all steel. He didn't look human to Ri anymore.

"I want to know what it is you know, little Etryan bird."

"About what? Gods, about *what*?"

The man moved like lightning. In a second, he was on his knees in front of Ri, meaty hand gripping Ri's face. Ri had thought every surface of his skin was dulled to pain now, but learned very quickly that his face was still more than capable of feeling everything at the highest levels. He gritted his teeth so he wouldn't give his captor the satisfaction of a noise.

"Everything," the man said. His breath was hot and it stunk. Ri figured he had little room to talk in that area, but they had done this to him. This man seemed to live this way. Ri recoiled.

"You're winning," he said. "You're winning your damn war; why do this?"

"Because you are no ambassador."

"So what if I'm not?" said Ri. His voice sounded strangled even to his own ears. Exhausted, pleading. But every breath hurt. Every thought hurt. They had hit him and burned him and forced him to piss in the corner, arms stuck behind him to the wall. The smell of his own filth had assaulted him at first, but he could hardly smell it anymore. How fast did that happen to a person? An hour? A day?

The man's heavy eyebrows rose.

"So what if I'm not?" Ri repeated. "Say I am a spy. Say I am an assassin. Say I am a pirate lord. What difference does it make? Why don't you just kill me?" The moment he said it, he regretted it. Wished he could swallow the question back into his throat. Despite all of this, Ri did not want to die. A cold fear settled over him—a fear that had nothing to do with the man's bloodied fists and knuckles, and everything to do with the blade he had just now noticed, flashing in a very large hand.

"I will not kill you yet," said the man.

Ri relaxed a bit.

"I will not kill you until I know everything you know."

Ri shook his head and shut his eyes, leaning his head back against the wall. Because when it came down to it—when it came down to the security in Etrya, the secrets, the battle plans of a queen, Ri didn't know shit.

He liked to think he wouldn't have given it up, even if he did.

So did every traitor to their country who cracked under a knife.

A low rumble came from the man in front of him, and a frown flickered across Ri's brow.

"Hm," the man grunted. "Well, a person has got to eat," he said, and he stood, patting the place from whence the growl had come.

"Yes," said Ri. "A person has."

The hulking man only laughed at Ri's obvious request. "I will be back for you later." He pointed the knife at Ri when he said this, smiling with all of his perfect white teeth, and left Ri alone, cell door clanging behind him. He wasn't sure why this place had bars at all; it wasn't as though he could get up and walk out of it, not with the iron at his wrists. And they were impossible to break.

He'd tried.

A lot.

He shifted, trying to find a comfortable divot in the stone for his head to rest. There was one somewhere along the wall—worn down and rounded, probably from this cell's previous occupants. He thanked them silently, and then cursed them when he couldn't find it right away. He didn't want to die, but there was nothing he could do about it right now. So he might as well let himself slip into unconsciousness.

It was easy enough to do, even with the pain blanketing his body—when a man was hungry enough, falling into oblivion rather than forcing himself to keep his eyes open wasn't terribly difficult.

Just as consciousness began to slip away, a pain gripped him so hard he physically recoiled from it. He jumped back, head hitting the stone behind him, and his eyes opened far too wide, far too fast.

Food.

He could smell the spices from here, though he couldn't see them. It didn't matter that Andran food was notoriously bland, that the only spices they used with any regularity were salt and pepper, or that the only meat they tended to eat was chicken. It could have been dry as jerky and to Ri, it would have smelled like fish drowned in garlic and herbs and creamed sauce. It physically pained him to smell.

He jerked once against his shackles, though the effort was pitiful. It wouldn't do anything. Not when he was in peak physical condition, and sure as hells not now.

For the first time since he'd been down here, he wanted to cry. A hint of food had reduced him to that. Perhaps some guard was walking by just to torture him with it. And right then, if he'd been asked, he might have told them everything. This was worse than them burning him.

"Hello, prisoner," said someone with a smallish voice.

Yes. That was exactly what they were doing. Gods, he wanted to gut them all right here.

He refused to speak. Not just because the roof of his mouth was currently glued to his tongue for lack of water.

A person the size of their voice opened the bars and walked in, carrying a tray of food and a large cup in one hand, a pitcher of water in the other. Ri focused on their fine-boned face so he wouldn't have to think about what they held, that he would not be able to take.

Ri's entire life, it seemed, had consisted of the universe holding things out in front of him that he could not have.

He looked at *them*. Drowned out the smells as best he could, and focused. Their features were all very sharp and very small. Not just on their face, on all of them. They were assessing. A thousand things at once—Ri could practically feel it. They were attractive. Short, dark hair, shaved at the sides, small blue eyes. Yes, attractive. But he was not so captivated by that as he was by the raw intelligence just spelled out on their face. He could read it there on them as well as he read a book. When they looked at him, they weren't just seeing. They were calculating.

They sat, cross-legged on the floor, and when the plate clattered on the stone ground, large goblet of wine beside it, Ri couldn't not look at it. He actually *whimpered*. The high sound rattled in his throat, and he wanted to be embarrassed, but he couldn't be.

"Hungry?" said the newcomer, cocking their head and pinching a bit of chicken between their thumb and forefinger, then sucking it into their mouth.

It wasn't dry. It wasn't spiced well, he could see, but it was moist, and surrounded by buttered vegetables, a lump of potatoes.

"Fuck you," Ri hissed.

"Oh, not likely," they said, smile on their lips. Ri wanted to bite their lips right off them, if only to get a taste of that chicken. The person's tiny nose wrinkled. "It smells a bit like shit down here, doesn't it?"

"Yes, well, that would be my shit. In the corner," said Ri.

They laughed.

"You never answered my question," they said.

Ri narrowed his eyes. "Am I hungry?" He considered saying no. If this was torture, he didn't want to give them the satisfaction. But what if…what if… "I'm fucking starving," he said.

And maybe it was a dream, but they pushed the plate toward him, close enough that he could eat with his toes. Usually, the guards brought him nothing but bread, and fed it to him; he didn't need to worry about what to eat with.

Thanks the gods he was flexible and very good with his feet. Ri gripped a piece of chicken between his toes and brought it to his mouth, almost collapsing when it touched his tongue.

"Wager you'll have trouble drinking the wine," they said.

"Water," Ri rasped. Everything in him screamed *Trap, trap, trap*. But his empty stomach and paper-dry throat screamed louder. "I will *beg you* for water."

They shrugged and lifted the pitcher to his lips. Little bits dribbled over his mouth, down his chin, and Ri thought he had never tasted something so sweet. He could feel his throat opening little by little as his savior or something like it poured the water into it, could feel himself beginning to breathe again. He could feel something that wasn't just his body crushing in on itself.

Then he pulled back when it was too much. He needed to eat. Wanted to eat more than he'd wanted anything in his life.

He continued working at the plate with his toes, bit by bit filling his stomach.

"Why?" said Ri, food in his mouth. But he didn't care about decorum. He cared about surviving. "Are you doing this so I'll remember food, and how much it hurts when it's gone?"

The person smiled.

They smiled like a knife.

"I assure you, I remembered just fine," said Ri. "Not that I'm complaining."

"No," said his captor-savior. "I'm not here on behalf of them."

Ri raised an eyebrow. "You're not."

They shook their head and stretched their arms out, reclining on the stone. This little person was in a dungeon with a criminal, and looked like they were lounging on their living room floor. "No," they said.

"How did you get down here then?"

"One does not have to be in allegiance with someone to get what they want from them. I'm sure you know."

Ri considered this, and dipped a toe in the potato, then sucked it off. He didn't care that his feet were filthy. Couldn't bring himself to care about much beyond the stabbing pain in his stomach that was finally receding, and the illusion in his limbs that said he could move.

"I'm here," said the person, "because I know exactly who you are."

"There it is," said Ri. "Bait me with food and a tiny, unassuming frame, and then reveal that you're an interrogator too. Have you got needles for my fingernails hidden somewhere in the folds of your tunic?"

They laughed again. "No. I'm not here to trick you, prisoner. Haru, they call you? Though I doubt that's what *you* would call you. Am I right?"

"Mm. Getting me to trust you with the food, then. I see."

"No. I am not here to trick you," they said. They leaned forward and took a sip of wine. "I'm here to bargain with you."

Ri blinked. Every nerve in his body was on high alert, thoughts in his head jumping and bouncing around in his skull. Perhaps he was hallucinating. He must have been, because there was no way in hells an Andran citizen was down here, asking to work with him.

He ate another large bite from his feet without answering. Then they offered him the wine. He could feel the sharp edges of his mind soften when he let himself drink. But what did it matter? What did any of it matter?

"What time is it?" said Ri, shutting his eyes to savor the last coating of wine on his tongue. He wasn't answering their question.

"Midday."

"Mm," he said, taking another sip of the wine as they held it out for him. He shut his eyes. He could feel it coat his throat, warm his belly. Perhaps it was loosening his tongue as well. But it was also giving him relief from the pain. And that was a powerful bargaining chip. Powerful enough that he simply didn't care. "Hard to tell in the windowless dark."

"Yes."

"How long have I been down here?" He drank again.

"No. You'll talk to me about what I want to talk about now."

Ri narrowed his eyes, stab of irritation needling through his stomach.

"You're the one in chains, Haru," the person said. "And I'm the one with the power to wash your wounds. Unless you're flexible enough to lick those too."

Ri leaned back and made a noise that was not quite a laugh. The stranger poured a bit of the remaining water in the pitcher onto a cloth that came from somewhere Ri hadn't seen, and ran it over his face. He hissed when they kept catching on scabs and fresh blood combined.

"Why are you doing this?" he said, eyes shut. He was leaning into their hand, leaning into a gentle touch—the first he'd felt in days. Gods, was he this weak already?

"I'm doing *this* because I can't stand the sight of blood."

Ri snorted

They continued, "And I'm helping you because I believe we can help each other."

"And how is that?" said Ri. Everything felt so slow, so dull. There was something in the wine, perhaps. Something he would pay a hell of a lot for if he had the capability. The stranger moved with their cloth to his arms, which were as bloodied as the rest of him.

"You, Etryan 'ambassador', have not come from Etrya. You've come from Va'al."

Ri's pulse spiked, even through the haze of the too-potent wine, and he shifted, but his eyes remained shut. "Tell me what makes you think so."

"Your Etryan horse," they said. "He's shod in bronze."

At that, Ri looked up. Suddenly, he was sharp and hard as a razor again.

"That's Va'alian, my friend," said the person. It suddenly bothered Ri very much that he didn't know their name.

"*Friend.*" Ri sneered. "What were you doing with my horse?"

"Oh, I doubt very much he's your horse. Your employer's horse? That's of no relevance to you."

Ri swallowed hard. The hairs had risen on his neck, and he was clenching his jaw with just a bit too much force. They smiled and continued cleaning his wounds. He was nervous, and they knew it.

"I also noticed that you brought seven water skins with you. Seven is quite a lot for such a short journey. Twice as much as you need, I'd figure."

"I try to stay well-hydrated," Ri ground out.

"No," said the stranger. "You haven't had more than a swallow of water in four days, and yet I offer you a pitcher and you leave enough that I can still wash your wounds? You, *ambassador*, are a man used to going without."

Ri's teeth crushed and slid against each other, and they moved to his legs. He jumped when they reached his thigh. "That hurts," he breathed.

"Please," they said. "Gods, these are nasty. What did you say to him?"

"A good deal of things," Ri growled. When the man had brought out his blades, Ri had waited in silence for about thirty seconds before he'd started spitting out whatever he thought had a chance of making the torturer put them back. When Ri had gotten furious enough at the pain that he'd lost his mind, he had started saying vulgar things. *Where did I hear these foul phrases? Oh, your mother whispered them in my ear just last week.* And it was at that point that the guard's cuts had begun to deepen.

"As I said," the Andran started again, "I know you didn't come here from Etrya, though you certainly have a strong background there ethnically. And I heard you swearing in what sounded like Etryan, so the odds tell me that you *are*, in fact, Etryan, though you were sent by someone else." They moved to his left thigh and upper leg. Ri hissed and jerked back. These were where the cuts after the ill-fated mother comments had landed. The towel was almost drenched with his blood at this point; luckily they were nearly done. Or Ri figured they were, at least. "Obviously, being Etryan, the very last place you'd want to come is here. Here where just looking like you could very well get you assaulted in the streets." They glanced up at his eyes, and saw a flash of something—fear, sadness, apprehension—in them. "Am I close?"

Ri was silent, staring straight ahead. Because fuck the Andran at his feet. Fuck all of them.

"Just say nothing if I'm right."

Ri narrowed his eyes and said nothing.

The stranger laughed. "So, you know as well as I do that Etrya is getting crushed. I've wondered if perhaps you've more allies than you've let on, if this war will cost Andra more than it gains us, but I don't expect you to divulge that information. I expect, in fact, that you don't know."

The person, whom Ri now suspected was a servant judging by their shabby dress and willingness to get their hands dirty in subservience, drew back from his legs. They were mostly clean now, though they burned like hells. They dripped a bit, and pale pink ran off them onto the floor.

The Andran ran their hands through his filthy hair. Ri didn't lean into their touch this time, though he had to consciously fight the reaction. They poured most of the last remaining water from the pitcher over his head, and it ran brown over his collarbone and neck and chest. He shuddered.

"You've come here from Va'al, and are originally from Etrya. So why, I wonder," the servant, who was perhaps also more than a servant, continued, "would Va'al hire an Etryan mercenary to go to Andra on their behalf? Well, I was also made aware of a sudden, secret peace treaty that Va'al has brokered with us. Trying to keep us off their trail, I figure. Secure an ally? Though I presume it to be false. It didn't make sense to me when I heard it and it doesn't now. Va'al, I wager, is angry."

"How do you figure?" said Ri. His voice was lower than a whisper now, and every part of him was rigid with nervousness.

"Well, after Andra, Va'al was next in line to be joined with a king. The most powerful king in the world. Only the Farowfin queen and the Andran princess, Chaya, have a hope of enticing King Reyan away from Va'al's prince. And times are desperate, aren't they? All Va'al needs to become a major player in the world is to put their man on the throne. And Va'al is awfully close to that creeping pestilence of darkness. Awfully, awfully close."

Ri was shaking now. From the cold of the water, one. But more than that, from fear. This girl knew everything. Every damn thing. Which meant things had gone so terribly wrong that even if he somehow managed to survive this, he could not expect to right them.

"So they sent you," said the servant. "They sent you to Andra, which is curious. Or I thought it was. Why, oh why, send an Etryan to Andra when what they really want is a place in Jaelen? To kill Chaya, perhaps? But that leaves the esteemed Jaelenian queen alive. And why, then, would you come so out in the open? A real puzzle."

Ri blinked up at her as they poured the last remaining water over his head. This time, it ran nearly clear. They offered him the last half glass of wine in his goblet and he downed it all at once.

Then something in his dark eyes split. His heart simply cracked open. As though it had been waiting to do so. "My people are dying," he said. *My people. My friends. My brothers. My littlest sister.*

"Va'al?"

"Etrya." He was too tired to be embarrassed when his voice cracked on the word. "You win," he said. Exhaustion pressed down on his shoulders at simply letting the people he loved into his head for more than an instant. And there was nothing in his chest but the desperate desire to be heard, not to be hurt anymore. "They said they would help us—I want to say your name, but I don't know it."

"Shev," they said. "And yours?"

"Ri." He had nothing to lose by giving his name. Not now, with his secrets on Shev's tongue and his back against the wall.

"Va'al, Ri? Va'al said they would help you? If you…if you killed Chaya."

"Your princess? No," he said, almost laughing. "I hardly know Chaya's name."

"You need to kill the Jaelenian queen. Of course. But that means nothing if Andra is still an opt—oh." Understanding washed over their face so quickly, warring with euphoria. Ri could have sworn he saw their eyes glaze over. It looked like they'd ingested a drug. "You're not here to kill the princess."

Ri's eyes sharpened. "No."

"You're here to broker peace, and then to leave for Jaelen."

Ri was quiet.

"When you're there, you'll murder the young queen. And you'll frame us as the ones who've done it."

He said nothing. The servant's eyes were bright—so very, unsettlingly bright. He wondered so many things in the moment of silence that thickly followed. How they'd bribed the guards into letting them do this. Why a servant looked so excited over information. If they would take pity on him or kill him, or if perhaps the two were not mutually exclusive.

They could kill him right here, if they wished it. All it would take was fetching a knife, then jamming it into his throat. He was committing espionage; that would be the most sensible choice for them to make. Gods, he was so damn tired.

Shev dropped the soaking cloth at their side and studied the ground while Ri studied them.

"You have me," he said after minutes of waiting. His voice was a growl now. "You've won. What will you do now, Shev?" Ri's fingers dug into the cool wall—hard enough his hands whitened, hard enough he could feel little pinpricks of blood welling up under his nails.

"I don't know," said Shev.

"I don't believe you."

Shev chewed on their lip. "Perhaps I wish to do nothing to you," they said.

"I'm a spy. Come to ruin you all," he said. "How can nothing be my sentence?"

"Do you have a death wish, Etryan?"

Ri's eyes shuttered and he glanced at the dark grey ground, shimmering with water and his own blood. His heart surged at the thought, jerked dangerously. *No,* it said to him. *We will not go this easily.* "No," he said quietly.

"Then perhaps you should stop talking."

He did.

"What if I wanted to help you?" Shev said.

Ri's eyebrows shot up high enough that they disappeared into the hair than hung over his forehead. "Help me?"

"Yes. What would you say?"

Ri shrugged, disbelief winding through him. "I would say I'm in no position to turn down any offers."

"What if I could get you an item? An item you could have on your person when you killed the Jaelenian queen, one that proved beyond a shadow of a doubt the country from whence the assassin had come?"

"You would..." Ri faltered. "You would get that for me? Something Andran? Something to frame your own country?"

Shev merely stared at him. They didn't blink. "What if I could? What would you do?"

"Nothing," said Ri. "I'm chained to the wall in a dungeon."

Shev smiled. "Let me take care of that. If you were free, Ri. If you were free, and I could get you a trinket, and you could get everything you'd come for, what would you do?"

"I would ask why."

"Only a fool asks why when he's chained to the wall."

"Then I am a fool."

Shev said, "Because the shadow is coming. And when it comes for Andra, I want friends in high places. I want Jaelen to war with my country, so that we will be evacuated, and *I* want to be welcomed there. I want to be welcome wherever Va'al is, and that is where they will be when Va'al's prince sits on Jaelen's throne."

Pain flashed hot and quick in Ri's gut. Then he forced it away. This was no time to consider the prince. He needed his mind working, and that was the only thing that mattered. "You want immunity in Va'al. For helping me. That's it."

"I want immunity," they said. "And I want a position of authority."

"I think…" said Ri, glancing up at his hands trapped in the shackles, "I think that can be arranged."

Shev stood, taking the empty cup and pitcher and plate with them.

"Wait," said Ri. A sudden panicked desperation clawed at his throat. "Where are you going?"

"I don't have it yet, assassin. But I'll be back."

Ri blew out a slow, measured breath as Shev turned their back.

"Careful, though," said Shev. "I wager all of this will only make everything hurt worse when the pain comes tomorrow."

CHAPTER FIFTEEN

"**I** WANT TO SEE the records on the prison," said Kasia.

Her voice bounced off the walls in the small stone meeting room, and her echo was all that answered.

"Did you not hear me? Pro—" She hesitated. She'd only heard the king say his cousin's name once or twice, if even that. All she could remember was seeing it written. "Proch?"

The sharp-boned young man raised an eyebrow. "*Proke*," he corrected. "Not…Protch." He mumbled something under his breath, too quiet for Kasia to hear, but she made out the words "damned Farowfin language," and tightened her fingertips on the arms of her chair.

"Give me the records," she said, and her voice came out like steel.

Proch blinked slowly and shifted his tongue in his mouth in a way that was irritating—nearly dismissive. "You want a list of everyone in the prison cells?"

"I will not repeat myself."

"I could save you a great deal of effort if I knew what you were looking for."

"The men at the gates."

Proch nodded, firelight casting shadows over his cheekbones. "The soldiers?"

"Yes."

He leaned forward, black hair hanging beside his chin, fingers lacing together, and said, "What use would you have with such names?"

Kasia's face did not move. "Are you not a royal advisor?"

"I am the king's advisor."

Kasia ran her left hand over the chair's arm slowly, grounding herself. It was hard and wooden and real, and she needed very badly to focus on something entirely neutral. Entirely physical. "It is not your job to question me."

"With all due respect," he said, bowing his head until the tips of his hair grazed the table, "neither is it my job to answer to you."

She could feel the slow rise in the temperature of her blood.

"Then whose job is it?"

"Advisors will be assigned to you, highness."

"When? I've been here over a month."

Proch shrugged sympathetically.

"Do the king and queen not share these things here?"

"This is a matter you should discuss with the king."

"Gods dammit, I am the queen."

Proch did not blink. He leaned back in his seat and said, "The last queen, Reyan's mother—she did not care to be so deeply involved in the politics of ruling. Apart from one or two issues that mattered to her, she left most of the day-to-day drivel to the king."

"I am not Reyan's mother," said Kasia.

"No." Proch nearly laughed, and it was impossible to tell if it was with her or at her. "You are not."

"I wish to know which advisors answer to me, and—"

"As I said, I suggest you take this up with your husb—"

"No," said Kasia. "I will take it up with you. And if you do not *listen* to me, I swear to Plynos I will have the answer taken out of your skin. I am quite sure I can find a servant with a flogger who will listen to me."

"Queen, I am royal as well," he said, a quiet note of danger in his voice. But his mouth curved into a misplaced smile. "Oh, I like you."

Kasia raised an eyebrow.

"Seems the gods put a whip where your tongue should be."

"Mm," said Kasia. "I've been told that whips hurt less."

At that, the king's cousin threw his head back and laughed. "What was it that you wanted? A record of prisoners?"

"Yes," said Kasia.

"It's here." Proch stood and rummaged in a large bloodwood cabinet in the corner of the room, then tossed a scroll to her. She wasn't sure if she'd frightened him or charmed him into giving it to her. Her intention had been the former, but if she had to wager, she would have placed a bet that it had somehow been the latter.

"Thirty-five men," she breathed, tracing a finger over the ink that named each soldier being held behind bars in the dungeon on the palace grounds.

"Thirty-four," said Proch. "First name on that list is the dead man. That's why it's been etched over in red."

"Then you are quite familiar with this list."

Proch met her eyes, and for once, his were dark and entirely serious. "I am."

"Do you not think the king is being influenced by his own grief to hold them there?"

"Don't ask me such things."

"You advise my husband. Has *he* not asked you such things?"

The knot in Proch's throat bobbed when he swallowed. "Queen—"

"I want them released," she said.

"Excuse me?"

She enunciated very carefully, voice low, "I. Want. Them. Released."

"I cannot do that."

"I thought Jaelen was hailed as this bastion of equality."

Proch shook his head, lips pursed. "I know how it is in Farowfin, but I swear to you, lady, this has nothing to do with your sex. Were you a man and Reyan a woman, I would hold the same convictions. The fact remains that not only are you new, you hail from a country that Jaelen has long been on shaky ground with. And you and Reyan are not...you're not even bound."

Kasia's lips thinned and a breeze made the candles in the room flicker. Perhaps it had risen from her.

Proch glanced up at them, then locked his gaze back on hers. "I do not care if you had been queen for a decade, I could not release the king's prisoners on your command alone. Just as I could not release yours on his."

"Will he kill them?" said Kasia.

"I don't know."

She couldn't decide which she was more frustrated over—these men imprisoned on her own palace grounds, and nothing she could do for it, or over the very fact that she had all the authority in the world, if a person glanced at her. But that when it came down to it, she was entirely powerless.

She did not thank the king's cousin when she stood and left the room.

Instead, she found herself in the surprisingly modest libraries of the castle, and settled herself in a nook beside the fire. She'd smashed her way into power when she was a girl, and she would do it now, in the same way: through knowledge, and its ravenous pursuit.

She lost herself in the dullest, largest tome she could find: Jaelenian law. Eventually, she would know it better than the king, then let him and his unbearable cousin cross her.

Wits was a game she knew she could play.

"King—"

"Yes, I am aware of your interest in the prisoners."

Kasia closed her mouth and approached the throne. "You are."

Reyan breathed in through his nose, out again slowly. "My cousin does not keep secrets from me."

Kasia could not decide whether to sit on her own throne beside him to have this conversation, or to stand in front of him. She would be damned if she would kneel.

"Next time you decide to involve yourself in matters that could incite unrest, I do wish you would do it to my face." His face was granite.

"Oh?" said Kasia. She made the decision to stand. Inches away from him, she could look down at him, see the particular tension in his fingers, the drawn lines of anxiety in his forehead. "Like you consulted with me over slapping Farowfin in the face?"

"Oh gods," he said, rolling his eyes. He stood and walked right past her, quickly enough that Kasia nearly stumbled getting out of his way. She cursed herself immediately. Why should she have been the one to move? Let him bruise his shoulder knocking into her.

Kasia caught up to him quickly, matching his long strides, and he glanced over his shoulder at her, coolly appraising. The king wore grey today. It was so different from the bright teal of Kasia's dress. That was a difficult thing to get used to. Outside, Jaelen was tropical. Smothered in humidity, which meant that the forests were bright green, and the flowers and bugs and trees were so many intense shades of pink and red and blue that it was dazzling. But the people tended to wear colors that were muted and sharp all at once. Deep, fathomless blacks and silvery greys, bright whites. Some deigned to venture out and wear dark blues, and Kasia had seen one or two in dresses that suggested some sort of color, but Reyan always wore the colors of the rocks that lined the cliffs. White and grey and obsidian.

All Kasia owned were bright, indulgent things. She supposed they were oddly alike in that way—he dark against the brightness of his country, and she, bright against the cold white of hers.

"I saw the ledgers," she said.

"And?"

Kasia clenched her jaw.

Reyan pushed out of the massive doors of the throne room and they walked through the halls. He sighed finally, and stopped, turning toward her when they were near the kitchens. "I did not think it wise to waste money on helping to fund a frivolous festival when we have more financial trouble now than we've ever had. The damned grey is destroying our funds, Kasia."

"I know," she said. "As I told you, I saw the ledgers."

Reyan raised a hand in question, letting his fingers brush the air for a moment, raised his eyebrow.

"It is tradition, King."

"I am well aware."

"The whole world goes to that festival. Your kingdom contributes money to its allies when they must host every year. And yet the year you are allied with Farowfin, with whom you have a reputation, by the way, of being less than hospitable, you rescind all your financial support?"

"I do not know what you wish me to say."

Kasia let out a little laugh.

Reyan stood a bit taller and clenched his jaw. "We do not have the funds to share. Perhaps if your country took the threat that is devouring the earth more seriously and endeavored to house a *fraction* of the people we've been saddled with, withdrawing my support wouldn't be necessary."

Kasia bristled under the weight of a biting truth. "Our support," she said.

Reyan nodded once in acknowledgement of the correction, then pushed open the door to the dining hall.

"Where are you going?"

Reyan cocked his head. "Food," he said. "I'm starving." And he let the door close without inviting her in.

CHAPTER SIXTEEN

EVERY TIME GALLIEN KNELT before the Va'alian king, she wanted to throw up on his perfectly polished floor.

Her whole life, she had slowly allowed herself to acknowledge, revolved around bowing to him. And if she tried to stand, he would jerk her back down by the throat.

He'd done it before.

"The assassin is not here yet."

Gallien frowned. She was only a day early; that seemed strange.

"You may stand," he said, and she stood. She was so much taller than him, so much stronger, so much more suited for war. The lazier the king had gotten, the less he'd worked his gift of water. When he was young, Gallien was sure he could have flooded this room on command. But now, his languor made Gallien wonder if he could even soak her head from here. It would be so horrifically simple to kill him at this very moment, if guards weren't stationed at every corner of the room.

The only time he ever let her in here entirely alone was when the assassin was there too—a quiet, and somewhat ironic, insurance policy.

Fire burned through her veins, and it smoked in her eyes whenever she looked at him. He would had to have been a fool to feel safe with her. And if there was one thing the Va'alian king was not, it was foolish.

"The assassin will be here. You will wait for him."

"Yes, King," Gallien said, staring him straight in the eye. She locked her jaw and stood tall, now that she had been allowed, because something in it felt like freedom.

"Leave me," he said.

She left.

When Gallien made it to her little house just south of the palace, she felt her very skin begin to relax. It wasn't a large place, just a one-bedroom cottage, really, surrounded by trees. The land had been her father's, back when he'd been a captain in the king's navy. Back before battle had taken his life and buried him beneath the sea. The cottage, she had built herself.

Leylya was waiting on her front porch. "You and I need to talk."

Gallien scowled. "I don't know what about."

It was not simply about Leylya. It was about the prickling emptiness she'd felt ever since she'd driven back the grey. The emptiness that she'd been trying to ignore, had had perfectly good excuses to ignore, until now. The emptiness that haunted her—a vacuum where her power had been.

She'd used it before, of course, and she'd always known when she'd hit a limit. It felt like a sort of gnawing in her innards that said *Do not take more than your god gave you, or it will come out of your bones.* She'd never edged farther than that. She'd heard stories of practitioners gone mad or so weak they couldn't function after overspending power past what they'd been granted. So she'd never so much as tiptoed past the warning.

And every night after, she'd wake to find that well refilled. Sometimes a little earlier, sometimes later, but always, *always* the power was hers again.

This gaping pit in her stomach where she usually felt the blessing humming, it spoke of emptiness.

She could still light fire. Her power hadn't been spent.

It was just…less.

Missing.

Not enough to send her into a panic, but enough to make her crave being alone. Enough to make her furious that Leylya was here.

Leylya breathed out a little disbelieving laugh, and followed her when she went inside.

"I did not invite you in," said Gallien.

"Fuck yourself," said Leylya, and Gallien tried not to smile at the vulgar insult coming from such pretty, feminine lips.

Perhaps she shouldn't brood, not just yet.

Perhaps she wished to be distracted.

Gallien turned on the water in the small basin and came out in a trickle. "Light a fire for me," she called over her shoulder to Leylya.

"What for?"

"Tea."

Leylya laughed, and Gallien shut her eyes and fell into it. "I've never seen you drink anything but alcohol."

"Well," said Gallien, choosing to worry about the things Leylya had seen rather than the quiet things she felt. That seemed less dangerous, somehow, "you've learned a great many new things of me recently then, haven't you?" She pursed her lips. There she was, trying like hells to deter Leylya from bringing up the incident on the sea, and she'd opened the door for the conversation herself.

She was silent as she moved her iron tea kettle to the fire the second Leylya had it lit.

She sat on the wood floor she hadn't swept since she couldn't remember when and Leylya sat with her. She never had guests and stayed on the land as little as possible; Gallien had never had much reason for living room furniture.

There was no sound in the room but the crackle and pop of flame. And so fire was all there was left to discuss.

"You have to tell me," said Leylya.

Gallien did not look at her. "I don't know what else there is to say."

"Captain."

"You can call me Gallien. We're on land, now." Gallien glanced at the girl, who was sitting very close to her, and Leylya nodded, once.

"How long?"

Gallien blinked at the fire, smoke swirling up into the chimney, little wisps spreading out to sting her eyes. She swallowed hard and shut them. "A decade."

"What?" Leylya's voice was usually so very soft, but this was a roar.

"Longer now, I suppose. Eleven years? I was twenty when it happened."

"*How?*" said Leylya, and she grabbed Gallien's arm. Gallien narrowed her eyes but allowed her first mate to turn her.

"How what?"

Leylya blinked at the ground, shaking her head slowly and blubbering. "Eleven years. How did you…how did you get it? And how did you hide it for so long? Gallien, this is impossible."

Gods, Leylya never used her name. She curled her fingers into the wood floor.

"I had no choice but to hide it, Leylya."

"It's illegal," she whispered.

"I know."

"Do you understand what they'll do if—"

"Nothing," said Gallien. "The king has already taken everything from me that he can."

"I don't…"

Gallien sighed heavily and removed the kettle from where it hung over the fire. She poured the orange and rose water into cups for them both and drank. "I was sixteen when I joined the king's navy," she said.

"That long?" said Leylya. "Gods, I hadn't realized."

She'd met Leylya when she was twenty-six, hand-picked her for her crew. But Gallien had endeavored never to share a single detail of her life before then with anyone. It wasn't their business, and it could get someone killed if she wasn't careful. "Of course," said Gallien. "Everyone serves as *something* at sixteen; were you not always in the navy?"

"No," said Leylya. "I taught, actually. Two years. Languages. Then I joined up when I felt I was ready."

"Not me," said Gallien. "Father was a brilliant officer, and my older sisters had done their duty on the ocean, so it felt right that I would do the same. Of course, I was more brilliant than my father ever was."

Leylya smiled into her scar and sipped her tea. "And so modest."

"At eighteen, I was going to leave the king's navy. I loved the sea, and I was a good fighter. But sailing without the freedom to go where I wished, do what I wanted, made me…gods, it made me *sick*." She felt that old familiar sickness sinking into her bones now, just thinking of it. How unimaginable it had been then, how intolerable it was now. "But my father…he was killed. One of the king's many, many battles." It had been such a long time, but it stabbed like a thick needle to her heart, just the memory of it all.

"Vashkaree," said Leylya, a Farowfin swear in frustrated affirmation. The Va'alian king had never shied away from conflict.

"So I stayed. I thought I would stay on a couple of years, earn money as I was advancing incredibly, then go back to my mother and sisters with it all and figure everything out from there. Become a fisherman, something. I sent word that I would be leaving, and got an audience with the king himself in response. He begged me to stay. *Begged* me, Leylya." A vicious satisfaction wound through her chest at that. He had begged. And she had said no. What a fool, to think she could refuse a king. "I turned the tides of wars, you see. Won or lost battles by my presence or lack of it. And I knew it. I'd trained at weaponry and the seas since I was a girl and I was...good. The king pleaded, offered me money, a ship, a command...but I didn't wish for the freedom of the sea under the thumb of a man. And I wanted to go home. It had been two years and I hadn't been allowed to mourn the death of my father. I turned him down."

Leylya looked down into her cup, ran her teeth over her lip.

"And this, my friend, is the part you can never tell."

Leylya met her eyes. "Friend?"

Gallien's eyes shuttered and an unfamiliar tangle of nerves expanded in her stomach.

But then Leylya smiled, and the tangle dissipated into nothing.

"On my life, I swear it."

Leylya had already seen the biggest secret she'd kept all her life. The time for mistrust was long past. And it clawed at her. Now that she'd shown another human one thing, she wanted desperately to show her everything. Intimacy was quickly, dangerously addictive. Still, the words clawed in Gallien's throat, hanging on so hard she had to rip them out. "Three weeks later, I found myself returning from one of my final voyages to word that my mother and two sisters had fallen ill. Something had swept through their village, the messenger said, and there was nothing to be done. They were already dead." Gallien had never been able to forget the violent sickness in her stomach, the hurt behind her skull. The particular pain of a heart being ripped in two.

She'd gone to the king. And she'd knelt before him, known that it had been him who had done this to keep her. He'd held her in chains with a glance, and a friendly set of condolences. "I was very sorry to hear about your family. How tragic."

"Thank you," she had said, heat burning in her face, her ears, her gut. Her fingers had ached for a sword.

"Circumstances being what they are," the king had continued, and his voice had once been as smooth as velvet, "I wondered if you had reconsidered my offer."

"Yes, King," she'd said. "And I accept."

He'd promised her her own command, the best ship in his navy, more money, nearly free reign of the sea when she was not fighting for him—and all of it felt like blood.

"Gods," said Leylya.

"The moment I took my command, and I insisted on choosing my own soldiers, all women, the first battle I fought, a god took notice and gave me this." Gallien let a little flame rise from her fingers and then watched it die.

"Which god?"

"I never bothered to ask."

Leylya had stopped drinking and the tea was growing cold. "Why do you sail for him?"

"Because," said Gallien simply, "the threat was clear enough. If I didn't, then I would find myself sick as well. And because this is very close to freedom. And because..."

Leylya shifted closer to her.

"Because someday, perhaps I will find myself in a position to steal back the ship he really promised me. The best one. And perhaps I will take from him *everything* he took from me."

"That's treason," Leylya whispered.

"So is hiding a gift from the gods."

"Do you know what the king did to the last man who was found hiding his wind, Gallien? He had him whipped, then boiled the man's husband in oil. In front of him."

"The whipping is nothing. If he finds out, he can do what he wishes to my body. No one gifted ever gets *truly* harmed. That in itself would be too much a slight to the god who gifted them." The only ruler who had ever tried executing someone for hiding their powers had been a Jaelenian queen, ages and ages ago. She'd thought to make an example of a woman who'd been blessed with water and hidden it away, by surrounding her in blue—the color of the water. She'd buried her publicly in vorissus blossoms—beautifully fragrant, and they melted flesh if that flesh brushed against them. The queen had woken the next morning to find herself so badly burned that her skin was just this side of stripped from her body. Everyone took it as vengeance from the gods, and the punishment had been rewritten across the world. "You and I both know the real risk isn't in a few lashes. It's what they do to the people you love."

"No one has been caught hiding something like this in decades, Gallien."

"They will force me off the sea and into nobility, Leylya. And I will wither away. They may as well just slit my damn throat. No one does it anymore because everyone has people they love too much. But the people I love? Are all already gone."

Something that might have been hurt flashed in Leylya's eyes, and panic gripped at Gallien's throat suddenly.

"Don't...I...you need to leave," she said.

Leylya blinked. "What?"

Gallien stood. "*Leave.*"

"Captain—"

"Gods, Leylya!" she yelled. "Go!"

Leylya jumped up, her teacup discard on the floor, and said, "Y-yes, Captain." She left.

`Gallien poured herself another cup, shaking. *The people I love are already gone.*

How carefully and how long had she worked to make sure that were true? It was. It was true. Dammit.

She did not think of Leylya's fingers, and what they would feel like trailing across her throat, her collarbone, and that night before she fell asleep, she did not imagine them trailing lower.

There was no room in her veins for anything like that—there *couldn't* be. There was only room for the ocean, and the swords in her ship, and the cold certainty that someday before he grew old enough to die, she would destroy the Va'alian king.

CHAPTER SEVENTEEN

K ASIA SHRUGGED ON A coat—too heavy for the season. It was thick and dark and fur-lined, and absurdly impractical. But it was soft, and she wouldn't be wearing it for long.

She hooked a blade in a sheath attached to her belt, and tied her thick curls of hair back, chin held high as she passed her husband in the large foyer, who followed instantly.

"What are you doing?"

She didn't answer, merely pushed out the massive double doors that led to the courtyard, and made her way across the grounds to the stables. She smiled to herself when she heard footsteps behind her—hurried and heavy.

"Kasia," he said again, grabbing her arm and turning her toward him. "What are you doing?" He glanced up and down her body. "And why in hells are you dressed like you're going to spend the night in a snowbank?"

Kasia looked at him coolly, and jerked back from his grip. It was hot as all hells at the moment, and she thought with the heavy coat crushing her chest and the humidity filling her lungs, she might actually suffocate shortly.

She opened her horse's stall and set a saddle upon her back, then led her out onto the grass.

"Answer me," said Reyan. He ground his teeth together when he shut his mouth; she could see them moving behind his lips.

"I'm going south, and I'll need it when the nights get cold," she said. She adjusted the straps of the saddle on the horse, empty food bags and water skins hanging from the animal. Kasia prayed Reyan wouldn't test them. As it was, she didn't seem to be in much danger of that; Reyan was backed into the shadows of the stable, hand on the door of a stall. He stood on the balls of his feet; if she took off, he was ready to follow her.

"South," said Reyan.

"Mmhmm."

"And why, my beautiful, delicate sun petal of a wife, would you be going south?" Sarcasm ran from his words like water.

Kasia raised her eyebrows and smoothed her horse's mane down, then hoisted herself on top of her. At that point, Reyan opened the stall. His muscles were tensed, veins standing out in his neck. "Well, we've a bit of a problem down there, don't you think?"

"And you're going to solve it."

"I am," said Kasia.

Reyan barked out a laugh and said, "How do you plan on doing that?"

Kasia said, "Don't concern yourself with my business, King. Why don't you go back to your shrine and *pray*?" At that, she kicked her horse, and the animal galloped off. Kasia made out one very harsh swear from Reyan's mouth before any sounds he made were drowned out by her horse's hooves.

She was certain he would be on his own horse and galloping after her within seconds; he'd practically been jumping to mount his animal back in the stables anyway. She was further sure that there was a host of guards following along out of earshot. But that was fine. Kasia had no intention of riding alone to the south; she wasn't mad. She had no plans to try to dispel that all-consuming grey by herself. People had been blessed with abilities before her, and they would be blessed with them still after, and no one had been able to drive it back by themselves. There was nothing she could do completely on her own. And truthfully, it wasn't altruism that drove the desire to do anything about it anyway. Not entirely.

What she really wanted was a people under her who didn't sneer when she walked past. Who bowed as quickly to her as they did to their king. She wanted a country that saw her power—both of their powers combined—and found themselves stricken with awe. With nerves, with fear, with hope. And right now, as it was, they had none of those things. Right now, all the people did was grumble. Grumble at a union that was supposed to have been so powerful, would make such a difference.

And yet, for a week and a half, prisoners sat, undealt with, from the last town the darkness had claimed. The blood from their altercation had been cleaned up, the bodies moved, but it was fresh. And all the people wondered, as Kasia wondered, if perhaps it had been preventable.

The fact remained—she could do nothing about them, and she could do nothing about the endless shifting dark. Not without the king.

Her horse slowed at her behest; she needed to allow Reyan to keep up, to stop her. And he would; he had married her for *some* reason, though that reason was currently entirely unknown to her. But she was betting on his wish that she not ride somewhere ridiculous and get herself killed.

Soon enough, she heard the thunder of hooves behind her and smiled, her own dapple moving along at a steady trot.

Reyan moved alongside her. "Stop," he said.

Kasia laughed.

"Gods, stop," he said again. He moved his horse in front of hers, bullying her grey into turning toward the wood at their side. Kasia let it happen.

Reyan moved close enough to her that he was able to grab her horse's reins.

"What are you doing?" he said. His voice came out very tired. More than tired.

The horses slowed to a stop in a little clearing, where the trees were tall and the shadows long.

"*Something*," she said.

Reyan let out a sigh and his shoulders dropped. He kept his eyes on her and slid to the ground, bright green leaves bending and crushing under his feet. Not once did his gaze waver; if it did, perhaps she would run off.

She wouldn't. But of course, he didn't know that.

Kasia got off her horse without asking for his hand. By now, he knew better than to offer it. He tied the horses to a tree.

"What are we to do, King?" she said.

Reyan slid a glance over at her. "About what?"

Kasia just laughed. Perhaps another king would have tried to kill her for it. But if it hadn't been Reyan, Kasia would very likely have tried to match with a queen anyway. Queens understood each other without death threats.

Perhaps she still would. If they hadn't even bound with one another, then perhaps all of this wasn't final. She would leave him sitting on his throne and go straight down to the Andran princess. Fuck Jaelen, and fuck its king.

If she couldn't get him to give her *something*, then perhaps she would go back to the palace, and quietly pack her things away.

Kasia sat on the leaves beneath her feet. Reyan hesitated on his way to her, but sat as well. "I am going to ask you a question, Reyan, and I believe I am owed an answer."

Reyan glanced down at the ground, nostrils lightly flaring. Then he met Kasia's eyes with his own, so dark they were nearly black, and she was struck again at how bright they were—how fiery and cold all at once. "Ask," he said, "and I will answer."

"Why do you refuse to bind with me?" she said.

Reyan was quiet.

"I think it is me, partly. But I know it is my country you hate more than my sharp tongue and my tendency to laugh at you and not treat you gently, as all men treat kings. What is it that you detest so thoroughly that even as I ask you this question, you cannot bring yourself to look at me?"

Reyan's jaw shifted, a hard line. His eyes moved very quickly from frozen to stormy. On his face, Kasia saw something she hadn't yet: pain.

"You are exhausting," said Reyan.

Kasia's lips curved into a smile. "Now that, I have heard more than once."

"You're disrespectful and temperamental and...a thousand things that, quite honestly, make me tired just thinking of them. You are everything I hate about Farowfin."

"And what things are those?"

"Gods."

"You hate our gods? Careful, they don't talk back, but they hear every-thing."

He was quiet.

"It must be something more," Kasia continued. "You're not a child. I do not believe that a king as powerful as you is so petulant that he wouldn't fuck a woman he hated *once* if it meant he could save the very world."

Reyan blew out a breath, veins standing out in his hands that splayed on the ground.

"You're very tense."

"Yes," Reyan ground out.

"Almost always."

"I don't trust you," he said.

"No?"

"Our power will be *monstrous* when we bind, Kasia. Surely you can feel that. And there are so many things about you that I cannot put my faith in."

"Perhaps that is something you should have considered before you married me."

"Perhaps."

Kasia brushed her fingers over her lips. "I think that you are afraid. Of what we will be. Of the permanence of such a thing."

Reyan laughed hoarsely. "With you? Yes. I am." He paused, shut his eyes. "My father begged me not to marry a Farowfin girl. He *begged* me."

Kasia stretched her arms over her head and leaned against the tree at her back, utterly languid. "And why did he beg you?"

"Because your country is filled with thieves and murderers."

"Far be it from me to call you a bigot," said Kasia.

He laughed without humor.

"Oh," said Kasia suddenly. "This is personal for you."

Reyan slid a glance over to meet hers.

"Did they do something to you?" Her tone was mocking, just this side of playful. She was baiting him, and the king, with her at least, was so easily baited. "Did you fall in love with a Farowfin girl and she broke your heart? Did they *steal something precious*?"

"Yes," he said very quietly. Quietly enough that Kasia wasn't entirely sure he'd said it. But there was a deep, almost fathomless pain in his eyes. She couldn't look away. "Yes. They took her."

"Who?" Kasia whispered, voice no longer light or playful.

"My mother."

Kasia's face softened. "I am sorry."

"You cannot imagine what it's like to be nine years old, having just played a game of Cathoon with your mother the night before, and to wake up, and walk into your mother's rooms, and find a bloom of crimson under her body. Dripping to the floor, her arms—these arms that held you a thousand times, limp and lifeless. I was the one who found her. And when my father returned from a hunting trip that morning to the news, he couldn't get out of bed for weeks."

Kasia's face had drained of color.

"There was more than one of them; of that we are certain. We caught one. Hung him on a pike. It was political maneuvering; she was in favor of closing off trade with Farowfin because of their policies on slavery."

"We didn't trade with Jaelen."

"Not after that."

"Why didn't this start a war?" said Kasia.

"Couldn't prove anything. We knew it, but nothing would get the assassin to talk. And my father was…weak. He was not one for war."

"I'm sorry," said Kasia.

Silence hung between them for some time. Then Kasia said, "You know, most of us hated that king. The one you hate me for. He was the one whose body I—"

"I know," said Reyan. "It's what made me think of you in the first place." He looked sharply at her again. "I married you against his wishes. Because I knew it was right. I knew it was best for Jaelen—opening up an alliance with Farowfin, particularly should the time come that we ever need to flee north. And I knew…"

Kasia said nothing. She waited.

"I knew that you and I specifically would be…" He caught her eyes with his. "But I can't, Kasia. Every time I look at you, it's like a betrayal. To my father, to my mother, to everything I've believed since I was a child. It's maddening to think of touching you. To think of sharing this massive thing I know we will have with someone who said herself she never gave a shit about the darkness. To ignore everything in my gut that says that you cannot be trusted. I thought I could do this and I can't. I look at you and I want to shove a dagger in your heart, or mine, one."

"So do it," said Kasia.

"What?"

She stood and stripped off her coat; it was stifling in the wood anyway. "Draw your sword; I know you have one. Let us settle this as foolish men settle all of their arguments." Kasia drew her long blade from her side. "Fight me."

CHAPTER EIGHTEEN

"THIS IS RIDICULOUS." REYAN refused to stand.

"No more ridiculous than you holding the sins of a country against your wife. Stand up or I will drive this into your heart."

"That," said Reyan from the ground, "is treason."

"So is admitting you wish to kill me every time you look at me."

Reyan shook his head and leaned back against the tree, eyes shut. "You, Kasia, are very young."

"And you are unreasonable."

"Trust is an earned thing, Queen."

And at that, he felt the cool of her blade against his throat.

His jaw locked, and he opened his eyes.

She held the hilt very close to his neck and stared back at him, eyes dark and hard as flint. Reyan grabbed her wrist. "Stop," he said, voice deathly quiet.

She pushed.

He drew his sword.

"This is foolish, Kasia," he said, but she backed away a pace and he got to his feet. "If you think my guards aren't waiting just outside this forest—"

"I suppose you'd better kill me quick, then."

She lashed out.

Reyan jumped back, sword brandished. "I don't want to hurt you," he said.

Kasia slashed again, twice—wild and moving closer to him with each swipe of her sword. It was long and thin and matched her very well, as though the blade had been made for her, or she for it. "You said you wanted to shove a blade through my heart."

Kasia stabbed straight for his chest, and he blocked with his blade, eyes going wide. The sound rang through the trees.

"Fight me or I will kill you here, King," she said, and when she lunged, something burst in Reyan's chest. He swung for her with all the force in his arms and she stumbled when their swords connected.

Reyan pulled back and stabbed for her again, point aimed at her chest. She parried, dancing back like she'd done this all her life. Her body moved like it was used to this, like it welcomed it. Like it was aching for a challenge. Fine, he would give it to her.

Kasia leapt toward him again, both hands on the hilt of her sword, and swung with everything she had. Her face was red already, and Reyan could feel the sweat popping up on his brow. He met it, and pressed against her, flipping her so that she wound up, back pressed against the tree. They were so close, close enough that he could smell the lilies and lavender perfume she'd oiled over her neck that morning, could detect the faintest hint of strawberry wine on her breath.

Their bodies pressed against each other, clean lines melding with curved ones.

Kasia ducked just as he let up pressure, and his blade slipped, digging into the tree. He yanked it out and spun just in time to catch Kasia's sword flying for him. It caught him in the cheek, drawing a thin line of blood. Kasia did not even have the grace to look sorry.

Reyan reached for it, and his fingers came away red and sticky.

These were real blades, and either of them should have been prepared for damage. Reyan made for her again, this time, not worrying about restraint. He didn't see her, he saw Farowfin. Not her skin, but his mother's—cold and rigid. When he nicked her arm, it wasn't Kasia's blood that dripped onto the leaves, it was the blood of his mother. He let a rage he had never allowed himself to really feel uncoil inside him until he was blinded with it, choking on it. Consumed by eighteen years of hatred for people he could never even touch, never get vengeance upon.

He swung, and swung again, and again, until his arms burned and the sound of metal on metal filled the trees. One more powerful lunge, and Kasia fell. He blinked, and suddenly he saw *her*. In this moment of startling clarity, he saw Kasia. Her eyes sparked with passion, with fire, with fierce determination. All Farowfin traits, these things he thought he despised. But there was his wife on the ground, devastatingly beautiful and determined, dark eyes flashing, and something sliced through his chest, something that was not hate.

Kasia took the pause for herself and shot her hand out into the air, sending a gust of sharp wind behind Reyan's knees and knocking him to the ground.

He hit hard, knees cracking against little sticks and crushing the grass down to the dirt. He caught himself with his hands.

"You cheated," Reyan breathed, sitting up, and resting for a moment on his ankles

"It's not cheating to use my advantages. You've got six inches and forty pounds on me." She dropped her sword and lunged for him, powerful, frigid air gusting from her fingers and dizzying Reyan. It caught the dirt on the ground and peppered him with it, and he fought a yell. If he cried out, the guards would come.

And he didn't want that.

Vicious wind swirling around him, Reyan dropped his sword as well, and caught his wife's hands as they made for his neck. He gripped her wrists hard, and cold poured through him, freezing her skin.

When she looked down, he flipped her over and dug his knees into the ground, one between her legs, one outside, pinning her arms over her head.

Cold poured through him, and the wind through her, and she shifted beneath him. His leg stayed still against her thigh and he clenched his teeth. Kasia gasped when he let another surge of cold spread from his fingers, and arched her back, and Reyan fought his own body's not entirely appropriate response to that.

To that, and to the heady combination of his power winding together with hers, crackling and amplifying and washing over both of their skin in waves. It only rose in intensity, until it had become such a part of him, such a part of her, that Reyan could hardly breathe.

What would it feel like, he couldn't stop himself wondering, if they joined their bodies? If they completed the binding that the wedding ceremony had started?

He stopped, fighting a shudder, and unhanded her wrists. And Kasia just breathed there on the ground beneath him. The wind died with the cold.

He slid off her, forcing his mind back to a neutral blank, and tasted the bloody tang on his lips—that scratch from Kasia's blade. Kasia rose beside him, knees digging into the earth before him. Her dress was destroyed, hanging in tatters around her bruised shoulders. Reyan was positive his skin would be similarly marked if he looked in the mirror.

"Reyan," said Kasia, and she grabbed his sword from where it lay on the smoking ground. It smoked because of them. "Do you want to kill me?" Her voice was so shockingly gentle. She brought the point of the blade to her chest. He could see the redness on her skin where it dipped down into her ruined dress. She was breathing hard, and so was he.

Reyan took the handle from her, point digging into her skin. One little move, a small application of pressure, and she would be dead. He never really would have done it; it would have been political suicide. Utterly foolish.

But here she was, begging him to, and no part of him even wanted it. He locked eyes with her, and drug the sword down from her chest, over the fabric, splitting little threads as it went. Then he let it rest on the ground.

Kasia moved so that she knelt between his legs, knees pressed against his thighs. She slid her small hands up his neck, framing his face, fingers feathering over his ears. Reyan fought a shudder. "Reyan," she said.

"Yes?" His voice was hoarse.

"I am sorry about your mother." He could feel her sincerity sinking into his chest. She rubbed her thumb across his face and he didn't want to press his face to her fingers. But he did. "I am sorry about my countrymen, and I am sorry that your father left you with the guilt of having to choose between your country and your loyalty to your family." Her fingers wound in his hair. "I am sorry," she said—simply that. She searched his eyes—for what, he didn't know. Didn't need to.

He was so, so tired.

He shut them, and leaned forward to touch his forehead to hers. Maybe he was sorry too.

The energy was different now, between them. They moved around each other without a ramrod sort of stiffness in their shoulders, and Reyan didn't feel the need to clip his words in every sentence he spoke to her. It was still less than tolerable; she still had that tongue, all those things that reminded Reyan of a deathbed request he'd shattered, that spoke of the worst traits in a country he despised. He still found himself unwilling to turn his back to her, unable to trust her the way he needed to.

But it was chilly now. Not frostbitten.

"You're different," said his cousin.

"How?"

"I don't know." Proch shrugged and drew on his bow, black strands of hair falling into his eyes when the wind blew. "It's enough to make me think you're finally finding a way to loosen up a bit." Proch waggled his heavy eyebrows and Reyan rolled his eyes.

"Hardly."

"I didn't say *how*; that's on you, cousin. What if I meant knitting?" Proch loosed an arrow toward his target just as a wind kicked up and missed completely. "Dammit."

"My turn," said Reyan. He nocked an arrow and stared down the line.

"Why don't you get your wife out here to calm the wind? That's a thing she can do, right?"

"Kasia has never used her abilities to calm *anything* in my presence," said Reyan.

Proch laughed. Reyan fired and it hit just left of center.

"Oh, impressive," said Proch.

"That's what they say."

"Pompous ass," Proch grumbled, and he drew an arrow from his quiver.

"Not pompous if it's true." He grinned at the particular irritated slant of Proch's eyebrows, the thinning of his lips.

"Did you hear the latest from Parien?" said Proch. He was waiting, clearly gauging the wind.

"No."

"Queen's on her deathbed. And her husband died years ago, you remember. Seven children and not one of them gifted."

"Hells," said Reyan. He fired another shot, just to irritate his cousin. It landed just left of center.

Proch pursed his lips, and looked up at the clouds. As though they would help him. "They're holding a proving just next week. Three commoners are of age, though one just barely. Haven't seen someone without a name ascend anywhere in how long?"

"A long time," said Reyan. Simple, inconsequential gossip was relaxing him, for once.

Proch aimed, face stilled in concentration. Another light breeze, just as he fired. "What in hells," he yelled. "I tire of this."

"If you can't fire through the wind, you're a piss-poor archer, Proch."

"And you, King, can kiss my royal ass."

Reyan laughed and hooked his bow across his back. "Tired of this, then?"

Proch paused for a moment. It was very clear to Reyan, suddenly, that Proch had something he wanted to ask. Something that made him nervous. "What are you going to do with them?"

A frown flickered across Reyan's face. "With whom?"

"The men in the dungeon."

Reyan sobered instantly. "I didn't come out here to talk politics with you, Proch. I came to get away from that for a moment."

"Well, my apologies. But those men are rotting in a cell, and the people are afraid."

"Oh, and you know this how?"

"I have my sources."

"Dalliances, probably," Reyan spat.

"Information that comes in the form of someone I've slept with doesn't make that information less valuable. All I'm telling you is what I've heard. The people are worried about the shadow. They're worried about the battle outside the gates, and they're worried it's going to come to them. They're worried that—"

Reyan waited, and when his cousin didn't finish his sentence, Reyan said, "What? They're worried that what?"

"That you are their king. And you've done nothing about it."

"Nor have any other kings or queens."

"Those kings and queens are old. No one expects them to give a shit." He shook his head once. Then met Reyan's gaze. "Those kings and queens don't run the most powerful nation in the world, Reyan."

Reyan swallowed hard, and looked over Proch's shoulder at the skyline. "And what would you have me do? What my father couldn't? What no one else in the world seems to be able to do, or *has* been able to do since all this began ten years ago?"

Yes. Gods, yes. Of course that's what he needed to do. If he wasn't so fucking paralyzed by fear all the time, he would have done it already.

Proch shrugged. "You could start by *binding with your wife.*"

Reyan shook his head. "Would you trust that woman with a power so great? Once it's done, it's done, Proch. There's no going back once we do."

"Reyan. You know what you need to do."

Reyan's jaw locked. "What I do with Kasia is none of your—"

"When it could give you the power to fight back the force that is crippling the world I live in? Yes. I would say it's my concern."

"Not only could she be an adder. But binding with Kasia, Proch, requires *fucking* Kasia, and I can't—" Gods, why did it matter? Why did the thought of that hurt so deeply in his chest? The mood had darkened considerably, and Reyan was no longer terribly concerned with spending the day with his cousin. He said, "I am not required to answer to you."

Something like pity—or the combination of pity and anger—shone in his cousin's eyes. And it was unbearable.

Reyan simply said, "I have things to attend to."

Proch pursed his lips, but nodded. He bowed, turned on his heel, and left.

On his way to the gardens, Reyan caught a flash of something dark out of the corner of his eye, and turned to see Kasia, hiding in the corner.

"Was it...how long have you been there?"

"Not long," said the queen.

"Was that you? Were you...manipulating the air when Proch shot?"

Kasia smiled, all sweetness and innocence. "King, I have no idea what you're talking about." And she let a little breeze float the leaves around her as she walked away.

CHAPTER NINETEEN

S HEV HAD BEEN RIGHT. Everything was worse. Deliberately, intensely, agonizingly worse. When Ri had *just* tasted food, the lack of it was astonishingly painful in his stomach. The wine wore off too quickly, and everything was back with startling clarity—the ache in his head, his teeth, his gums, dying for lack of water. The raw red at his wrists, the cold stone at his back.

And worst of all was the hope. The hope that that Andran had somehow been telling the truth, that they would come back for him, let him go, help him complete this mission and sabotage their own country. The most painful was not knowing when, and figuring it would never happen anyway. Knowing that a chain and knuckles and knives hadn't been able to loosen his tongue, but the simple promise of under seasoned chicken had done it.

He had withstood so much and traded off his integrity for so little. It didn't matter. Ri had never been much for integrity. But something in it stung at his pride. There was nothing to do down here in the damp dark but contemplate just how it had happened that he'd managed to fail so thoroughly. He'd ruined Va'al and Etrya in one fell swoop. It was almost impressive, really.

Ri thought of nothing but that, —his country, his family and friends, dying, and his role in it all—and very occasionally, he allowed himself to think of Adè. When he wasn't racked with guilt and tremoring with hunger, he sometimes shut his eyes, though there was hardly a reason down here in the dark, and pictured Adè's massive arms, folded across his chest, his dark, dark skin that glinted in the sun, his bright white smile and the way his laugh rumbled in his chest. Adè had very deep dimples. It was something most people didn't know about him. People noticed his size, his smirking mouth, his quiet, authoritative presence, his position in relation to the power of the world. But people didn't look closely enough to think about his dimples.

Ri did.

It had been endlessly frustrating, just trying to be around the man. They'd first met months ago, when nothing but whispers of war had plagued Etrya's shores. He'd come to Ri's home with his family, on some sort of political visit. The nobility had held a ball, and Ri certainly wasn't noble, —even more certainly wasn't royal—but he knew enough of them far too intimately for at least someone not to have been pressured into inviting him.

Ri had met the prince at that ball. He'd seen him stride down the stairs in a close-fitting suit and sharp, laughing eyes and almost choked on his wine. Nothing had happened between them; nothing had *ever* even begun to happen between them. But they'd spoken. And they'd spoken enough.

Enough that when war broke out, and Ri was called to Va'al, the prince sought him out, again and again. Enough that though they did nothing but talk, within two weeks there, Ri knew the way to the prince's rooms in the pitch black. Enough that the thought of killing that Jaelenian girl just to set Adè up on the throne joined with that brat king felt like licking the sharp end of a knife.

And there it was again—the sharp, shuddering pain of existing.

Ri waited, and waited, and waited for what might have been a day. Or it might have been six. He had no idea except in as far as he was beginning to lose his mind. Beginning to see shadows dancing on the walls, to feel things that were not stone beneath his hips, beginning to hear sounds that he knew were false. Surely birds didn't sing in dungeons.

And when the door opened to his cell, and the figure who walked in was small, with short, bright hair and a pointed smile, Ri assumed that was part of his descent into madness as well. It certainly wasn't his fortune come to fix his life.

"Ri," said the small person, and Ri did not answer. Why should he humor his own cracking mind?

Shev knelt before him and poured water into his mouth once again. Enough that he could feel it cooling his veins, nearly shuddered in pleasure when a little dribbled from his lips over his skin, which was too hot and too cold all at once.

"How long?" he rasped, when he'd determined that Shev was either real or the sort of illusion he was desperate to dream.

"Three days," they said.

"Gods. It feels like I've been here forever."

They hadn't brought a feast this time—just some dried fruits and meats, a hunk of bread which he would gladly rip into now if his hands were free.

"The rest is loaded on your horse," said Shev, gesturing down to the food in their hands.

"The rest?" said Ri. A frown flitted over his features. He struggled to breathe; he'd been locked in this position for far too long.

"Yes, you idiot," they said, reaching into the front pocket of their leather pants. "Have they gone for your brain as well as your body now?"

They pulled out a key, and Ri could practically feel his eyes dilating just looking at it. Could feel his skin begging for it. Such a small thing, promising something so very large.

"Don't try anything," Shev said, and they stuck the key in his right shackle. They moved immediately to his left just as his right dropped to the floor. The feeling of his muscles uncoiling was agony. Sweet, perfect agony. As though a tiger had stretched, and run its claws down his biceps, then gnawed on his wrists. Ri let out a strangled cry when his arms hit the dirt.

He grabbed for the hunk of bread the moment he could get his stiff fingers to cooperate and tore into it the way an animal tears into a kill.

"You're really helping me," he said. He was unreasonably embarrassed at the sudden tears stinging his eyes.

Shev shrugged.

"I could kiss you," said Ri.

"If you value the use of your tongue, and from the reports I've heard, you certainly do, that is not a course of action I would suggest taking."

Ri let himself smile, just for half a moment, and his lips cracked. He tasted blood immediately, but that was nothing new.

"How are you doing this? Is this not treason?" said Ri.

"Why in hells, captive, do you keep trying to persuade me not to save you?"

They looked at him quizzically, head cocked, but with a sarcastic tilt to one of their eyebrows.

"I only wish to know how," said Ri.

"It is none of your concern how. There are people I know and people I know a good deal *about*, and all men will shatter their convictions for something. Most often, something intangible. Though for you, that price was apparently food."

Ri made a vulgar gesture at them, and they laughed lightly.

"The guards have stepped away for the next eight minutes. They will say they came down here and found you dead. You're in no condition to ride on your own without a little rest, so you will come to a friend's, sleep, and in the morning, you will go. Do you understand?"

Ri nodded quickly, and just that small movement was enough to make the ache in his head flare. He winced.

"Gods, you're in a bad way," said Shev, and they jerked their head toward the cell door.

Ri stood slowly, legs shaking and prickling. They could hardly support him.

Shev looped an arm around his shoulder, though they were much shorter and smaller than he was—he doubted they would be of much help. And the two silently left the cell.

Shev grunted under his weight and hissed, "No wonder they didn't feed you. I should've left you down here longer."

Ri rolled his eyes and worked on supporting more of his own weight, though it sent screaming pain up his shins.

They ascended the stairs into the air and dim moonlight, and Ri nearly started crying right there. He hadn't been under for long, but it had been long enough. Long enough to make him wonder if he would ever see the sky again, or if he would draw his last breaths in a stone cavern that smelled of his own piss and shit.

"Don't fall apart yet, assassin. We haven't the time for it."

Ri dragged his feet across the limp grasses, just breathing, breathing, breathing. They kept to the shadows; not getting noticed was not difficult. There were few guards around, and Andra did not have a reputation for keeping many prisoners.

Shev had taken care of the only guards that mattered.

They stopped with him just outside the quarters reserved for the dungeon and let out a low whistle.

"You're going to get me killed someday, Shev. You and your damn schemes," Ri heard someone grumble.

"Harlin. Shut it. You know you love me."

A young man appeared around the corner with two horses: one for himself, Ri figured, and one for, perhaps, Shev and Ri?

Shev hopped up onto theirs, and Harlin had to boost Ri to get him onto it with them. He was just too weak. Too weak and too in pain and just this side of entirely disoriented.

He didn't ask where they were going, didn't ask how far; it didn't matter. All that mattered was that he was out of that hellhole, and wherever he was going could not possibly be worse.

It wasn't. They took him to a little cabin far enough from the palace grounds that no wandering eyes would find him, and a well of anxiety opened up in his chest. There were a hundred ways this could go wrong. But Ri was almost too exhausted to feel it. Too exhausted to feel suspicion, or worry, or anxiety, or anything that wasn't gratitude, and lust for a soft bed and a cup of something hot. Something that would soothe his raw throat.

He slid off the horse after Shev, and Harlin caught him, grunting. It wasn't that Ri was particularly large; if anything, he'd always hated how thin he was. It was that he was tall, and nothing but muscle wound beneath his skin. He was heavy.

They made their way into the little house, and Shev went to tend the horses. Ri tried not to collapse on the living room floor.

Harlin's nose wrinkled after a few moments of awkward silence. "You smell like shit."

"I'm quite sure I do," said Ri.

"Harlin, leave him be. Gods. Ri, there's a bathroom in there, just at the end of the hall. Clean yourself up, and then we will talk."

Ri didn't have to be told twice. He braced himself on the wall and made his way to the bathroom, legs shaking the whole way. The room was...shockingly extravagant, compared to the rest of the house. Several soaps, a mirror, it even looked like...did he have running water? That was uncommon among those who were not wealthy.

Ri turned a dial over the bath, and water came falling out. A knot formed in his throat, and he stripped out of his mess of clothing. He couldn't even remember what their original color had been.

The water was tepid—just warm enough to be tolerable. But it was paradise. He shut his eyes and leaned against the stone, lying so flat on his back that the water soaked over his face. Perhaps he would drown right here, and he wouldn't even protest. Ri blew out a breath that rose to the surface in a bubble and let the water soothe his skin. The soap burned like fire as the bubbles found their way into the little cuts he had everywhere, the gashes on his legs. It burned the worst around his wrists, but even the pain felt good. Ri welcomed it. Because his skin was tingling with perfect emptiness, and the soap here smelled like honeysuckle, and for a moment, it was all right.

He wasn't going to die.

It was all right.

He pushed his head to the surface and sucked in one sobbing breath, and that was all he allowed himself.

When he exited the bath, still dripping, there were fresh clothes laid out for him, and his others were gone. He hoped they'd burned them.

The soft linen shirt was big in the chest, and the dark pants were loose around his hips and didn't reach farther than his ankles, but Ri didn't mind. It didn't matter. None of it did.

He walked slowly into the living room, fingers at the back of his head. He needed something to do with his hands. In the deafening silence, the strangeness of the situation hit him.

There was cheese and bread and fruit set out on the little table in the living room, wine, which he normally would have worried was drugged. Ri was on his guard at all times. But tonight, he couldn't afford the mental exertion. So he sat in the quiet room with Shev and Harlin and ate. And drank. And ate and drank until his stomach was no longer racked with pain.

"You'll stay here," said Shev.

"This is your home?" Ri's voice was still rough with disuse, with pain.

"It's mine," said Harlin. Harlin had kind eyes—kind, and terribly cunning. A combination Ri did not typically find at a glance. He leaned back against his couch, arm draped around the back, one ankle crossed over the other. He looked older than Ri wagered he really was. Though he was certainly wealthy enough—perhaps he *was* quite a bit older. He had one of those faces that no matter what his age, the number would have seemed wrong.

"Why are you letting me stay here?" said Ri.

"It's only for the night. And I'm doing it for them." He inclined his head toward Shev. "Don't touch things that aren't yours. And I expect you gone in the morning."

Ri swallowed hard, and Harlin left for his room without another word.

"Don't worry over him. He's grumpy when he's tired, and he's tired about seventy percent of the time. Worry over me." Shev leaned forward, eyes shining, and said, "You will take one of his horses. She's old, and she's shit, but she'll do. You can't take yours; she's Andra's now. Otherwise, no one will believe you've died."

"I'll just take it," said Ri, skepticism flatly coloring his features. "His horse."

"And you'll leave payment."

Ri shrugged. "I'm sure they took all I had."

"No," said Shev. "That money would belong to the king if you were found a spy, and no one could legally lay hands on it until you were dead or convicted. It hasn't even been counted."

Ri raised his eyebrows. "So it's—"

"Safe. With me. Enough to cover Harlin's horse. And there are a few gold pieces on your horse. The rest of it stays. Sorry; can't risk anyone finding out, and if it's suddenly gone, well, that's someone's head."

Ri felt his shoulders curl in. If he'd been just a hired sword, he would have cut his losses, taken this horse, and fled back to Etrya. It wasn't worth the money. Not when he'd been caught, tortured for a king to whom he had no allegiance, and now, robbed. Everything hurt. Everything felt hollow, except for searing anger, burning out from his stomach to his limbs. If it hadn't been for his father and stepfather back at home, his brothers, and his damned patriotism, he would be rid of this entire business. But Ri without those things was not Ri at all. And so it was a fantasy spiral of thoughts.

"What you will do, Ri, is take the horse you've bought, and supplies which I will provide for you at dawn, and you will go back to Va'al, and you will carry on with whatever plan you'd intended to carry out in the first place. And I expect you to honor our bargain."

"On my life," said Ri. "You will have protection from Va'al when the time comes."

"I, and Harlin," they said.

Ri glanced over her shoulder toward Harlin's bedroom door, which was shut. "All right," said Ri. He was making promises for which he had no authority, but he would do whatever he needed to make sure they were fulfilled. This person, however grey their hidden motives, had saved his life. And he would be damned if he didn't repay them for it.

"There is antiseptic in the kitchen. And several salves and bandages, should you need your...miscellaneous pain dulled when you ride out in the morning. You will leave when the light is grey. I will be awake, and I will be here. When you leave, I will give you the item you came for."

Ri nodded, and Shev rose to leave, turning toward Harlin's room. Ri caught their arm, and their eyes widened in what might have been alarm.

"Thank you," said Ri. "I am forever indebted." He dropped to a knee before them, and discomfort flashed in their eyes when he looked up.

"Do not thank me yet. When the time comes, and I have safety from all this shit that's coming, we will be even."

Shev didn't look at him when they left this time. Just disappeared behind the door and softly shut it. He wondered if Shev and Harlin would sleep tonight, or if they would both lie awake, listening for the turn of their doorknob, an assassin slipping into their room. The opening of the front door, if they were wrong, and he'd come to kill their princess.

Ri had never aspired to be feared. But here he was.

He moved into the kitchen, taking one last bite of sharp cheddar, one final swallow of the some of the richest wine he'd ever had—the only positive piece of Andra's reputation in food and drink. Then he stole away with bandages and antiseptic to the bedroom that connected with the bathroom.

He stripped out of the clothes they'd given him, down to nothing, and poured the stinging liquid in every scrape, every cut, hissing and breathing hard. His whole body burned.

Then he rubbed his legs with herbal cream, a few wounds on his back—the places he could reach, at least. His face. He spent a good deal of time with the salve on his wrists.

Ri didn't bother putting his clothes back on. He crawled slowly into a bed that was softer than anything he'd ever felt. Blanketed in quiet and dark and the air that felt *safe*, Ri slept harder than he had in his life.

CHAPTER TWENTY

K ASIA'S BLOODLINE RAN WITH fools. Her brother was a drunken idiot, and her parents were both good at business but not much else. Her mother was naïve, and her father only succeeded at things he had inherited.

So it was eminently frustrating that the Vanes were known from street corner to street corner in Farowfin, and here she was, the only one with a single wit among them, hidden quiet behind castle walls.

Kasia had been called many things as a girl, but "content" had never been one of them. She was so young to desire a throne, but her teeth ached for it. She'd pored over tomes on history and rulers and a thousand things that couldn't matter, really, because everyone knew the gods only blessed with powers those who were deemed worthy enough to rule. They could be noble, or they could be peasants. But it was law; no one was allowed to rule who had not been blessed.

Kasia had manipulated and betrayed and befriended and ruined person after person, as a child. She had been slippery and charming and absolutely single-minded. Not cold, but calculating. She would do what needed to be done. And so many people in her classes, down the street, in her vicinity in any way, had wound up bleeding or as ruined as a nine-year-old could be when they'd stood in her way.

Above all, Kasia *wanted.*

It wasn't that she had no friends, exactly. She grew up eventually and learned that relationships mattered in their way. But she was devoted. Unstoppable. Kasia was like death itself: singular in purpose and the harbinger of her own power.

She quietly clawed her way, as a very young girl, to a position at the top of her father's financial business, until she knew more than anyone, and even the tallest, oldest men, found themselves bowing to her. With Kasia whispering in his ear and losing sleep to puzzle out the inner workings of business, of money, of leadership, they thrived. And one night, Kasia had caught her father's business partner stealing from the coffers. She'd waited until the annual holiday ball to confront him with it. To let him know that he could secretly yield his half the business to her, or she would ruin him. He'd conceded. And he'd bowed when he did.

Just like that, a seventeen-year-old girl had her hands on the pulse of the entire city. Half the money in the region went through the Vanes. Her father had been half-furious, half-proud. She'd smiled quietly and gone to bed.

The next day, Kasia had woken up, and it had been her monthly bleeding, and she'd been very angry about it, because it was particularly painful this month. And she'd fallen right out of bed, doubled over with the pain of it all, and cursed being a woman, when suddenly, the pain and rage flew out of her in a wind.

The air had just rushed through her and burst out her hands and arms and feet and the top of her head. It had roared so loudly, so powerfully, that Kasia had wondered if she was going to die. She'd been terrified out of her mind when her mother had rushed in the room, taken one look at her seventeen-year-old daughter, all her things flying about her head in a small tornado, and said, "Oh. The gods...the gods have spoken. Sweet Plynos, they have spoken."

And after that, everything had changed.

Most blessed people were born with power that showed itself when they were toddlers, or they didn't have it at all. And many of them came from royal bloodlines.

Not Kasia.

Kasia's power had come late. And her parents had been no one. She, by extension, had been no one.

Some girls were born with a place in the world, and some girls carved the earth so that it would make a place for them. Kasia was a carver.

And gods damn her if she wouldn't find a way to carve a place for herself here. No matter how much they all hated her.

"Milady?"

Kasia jumped and turned around at the sound of her handmaiden's voice. "Yes?"

Nagonia bowed. "I only wished to know if you needed anything. I am taking a night to attend a play, but I don't leave for another two hours."

"A play?" said Kasia, arching an eyebrow and smiling.

Nagonia blushed. "Yes. One of—of the king's guard is taking me. It's supposed to be dreadfully romantic."

Kasia's smile softened into something almost real. Nagonia wasn't her friend; she couldn't be, given that Kasia was her employer, and Kasia wasn't particularly interested in friends. But it seemed like she cared.

"Would you have the time to braid my hair?" Kasia said. She could have demanded it; she didn't have to ask. But she found herself being very gentle with Nagonia. Something about the girl suggested a delicacy Kasia wasn't used to dealing with.

"Yes. Of course," Nagonia said, and Kasia sat at her desk, surrounded by beads and scented oils. Nagonia ran her hands through Kasia's hair, saying nothing, just braiding. She'd chosen something complicated—Kasia could feel it in the heaviness of her hair. Something with beads and pearls and a scent like peach and honey.

"Thank you," said Kasia. Nagonia bowed, taking it as the dismissal it was, and left, presumably to prepare for her evening.

Nagonia had no shortage of lovers, it seemed. Kasia remembered the night of her wedding, when she'd seen a sharp, handsome Etryan man with his teeth at Nagonia's ear. And now she'd managed to catch the eye of a knight.

Kasia laughed. How did a servant have enough time for multiple, ever-changing lovers?

Perhaps that was not a reasonable question. Kasia was a queen, after all, and she'd had time for all that and then some if she'd wished it. Time enough for a thousand meaningless things.

Perhaps she would take some of it to play her violin. Or perhaps she would beg favor from her god. Or direction. A reason to stay or a sign to leave.

She rose from her desk chair and slipped something new over her head—an emerald green dress that just grazed her knees. It was simple, and

Kasia rarely preferred simple. But at this moment, she did. Her hair was elaborate enough on its own.

She walked in bare feet down the hall to Reyan's private shrine, which she assumed was hers as well. And if it wasn't, perhaps he would catch her and try to kill her again. At least that had been *something*.

It was very small, she realized when she stepped inside. The silence didn't feel heavy in here; it felt close. Comfortable. Candles flickered already, casting shadows on the polished wood. This looked so different from the bright, open shrines they had in Farowfin. Then again, perhaps the king and queen's shrine looked exactly like this; she certainly had never been in it.

Kasia approached the front of the room and knelt on a pillow, holding her hand over the largest open flame. She would wait until it started to hurt, and then she would pull it back, wrist smoke-blackened to show her reverence. She'd done her left last time, so tradition called for her right now.

She'd resented it since she was a child. But she locked her jaw, blocked the quiet rage, and did it. When the heat became nearly unbearable, Kasia jerked back with a hiss, then fell prostrate on the ground.

"I thank you, Plynos, for blessing me. For keeping me in power and in strength, and in wisdom, in all your great knowledge." Plynos was the god of wisdom, and she recited these words mechanically. She'd almost begun to forget what they meant. "I thank...I thank you for..." Tears stung at the corners of her eyes again, and she gritted her teeth. She shouldn't have been worrying about this now. Certainly shouldn't have been *crying*—dear gods, she wasn't a child. And it was disrespectful. She was praying. But the tears came. These weren't tears of sadness; they were hot tears of anger. Anger at being made impotent, when the gods themselves had chosen her. Why had they chosen her at all, if she was meant to simply languish in a castle and do *nothing*? Her fists tightened on the pillow below her, and she said to the ground, but for Plynos' ears, "Sometimes, I wish you would talk back."

I'll talk with you.

Kasia froze. "What?"

I said I'll talk with you.

His voice was wine. Dark and rich and liquid silk. She could almost feel it on her skin. Kasia kept her head bowed.

"Who are you?" she whispered, voice breaking the moment she chose to use it. She'd heard they did this here—the gods, sometimes. Had believed it intellectually, but had never thought... "Are you Reyan's god?" If he was, she wasn't interested. She hadn't come from Farowfin simply to trade her gods for her king's, no matter the delicious chill that swept over her skin at the thought that a god had chosen to speak with her.

Suddenly, laughter filled the room. Breathy, like a scratch over wood. Darkly amused.

Thakros?

No.

I am not Thakros.

Kasia waited.

Who are you?

Kasia moved a bit, glancing up from the ground.

Do not bow to me unless you think it comfortable.

Kasia hesitated, then slid up to a seated position.

"Do you not know who I am?"

Of course I do. His voice, coolly entertained. *But I want to hear it from your lips.*

"I am Kasia Vane," she said. "Queen of Jaelen."

So you are.

Kasia Vane, who clawed a blessing from the gods.

Yes. I know of you.

"Wh-what?" she said, then she snapped her mouth shut. She never stuttered.

Is that your full question?

"You know of me?"

Yes.

"Clawed a blessing from the gods?"

Yes. The story is well-known. We all know you. What a playing piece, Kasia Vane.

She shivered, then, and he laughed again, the sort of laugh that brushed its fingers over her, tickling her back.

Does that thrill you?

"Yes," she whispered.

You are the girl who was not born to power but wanted it so badly that she would get it at all costs. You were not destined for this.

That stung for a moment.

But then: *You have earned it.*

Kasia shut her eyes, so she could hear his voice more clearly, so she could *feel it*, wrap herself in it like a coat.

"What use is power when you're shackled and cannot wield it?"

Oh, he said. That unmistakable amusement again. *I seriously doubt anyone could ever shackle you.*

Her heart was pounding, pulse a roar in her ears.

Who was she, to be spoken to this way by a god? Young and impetuous and driven by passion. She was—

Something. You are something.

The liquid voice finished her thoughts.

"How many do you speak to this way?" said Kasia, shaking everywhere.

No one.

"Are you lying?"

I couldn't if I wanted to.

Kasia was quiet again.

I haven't spoken to a person in a thousand years.

A frown flickered across Kasia's features. "I thought the Jaelenian gods spoke back."

They do.

"And yet...then what are you?"

A small breath of air as the door to the shrine opened and Reyan said, "Oh. I'm sorry I...I did not wish to interrupt you."

The god, who was most assuredly not Jaelenian, did not need to answer her question aloud, and Kasia knew he wouldn't, not with Reyan here. He didn't need to, because she felt it, suddenly. Felt it like a heavy cloak sinking onto her shoulders, lips brushing against the shell of her ear—the cold slip of a lover's fingers down her spine:

Death wrapped around her.

CHAPTER TWENTY-ONE

R EYAN COULDN'T BREATHE. JUST for a moment. Just for one heady, heart-stopping instant, when he saw her kneeling there in his shrine. In the place reserved for he and his wife—one of his favorite places in the world. It struck at him, something he should have been irritated at, something he should have been elated at. Something he should have...well...*something*.

She sat there so peacefully, bathed in flickering shadows and candlelight. Gods, the lines on her face were incredible. And the way that dress accented the very particular curves on her body, the swell of her chest, the softness in her stomach, the arch in her back when she knelt there. The dress was short enough that it skated up her thighs when she shifted, and Reyan set his hand on the doorpost to balance. He did it casually, as though his heart wasn't wedging itself in his throat. As though he merely wished for something to lean against, not to keep him upright.

"They're serving dinner soon. I came here to pray, but I'm..." Reyan blinked at the ground. "I'll leave you to it."

He turned, catching just a flash of the confusion in her eyes before he fled the room. Quite literally fled it. Because her bewitching, dark eyes blinked in his mind, but every time he started to let himself fall into them, his father's overlaid them. And they pierced him through with accusations of betrayal.

Perhaps it would have been easier if he'd felt indifferent toward her. If the first time they'd met, she hadn't made his blood run hot with frustration. If when he'd seen her walking down the aisle toward him, his knees hadn't nearly buckled with how stunningly beautiful she was. If he'd ever been able to look at her with cool indifference—not with anger, wildness, fascination. Then, perhaps everything could have been clinical, removed, no guilt, or little of it. But never had Kasia inspired any feeling in his bones that wasn't taken to its extreme.

He'd always hated her, and that was the problem.

Love and hate were separated by a knife's edge.

He walked down the hall from his shrine like it was crumbling behind him. Cool relief when he crossed away from it into the main palace and over to the dining hall. The smells wafted from the kitchens over to him, and he shut his eyes, inhaling deeply. Let the smells of roasting meat and sweet potatoes fill his lungs so that they could spill over into his mind and wash away the thoughts of Kasia.

Reyan slammed the doors to the dining hall open and sat, though the food wouldn't be set out for another half hour. He leaned back in his chair and closed his eyes, raking a hand through his disheveled curls and leaving it there.

His tangled feelings for his wife were not the only things lighting an anxious fire on his skin. Thakros's voice haunted him.

She is a gift from me.

Reyan hadn't been able to stop playing his god's words in his head, over and over and over. *She will drive you mad with power and tear down the world.* If that were true, then his wife was something extraordinary. And very possibly terrifying. And together, if they were bound, they would be something dazzling. He knew it like he knew the color of his own eyes and every childhood scar on his body. If Thakros had done this, then it meant something. But that was highly troubling all on its own, because the shadow in the world had only popped up a decade ago when the southern gods had conspired to make their rulers a combined force. The gods themselves had sent a plague on the enemies of several southern nations and strengthened their own rulers in such a massive power play that they had destroyed the rules of whatever games gods played. And the world had been ravaged for it.

Reyan had never understood why celestial misdeeds gave way to punishments that affected people, but it was a punishment. Taking the gods' playthings. And *I gave her to you* screamed of cheating again. Of a god overreaching. Trust was a delicate and mind-boggling issue, because he knew in his bones that together, they could save the world or destroy it. It was all too much, playing with the gods. The power was too great. But perhaps holding back a decision on the binding and clinging to the ability to turn back was his father. Perhaps it was weak. His head hurt.

"Cousin?" came a smooth voice from the doorway. Reyan could hear the smile in Proch's tone, and it set him more on edge, if that were possible.

"What?" said Reyan. He made no effort to conceal the frustration in his voice.

"Oh, testy, are we? Suppose I was wrong about your finding a consistent method of stress relief."

Reyan didn't open his eyes. His voice was flat when he said, "Do mine ears deceive me, or did you just admit you were wrong?"

A chair shifted to Reyan's left, around the corner of the table where he sat. "You're clearly under some sort of emotional duress," said Proch, "so should you bring this up later, I'll discredit your memory of it all thoroughly." The chair creaked; Proch was probably leaning back in it. He'd ruined at least three chairs in Reyan's memory, sitting in them all wrong, and the legs would just snap beneath him. Reyan would have rolled his eyes if he'd decided to go to the trouble of opening them.

"What's got you all...like this?" said Proch, and Reyan cracked one eye open to see Proch gesturing flippantly with his fingers in Reyan's direction. "Oh. The king awakes." Proch grinned, and Reyan reluctantly opened his eyes fully. Proch was always grinning, always effortless. His clothes always looked like he'd just rolled out of bed and fallen into the first thing he'd found, hair long and stick straight, brushing the tops of his unusually light olive shoulders in a way that looked lazy and refined all at once. He was a rather beautiful person, Reyan had always thought. It was something he'd been jealous of as a boy, when the girls cared more about your hair and the dimples in your cheeks than they did about who would rule the world next. Now, his cousin's handsome face was not something he envied—that feeling was reserved for the way that it always looked relaxed. When was the last time Reyan had done anything that allowed him to look like that? Apart from sleep, and even then he wasn't sure.

"What's that ridiculous thing around your neck?" said Reyan. He was grasping for anything that wasn't exhausting to talk about, and currently,

Proch was wearing a very gaudy chain of truly *blinding* gold around his throat. It was not atypical.

"Don't make fun of my relics just because you don't have the connections to get hold of them, cousin. This *thing* is ancient. They wore it hundreds of years ago, all the way down in archaic Va'al." His eyes sparkled with pride.

Proch had an odd affinity for old things and ancient culture.

"Now," he said, "enough about your jealousy over my jewelry."

Reyan groaned. There was nothing left to grab as distraction, and if Proch was not to be thrown off course even through discussion of his own reflection, then his cousin was not in the mood to be distracted anyway. After a minute of silence, he said, "What am I to do, Proch?"

Proch set down his glass of wine and leaned forward on his elbows, lacing his fingers together and resting his chin on them. "About what?"

Reyan wasn't entirely sure. Anything. Everything. All of it. But he said the least embarrassing thing, the least personal. "The men in the dungeon. What am I to do about them?"

"How am I to know? You're the king."

"Don't offer me advice then bristle when I ask you for it."

Proch's lips thinned into a line. Reyan wanted to be in the mood for his cousin's carefree attitude, his lazy refusal to commit to any decision, one way or the other. But he was not.

"Fine," said Proch. "I think it's ridiculous that this is even a decision for you."

Reyan's brow furrowed.

"And I think by keeping those men locked away for being *afraid*, you're being an absolute prick."

Reyan coughed. "Excuse me?"

"Sorry, I just love an excuse to malign a king with minimal fear of retribution. You're being an absolute—"

"I heard it."

Proch shrugged.

"Those men murdered my captain, Proch."

"No," said Proch. "*One man* murdered your captain. And he has been dead for two weeks. The rest of them participated in a battle that was not theirs, fleeing from a threat that was not of their making. It's barbarous to keep these men locked up for nothing and teach them to hate us. How long do you think you'd need to keep them down there before, by the time you let them out, they'd want nothing more than your head on a pike?"

Reyan's jaw locked. "So I should just release them all? With a slap on the wrist?"

"Two weeks in our dungeons, cousin, is a lot more than a slap on the wrist."

The room was silent.

Proch's face twisted into an uncharacteristically vicious mask. "Though if you disagree, you could just go kill them all right now. Slit all their throats 'til the stone dungeon floors are a crimson lake. I know you like to do these things yourself. Best go now, get it done in time to wash up for dinner."

Reyan almost laughed then, if it could be called that. It was a dark sound, angry. Tired. He rose and braced himself on the table, arms shaking. "You think I enjoy it? Killing them?"

Proch said nothing, only stared at him, gaze unflinching as iron.

Reyan turned to leave; he didn't know where for—only to somewhere that wasn't here. He wasn't safe in his shrine, wasn't safe in his dining room.

Kings were not safe anywhere.

"Don't leave on my account," said Proch. His face had darkened, and he was staring at the table.

"He's right," came a voice from the doorway. Reyan looked up, and his stomach dropped into his feet. Kasia was still in that simple, pale dress, neck still long and elegant under her hair. And the room suddenly smelled like honey.

"Those men," she said, "do not deserve to die for rash actions borne of fear."

Reyan gathered himself and said evenly, "I do not recall asking your opinion."

Kasia raised her eyebrows. "And I do not recall ever promising to wait until you asked."

She passed behind him slowly, brushed her fingers over his back, and Reyan stiffened.

Proch's face had lightened considerably in a moment, and he was now fighting a smile, covering it with his hand.

Reyan looked to the sky, begging the gods for assistance. And he sat. Because when Kasia sat, her presence pulled him there.

"I'm sorry," said Reyan, and Proch nearly choked on his wine.

"For what?" Kasia's face was entirely impassive at his apology.

He looked at her, then, in a way he hadn't allowed himself to look at her. She was bold to come in here and challenge a king. She'd been challenging him from the beginning. And not even to question him, then retreat. No, Kasia walked into the room and did not move for anyone; they moved for her. If she said what she was thinking, she stood firmly behind it. They could cut out her tongue, and still, she would speak her mind.

She was a force.

She *believed* in things, no matter how hard he'd been clinging to his own doubts.

And she was right. Those men were waiting in chains because he knew that when the time came, he would not have the gall to take their lives with his own hands. But he did not want to contend with the idea of releasing them. Did not want to wrestle with the guilt of knowing that they were only here because he had not cemented his bond with Kasia, had not been fighting with every tool at his disposal to drive back the jaws that were eating the world.

It was his fault that they had had to come to Jaelen at all. His fault that they'd been driven from their homes by a nameless dark. His fault that...his fault that Cariq, captain of his guard and the man he'd looked up to since before his mind could form memories, was dead.

He blinked down at the empty table and found that he was not hungry. The smells that wafted in strongly from the kitchen now did nothing to ignite the hunger in his belly. There was nothing raging in there but guilt—stark and cold and fast.

Reyan shoved back up from the table and left without a word.

He marched down the hall, ignoring the bows and greetings from a hundred nameless faces shuffling through the palace, suddenly choking on regret, on panic, desperate to be in his rooms. He needed to be away. From them all.

He hardly paid mind to the footsteps behind him. They were small and quick and plagued him constantly, so he could not worry about them all the time. Couldn't think about her every hour of the day. He didn't have room in his mind, now, anyway, for a single thing that wasn't grief.

He burst into his rooms without shutting the door behind him—it was no use; Kasia would open it anyway—and stopped in the farthest corner, by the window. Reyan blinked up through it at the vast landscape of stars that fought against the dark. And he forced himself to breathe. Not to think of a hundred faces that lay dead and rotting in the grey that was slowly, slowly, slowly coming this way. Not to think of the terror in the soldier's eyes just before Reyan had slashed his sword across the man's throat for killing his captain. He tried very hard not to think of Cariq, with deep wrinkles beside his eyes and lined across his brow, and a serious, hard voice that had often made Reyan wonder if the man had liked him at all.

Cariq had been there when his father hadn't. Had taught him strength and honor and things innumerable. And now he was dead. He was dead, and Reyan felt the blame weighing down on his shoulders like a physical thing, pushing him to the floor.

He nearly gave into it, nearly welcomed the excuse to just kneel for a moment. But then he felt Kasia's small hand on his back, and every muscle in his body jumped to high alert.

"King," she whispered into the light fabric, breath drifting over his skin.

He was so tense that he couldn't swallow. So wracked with grief that he didn't know how it was possible that he wasn't crumpled on the floor.

Ice spread through his veins, and Kasia gasped at the sudden cold on his skin. He turned around.

"I am sorry," he said, voice rough, "for a thousand things. I am sorry, and I cannot name them all. I am...I can't pin the nature of all of this with words any more than I could wrap my tongue around the nature of you. But I am..." He drew in a quick, shuddering breath. "I am sorry." His voice cracked, and her arms wrapped around his body.

Reyan did not eat.

He waited in his rooms until Kasia fell asleep. Then he slipped out, in the middle of the night, and stood before the guards in the dungeon. And commanded them to release every soldier in it.

CHAPTER TWENTY-TWO

H E HAD BEEN RIDING for nearly four days. The journey from Va'al to Andra had initially taken him this long, only because of the odd route he'd had to take to forge an entry from Etrya. This time, it took so bloody long because everything hurt. The summer sun had baked into Ri a rather sour disposition, and by the time the journey came to a close, he was ready to tear the head off anyone who came close.

He was tired. His lips were cracked and dry, on the ragged edge of bloody. The hair of his horse scraped against his wounds in a way that made him want to hop off her entirely and make the entire rest of the journey on foot. Leave the damn horse out here to die; she'd hardly been worth whatever the hell it was that Shev had taken from him.

That was another thing: if he'd had a horse that was actually physically capable of *making* the trip, that would have been nice. Perhaps he would have been riding across the Va'alian border early this morning instead of in the cool, dark evening, as he was now.

The last few yards to the city felt like an eternity, and the trip from the city's edge to the palace itself was nothing short of murder. He stopped by the stables and let the rotten animal into a stall, removed her saddle, gave her some water and food. She was just this side of useless, but she'd done the job. He was alive, at the very least.

Ri did not go to the king. He didn't go to the prince, didn't seek out a single human. He sought out the royal bath house. He'd ridden across the entire gods damned desert in Harlin's too-short pants and too-loose shirt, and the fabric was peppered through with sand.

Ri had been in better moods.

He yanked the shirt over his head when he stormed inside the bath house, unable to even find the leftover emotion to feel glad that it was empty, and loosed the string that was barely holding the pants up over his hips. They fell to the floor and he sunk into a bath.

A fucking hot one.

When he was clean, and his muscles weren't on fire from riding, he dragged himself out of the water and to his quarters. His inner thighs were bruised as all hells, and gashes still lined his calves, still curved around his eye. But he didn't smell like sweat anymore, and he wanted nothing more, at this moment, than to pick a fight with a king.

He stalked across the castle grounds in his own clothes, which were too big for him now, and the guards moved aside when he made for the door. It was late, but not so late that anyone had gone to sleep.

Or Ri hoped that were true, for their sake. Because either way, he was pounding on the door at the end of this hallway, and he was doing it imminently.

He pounded.

The king's head servant opened the door, hair disheveled, bleary-eyed, and Ri's stone face did not move.

"My lord," said the servant.

"I will have an audience with the king."

The servant blinked the sleep from his eyes and stood a little taller. "Do you know what time it—"

"I don't give a camel's steaming pile of shit what time it is. I will see the king, and I will see him now, or you will find yourself staring up at me from the ground with hand marks around your windpipe."

The servant scoffed, face going pink with rage, but Ri simply folded his arms and waited.

The man moved past him, and within silent minutes, he was shown into the throne room.

He could hardly force himself to bow when he saw the old man; perhaps the man should have been bowing to him. But he dropped to a knee, grinding his teeth against each other, and looked at the stone floor, hair hanging around his ears. Just looking at that grey stone was enough to make nausea roil in his stomach.

"You're late," said the king.

Ri wanted to pull Shev's enchanted Andran dagger from his thigh and plunge it into the man's stomach. He rose. Let the king examine the wounds on his face, the swelling, the thinness in his arms. He wondered if the man could make out his ribs through the fabric.

"Well?" the king demanded.

"I was indisposed," Ri ground out.

"Hmph," said the king. The damned king.

"I was taken when I arrived," said Ri. "I just barely escaped, and they took my money, my—"

"That is not my problem, Etryan." The man's voice echoed throughout the throne room.

"I beg to differ."

"Challenge me again, boy, and I will show you what it truly means to beg."

Ri looked at the ground again, rage licking through his chest.

"I do not care," said the king, "about your financial problems, or your squabbles in Andra, or a single thing apart from you doing the job I have paid you to do."

"I told you," said Ri, "half the money you gave me was robbed by the Andran government the moment I set foot in the land. And—"

"And what? I should pay you back for your own incompetence? Will you walk away, Ri? Leave your country to suffer and die beneath the sword of Andra for your own greed? No. I don't think so."

Ri drew in a shaky breath. It was like scraping shards of glass over his lungs. Perhaps he *should* abandon all of this. Just walk away and leave the ship behind, and go back home empty-handed.

He almost laughed. The king had him by the balls. That was something he absolutely could not do. Not when the lives of his family and the fate of his country were in the palm of his hand.

"I tire of this," said the old, crumbling king. "Go home. Tomorrow you will set out with Gallien; she's been waiting days for you. And you will finish the job I have paid for. That is all. You are dismissed."

Ri bent at the waist, jaw juddering with furious tension, and spun out of the room before he could say something he would regret. He had no intention of winding up shackled again, and whatever words he had for that king would send him there if he spoke them.

Ri did not look at a soul when he crossed the way to his quarters. When he was there, he found himself unable to sit. Unable to even stand still. He changed into soft nightclothes—a threadbare white shirt that had once been snug around his chest, loose grey pants that now hung off his hips.

Then he paced. He raked his hand through his hair almost painfully hard and paced. And paced. Fuck the king; Ri would love to kill him himself. Watch his stupid wrinkles deepen in shock when he felt his heart stop beating because Ri had stopped it with a knife.

He reached for the ceremonial knife he'd strapped to his thigh—the one Shev had given him. It was enchanted, they'd said. By the moinchire. A race long since dead, but whose magic still ran through the earth in echoes of what it once had been. Or so they said. It was a famous, ancient weapon designed to interact with the blood of anyone blessed with magic in a terribly unpleasant way. The knife was jeweled and curved, bronze dripping down between the glittering colors. It was stunning. And soon, it would drip with the blood of the Farowfin queen of Jaelen.

Ri would have done nearly anything, at this moment, to watch it go red with the blood of the Va'alian king. He would have licked the fucking blood off and enjoyed it, if it were a possibility.

Ri tossed the dagger back into the drawer and slammed it shut. It wasn't possible, and looking at it only made it worse. That gnawing anger in his muscles wrapped its fingers around his throat.

His door creaked behind him, and Ri knew that in the doorway was a face he currently had no desire to see. The prince looked too much like his father.

"Adè."

"Ri," said Adè.

"What did you come here for?" Ri still would not turn around to look at him. He was too busy clenching his jaw and staring at the wall.

"I wanted to see you," said Adè in that low voice that rolled over Ri like thunder. "I was... I was worried when you—"

Ri turned then, and the moonlight outside the still-open door spilled over half his face.

Adè's eyes widened, but Ri's face remained hard, impassive.

"What happened?" the prince breathed, shutting the door and crossing the room to come to Ri. Adè ran his thumb over the gash around Ri's eye, and Ri hissed—from the pain, and the surprise of Adè touching him without warning. Adè immediately dropped his hand back to his side and looked over Ri, from his head down to his feet. Ri could feel that his pants were too low now—that that little strip of skin just below his navel was exposed, down past his hipbones.

Adè's gaze caught there. "Ri..." he breathed.

Ri knew. There were, mottled low on his stomach, scrapes and the angry red line of a knife. It had nicked the bone, Ri was fairly sure, but at the time, he'd just been grateful that the man hadn't slashed a little higher and spilled his innards.

Adè brushed his fingers over it, and Ri jumped back. "What in hells—stop touching me where I'm *hurt*." His voice cracked, and he braced himself against his dresser, arms suddenly shaking.

"Are you all right?"

"Why do you care?" said Ri.

Adè recoiled as though Ri had physically punched him. But the question was valid, or close to it. Adè had never touched him before; Ri didn't know why it was that he should touch him now.

"Maybe I don't want to discuss it with you," said Ri. His voice dripped venom that the prince had probably not earned. "You have your father's face, and your father..."

"You do not need to tell me of my father's transgressions. They are many. I know."

Ri felt a little needle of guilt. Of course Adè knew. Better than anyone. His father was king first and father a very, very distant second.

Ri let out a sigh. "I want to watch his ancient face crumble into dust, prince. And yet here you are, with a prettier version of it, standing in my room and reminding me of all my injuries." And just like that, he was furious again. "Maybe," he said again through gritted teeth, "I don't. Want. To discuss it with you."

"I was *worried*," said Adè. The pain in his voice was strikingly evident. "If you hadn't come back tonight, I would have ridden out tomorrow myself."

Ri blinked. "Why?" he said.

Adè just looked at him, gaze touching all his injuries. "How did you get these?"

Nothing.

"Are there more?"

Nothing.

"I can see them under your shirt."

Adè crossed the couple of steps and pulled Ri's shirt over his head, then dropped it to the floor. So he stood there in nothing but bruises and scars and pants that hung too low on his hips.

"Hells," Adè breathed, circling Ri to get a full inventory. The scratches everywhere, the deep gashes, the raw, violent red around his wrists. "What did they do to you?"

"What in hells do you think they did to me, Adè? They took me the minute I arrived. Said I was a spy. Interrogated me, tortured me, hardly fed me. I thought I would die. That's what they did. Are you happy? Does the story lend some excitement to your evening? And are you through looking? Can I put my shirt back on?"

Adè's face flashed with hurt again, and Ri instantly regretted saying everything. Everything. He opened his mouth to apologize, and Adè said, "Of course, put on your shirt if you're uncomfortable. I just wanted to—I wanted to see."

"And?" said Ri. His throat was hoarse.

"And I wish I'd ridden there sooner."

Ri didn't know what it was he'd wanted to hear, and if that sufficed or not. He didn't know. But he didn't put his shirt back on either.

"I leave tomorrow," Ri said through a sudden thickness in his throat. He crossed Adè, so that he was between the beautiful man and the door, and said without looking at him, "Thank you for coming to check on me. It's very thoughtful."

"Ri—"

"I should sleep," said Ri. He looked up at Adè, who was staring at his eyes with such intensity that Ri felt the gaze like a physical thread, linking them.

"If you don't come back this time, I will cross the sea to find you," said Adè.

Ri almost choked. He looked at some invisible point over Adè's shoulder and walked, arms brushing lightly over the man's chest when he went to open the door and make him leave. But then there were strong fingers gripping his arm. Ri looked up.

Adè locked eyes with him and pushed him back into the closed door, hard enough that Ri's bones rattled. Urgently enough that Ri was desperate.

Ri breathed in shakily for a beat of silence, then jerked his arm back so that Adè fell into his chest. And Ri caught him with his mouth.

Adè didn't hesitate for a moment. He took Ri's face in his hands and kissed him, sliding his tongue between Ri's teeth like he had been the one who'd been starved.

For the first time since he'd ridden to Va'al, and perhaps since long before then, Ri relaxed. He let his muscles uncoil under Adè's, ran his fingers up his back, knit them in his hair.

Adè moved his hands from Ri's face and slid them down his chest, so gentle Ri could hardly feel them, and he knew it was because of his injuries. No one had ever touched him like that. Like perhaps he was breakable. And perhaps that mattered.

Adè had never viewed him that way, but he did now. Ri hardly moved, except to kiss him, except to let his tongue tangle with Adè's, except to just allow himself to be touched.

And Adè opened his eyes.

Ri stared back at him.

"Do not die in Jaelen."

"Why not?" Ri said, throaty whisper oddly high with pain. "When I kill that girl, you will marry Reyan."

Adè blinked and looked down at the ground. Then he brushed his lips over Ri's cheek and left.

Ri hardly slept.

CHAPTER TWENTY-THREE

K ASIA AND REYAN DANCED around each other now. He still didn't ask her opinion in a good many things he should have, and Kasia didn't bow before him or kiss the ground he walked on. But it was a dance now, not a vicious thing.

She could feel him looking at her from across the room, sometimes. Dark eyes resting on her hips, sliding up to her face, slipping down again. And she would be lying if she said her breath didn't catch every time he passed too closely. Two nights ago, she'd caught him half naked in their rooms, and she couldn't remember the last time her face had gone quite that deep a shade of scarlet.

Her face still burned from it, which was ridiculous. She'd been with people before. A far cry more than one, in fact—certainly seen them naked. But none who looked like him. And none who made her bones itch with nerves every time they so much as looked at her too long.

She finished the wine at dinner and left the table; Reyan was long gone, retreated back to bed, she figured. He tended to arrive to anything social late and leave early. She smiled, despite herself, at the little trait. She didn't even know what it was that she liked about it.

Kasia moved through the winding halls, slow, relaxed steps until she reached her rooms. Maybe she would have a bath tonight. But she'd had one the night before; maybe not. She blew out an irritated breath. Queen of a country, and the biggest decision she had to make tonight was whether or not to have a bath.

She pushed her door open quietly, and shut it behind her, looking slowly up to find Reyan, hands clasped behind his back and staring out the window. It was pitch dark outside; she had no idea how he could really see anything.

But perhaps seeing things was not why he stood there. Perhaps he simply stood there to wonder.

"I heard what you did," said Kasia, and he jumped.

"I'm sorry, I didn't know you were here," he said.

She laughed.

"What did you hear?" he said. He didn't turn around.

She walked several steps closer, close enough to lower her voice, but not so close that he could touch her. "That you released those soldiers."

"Yes," was all he said. His fingers remained carefully clasped, and he stood straight, staring at who knew what. He was wearing black—crisp lines from his heels to his shoulders. Kasia's pulse spiked just from looking at him. "Thank you," he said softly, just as the silence had swollen so large that Kasia had considered going to have that bath and leaving the impossible man to his beloved quiet.

She blinked and stepped closer. "For what?"

Finally, Reyan turned a fraction of an inch, and the relative dark in their room did odd and beautiful things to the lines of his face. "For telling me what you did. For the fight in the wood. For not…" He moved into the flickering light, just beside her. "For not being afraid of me."

Kasia blinked slowly, nodded, and turned to leave. Her hand brushed his when she did, and he linked a single finger in hers.

She stopped.

Turned, raising her face to look at him. Wondered if perhaps it had been a mistake. But he didn't move.

She swallowed, pulse suddenly pounding in her throat. His gaze swept from her eyes down to her collarbone, and slowly back up, catching on her mouth. Kasia's lips parted, and Reyan's eyes darkened.

He pulled her suddenly into him, and she let out a gasp when she hit his chest. His mouth was on hers in an instant, hands pressing into her back, tongue slipping past her teeth, laying claim to her mouth. Her fingers dug into his shoulders as he kissed her. He tasted like the cold.

Reyan slid his hands down the silk of the back of her dress, to catch the backs of her thighs and lift her, so that her legs wrapped around his hips. He kept one hand there, and slipped the other up, fingers threaded through her dark curls, hand gripping the back of her neck.

He drew back when she was utterly breathless with all of it, and slid his lips from her mouth to her jaw, up her neck to bite her earlobe. She gasped sharply, and she could feel him smile against her skin.

"Reyan," she whispered, and he stilled. Her heart was so loud in her ears, she thought they might burst. Her skin was on fire with the closeness and the cold of him. And he was completely still, and it was torture.

Slowly, the king dropped her down his body, so she stood on the floor, staring up at him.

He took a breath, face set in such a way that it said he was confident. But his eyes were too wide, he was breathing too hard, for him not to have been the slightest bit afraid. Nervous. The king. Scared of her. Desperate for her. This, Kasia thought, was how it felt to be truly intoxicated.

"Do you want this?" she said. The king was completely unable to stop looking at her mouth.

Reyan said, "Yes."

"It will bind us. We can't go back after this."

"*Yes*," he said, and his voice was raw with the want of it. "I am…gods, I am not my father. I am through."

"With what?"

He blinked down at her, then brought a hand to the thin, gold strap that held her dress up. Linked a finger in it, and slipped it down her shoulder. He ran his fingers over her collarbone, so slowly she wanted to die. Perhaps she would. He trailed it past her heart, across her burning skin, until her knees began to shake—and did the same to the other.

"Being weak," he said.

All she had to do was move her arms, and the dress would fall to the floor. She wore nothing under it, not tonight.

Reyan waited, chest rising and falling rapidly. His fingers trembled against her skin. Kasia was suddenly, paralyzingly, nervous. She struggled to breathe, struggled to swallow with him looking at her like that. It wasn't cold, wasn't ice or stone. He looked like he wanted to devour her whole.

Reyan's throat bobbed, and he reached for a tendril of her hair. She moved. Her dress fell to the floor.

Reyan stepped back, eyes taking a hundred years on every part of her body. He brought his hand to his mouth, then rubbed it across his jaw.

"Gods," he breathed.

Kasia raised a dark eyebrow and stepped out of the puddle that was her dress. And Reyan breathed something unintelligible.

Kasia moved toward him and reached for the buttons at his shirt. He straightened, heartbeat quickening under her hands, button by button, beat by beat. She slid the shirt off his shoulders so he stood there in nothing but his pants, which hung so that she could just make out the ridges of his hipbones, the shadows and trail of black hair that made her wonder what exactly he would look like in nothing at all.

Kasia's mouth went dry.

Reyan caught her to him again, pulled her easily up so she wrapped around him, chest pressed against the muscles in his, then walked her over to the bed, and laid her down. She untangled her legs, and moved for his pants, but he grabbed her wrist, pinning it, lightning fast, to the bed.

Gods, he was strong. He was strong, and his eyes said that this was not perfunctory. This was not cold; this was not just for the gods. This was for him.

And truthfully, it had been for her since the moment she'd laid eyes on him.

Reyan climbed up onto the bed with her, knees on either sides of her hips, and slid his hands agonizingly slowly, too light, too everything, from her shoulders, whispering over her breasts, her stomach, down to her thighs.

Kasia arched her back just at that feather-light touch, fingers fisting in the slippery sheets. She could feel the air crackling between them, like the world itself was on fire, and Reyan braced himself over her, smiling. Wry, like she'd never seen him.

"I thought," said Kasia, then she stopped, thought better of it.

"Thought what?" Reyan whispered in her ear, teeth catching on its shell.

A flare of heat shot through her veins.

"I thought," she whispered, "that you hated me. Because of Farowfin."

Reyan pulled back for a moment, lip ticking, and growled, "I'm not touching your country; I'm touching you," then his fingers were at the tops of her thighs, and then—and then—and then—

Kasia shut her eyes, legs brushing over him when he slipped inside her, breath hitching. Everything was sensation; there was nothing but feeling. Nothing that could ever exist but this feeling. His fingers.

He wasn't gentle, and Kasia didn't want him to be. Somehow, he had known not to be gentle with her, that he didn't need to be, and so he was teeth at her throat, fingers bruising at her thighs and elsewhere, until she couldn't stop moving under him. Until if she stopped moving, she thought she would die.

Suddenly, he pulled back, and Kasia opened her eyes. He lay on top of her, his chest matched to hers, and brushed the hair out of her face. "Farowfin girl who will tear down the world," he said, and he pressed a kiss to her temple.

It was then that she realized that at some point, he'd slid out of his pants. She met his gaze for a long second, and saw an instant of fear there, an instant of worry, of concern to be laid so very bare with her.

"Have you ever—have you ever done this?" he said. And where his voice had been smooth and commanding before, here, for a moment, he was...nervous. Terribly vulnerable. It made Kasia's heart clench.

"Yes," she said, struggling not to laugh. He grinned. "Have you?"

The grin went wicked, and Reyan bowed, head on her chest. As though she were someone to be bowed to. He kissed her chest and she ran her nails lightly down his back. He shuddered, then caught her nipple in his teeth.

A high noise escaped the back of Kasia's throat, —she felt it all the way down to her core—and she shifted, then felt Reyan's hand on her shoulder, pressing her into the sheets.

He trailed kisses down her chest, to her stomach, teeth and tongue running over her hipbones so she couldn't breathe.

Licked his way back up to her shoulders, her throat, that hollow just below her ear.

Then with an agonizing slowness, he settled between her legs, and there was nothing between them.

Kasia felt the bind instantly—a shock of cold and liquid heat. A breeze blew up around her, winding itself through Reyan's hair. Reyan glanced up and kissed her, and they moved together—two bodies completely lost in sensation, lost to each other.

Kasia could feel their energies crackling together—his cold, her wind, slipping back and forth between their bodies into something wild and unpredictable and completely, utterly, addictive.

Power was sparking everywhere. And Reyan's skin was fire—Kasia's was a million nerves jumping at once, and she needed, more than anything, for him to be closer.

She dug her nails into his back and bit into his shoulder. This man, this king who had ordered her and everyone else around her, who thought nothing of taking a man's life in a public square, but who had wept and held onto her like she was a lifeline just nights ago. She had seen him strong, and she had seen him weak. And when he looked at her, eyes glazed, she knew she had never seen him quite like this. As though he'd woken up this morning and realized that Kasia was everything, and she had the power to shatter him.

Reyan slipped his hand between them and everything tightened. Kasia fought a scream and Reyan dipped very close to her ear. "No," he whispered. "I want to hear you." Kasia drew in a deep, shuddering breath. "I want to hear you say my name," he said, breath cool on her ear.

Kasia turned her head and bit his bottom lip.

"Shit!" he said, then he was laughing like a boy.

He slid his hand back down again, though, light and quick, moved his fingers in such a way that she couldn't think. They both stopped laughing. The wind poured out from her skin and the cold from his, whirling together and heightening every nerve, every pinprick of movement, so that Kasia was nearly coming out of her skin.

He whispered, "Queen," in her ear, and she came undone.

And Reyan heard his name on her lips.

Seconds later, he tightened his grip on her on her side, her hip, and Kasia heard hers as well.

The winds kicked up with the snow—the frost that had been coming off his skin. Outside, there was a pop, and wind poured from their room, ice and snow fleeing out with it. Kasia could hear it almost, could feel the rush of energy that hummed out of her, of him, and that now rested in both of them, burrowed new in each of their very depths.

Everything had changed.

Kasia lay back into the sheets, and Reyan lay on his stomach, breathing beside her.

The whole room was coated in frost. Kasia grinned and wondered if the entire palace was.

"Are you all right?" she said, running her fingers up and down his back.

"Yes," he said.

"With a woman who is Farowfin."

"No," said Reyan, catching her stare with his and brushing a finger over her cheek. "You are not Farowfin's. You are mine." He laid his head back down and said, though his face was a bit muffled by the pillow, "And I, Kasia Vane, am yours."

PART TWO

The world cracked. In less than an instant, everything changed.

The black beyond the window was the same. The stars still shone, and the moon still governed the night.

But the earth itself felt it. In the sudden burst of cold and wind and the fear that came with knowing there would be a price, and it would have to be paid.

Every god in the world felt it—that massive fissure that could only have been caused by Death.

They had played games with the world for centuries. Millennia. Had given them magic and taken it back and given it again.

But in something less significant than a moment, the door between them had been closed.

Death did not smile when he split the world.

This was nothing pleasurable; this was the order of things.

The natural response.

Because Thakros had cheated.

CHAPTER TWENTY-FOUR

THIS WAS THE SECOND time Ri had made her wait.

Gallien sat in a dark corner of the tavern, watching the women of her crew get drunker and drunker, and less and less steady on their feet. She sipped her ale—silent. Where in hells was Ri? Perhaps when he deigned to show back up in Va'al, she would get her girls to show him where their talents for hospitality really lay—in their knives.

"Oh, Captain. So mysterious—the shadowy traveler in the corner of the room sipping on what? Rum?" Leylya was slurring, arm thrown around Nazalie's shoulder.

Gallien smiled tightly. "Going to be able to walk tomorrow?"

Nazalie and Leylya both burst into a bout of high laughter and looked at each other conspiratorially. "Who knows?" Nazalie said.

"Hells, you should really have more fun every once in a while," said Leylya. She reached for Gallien's arm, shadows deepening the picture of the scar that split her beautiful face. Somehow, it only made her prettier. Gallien snatched her arm back when Leylya made for it, and a frown flickered across Leylya's face. "I don't dance," said Gallien. She didn't know why she'd pulled back like that.

"All right," Leylya said, and she took a step back, disappearing into the throng of unwashed bodies in the tavern. Everyone was so damn drunk. Gallien wanted to drink, but she also wanted to be stone sober, because she was almost enjoying being angry at the stupid, inconsiderate Etryan. And because she worried that if she let herself loose for more than a minute, she would find herself alone with Leylya again, and Leylya would start asking more questions she was wholly uninterested in answering. If they were alone, Leylya would want to talk about her fire, or her tragic past, or the consequences for her secrets. And Gallien would refuse to answer, or wine and the girl would loosen her tongue and she would spend the evening embroiled in a topic that scared her to her very core. One that was ultimately a massive risk to her and anyone else she ever let herself slip into giving a shit about.

So she kept to herself and stewed and sipped very slowly while everyone else lost themselves completely to drink and, probably later, to each other.

She stalked out of the bar before anyone else, and she chose not to sleep in the room the king provided her. She slept alone in her cabin on the docked ship.

When Ri showed up the next morning, pale as death, bruises littering his face and body, Gallien decided she wouldn't kill him.

A messenger had showed up at the *Horizon's Promise* and let her know he was finally here, so she'd gathered her crew (which had seen better mornings) and had been waiting since dawn.

Ri didn't get there until late in the day, and by that time, Gallien had been waiting at the helm, sharpening her knife.

But he crept up to her ship like a shadow—slight and dark and angry enough to make even Gallien sit the slightest bit on edge. "He arrives," she said.

Ri's lip ticked up, and he shot her a look so vicious she felt it lance through her.

"And he's got new scars," Gallien said.

Ri ground his teeth together and glanced up at the sky. "It's a good day for sailing" was all he said.

Gallien stared hard at him. Where had this man been? The new hardness on his face made him look younger or older—Gallien couldn't quite decide. Older in the way of experience. But younger because the dark, simmering anger made him look like a boy playing dress-up with his father's countenance. He wasn't ready to set his eyes like that, wasn't ready for the heavy tilt of his brow or the hard clenching of his jaw. Gallien had seen him not three weeks ago, and yet she hardly recognized the man in front of her.

Gallien watched him go and made her way around the ship. They would set off shortly.

The women prepared, and they set sail. When the shoreline melted behind them and they sailed on open ocean, Gallien smiled. This was always her favorite part—when the land disappeared, and the only things left were the sky and the sea. Some might have found it claustrophobic, being trapped on a vessel like this.

But all land was surrounded by water, too. Land that didn't move under your feet, that held you in place.

That had always felt a hell of a lot more claustrophobic to Gallien. This, though, this left her with nothing but possibility.

When the sky had just begun its descent into the evening dark, and the particular high of escape had finally dulled, Gallien followed Ri below deck.

"What?" he growled, spinning around and hiding something on the small table behind his back.

"It's time I was let in on your little secret. Whatever your business is with the king."

Ri laughed. "I owe you nothing. My business is between the king and me; my *passage* is the only thing that has to do with you."

Gallien shut the door behind her. "We're on open water, Ri. Out here, I *am* the king."

Ri's fingers twitched at his side.

"I want to know," said Gallien, "why it is I've been made to wait. Why it is that the king deems your services so worthy of *my* time." She swept a casually assessing gaze over him—over his lanky frame and the slightly hunched way he now stood (when he hadn't before), the sharp cunning in his eyes. He looked almost like a snake—ready to strike at any time if it were necessary.

Perhaps Gallien should have simply shut up and let him ride in the *Horizon's Promise* and questioned nothing. But that had never been Gallien. And she got the sense that war was rumbling straight for them and that she was leading the charge without knowing.

Gallien was a good fighter, but she'd hardly had a breath since the last fight she'd been thrown into. She was very good at killing—she did not relish it. If they never got into another war as long as Gallien lived, she still would have experienced enough bloodshed to overfill a lifetime.

And something in the Etryan's eyes spoke of blood.

"I do not owe you my secrets," said Ri.

"Doesn't matter much who's owed what out here."

She tried to see around him, get a glimpse at what it was he was hiding.

Ri shifted to block her view. The corner of his mouth turned up, and his fingers twitched again, almost imperceptibly. "I can guarantee you, Captain, I am not a person you wish to fight."

Gallien flashed her teeth when she smiled. "Neither am I."

Ri opened his mouth to speak, and that was when they all heard it.

A sharp snapping in the air. Big enough that the ship shuddered around them. It was as though a whip had cracked through the very sky.

Gallien frowned, and the item Ri had been hiding toppled off the table behind him. Gallien recognized the blade instantly. It was a famous item. How she would have loved to have gotten her hands on that. Traded it to her wealthiest contact in Jaelen; gods, that would fetch a price.

"Using that blade for something?" she said.

The ship jolted and shook again, and Gallien's attention snapped away from the ceremonial knife on the floor.

Ri's hands went immediately to his daggers as though whatever it was was something that could be fought off with a knife.

Gallien whirled around and exited Ri's room, running up onto the deck. Ri followed.

The deck was a flurry of activity; Gallien could taste the tang of fear on her tongue. "What in hells..." she started, but her half-question was answered when she glanced toward the west. There it was, rolling toward them and blanketing the sky like—the shadow.

"Shit," Gallien hissed. "Shit, is that—?"

"Yes," Leylya screamed. She was scrambling for the sails; they needed to get out of open water, hug the coastline, move northeast. As it was, it was coming right toward them. It had never moved this fast, never in history. But it was right there, spreading silently over the world like blood in water.

Gallien was frozen. What in all hells could have happened? What—

"Do something," Leylya screamed as every able body worked to speed the *Horizon's Promise*, to redirect it so they did not all become withering skeletons. Gallien realized, then, that Leylya was not screaming at everyone; she was screaming at *her*. Because she knew. Leylya knew what Gallien was capable of.

Gallien almost laughed. She could perform little tricks; she couldn't drive back the force that was devouring the very world. And she didn't—she couldn't let them all know. Couldn't let it get out that she had this, or they would force her into a palace and take her sword and give her a pen and inkwell.

And she couldn't get rid of the feeling nagging at the back of her skull ever since she'd come face to face with the grey not weeks ago—the feeling that something was gone. That something was missing and could not be recovered. That she was just a little weaker than before.

It tugged at her, a warning, whispering frantically in her ear.

But the grey spread, quieting the sky and the waves with it, and the weight of everything crushed down on Gallien's chest until she couldn't breathe; she couldn't breathe; she couldn't—

"Captain," she heard someone say, desperate, and she wondered how many times the girl had said it. Leylya was in front of her suddenly—her soft, lightly brown features shadowed into obscurity the closer the shadow came. Her eyes were this dark, stormy grey, wind whipping her hair over her face, and there were tear stains over her cheek. "Gallien," Leylya said.

And Gallien blinked back to life. Leylya ran her fingers up Gallien's shoulders, trailed them past her collarbone, over her neck. They rested below each ear, and Leylya said in a whisper that raised goosebumps on Gallien's skin, a whisper meant only for her, "You can save us." She swallowed hard, glanced up into the sky. Her voice was hoarse, "You can save *me*."

Leylya knew. Leylya *knew* how she felt about her; Gallien could feel it on her skin that she knew, and it shouldn't have mattered at this moment, but it did.

She knew she was being manipulated.

And still, it mattered.

"We'll die," Leylya said.

And Gallien blinked down at the deck. Then she stood.

You can save me.

She pushed past the panic strangling her and faced the storm. The waves whipped around them, the sea's answer to the dead silence coming from the west, and Gallien looked right at the grey and let the fire whip through her veins then swirl up around her hands in a smoky crackle of release.

She threw her energy behind the ship, and the darkness recoiled for a moment. The fire warmed her skin, blackened her fingertips, and the world roared and quieted both, depending on where she turned her head.

The grey bounced back, pushing for her again. Pushing for her ship.

She was desperate, frantic.

You can save me.

Gallien forced the magic to pop through her, though it ripped through her body. She wasn't used to this, hadn't done this enough, wasn't strong enough. The dark kept coming, pounding at the edges of her fire, and Gallien let out a sob and fell to her knees.

It stayed away from her magic and encroached on the ship. No, no, no, hells, no.

They weren't going fast enough; they needed to move.

The grey reached its fingers over the ship, and Gallien yelled, releasing a blast of flame toward it. If they could just *move.*

She could feel the power draining out of her blood. What did she have left?

Several screams rose up from the area of the deck that was smothered in the color of smoke on bone, and Gallien ignored them. She had to. She wondered if she could throw enough flame out that the magic would begin to eat into her very spirit. If she could die. The fire was agony in her veins now; she was too tired, too tired.

And then it stopped. The dead grey quit where it was, little ink moving out and receding with the breeze.

And she collapsed to the sopping floor.

She could hardly keep her eyes open, though she was soaked to the bone. And she fell into a heavy sleep, right there outside, when Leylya slid her soft lap under Gallien's cheek, and stroked her hair softly.

"You saved us," she said. "You. Sleep. I will be here when you wake up." Leylya leaned down and whispered in her ear, "I'll be here," in a breath like a butterfly's wing. And the world darkened.

CHAPTER TWENTY-FIVE

"**T**ELL ME A SECRET, Farowfin girl," said Reyan, running his teeth lightly over Kasia's shoulder blade. It was so quiet and still in here now—the room, the palace as a whole. Everyone slept but them.

"Thought you said I wasn't Farowfin's."

"You don't *belong* to them." Reyan said it into her skin. "I said that I was yours, that you were mine...But I don't know—I don't know that you really belong to anyone."

He felt her body shake against his when she laughed lightly and had to fist his fingers in the sheets to divert some of the instant ache at the feeling of her skin.

"You want a secret," Kasia said, and Reyan smiled, laying his head back on his pillow. He hadn't felt this relaxed, this safe, this...as though everything was *right*...in how long?

Too long. Reyan traced lazy patterns on his queen's bare back.

"When I was a girl," she said finally, her voice gravelly with sleep and who knew what else, "they all thought I was trouble."

"That," said Reyan, biting her shoulder hard enough that she smacked him, "is not a secret."

She ignored him. Unsurprisingly. "I was a bit of a force for a young girl, and my brother, especially, hated it. He's older than me, and an absolute ass. Thinks he's the gift of the gods, which I always thought was amusing since he isn't even actually gifted himself. They all teased me, especially him. So one night after he'd fallen asleep, —hard, partied too late into the night and drunk too much wine—I snuck into his room and shaved his head."

Reyan snorted.

"He was so proud of his stupid, blond curls, and always made fun of my dark ones, and I don't know. I was cursed with just the absolute worst brother. The terrible thing of it is I'd dipped the razor in this solution, this enchanted, allegedly moinchire herb that was supposed to have staved off its growth forever."

"Oh no," said Reyan.

"And it apparently worked. Not as well as the shopkeeper promised me but well enough. He was furious when he woke up, had no idea it was me. And waited and waited for these beautiful locks to grow back. But now they won't go much past his scalp, and they're this light, hardly blondish brown. It's been *years*."

"That's awful," said Reyan, smiling.

"Yes, I feel terrible about it." Her tone suggested that in fact, she did not.

Reyan found that now that he'd tasted it, he couldn't keep his mouth away from her skin. He trailed teeth up her spine, running his fingers down her ribs, over the gentle curve of her waist. She wasn't slight. She was smaller than he was, but soft, all swells and arches—and he couldn't stop touching them. Didn't want to, at least. Kasia had been exhausting to the point of rage before, and now, she was entirely addictive. "What did they make fun of you for?" he said into her back.

"Reading. Studying, mostly. I wanted so badly to be someone the world feared. Someone they looked to when they needed something rather than looked down upon because I was a young girl in a world made for men."

"Is that the way of the world, then?"

"Not everywhere. But in Farowfin? Yes." She sighed, dreamy quality laced in her voice. "I hear down in Etrya, it's the opposite. Everything is run by the women. And elsewhere, I don't know."

"Ebbs and flows, I suppose," said Reyan.

"Not where I'm from."

Reyan pursed his lips. He had a difficult time imagining any world that was not built for someone like Kasia, no matter her gender. No matter her anything. But Farowfin was a different kind of place.

"I'll tell you a secret," said Reyan, and Kasia turned over.

His eyes darkened when the cover fell from her chest to pool around her waist. He ran a thumb over those particular curves, brushed it over the shadow under her breast, the soft swell of her hip, and Kasia's mouth tilted up. "Tell me," she said.

"You'll laugh."

"I won't laugh."

"If you do, I shall have to divorce you. My pride won't be able to take it."

Kasia did laugh then, low and throaty. "If pride is an issue for you, you'd better just cast me out now."

Kasia's fingers trailed absently up his chest in the dark, quickening his pulse. "I like to read as well," he said.

"Lots of kings read."

"Well," he said, "histories, war strategies, philosophies. I read…fiction."

Kasia did laugh then and Reyan caught her fingers in his. "Gods, breaking my rules all the time. Get out of my house, devil woman."

She bit her lip, then nipped his ear. "I'm not laughing because I find it foolish. Just surprising. What stories do you love, Reyan?"

"All of them. Magic and betrayal and war and love and blood. I love them all. They've always been something of an addiction, and my father hated that. Said it was a waste, filling my head with things that weren't real." He shrugged, setting one arm under his head. "I've got piles of books hidden around the palace."

"Do you?"

"Check under the bed."

Kasia raised an eyebrow and slid off the sheets, then bent to peek under their bed, where Reyan really did have part of his collection stacked, and when she rose again, grinning, Reyan joined her on the floor and caught her with one hand around her waist, the other at her wrist, pinning her against the wall.

"Knave," she said.

He kissed her, and her knee slipped between his legs, fingers digging into his biceps. She moved her mouth from his lips to his ear and whispered, "Tell me a story, King."

He slid his teeth along her jaw and his hand up her leg. "My favorite," he murmured, "involves a moinchire thief and the mortal boy she loved." *Moinchire.* The Undying. They were long dead, and most stories of them and their power had faded into myth, but they were his favorite. His mouth was at her collarbone now, and he could feel the temperature rising on Kasia's skin by degrees. "She watched him from afar, you see, never spoke to him, never touched him. But she was in utter, foolish, mad love with the way he approached the world. She was immortal but crept about in the shadows, terrified of being caught with the way she lived, since she broke more laws than she kept. The moinchire are not kind to rule-breakers, you see. This boy was fragile because he was mortal, but he took the world by storm—did everything as though he wasn't afraid to die."

Reyan pushed her other wrist into the wall, catching both in one hand, and pressed his leg between Kasia's. She was hot as fire against his thigh. "The thief broke a rule, and went to speak with him; she could not control herself any longer. Couldn't stand withering and watching him, wondering. And while she was with him, she stole something most precious to the boy. As a memento, not knowing, of course, the value it held to him. He vowed to kill the girl if he saw her again. The boy didn't know she was moinchire."

Reyan dipped his head down to her chest, hair tickling over her skin, and slipped his fingers higher on her thigh, high enough that his fingers found slickness. He smiled and licked over her breast, caught her nipple between teeth, and when she drew in the smallest breath, he bit harder. Hard enough for a proper gasp. He let it go, grinning against the red mark on her chest, and spoke into her skin. "In his hunting for her, he found himself in a very bad situation and wound up with his throat slit. She found him bleeding out on the ground and wept. And Death came to make a bargain with the moinchire thief." Kasia's breath caught when he trailed his fingers as high as they would go, and he slid two inside her.

"Reyan," she whispered, voice strained.

He moved in her, skin electrified with her touch against him, the high breaths and flush of her skin under his mouth. "Death said, *What is that you have in your pocket?* The moinchire thief ran her fingers over the boy's trinket and said, *All I have left in this world. All I have left.*" He slid a third finger inside her. Kasia gasped. Her hands dug into Reyan's back, and he smiled. "And Death said—"

"King!" The door to their rooms crashed open, and Reyan nearly fell backward at Proch's voice. "I'm sorry to wake you, but—oh." Proch's eyes took on a wicked light as he glanced at the king and queen, smile like a razor, and he said, "Oh."

"Get. Out," Reyan growled.

Proch raised his eyebrows, choking on a laugh, and turned to face the door. "My sincerest apologies, cousin. And queen. But there is a matter that demands your *urgent* attention, and—"

Reyan's voice was still rumbling and vicious. "In the middle of the gods damned night? So urgent that you couldn't bring yourself to *knock*?"

Reyan heard his cousin snicker, and if he were standing there in a shred of clothing, he would have very seriously considered leaping over the bed and strangling him.

As it was, the option did not seem entirely appropriate.

He caught Kasia wrapping a blanket around herself from the corner of his eye.

"What have you come to say, Proch?" said Kasia. Her voice would have sounded steady to anyone, probably, but Reyan was close enough to catch the light waver, the shallowness of her breath.

"Your highness." Proch's voice was more serious now. "Something has happened outside. The world...the sky...it...you are *needed*."

"All right," Reyan said. "Out."

Proch did not linger.

"What in hells..." Reyan grumbled. "Do you suppose we have time to—"

"Reyan," Kasia breathed. She was standing by the window, illuminated by the soft white moonlight that glowed through it.

"What?" Reyan pulled a heavy throw from the chair in the corner of the room and tucked it around his waist.

She didn't need to answer; he could see it plainly. The sky was dark, twinkling with stars. But in the middle, spread from one end of the sky to the other, was a crack—split across it, completely devoid of light. Dead.

CHAPTER TWENTY-SIX

KASIA PULLED THE LAST dress she'd worn over her head and ran her fingers quickly through her hair. As though that would do a thing to distract from the flush in her cheeks and the teeth marks at her jaw. She gave up entirely—one of the advantages of being a queen; no one was allowed to give a fuck. She followed the king, in bare feet, to the throne room.

There was a host of people gathered there already. People who looked as exhausted as Kasia—red-eyed, in clothes more suitable for bed than for a meeting in the throne room. What in hells was happening, and how had she missed it completely?

"King," said Proch, dropping to a knee and bowing. "Queen." He was all business now, mirth gone from his eyes. Kasia could almost forget that the man had seen her naked, back arched over Reyan's hand, minutes ago.

"*What*," Reyan said, voice quiet and blanketing the chaotic room in stillness, "is happening?"

Kasia eased up onto her throne beside him. It was so strange to be in here when it was this dark—black streaming in through the windows, the only light flickering from torches that lined the walls.

"Did you..." Proch frowned, head still bowed. Shadows danced across the deep furrows in his brow. "Did you not hear it? Or—or feel it? It shook the world, King."

Reyan glanced over at Kasia, little wrinkle between his eyebrows, then slid his fingers over the arm of his throne. Kasia could feel the tension radiating off him. She looked down at Proch, at the rest of the gathered currently fidgeting silently before them. "What do we know about it?"

Proch kept his head down, which in and of itself meant that things had gone very, very wrong. "Only that the sky has split. It hasn't reached us, thank the gods, and since the crack that you two apparently *somehow* missed, it hasn't spread. But it's *close.* It looks like the shadow in the south has grown. Monstrously. Just...just look."

The sky itself. Gods, it had never reached the air above them. Never spread so far, so fast, not like that.

Reyan and Kasia vacated their seats at the same time and headed together for the doors, trailed by guards. Kasia moved ahead of Reyan, pulse rising when they left the throne room and approached the doors to the gardens.

She pushed through them and stared at the ground as she walked. She wasn't ready to look at the sky, not without a pane of glass between it and her. But she stopped. And looked up.

"Holy gods," she breathed.

Reyan's nostrils flared when he looked up with her.

It was worse than it had looked from inside. Out here, it felt raw. Like the very world was aching. The black of the sky was so different from the air in the split. In the sky, it felt like possibility. In the split, it felt like...death.

Doesn't it just?

Kasia stiffened.

Don't respond aloud. Or do. I suppose it doesn't matter either way, but your beautiful king will, of course, think you've lost your mind.

Kasia glanced over at Reyan, who was currently quite occupied with the sky. And it seemed, so was everyone else. Reyan ran his tongue over his lower lip, and Kasia could feel the tension, see it in the hard set of the muscles in his arms. But he did not seem to be hearing anyone.

He isn't. I do not choose to waste my time on Reyan. It was the first time she'd heard him waver from cool disinterest. To...almost disdain.

Kasia clenched her teeth and tapped her fingers at her side.

None of them hear me. None but you.

"What has happened?" said Kasia, staring up into the air with the rest of them. She directed her question at the people who stood beside her—the ones with bodies.

I could tell you.

Her pulse was thumping through her. Either she really was going mad, or this god, most powerful of them all, was volunteering to speak with her. And not just in the shrine. And he could tell her what was happening.

Yes. I could. The god of cold has been...meddling.

Kasia furrowed her brow. "Thakros," she whispered.

Reyan's head whipped around. "What did you say?"

"Nothing."

"No," said Reyan. He gripped her arm and bent very close to her. "You said...Thakros. Why?"

"Reyan—"

"That can't..." Reyan glanced up at nothing. Thinking, she figured. Then he blew out a breath and said, "Shit." He released her and stormed back into the palace alone. Most of the guard followed.

Kasia had no desire to go with him. "You may accompany me to my shrine," she said to the two guards remaining. "And then, I wish to be left alone."

"Yes, your highness," said the woman nearest her. They trailed her, not quietly, all the way to the shrine.

She slipped inside and shut the door behind her without so much as looking back at them. There was an urgency, a quickening in her veins, that begged her to hurry. This was a hundred terrible things happening at once: the consumption of more southern land, probably an influx of refugees from gods knew where, years taken off the time they'd thought they had to fight it back in a single night, and the world, which was being slowly—and now quickly, it seemed—eaten. Nothing had ever warranted more of a hurry.

Kasia fell hard to her knees in the shrine that had been built for another god, candles flickering and warming her. She reached her left hand for one of the open flames, intending to blacken it on instinct, and someone snorted in her head.

You don't need childish rituals for me. Unless you were planning on speaking to someone else?

"I'm sorry," she said.

Don't apologize.

His voice was so slow, so languid, and she felt like she couldn't keep her own words from tumbling out over one another in a rush. She forced herself to calm down, her pulse rate to fall.

Kasia stared at the floor then glanced around the room. As though he would appear. As though the owner of that liquid voice would simply walk through the wall in the corner of the room and say hello. "It's so odd speaking to someone you can't see," she said.

Is that not the basis of all religion?

"I suppose."

Don't worry about seeing me. I'm here to talk with you. And as long as you can hear me, you'll have what you need.

"Who are you?"

That soft, throaty laugh, like wind rattling through leaves in autumn. *Why are you asking questions to which you already know the answer?*

Kasia dug her fingertips into the hard floor. Needing to ground herself. Needing to feel the floor. "Did you do this?"

The sky?

Kasia's eyes narrowed. "You know I mean the sky."

Well, well. Such boldness, girl. When you know to whom you speak.

A cold shiver of fear dripped down Kasia's spine. But her face remained hard. She was quite certain she wasn't fooling him.

Yes, he said. *I did.*

Kasia nearly choked. Of course this god had been the one to break the world. But there was something unbelievable about hearing a single person—being, something—take ownership of the destruction of existence. "Why?" she said, voice hardly above a whisper.

The god was quiet for a moment. Then he said, *Ask your king.* And this time when he spoke, his voice blanketed the room in velvet. It wasn't just in her head anymore; it was *there.*

"Reyan knows nothing of this."

She could have sworn she felt his lips at her ear when he said, *I think he does.*

"Why are we speaking of Reyan? I thought you wanted to speak to *me.*"

Why shouldn't we? he said. *Your king certainly speaks of me.*

Kasia furrowed her brow. "When?"

He whispered about me, into your chest, when you were pressed against the wall not half an hour ago.

Kasia flushed. *"And Death said..."* Reyan had murmured into her skin.

Ask your king about his god. Ask him what they whispered about you weeks ago when he sank to his knees and dripped blood in this shrine. I believe you're kneeling on the stains.

Nerves crept up Kasia's legs, wound up to her throat. "What they whispered about me?"

Mmm.

"But you were the one who did this."

Yes.

"And you could tell me how to stop this?"

I certainly could.

"But you won't."

No.

"Why not?"

So bold. Such a tongue. Making demands of Death. If I were Thakros, I would make you cut your skin.

Kasia went cold with fear. There were few things she feared, but blades were one of them.

I'm not a barbarian.

Kasia blinked at the ground, instinctively keeping her eyes averted, though he was nowhere in the room. And he wouldn't ask her to do so if he were.

"But you've killed people. And you plan to keep doing so."

When he laughed this time, it didn't rattle. It was loud and smooth and clear. Rolling over her back and filling the room like dark, melted chocolate.

I am Death.

"So you enjoy it."

My enjoyment or distaste is of no consequence. I do not control death, girl, as Asha controls the waves. Or as Thaestra works the winds. I do not command death; I am Death. You would not like a world without me. And this? This consumption of the earth? It will continue until the gods' debts are paid.

"A god broke a rule, and now the world will end for it?"

Death waited. *These were rules written in the dust of the earth as it was formed. I exist to balance the gods. And they are not to change the fabric of humanity. They play their games, and make little moves here and there, and I pay them no mind. But you, dear one, you and Reyan should not have come together in the way that you did. Not that way. It is a grave imbalance of power. An unforgivable offense.*

"I have no idea what you mean." Suddenly, she was so tired. The cataclysm outside, the past couple of months, the fact that all of this was happening in the middle of the night, and Death had taken it upon himself to speak to her, and lay the blame for the ruination of the world at her feet. She wanted to collapse right there.

Farowfin does not speak much of gods, do they? I forget. But you are in Jaelen now, and Jaelen is well, well aware. Speak with Reyan. I tire of this conversation.

And like the room had been sucked dry of a physical thing, he was gone. Everything was empty.

Kasia stayed there for too long. Hoping he would come back to speak to her, hoping he wouldn't. She didn't know what she hoped for any more than she knew how to fix the dying world. And when it had been an hour, perhaps more, Kasia rose, legs and knees complaining with stiffness.

She slunk outside into the gardens, which were empty, and across the grounds that bordered the forest. She wandered until she found herself in a hidden corner, just past the tree line. Still on palace grounds, but nearly outside them. A little stable, almost completely hidden from view.

She crossed over to it under the split sky and moon, to a shadow who stood alone, one hand in his hair, and one on the muzzle of a massive horse that stood a full two hands taller than any other she'd seen.

"Reyan?" Her voice sliced more sharply through the air than she intended, and he jumped. His gaze landed on her, and he blew out a breath.

"The guards let you out here alone?" Kasia said.

"I could ask the same question of you."

She shrugged and moved to stand beside him. "These are your horses."

"Yes."

"Why are they kept in separate stables from the rest of them? And why are they...well, gods, they're the size of elephants."

Reyan laughed. "You've clearly not spent much time around elephants."

Kasia allowed herself to smile. Reyan's horses didn't matter, not really. But they felt *real*.

"They're moinchire," he said.

Kasia whispered, "No," and approached the ghost white horse at the entrance. When the horse looked at her, Kasia swore she was truly *thinking*.

"No one knows I have them. Apart from a few servants. They're not purebred, of course; moinchire horses haven't been purebred in five hundred years. But some merchants, you know, they'll sell you a tall horse and claim it has moinchire blood somewhere in its lineage. These? They truly do. You should see them run. Gods, it's incredible. They're so fast, a legion of horses couldn't catch one."

Kasia had never heard another person speak with such love for an animal. It was the way she talked about her violin. She laid her hand on the muzzle of the horse who was staring at her, and the horse nuzzled into it.

"There's magic running through their veins, no matter how small the amount. Leftover from a race I would kill to have gotten just a glimpse of. Can you imagine? Magic in your veins from birth? In your very blood? Someone immortal." He went still for a moment, fingers curled on the black horse's nose. Then he took several long steps until he was touching the silver beside Kasia's white. "I don't know what to do," he said, and his voice was tortured.

Kasia blinked slowly, looking into the horse's eyes. Calm and quiet and steady.

"Tell me of Thakros," said Kasia, and her voice left no room for refusal.

Reyan faltered, and his hand fell from the horse. "What?"

"Tell me of the rules written in the sand at the making of the world. And how your god cheated them, and you told me nothing."

His eyes hardened and shattered in seconds. "Kasia, I—"

"Reyan." Kasia caught his gaze and held it. "*Tell me.*"

Reyan blinked slowly and closed the distance between them, brushed his fingers over her mouth. And opened his to speak.

CHAPTER TWENTY-SEVEN

G ALLIEN AWOKE IN HER cabin. The ship gently rocked, sloshing and lulling her from sleep to wakefulness and back to sleep again.

After an hour of this, (or more—Gallien had no real way of knowing, given her tenuous grip on consciousness) she forced herself to sit up.

"Captain?" came a small voice from the corner of the room. Gallien nearly jumped out of her skin.

"What are—what are you doing here?" She glanced down at herself, blood rushing to her cheeks. She was in different clothes than she'd been in before: soft, dry. Clothes for sleeping.

"I shut my eyes, Captain," said Leylya, glancing at the ground. "I swear. It was only to make sure you didn't get hypothermia. You were soaked."

"How long was I out?" Her voice was rough with sleep and embarrassment. She didn't wish for Leylya to see her like this. Weak, tired, completely vulnerable. She didn't want *anyone* to see her like this. And up until now, no one ever had. Gallien gritted her teeth. She had to swallow her tongue not to order Leylya out of the room.

"Mm. Half a day," Leylya said. "It's evening again. We're just two days from Jaelen's docks now."

Gallien snarled. "Why didn't you wake me?"

"What for? You needed rest; you passed out. And we are more than capable of *steering a ship.*"

Leylya raised an eyebrow, and Gallien's lips flattened into a line. She glanced over at the wall and smoothed her arms over the ratty blanket that Leylya must have thrown over her.

"Is everyone all right?"

"Yes," said Leylya. "It was incredible."

Gallien said nothing.

"The way you pushed that...that thing back. You and I have fought in too many battles together, and you were always this mighty force of nature on the field. Towering over everyone and cutting them down, so that even armies of men cower at your name. But this...this was...I don't have the words to describe it."

"They all saw it," said Gallien.

"Yes."

Gallien breathed out heavily, nearly choking on fury when she tried to inhale. They'd all seen; they all knew. And short of killing her entire crew, there was no stopping it now. No one could contain a secret like this.

"What?" said Leylya, crossing the little cabin to kneel at the side of Gallien's little bed.

Gallien rolled over. She *hated* this; it was too much—lying here, looking at Leylya face-to-face. As though they were girls in school, whispering and giggling over secrets. As though they weren't the fiercest warriors in the water. And yet, Leylya's eyes were so bright, so sincere and focused, that Gallien found herself disarmed an instant at a time as she lay there. "They know about me, Leylya. About what I can do. I've hidden it since I was hardly more than a girl. And now it's all...dammit. Everything's ruined."

"It's not ruined, Captain."

Gallien breathed out a bitter laugh.

"No," said Leylya, and she slid her hand over Gallien's wrist. Gallien hoped she couldn't feel the newly mad pounding of her pulse. "Just because the gods blessed you does not mean that you owe it to men to do what they wish with it."

Gallien cocked her head and shifted closer to the edge of the bed. She wasn't even sure she was interested in arguing the point. Because Leylya's voice was like hot tea—warm and comforting and melting over her. And the words she said sure sounded pretty to believe.

"You know, in Farowfin—"

"You're from Farowfin?" That explained the odd Farowfin swear from the other night.

"My family was. Did I never tell you? Well. My mother was Farowfin, my father was half Farowfin, half Va'alian. I lived there when I was a very young girl, before we crossed the borders to come here, where my grandfather lived. And I'll never forget the moment I grew up. The instant the ladies started looking at me funny because I reached for the swords in the shops before I reached for the dresses."

Gallien smiled. "You love dresses."

"I love dresses. And I love knives. In Farowfin, they said I was too beautiful. That girls as pretty as me didn't need swords." Leylya pursed her lips, and blinked down at the floor. "That minute, I swore to myself that I would get out. That no one would tell me what my face would allow me to do. I didn't owe it to men to be a pretty petal without a bite, just as you don't owe it to anyone to waste your life making rulings and signing documents."

Gallien rolled over onto her back and stared at the ceiling as the ship moved back and forth under her.

"I suppose he was right, though," said Leylya.

And Gallien's eyes flickered when they met hers. "About what?"

"Too beautiful for swords then. And now one's split me down the middle of my face."

Gallien laughed, and said before she could convince herself not to, "And you think that anything about that makes you less beautiful? Here you are in my cabin, with your face marked by your courage, with your sword, in your pretty dress."

Leylya met her eyes, and Gallien set her jaw, glanced over Leyla's shoulder. Even saying that was stupid. An image of that man, the husband of the traitor gifted by the gods who'd hidden it away, boiling in oil, flashed before her eyes.

Leylya's opened much too slowly, and a smile turned her pretty lips. Everything about Leylya was pretty. The gentle way she spoke, the soft glow in her eyes, the shape of her that was so feminine and quiet, and the vicious side of her that screamed obscenities on the battlefield and tore the enemy to shreds in flashes of steel. Gallien could hardly breathe.

And Leylya knew it.

Gallien *knew* that Leylya knew it, and she further knew that Leylya was not interested, not really. That Gallien's thoughts likely only turned so maddeningly tender and idealistic toward her because she wasn't.

The girl's hand still clung to her wrist, —another tiny manipulation—and Gallien forced herself to exhale.

There were so many things Gallien wanted; well, there were things Leylya wanted, too. Gallien could guess at a number of them. She could guess at herself being merely a vehicle to them, not a destination on her own.

She was a fucking idiot sometimes, but that much, she could see.

"Are you…are you tired, Captain?" Leylya was so close.

Gallien wasn't tired.

"Yes," she said.

Leylya blinked once, eyes shuttering, then she nodded—something just this side of a bow. "I'll leave you then."

Gallien didn't answer. She was too afraid to answer. She didn't watch Leylya go.

She shut her eyes and tried not to think of the softness of the woman's skin. The bells in her voice when she laughed. Instead, she considered Farowfin, a beautiful girl who had been told she couldn't fight, and the fire in her bones that had said she could.

The gods had dictated that Gallien rule. Well, she did. She ruled this ship. She ruled these women. She ruled this sea.

If men had not been able to command Leylya, then neither would men or the gods command *her*. No one would.

CHAPTER TWENTY-EIGHT

"**I** DIDN'T THINK IT important—"

"Reyan," Kasia said. "I don't *care*. I only need to know."

Reyan's hand jumped for his hair, and he looked up at the ceiling. Beyond this fading, ancient wood was the strange sky. He could feel the reality of it now, opening his chest, digging under his ribs. It wasn't that he hadn't believed the threat was real before; it was that he'd only seen the *effects* of the threat—he hadn't actually seen it. And watching that emptiness snake across *his* sky, his stomach felt hollow. His bones felt empty. Never in his life could he remember feeling this dead, skin-numbing fear. So he swallowed and breathed in the hay-and-animal scent of the barn to calm his raging nerves and said, "I had no idea that anything would actually—I was only listening to my god."

"Thakros."

"Yes." Reyan's voice floated out cold. He could see it on the air—frozen like little crystals of not-quite snow, even in the relative warmth of the stables. "Do your people not know the story of the creation of the world?" His brow furrowed.

Kasia shrugged. "We have the story. But no one cares. We don't talk about it or about the gods, really. I have mine, and I will keep them. But they aren't important in Farowfin, not like they are here. We care about living, and about farming, and about making things count on earth. Not about legends of people in the sky."

"Well," said Reyan, chewing on this for a moment, "you need to pay them heed now."

"Tell me of the beginning of the world," she said.

Reyan took her hand. There was nervous energy running through his veins, and he feared if he did not touch something *real*, it would burst out of his skin. He ran his thumb over her palm, let it bump over the veins on the other side of her hand, and walked several steps. He needed to move. Needed something. Needed to be by his favorite horse—something that could not hate him for what he'd done. He leaned against Vii's stall door, guilt gnawing at his bones, silent, steady beat of his heart that pounding into his mind with every rhythmic thump, *Your fault, your fault, your fault.*

"No one knows how the world came to be," he said. His voice was so quiet. But the stables were quieter. "But we know the gods were there at the making of it. There are enough of them, of course, that I do not know all their names."

"For shame, royal," Kasia taunted. Her dark eyebrow was raised, red mouth turned up.

"Oh, you do?" Reyan's eyebrow arched in response.

"In the north, there are Yaalen, goddess of war, Proitius, god of light, Darthoce, goddess of stars, Thoriell, god of fertility—"

"All right," Reyan groaned. "I thought you said no one cares about the gods in Farowfin."

"No, but we at least bother to learn their names."

Reyan rolled his eyes and shifted, arm brushing against Kasia's. "Well. Either way. There are a great many. And they play with the world, but the rules of the earth bind them. They are not permitted to work things in their favor."

"What does that mean?"

"The gods may bless people. Hence, you and I. But beyond that, and beyond answering little prayers here and there, they aren't allowed to reframe the world. The gods have their regions, their countries, their favorites. And they compete. But they also have limits. Large moves, power plays, are not allowed."

"And who regulates that?"

"Death," Reyan said, and he felt Kasia stiffen.

"Death."

"Surely you must know this."

Kasia shrugged. "I never paid attention to mythology."

"It's not mythology, Kasia."

"Semantics."

Reyan pursed his lips.

"I read theory, Reyan. Of course I know what I've been taught of the gods and the way they run magic in the world, but the rules of their games never seemed relevant to me. Some of us were not born to power." He flinched. "Some of us had to spend our free time working the whole world in our favor and reading about things that *mattered* and doing all we could to step in the way of Death so that someone significant *might* begin to notice."

Reyan was quiet. Then he said, "Yes. Well. Death. He was made as a force opposite of all them. So that if they began to break the rules, he could...dole out consequence."

Kasia said, softly enough Reyan could hardly hear her over the soft breathing of the horses, "One god to combat a hundred?"

"Death runs the world, Kasia. It's no stretch to believe that he runs the sky as well."

"He is as powerful as all of them put together." Kasia breathed out long, as though this was a revelation worth all her attention.

Reyan's brow wrinkled. But he continued. "This break in the world, as you know, appeared years ago. The gods had become a bit too involved. You remember the massive slaughter in the south when they—"

"Of course I remember," Kasia said.

"We tore several shrines down here, and they followed suit in a number of nations to the south. Just to tempt the gods less, if this was the problem. Fear of these consequences—breaking the very earth—is why, we believe, the gods of some nations don't speak back at all. They don't want to be responsible if something happens to it."

Kasia was quiet.

"But now..." He didn't wish to say it aloud. Once he said it, he had to claim it.

"What do you know of it, Reyan?"

Reyan shuddered suddenly, stress of everything winding down his body, and he dropped her hand and turned, facing the horse. He needed to be farther from her when he said it. Because now, in the aftermath, it seemed so clear—so terribly foolish that he hadn't said anything to anyone. What had he been thinking?

He had done this. *He* had caused it.

Perhaps if he wasn't looking at her face, he could tell her. Could say it without shame strangling him until he couldn't speak. But she slipped between the stall and him, and he had no choice but to meet her eyes

"Is it these?" she said. She reached for his chest, just under the old linen shirt he'd thrown on to come downstairs to the throne room. And she traced one of the faint scars beneath it. Once, when he'd cut too deep—a raised line over his heart.

He swallowed hard. "Yes," he said.

"Why do you do this?"

Reyan's voice was rough. With stress. With fear. With deep, wounding resentment for his god. "Thakros demands it."

"You never did back away from your gods, did you?"

"Never."

Her fingers trailed across that scar to another at his shoulder, and the fabric shifted against his skin when her fingers glided under it. "For what does Thakros demand this penance?"

"Mostly the lives I've taken. Sometimes other things."

"That doesn't seem entirely fair," she said.

"Neither does this." Reyan grabbed his wife by the wrist and turned it so he could see the underside. The raised burns there. "I've heard the loyalty that the Farowfin gods demand as well." He pressed his lips to her scar, and her pulse quickened under his mouth.

"What did you learn from Thakros?" Kasia whispered.

"He said…he said he brought you and I together. That night—the one you saw me. Bleeding everywhere. When you tended my wounds…"

"I remember."

"I was paying penance. And I was…angry. Over my own damn decision, but nonetheless. I blamed the gods for cursing me with a Farowfin wife. And Thakros was furious. He said he brought you to me. That together. we would be incredible. More than powerful. That you would drive me mad with power and tear down the world, and who was I to question his gift?" The air cooled around Reyan, and a sudden breeze kicked up around them, rustling his hair. He brought Kasia's wrist to his chest. "It makes me wonder…"

Kasia said, voice low and even, "Do you think when we chose to bind tonight—do you believe that is what triggered everything? That Thakros cheated?"

Reyan took a shaky breath. "Yes."

He wondered if Thakros would strike him down right here, an icy bolt through the heart for speaking of him like this. But the gods were not allowed to kill.

He almost laughed. Rules had not stopped Thakros bringing them together.

"So," Kasia started. Then she shut her mouth.

"What?" Reyan looked up through the steam and found her eyes, tightening his fingers minutely over her wrist. "Tell me."

"If Thakros' meddling in our pairing was enough to crack the earth, the very sky, then you and I must be…"

She averted her eyes, little wrinkle showing between her eyebrows.

Reyan drew closer to her. "We must be *matched*, Kasia."

Her voice was hardly above a whisper. "How many times has that happened in history? It's absurd. People never find the perfect equal for their power. They never…"

"What if we did?"

Kasia met his eyes. "If we did, then we are responsible for this."

Reyan nodded, once, eyes cold and sharp as ice. "And it is our duty to fix it."

Kasia ran her fingers up his chest and back down, fingers bumping over his scars. She wrapped her hand around his neck, palm on the ridge of the freshest scar he had, and said, "This cut was deep."

"It was the one Thakros required when I called you a curse. Not a gift."

"I am no one's gift."

"No," he said. "You are your own, and you are a hurricane."

Kasia's fingers tightened on his neck, and Reyan threaded his fingers over her ears. He could feel the new power thrumming over both of their skin, the combination nearly tilting him into drunkenness. It found its way into his veins, and he let himself lose his mind over it, just for a moment.

"Did we break the world?" he whispered.

"I don't know."

"I couldn't even pick out the consequences. Here I am, a king, and I couldn't hazard a guess at anything beyond a black patch in the sky. Anyone could see it."

Kasia said, "You are not alone."

Reyan kissed her, drank her in. If this had been them, then he was terrified and electrified all at once. How was he supposed to feel?

"You never finished your story," said Kasia when she pulled back from his mouth.

"You want a story right now?"

"I've been held in suspense for too long."

Reyan pulled her against him, Vii's breathing too loud and warm over his ear. He breathed in the animal's earthy smell, and his mind relaxed into a familiar story. A story that would allow him to *breathe.* He whispered, lips against Kasia's ear, "Death said, *Give me the contents of your pocket, and I shall give you what you most desire.* And the moinchire thief hesitated. It is an uncertain thing, bargaining with Death. But Death began to fade away, and she grabbed for her lover's trinket and threw it at him. So Death smiled and kissed the moinchire thief. Such a kiss that she wondered if she would ever to be able to breathe again. And when she opened her eyes, he was gone, and her boy was alive. But Death had stolen her immortality. Her immortality for the boy to live. She loved him, and he loved her, and they lived, and died."

"That," said Kasia, "is a very sad story."

"No," said Reyan, kissing the hollow beneath her ear. "She was granted a life to live with the boy she loved. But you see, while she had been watching the boy, Death had been watching her. When she gave him that which was most precious to her, he left with a piece of her heart. And when he kissed her, he stole her breath. And the moinchire thief found that mortality was not frightening. Because she knew that a piece of her loved this dark thing as well as the boy. And that at the end of all things, perhaps she would dance with Death. When the world ended, she would fall into his arms."

Kasia smiled. "You are a romantic."

"It cannot be helped."

Kasia leaned into Reyan's chest, shivering the slightest bit with cold, and Reyan leaned into the stall door and wrapped his arms around her.

CHAPTER TWENTY-NINE

RI COULD HAVE DONE with a single morning that he didn't awake soaked in something. This particular morning, he wasn't so much soaked as he was covered—he was dry, which was an improvement, but yes. Covered. In salt, in brine, in whatever stunk in the sea. He hadn't come up onto the deck for two days. He'd changed since the storm—or perhaps "storm" wasn't quite the right word. Since the grey had reached out its fingers and grabbed for the ship—but there was no real way to wash here, on this vessel. He smelled like the ocean and sweat. Ri was so extremely tired of stinking.

The ship docked, and he moved silently up onto the deck, and even more quietly glided across it. Gallien didn't say a word to him—didn't even come out of her cabin. She'd slept most of the trip away. Which was more than fine with Ri. If she was asleep, she wasn't conscious to pry his secrets from his chest. As it stood, she held nothing more solid than the question of his secrets, and he held a certainty of hers.

A large one.

She'd used. Magic powerful enough to push back the dark; Gallien wasn't just a captain, and she wasn't just the leader of a band of warriors who split the hearts of armies when she came ashore with her swords. Gallien was chosen by the gods, and she was *very interested* in hiding it.

When this business was through and she was giving him transport back to Va'al, he would whisper it in her ear when she tried to threaten him at sea.

He had no interest in spreading her secrets across the world; if Gallien wished to keep it, she should. But she had no room to hold his over him anymore, and that was much more interesting to Ri than whatever it was that was special about her.

Ri shouldered his pack and wrapped his coat around himself. It was evening, and likely most of the tavern rooms around would be filled.

Well, Ri only needed one.

He moved through the streets of Jaelen's capital like a ghost—a quiet shape draped in black cloth that whispered over the sandstone roads. He dodged merchants hawking their wares, yelling at him to convince him that he desperately needed flatbread or shoes or moinchire herbs for his face. He snorted. The last whispers of moinchire magic were powerful, but he very much doubted that they would help removed wrinkles from a person's brow.

There was a tavern in the middle of town—and by the time he reached it, his muscles burned. Someone could have set him on fire and it would have burned less. Funny that tens of merchants could scream for his attention, but Ri wanted the only place that wasn't asking for it at all.

He moved through the open front door and approached the innkeeper, who wrinkled his bulbous nose at Ri. Ri threw up his hands in an exhausted shrug and said, "Have you an open room? Four nights."

The innkeeper raised his eyebrows—no doubt, Ri looked homeless. He reached into his pocket and dropped a small sack of silver on the counter. Adè had left it with him to fund his trip before he'd fled Ri's room.

Suddenly the disgust faded from the innkeeper's nose, and he was all smiles and kind, relaxed wrinkles. "Yes, sir," he said. "It's little and tucked in the corner past those stairs. Noise floats up from the tavern, and the bed is small, but—"

"Fine," said Ri. He paid his price, which he was nearly positive the innkeeper had raised when he'd seen Ri's money. But it didn't matter. He didn't care. He hardly cared about any of this anymore; he didn't have the energy at the moment.

Right now, what he cared most about was finding a hot bath. What he cared about was looking and smelling like a human. He placed an order for hot water to be sent to his room and left. He would worry about the rest of it later.

He shouldered his way through the heavy crowd at the bar, and had little trouble. Most people were wise enough to move out of his way so he wouldn't tarnish their clothes with fish oil and whatever else he smelled like.

The stairway was small and cramped, and each step groaned under his weight. When he reached the top and the key turned in the lock, he breathed a sigh of relief, then shut the door behind him. He was alone. And the tavern didn't rock or pose a risk of sinking. No one would question him.

Here, he could be alone. That was the only thing that mattered.

Ri went downstairs while his hair was still wet. It was cold and stuck to his forehead and ears, but it was clean. His clothes were clean, and his skin was clean, and that was such a small thing. But it made the entire night feel different. Ri had never really *hated* feeling dirty before. But he did now.

He found a table in the back corner of the tavern and called for rum, spiced and hot and buttery. His pupils practically dilated just at the thought of it.

And he waited.

"Cards, Etryan man?" someone slurred. He smelled like liquor and sweat, large beard unwashed and hanging past his chest.

"Not interested." Ri sipped his rum.

The man through his hands in the air and said, too loudly for Ri's taste, "Typical priss-ass Etryan. 'Fraid to wager a copper on a friendly game—"

Quick as a knife, Ri's hand darted out and he grabbed the man's sleeve. Five cards fell out and fluttered to the floor. Ri didn't bother looking at them.

The drunk man's face went white.

"Leave me the hell alone or I'm taking those cards to that table you've been working in the corner, then I'm shoving them down your throat and letting the people you've been cheating take their payment out of your skin."

The man's eyes went wide. Gods, his breath stunk. Ri felt a sharp surge of irrational fear at the smell and fought to keep his grip on the drunk. "Y-yes, sir," the man stuttered, and he bent to pick up his cards.

"Leave them," said Ri, voice low and ferocious.

The man braced himself on Ri's table, and the instant he left, Ri slid back into the shadows of his booth and drank his rum, much too quickly. His hands were shaking now. Was he so weak? Just the smell of someone's breath could take him back to that prison cell?

Piss-poor assassin. That was what he was.

His pulse was racing in his quiet corner, and he clung to his mug of spirit like it could save his life, and no one near him was any the wiser.

He wondered if the girl would show up while he was in the middle of a near-panic. She was supposed to be here. Or rather, he was supposed to have been here four nights ago. Ri was sure the message had been delivered to Nagonia—the maid he'd danced with on Kasia and Reyan's wedding night. She should have been waiting for him She'd be walking in the front door by midnight. Or at least he hoped she would be. Hells, perhaps he'd ruined everything by getting caught and staying in damned Andra for days, rotting in a cell. He thought, for the hundredth time, that he should have brought a guard. Curse it all.

She was a maid. It wasn't as though she spent every night out in the city. And four days was quite a lot of days to be late. Perhaps she wouldn't even be able to get away. Not after she'd maybe come here the last three nights for nothing.

A sick feeling welled in Ri's gut, potent enough almost to wash away the panic that had his hand shaking so badly that every time he took a drink, drops of froth and rum splashed up onto his face.

Without Nagonia, all of this would fail. Without her, he wouldn't know how to reach the queen's rooms, wouldn't know her routine, wouldn't know anything.

And killing queens wasn't something a person could go into blind.

He took another long swallow of the smooth rum and waited.

And waited.

And waited until the crowd got drunker and the lights got dimmer. He waited until his pulse had slowed entirely, and midnight had long passed.

His stomach went from hollow to clenched.

She wasn't coming.

Ri finished off his third rum of the evening and looked back over his shoulder to his room, which was beginning to sound very inviting.

"Aren't we looking mysterious this evening?"

Ri whipped his head around, and his stomach relaxed. "I thought you weren't coming."

Nagonia sat in the booth, knees brushing against his. "I nearly didn't. You're late."

"Yes. Well." He ran his fingers through his hair, and his sleeve fell back away from his arm. Nagonia's eyes caught on his scarred wrist, his forearm. "I was a bit held up."

A wrinkle popped up between Nagonia's eyebrows, but she didn't press. She simply said, "I wouldn't have come tomorrow."

"Then it's good that I arrived today." Ri downed the last of his drink and stood, then inclined his head toward the stairs. "Come to my room."

Nagonia raised an impeccably shaped eyebrow, clearly implying something lascivious, and Ri rolled his eyes. She followed him up the stairs, and he thought he saw the bartender's shoulders drop in relief.

He waited until Nagonia was in the room with him, then he quietly shut the door behind her. "Tell me what you know." He moved backward to sit on the bed, and Nagonia leaned against the door at her back.

"My lady rises at five. She was never much for religion, but as of late, she's been spending time in the shrine about half an hour after she wakes. She spends that half an hour praying. No guards with her. Just...alone."

Ri ran his thumb over his fingers and stared at the wooden floor. Something felt off about slipping into a shrine to take a girl's life. The gods saw everything, of course, no matter where you were. But doing it in their home was...different. "Any other times she's vulnerable? Alone?"

Nagonia shrugged. "Not unless you would like to kill the king as well. She's *very* vulnerable in the middle of the night, when she is tangled up with him." A grin flashed across Nagonia's face and Ri coughed out something that wasn't entirely a laugh.

"No," he said. "I wasn't paid to kill the king."

"This is the only way, Ri. You have that half an hour, or you have nothing. There are guards standing outside the building, close enough to the shrine that they could come running if they needed. I can take out two, maybe. A sleeping draught. But that leaves two for you. Lucky for you, the sun in Jaelen doesn't rise until my lady is already praying. It won't be dark, but it will be grey."

"I should kill them, then."

"Are you not an assassin?"

Ri sniffed and brushed his hand over his hair. "How much time do I have?"

"In days? Not many. Ever since that surge, the queen is getting restless. Keeps trying to convince Reyan that they need to go down there themselves and try to fight against it. He refused at first, but now...well...I don't think they'll be in Jaelen much longer."

Ri gave her a single nod. "All right." He considered, leaning his head back against the wall the bed was shoved against. "Give me two days. I want tomorrow—"

"You mean today?"

"Yes," he said, small smile creeping onto his face for a moment. Then it was back to solemnity. "I want today to recover from my trip. Tomorrow to prepare. The next day at dawn, I will be there. And the queen will die."

Nagonia bowed.

"I'll need you to meet me at the gates. Get me inside; show me where I'm going."

"Of course," said Nagonia. Then she knelt at the bed and curled her fingers around his neck and touched her forehead to his. Ri did the same. "For Etrya," she whispered.

"For Etrya."

CHAPTER THIRTY

G ALLIEN HAD NEVER BEEN content with acting as a simple transport. She was biding her time so that she could start a business, after all, and what chance had a business without a startup fund? Even if, or especially if, that business involved riding the sea to every rich asshole who sailed past and relieving them of their burdens. Businesses like that required capital—in weaponry, food, maintenance.

It was her ambition that meant that if she ran people from one end of the world to the other, she'd be damned if she didn't make a single gold more than the king offered her. No, Gallien had spent enough time at sea to know valuable shipments when she saw them, and enough time on land to know hunger in people's eyes when she saw *it*. The client she waited for was always hungry.

And Gallien's bag was always filled to the brim with tempting things.

He was very high up in society, royal even, which made everything feel more sordid somehow. It gave Gallien a wild thrill just watching him walk through the door. She always felt strange coming in here. It was a sight more reputable than the taverns she preferred, where she could sink into the background in her sea-stained clothes and ship-worn boots.

Here, she stuck out.

Here, the clientele smelled like money and pride.

She waited at a table in a private room as always. The man preferred both luxury and discretion, which were two things that often did not go hand-in-hand. People with gold in their pockets tended to have silver tongues, and gossips would speak for ages if they saw a royal and a pirate lord having any sort of regular dealings.

So, Gallien rolled her eyes every time she came to Jaelen, and agreed to meet in a place with ivory napkin holders, rich, velvet curtains hung from the floor to the ceiling, and air that always smelled a little of perfume.

"Pirate?" she heard before her ears detected the light creak of the door.

"Oh, don't call me that. It's so formal."

"But so illegal, which makes it a bit delicious, doesn't it?"

Gallien turned, and her mouth ticked up. The man was tall and lean, and his clothes always made very clear exactly what went where and which piece of him was sculpted how. Sharp-featured, a nose that made a statement on his face, and cheekbones that answered. He crossed his arms and leaned against the door, shutting it with his back, and propped his foot on it.

"Your hair's longer, Proch."

"It's a courtesy," he said.

"Courtesy?" Gallien raised an eyebrow.

"It's just so much easier to *pull* at this length."

"Gods, you're vulgar," she said, and laughed. "Sit."

Proch moved like a serpent. He was so relaxed in every room that sometimes it was as though the man didn't have any use for bones. He sat at the table across from her, and Gallien leaned back in her seat, arms behind her head. She kicked her shoes up on the table and Proch rolled his eyes. "It'll take them ages to get these scuffs out."

"Oh, you're good for it," she said, and he turned his middle finger up at her. She tipped her chin up at his neck and said, "That chain. Is it for pulling, too?"

Proch smiled in an almost predatory way and linked his fingers in the thick gold at his throat. "I could show you."

"Business first," she said.

"You know you were the one who gave this gold to me in the first place. Ancient Va'alian, correct?"

"Mmhmm."

"And what have you got for me today?"

Gallien looked him up and down and shifted so her boots scratched the table's shiny, dark wood surface a little harder. Proch winced. She hid a smile and bent to retrieve the artifact out of her bag. She'd gotten it months ago, and Proch hadn't been able to meet with her until now. It was nothing particularly useful—a cup. Tarnished with over a century's worth of life. Clay, which in and of itself made it remarkable it had survived this long, flecks of silver leaf and several colors—green, pink, teal, mostly—of which Gallien could not identify the material.

"Incredible," Proch breathed, immediately snapping out of his casual disinterest into fascination. That was always the way with Proch. He loved these things dearly and only bothered to do research into the items after he'd gotten them, if he did any at all. Most of that he got from Gallien who, being a pirate and occasional treasure hunter herself, given her profession, knew everything. But it was not the exact details or origins Proch loved. It was the story he imagined for it, and it was *touching* it. He loved laying his hands on pieces of history. Owning bits of magic. "What is it?"

"A cup."

He rolled his eyes and bobbed his head from one side to the other, rolling the goblet in his hands. "Obviously."

"Etryan. I'd wager around two centuries ago. Nothing magical, but see?" She leaned forward and tapped the spot beside the flecks of gold that barely clung to it. "That's silver. Expensive here and now, but plentiful in Etrya. Particularly back when this was used. If this was, say, a Farowfin item, I'd say you had yourself something of nobility, perhaps even old royalty. But the curve of the stem suggests Etryan, and with the silver and the clay base, this is probably a commoner's item."

"That's almost more interesting, though," said Proch. He turned it gently, as though he cradled something he could break if he simply touched it wrong. This was the only time she ever saw Proch reverent. "Who owned it? Mason? Carpenter? Prostitute? Pirate?" He grinned up at her, and Gallien smiled with her teeth.

"Haven't you had enough of pirates?"

"Never," said Proch.

It should have been an absolute no, doing dealings with one of the Jaelenian king's advisors, but she'd met the man on the docks one evening and started trading with him before she'd realized who he was. And it wasn't until several deals in, when he'd suggested they start meeting in a private room here, that he'd shown up in royal dress, hair black and perfect, skin oiled with cologne, and told her he worked with the king. Was, in fact, related to the king.

She'd reached immediately for the blade she kept under her jacket, but he'd assured her he had no interest in reporting her dealings. This was business, and this was what kept him from losing his mind in the quagmire of day-in, day-out politics and bowing and scraping.

They had been meeting for two years now, and they knew each other very intimately. His status did not worry her anymore.

"I'll take my payment now," said Gallien, after she'd watched him marvel long enough. She was usually able to watch for quite some time before she got bored; there was something fascinating about watching someone be fascinated. Particularly someone like Proch, who had seen everything in the world a hundred times and didn't know how not to be bored with all of it.

Proch's mouth curved, and he eyed the pouch he'd brought with him. He weighed it in his hands and tossed it to Gallien, and Gallien did not bother to count. Not anymore. Proch didn't cheat her.

He knew she'd cut off his balls if he did.

Honestly, he might enjoy that.

Gallien tucked the gold in her bag, and Proch wrapped the goblet in silk, painstakingly, then set it neatly in his.

He leaned forward. "Plans tonight?"

"A thousand," said Gallien.

Proch rested heavily on his elbows, eyes bright, mouth ten different shades of mischief. "I hope nine hundred of them involved me."

Gallien scraped her teeth over her lip.

"Meet me in an hour?" said Proch.

Gallien rolled her eyes but let him glimpse her lips quirking up as she turned to walk away.

His rooms were in the palace, which typically would have made it impossible for Gallien to have met him there. But rumor had it his cousin had grown so tired of waking to find various people of every gender hobbling through the halls half naked in the middle of the night that he'd allowed Proch to move to his own little villa on the palace grounds. Perks of promiscuity, apparently.

This had become almost as sacred a tradition on Gallien's trips to Jaelen as had bringing him trinkets and getting gold back. Gallien was very familiar with her route to his rooms.

She'd thought, after she'd left his presence, that she wasn't in the mood. Not tonight. Not with the hollow feeling in her stomach, five times hollower since her last confrontation with the grey. The one that told her she'd been right—that each battle she did with it drained her of her power.

Permanently.

She didn't know for certain and didn't know if it was truly gone forever, but what she did know was that she felt half the force she usually did running through her veins, and sitting alone in her rooms was going to do nothing to distract her from the dread.

So she approached Proch's door.

"So late?" he said, opening it before Gallien had had the chance to knock. It had been less than an hour. "I was sleeping."

"Shut that pretty mouth," said Gallien. She stepped inside and kicked the door shut behind her. "Or I'll shut it for you."

"Promise?"

Gallien grabbed him by his jaw and slammed him back into the closed door harder than she intended. Hard enough that his head rattled against the wood, and when she let go of his face to press her hands to his chest, he ran his tongue over his lip. It came away red. He smiled. "Gods, I missed you."

Gallien's grin was vicious. "Did you?" She linked a finger around the chain at his throat and pulled hard enough that he choked. She could feel the knot of cartilage bobbing over her knuckles. She felt it in the pit of her stomach. She felt it where she'd felt empty before.

The stirrings of power, of a different sort.

Who gave a fuck what kind? For once, she wasn't hollow.

"What?" he said. "You want me on my knees? I'll warn you; I bite."

Gallien needed no warning. Proch was extremely selfish in bed with her. After all, he had a reputation to uphold around the city, so he couldn't very well be that way with everyone at court. And here she was, a woman he only saw every few months at best—they didn't need to worry over reputations and who thought what and who was too slow to offer his tongue between a woman's legs. Gallien was impermanence and discretion and had no head for gossip. And when it came down to it, she was selfish, too.

Fuck, she loved coming to Jaelen.

"If I wanted you on your knees, you'd be kneeling already," said Gallien, and she led him by that necklace, which functioned quite well as a collar, to the bed. Want, pure and distilled, thrummed through her veins even as she walked like she owned him. Like she was entirely unaffected.

His bed was as ornate as that stupid restaurant he loved. But that was no surprise. It was iron, carved in what must have taken months of someone's time, silver silk sheets, all very clear marks of Proch. It was also obscenely large, which was not entirely outside Gallien's considerations every time she decided to fuck him. That much space led to nimble, memorable things, she'd found. Gallien kicked her boots off on the floor and stripped out of her pants. Proch hadn't been wearing anything but pants to begin with, so he crawled into the bed and simply waited.

He was very good at waiting.

He was less good at waiting whenever she pulled off her shirt.

Gallien smiled with her teeth, and Proch sat up immediately, back against the headboard. If his eyes had been playful before, they were hungry now. Mischievous, always, but hungry. "You may touch me," said Gallien, "ut not with your hands. Is that understood?"

Proch grinned. "Of course. Captain."

She pushed him back into the mattress and reached for his pants, and he kept his own hands fisted in the sheets at his side. She tried not to let her gaze linger on his hands, but god, she loved them. The sight of his veins sticking out like that, his long fingers clenched, the very obvious *effort* of waiting...it was difficult to fight past. Difficult not to just give up control, give up thought, and let him fuck her into oblivion.

The important thing was that Gallien did not need rope to keep him in line. She curled her fingers over him, and he sucked in a breath that sounded entirely masculine, which was what Gallien wanted. Because she'd seen Leylya and Nazalie walking out of rooms together more than once on the ship, and she wanted no unbidden images of that girl popping into her mind. Wanted nothing painful, no comparisons. Proch's voice wasn't particularly *low*, but the growls he always gave her were.

He was rock solid already, which she had opened her mouth to tease him for when he bucked his hips, and she fell forward onto his chest. He locked his leg around her thigh, moving more quickly than she'd ever seen him, and caught her lip in his teeth. Then he kissed her, and holy gods, could that man work his tongue.

"You're getting better. Your hands didn't even let loose of the sheets," Gallien said when she could catch her breath.

"Well," said Proch, and he slid under her, catching her breast in his mouth. He would stay there for a half hour if she let him. He bit down. Gallien's back arched. "I'm good at following directions."

Gallien shut her eyes and let him use that incredible tongue again, flicking over her nipple and tasting her breast, and froze when she felt his fingers on her hips, trailing up her back.

She narrowed her eyes.

"I said I was good," said Proch. "Not exceptional."

"Is that what the ladies of court say of you as well?"

Proch laughed and tightened his grip on her back, then flipped her over. He couldn't have done it if she hadn't allowed it; Gallien had a half-inch on him height-wise, and a good deal more muscle. But they both knew she loved it when he broke the rules. And he enjoyed her reaction to it.

"You'll pay for that," she said when he was staring down at her, wicked laugh in his eyes, his hair hanging over her ears.

"Oh, I intend to."

He kissed her. Again and again until she was dizzy with want.

"Can I touch you now?" he whispered in her ear. His hands were at either side of her neck, on the bed. He was certainly touching her everywhere else.

Gallien ran her nails down his bare back, hard enough to draw blood.

Proch hissed and yelled, "Fuck!"

"I said you'd pay."

He breathed out, shaky at first, then shut his eyes and grit his teeth through the marks she'd left in his skin. "I'll beg you if I must, Captain," he said.

"So," she said, "beg."

And he did.

CHAPTER THIRTY-ONE

"R EYAN, WE CANNOT AFFORD to wait another day."

Reyan locked his jaw. "You're being reckless. We've hardly worked with one another; you cannot expect that just because we're bound, we can waltz on down to the grey and magically wish it away without having worked together."

Kasia pursed her lips, hands fisting at her sides. "Reyan—"

"Kasia." Reyan rubbed the furrow between his eyes. His head had been aching for two days, having this exact argument again and again. It was clear; the very air was different. The bright of the green for which Jaelen was known across the world felt dull. Birds quieter in a ruined sky, a thousand things. Whatever they had done to the world had made it harder to *breathe*. But recklessness wouldn't solve anything. "Where in hells is Nagonia with that tea? I asked her ten minutes ago; my head is going to explode all over the grass."

Kasia shrugged and sat on the fountain, crossing one long leg over the other. "She's slow on her feet lately. Do you know she was out last night until nearly three in the morning?"

Reyan's eyebrows shot up. "Really?"

"She's got a wealth of suitors for a maid."

Reyan laughed. Then scowled again, at the pounding in his head and the casual look of power on his wife's face. That look said that she would get what she wanted, no matter what she had to do. And she was probably right. She would grind him down until he was dust, powerless to refuse her. Reyan sighed. "Come train with me."

She slid off the fountain. "Oh, well, this should be unfair. As your head is killing you and mine is being perfectly cooperative."

Reyan smirked. "That's the first time I've known a single part of you to be cooperative."

She pushed him. "Well, then I suppose I shall be uncooperative tonight. As I'm going to be verbally abused either way."

He caught her around the waist and drew her into him, biting her ear. "Careful with that tongue."

"Oh, you want me to be careful with it now?"

Reyan didn't often find himself blushing.

He found himself blushing.

Kasia walked ahead of him, toward the forest. The one that bordered their grounds and surrounded the bath house. It was private enough to really train, but the guards could stand just outside the wood if they were needed. As of yet, he and Kasia had only tried small displays here and there. Nothing too major, nothing too risky or conspicuous.

That was about to change.

He followed her into the trees, marveling at the way she glided over the ground. She was the wind, and she moved like it.

He stopped in the same small clearing they'd been in when she'd threatened him and leaned against a tree.

"Do you want to try it first, or shall I?" said Reyan.

"We're not holding back today?"

Reyan shrugged. "Not if you wish to go confront the tear in the world soon."

"Then I'm first," she said, grin slashed across her face. She dropped to her knees and shut her eyes. Then she lifted her hands and tipped her face toward the sky, which was half-hidden by the trees. At first, there was nothing, and then, Reyan could see them both swirling together from her fingertips—wind and ice. Kasia's eyes remained closed, and she whipped her hand around, a burst of cold swirling up into the air. It coated the world around her white; Reyan could feel the chill from here. With them combined, Kasia could whip the cold like a blade, and she flicked her wrist hard, sending a burst of whatever it was toward a tree to her right. It furrowed, bending from the force, and Reyan stood straighter. He watched, eyes dark and intent, as she scrunched her face in a way he'd only seen her do a few times—when she was with him. A burst of snow and wind sprang from her body, so hard and fast and in every direction that Reyan had to duck not to be injured by it.

Energy buzzed over his skin, calling for him. Begging him to join her. A note of fear licked up his spine at something he couldn't name. But it whispered over him—at the power, perhaps, that he could feel radiating off her. Pulling him to join her. It was so instantly intoxicating, Reyan could hardly think.

She looked like history. It all did. Like hundreds of years ago when the moinchire had walked the earth and left footprints of magic in their wake, and people the gods had blessed were so powerful they could change the very weather. Before the moinchire had been wiped out and the magic in humanity had been diluted as punishment. As balance. An ice princess could no longer coat the country in snow, and an earth prince could not split the ground from coast to coast. They were whispers of magic, just like whispers were all that remained of the magic of the moinchire.

But this...this looked like a legend. One he desperately wanted to be a part of.

He stood and lashed out with his hand, and it cracked like a whip, loud and sharp, weaving with Kasia's ice and wind. All of a sudden, the world was freezing. Power rushed through Reyan's veins as he gave himself over to it—to becoming hers, to her melding into him. It had been a frigid wind before, but now that both of them had combined their efforts, the energy shifted into a cyclone. Shards of ice stabbed out from it, and it roared in both their ears.

Kasia had stood now, backed to the other side of the monstrous whirlwind that whipped and spun between them. It tore through the air and through Reyan's veins—so strong it was almost alarming. If Reyan let himself weaken for just a moment, let himself be distracted for a half-second, perhaps it would spin out of control and rip a path through the woods, tear down the world.

He blinked at his wife through what they'd created, and she was smiling. Her hair flew around her face, dark and unruly, and he thought he saw her open her mouth to laugh. But the sound was drowned out by this thing.

It grew until Reyan could focus on nothing but this, could feel nothing but power pumping through his veins in place of his blood. He and Kasia both just allowed the storm to rage.

After minutes, Reyan's arms began to tremble, along with his legs. He stared over at Kasia, who was standing shakily as well, color beginning to drain from her face, and he shut his eyes and forced his body to rescind a heartbeat of the power he contributed, and another, and another, until it was only Kasia fueling it, and the storm was manageable once again. Her power faded as well, and then, it died.

For a moment, both of them simply stood there, blinking. At nothing—at the emptiness where something incredible had just been.

Reyan began to sit in the grasses, then froze, face draining when something moved through it.

Kasia frowned. "What?"

"Nothing," said Reyan, but he was shaking; there was no way she wouldn't detect it.

"Reyan—" She glanced down at the grass, then her lips flattened. "A snake?"

Reyan's nostrils flared.

"All of that and you're ready to faint over a little *snake*?"

"I hate snakes," Reyan whispered, and Kasia laughed.

"Gods, you're endearing," she said. "Control the weather, but snakes undo you. Sit down."

Reyan waited until the shiny black reptile had left and sat. It was unreasonable. But even kings feared some things.

After his breathing had calmed, he looked up at the sky, willing himself not to think of the things that slithered on the floor of these woods. "Maybe..." said Reyan, somewhat desperate to change the subject, "we can do this."

Kasia sat in his lap, damp with sweat on her arms, in her hair, and she threw her hands around Reyan's neck. He buried his face in the crook there, right at the bend between her neck and shoulder. They collapsed against each other.

"We can," said Kasia. Her whisper was too high, too thin. Like she was on the verge of tears. But maybe he was, too.

"There is a chance," said Reyan, sliding his hand up to hold his wife as close to him as possible.

"Provided there are no snakes in the south."

Reyan pinched her, and she yelped.

But this proved it. They had no choice but to go. Imminently.

It was the middle of the night when Reyan chose to enter the shrine. He hadn't been in here since the world had been cleaved in two. Hadn't been able to summon the motivation to speak with Thakros, hadn't known what to say if he could.

But it had been enough time now that he could think of his god without going rage blind. And he knew Thakros had noticed his absence. Perhaps he would make Reyan slice himself open just for the insolence of refusing to speak with him. Reyan's jaw locked, and he pushed the door open.

The absence of fury in his veins did not dampen the bone deep sense of betrayal just coming in here. His god had laid the guilt of the entire world upon him and hadn't even bothered to let him know. Of course, the worst part was that Reyan had known something wasn't right, and he'd looked past it. He was just as complicit in this as Thakros.

He dropped to his knees and looked up toward the warm wood ceiling.

"Thakros?" he said.

The silence was heavy. Thick enough to choke on.

A chill trailed down Reyan's back. "Did you know?"

That hadn't been what he'd planned to open with. But his heart had spoken before his mind could get hold of his tongue.

It was quiet in the shrine.

A scowl turned Reyan's face. Apparently, his rage had not dimmed as much as he'd thought. "You knew," said Reyan. "You knew you had cheated. That bringing us together was forcing too much power into the world, in *your* favor. That was not for me or for Kasia or for the sake of the world. It was for you." His voice cracked. "How many scars would I have to carve into myself to make up for the *catastrophe* that my actions caused? Would I have to rip off my skin?"

Thakros said nothing, and Reyan waited, and still, no answer came. He growled and stormed out of the shrine, wondering if Thakros would remove his favor from their house. If he would send a frost that would kill all the wildlife in the area and doom them to starve. Perhaps he would. Reyan couldn't bring himself to care.

It was one thing to be so deeply betrayed by a person. People were often not good for their promises or their intentions. But a god? That was something else entirely.

The simplicity of meeting her. The perfection with which it all fit together. Perhaps even his emotions on the issue had been compromised when he'd engaged himself to her initially; that didn't seem outside the realm of a god's power. And now, here they were. He didn't know if he was angrier at the god's manipulation or at his own trust in someone he had *always* feared would be untrustworthy.

Reyan fisted his hands at his side and marched across the grounds, skin burning with anger and with sorrow. He tore into the orange grove where he had taken so many lives.

The grove had always smelled strongly of citrus, especially this time of year when the boughs were heavy with fruit. But now, he couldn't quite shut out the overwhelming tang of iron in the air. The fruit and life hung in the air, but the ground had been drinking blood ever since Reyan had taken the throne.

He knelt in the very spot he preferred to make criminals kneel and looked down at his arms. They were scarred in several places, from his wrists all the way up to his elbows. A white, raised line snaked down from his collarbone, and more—at his neck, his shoulders. How much had he bled for this person? Thing?

He drew lines with his blade down his palms and let them drip into the earth.

"What do you want?" he yelled up at the sky. He didn't even know that Thakros could hear him out here, or that he was interested, even if he could. "How shall I make my penance?"

He turned the gold dagger from his hip to his own chest.

"Shall I give the name of my god?' Even to Reyan's own ears, his voice sounded thick with pain.

Silence answered him.

"I am not entirely sure," said Reyan softly, glancing at the black soil that bunched around his knees, "what name I would give."

He left the orange grove, several levels beyond exhausted, and slipped slowly across the grasses back to his rooms in the tower—leaving two deep knee prints in blood-nourished soil.

CHAPTER THIRTY-TWO

"WHAT I FAIL TO understand," said Kasia, "is why the gods' wars should be visited upon us."

You don't have to understand it. You only have to accept it.

Kasia's lip curled as she sat in her shrine, in a particularly unworshipful manner. Her legs were crossed, and she leaned against the door, hair spread out over the wood. She spoke casually with Death as she'd done the last several mornings. It was so odd for this to be a routine now. She didn't know if it was odder that she was choosing to speak to a god so regularly or that he was choosing to speak to her. She was glad he had deigned to do it this morning. She and Reyan had decided it last night—their power was too remarkable to waste, and the grey was affecting their world already. She could feel the death of the world on her skin. Like something was curling in on itself, waiting to eat the very ground beneath them, waiting, waiting...for something. It was enough to make her shudder into sleep every night. And the grey was coming alarmingly close to Va'al. If Va'al were to go down, the carnage would be unthinkable. And the fish trade would be irrevocably destroyed. Va'al was not a massive world power, but it was a country large enough that its consumption would have a global impact. Tomorrow, they would journey down to the grey. Who knew if pumping power into it would drive it away or kill them or destroy the world?

But too many were dying. And after they had felt the ages-old power between them yesterday in the grove, it had become clear. To whatever end, they would do *something*.

They had no choice. This had been exhausting them, all of this, since the crack in the world and the day they'd spent, watching their power blend and grow into something monstrous. It was an exhaustion neither of them could shake.

Kasia was quite certain that it would linger until their duty was done.

"Don't patronize me," Kasia snapped.

We're in a bit of a mood this morning, aren't we?

"Gods."

Just the one.

Kasia rolled her eyes and shifted so that her legs lay straight on the floor.

Not burning your wrist to speak to me has really taken all the reverence right out of you..

"Well, I won't be burning myself again, so you can get that thought out of your mind right now."

Death laughed that smoky, scratched laugh. But his voice was quite serious when he said, *Good.*

Kasia felt an uncomfortable niggling in her chest. A sort of fondness that she'd tried very hard not to feel talking with him. He was a god, after all, and gods were not terribly interested in the fondness of mortals. It was something that none of them ever returned. True loyalty to someone like him was dangerous. So Kasia refused to allow herself to develop it.

"Why this punishment?" said Kasia.

Punishment?

"You are entirely insufferable. Punishment. Consequence. Whatever you wish to call it."

He laughed.

"What did Thakros do that was worth *this*? All this suffering. You are destroying the world. For what?"

Did you not do as I told you? Did you not ask your king?

Kasia narrowed his eyes. "I did."

And he had no existential brilliance for you?

She ran a hand through her hair and sighed.

He waited. Then, finally, he breathed out slowly. *You and Reyan are like puzzle pieces—not in your souls, not in who you are. Soul mates, I am sorry to tell you, do not exist. But in your powers.*

"So it's true," Kasia breathed.

Yes. There are certain gifts that fit one another beautifully. Enhance the other's wildness rather than harness it. And certain gifts that amplify much more than they should when they combine. Yours and Reyan's are one of those instances. You should not have found each other, except by destiny. Except by chance or your own wills. You have a measure of power that has not been granted for centuries, because of the efforts of a god. It's cheating, Kasia.

Kasia was shaking, suddenly, and she didn't know why.

It's too much power for Jaelen, Death said. *And chance did not bring it about; Thakros did. So yes, the earth and the gods both must pay the consequence. It is the natural order of things.*

"Can we take it back?" she whispered.

No.

The room was blanketed in pressing, palpable nothing.

What will you do? he said. And in that odd way he sometimes had, it felt very much like he was there. Arm pressed against hers, pinky finger in that breath between touching and not touching hers. Every nerve in her arms rose to the surface of her skin to meet it, and she shut her eyes to picture him, though he was faceless.

Death stilled; she could feel it.

She jumped. Sometimes she forgot that he knew what she was thinking. Kasia could feel the heat rushing to her cheeks, and she shook her head and said, before he could, "Is there anything I *can* do?"

He waited a moment too long before saying, *Of course there is.*

"I feel, sometimes, that there isn't. I fear that Reyan and I will travel down to the terrible thing you created, and we will do all we can, and the darkness will not be driven back at all."

Death was quiet.

"It strikes me now that it is odd to discuss this with you. You set all of this in motion, after all."

The gods set this in motion.

"And you are the one who wants it to take the world. To take all of us."

What I want has no place in this discussion.

"So it stands to reason you would not be terribly interested in helping m—"

Death was so cool, so collected, that it startled Kasia when he spoke with a growl in his voice. *What I want is not to watch the world rot. What I want is for everyone to play by the rules. But I do not dole out consequence, I am the consequence. I do not look at all the people on the earth and laugh to take them from it. I am not the god of pain; I do not delight in suffering. Do you understand? I am balance. I am the equalizer. I am the order when the scales begin to tip, so do not accuse me of relishing the suffering of a million souls, because you could never possibly begin—*His smooth, silk voice cracked.

...Could never begin to understand me. Is that clear? Is that clear, Kasia?

Death did not say her name; he purred it, even through the pain he was so clearly experiencing, which in and of itself struck Kasia as terribly strange.

It is not unjust for the world to suffer for the power it's taken. And neither is it unjust that I have taken this game from the gods so that they are no longer permitted to play.

Kasia furrowed her brow. "What? What does that—"

I am leaving you today. I won't be back tomorrow.

Kasia sat straight up, chest suddenly tight with worry. Why—beyond that unanswered question that she felt she should have been able to interpret, the meaning of which was *just* beyond her reach—she didn't know, didn't particularly want to consider. But the thought that she would come here tomorrow morning and he wouldn't speak to her was maddeningly unnerving. Perhaps she had grown too comfortable, too quickly, with one of the most ancient things in the universe. Or perhaps...perhaps she had hurt him. Was that possible? For Death to bleed?

Kasia stood, glancing up, around, looking for that familiar feeling of his cool, dark presence. But she did not find it.

"I am sorry," she said.

And no one answered.

Kasia wandered by herself for a while. Well, as by herself as she could be at night in the market. Guards trailed her as they always did, and there were people bumping her left and right, people who didn't recognize her. She wasn't in any kind of dramatic, intentional disguise. But she wasn't looking to stand out this evening either. She'd worn pants—dark blue and close-fitting, and a lavender cloak. Colors that reminded her of home. Not that she bore any great love for Farowfin; she'd left for a reason. But something about home was comfortable, even though she didn't miss it all that much.

Tomorrow, they were headed to the grey. And so tonight, she needed home.

She walked in long, determined strides down the market streets, hood pulled up over her head, shading her dark curls and face—and her walk alone probably set her apart. Everyone but her shuffled.

It didn't matter, really, when it came down to it. All she'd wanted was a breath of air. A moment to be by herself, to sort her own thoughts from all the rest of theirs.

She'd gone back to her rooms and gotten her things together after the incident in the shrine, and now here she was. They were on the verge of something incredible, and Kasia, for the first time, realized that she was terrified.

She'd only ever had occasion to claim to be brave before. Never had much of an opportunity to fear what was coming, because up until this moment, no one had paid particular attention to her voice. No one had ever given her reason to be scared.

And here she was.

She moved through the crowd of people until she came to the end of the street, tall lamp flickering and casting shadows over the sandstone street. She leaned against the wall of a bustling tavern, outside of which a street musician played. A strange instrument, one she'd certainly never seen. It had nine strings, and a little hammer, and it made the most ethereal sound whenever the strings were struck.

Kasia shut her eyes, allowed herself to listen. Not to think about the darkness, or the king, or the gods and their game, or Death, and whether the abandonment was temporary or permanent. She didn't want to worry, only to clear her head.

The musician played into her heart until she felt nearly drowsy, and then suddenly, the door behind her opened, and she fell back into a body. She hadn't realized she'd been leaning against a door, and she cursed herself.

"My apologies," a man mumbled, and Kasia blinked up at him.

He was Etryan, dressed in dark clothes and…Kasia furrowed her brow when he stood her up and bowed.

"It's all right," she said, turning away. But his eyes were familiar. She was sure of it; she'd seen this boy before. "Do I know y—" she said, but when she turned to look for him, he was gone.

Kasia ran a hand over her forehead. Perhaps she was tired.

Well, that wasn't a truthful sentiment. She *was* tired. But perhaps she was more tired than she'd thought. They'd be riding all tomorrow, and the musician's song seemed to be winding down, so she turned, wondering if her guards had passed her and were trailing her already or if she would run right into them on the way back through the market.

Kasia hugged her cloak around her—coolness had come in with the night—and meandered back through the shops. She picked up a soap that smelled like jasmine and waved off a miracle cure for something or other that an old man tried to foist upon her, then stopped in front of an old bookshop. It was so small she might have missed it had it not been for the bright green paint that coated the windowsill and trim. A dim lantern hung over it, making the paint nearly glow.

Kasia smiled and went inside.

She'd never been one for books; Kasia wanted to make her own stories. And until she did, she figured she would only be jealous of whatever character was fortunate enough to have one. But Reyan was. She laughed to herself at the secret he'd divulged to her—a fondness for fiction.

Kasia slipped into the stacks without the person at the front so much as looking up and ran her fingers alone the spines. She pictured Reyan as a boy, tiny, curls shining, sneaking into his mother's collection of books to lose himself in a story, reading quickly so his father wouldn't take it before he learned the ending. What did he see, she wondered, in printed words on a page, that had been worth the risk?

The books were nearly all worn under her hand. All old. They had the feeling of rareness and the feeling of history. She glanced over several titles in history, a collection in romance, ran her fingers over fantasy—then stopped.

Death Takes a Thief.

Her hand froze over the title. She slid it out from where it sat, coated in dust, forgotten on a shelf with a hundred other books. Then she opened the first page and scanned what it read: the beginnings to a story of an immortal moinchire thief. And the boy she loved.

Her heartbeat quickened. It was a first edition; this book must have been absolutely ancient. And probably correspondingly expensive.

But she was a queen. She could afford what she wished.

Kasia smiled to herself and brought the old book to the man at the front. He looked nothing like the sort of person Kasia would have expected to work in a bookstore. He was very young, with hair coated in some sort of floral concoction that made it appear blue. Sparkling eyes and a shimmering smile. She would have expected an old man, white-haired and bearded. But she didn't know why.

The boy's eyebrows rose when he looked at Kasia's book. "This is a first edition," he said. "Of an extremely old book. The price is—"

"I don't care what the price is," Kasia said, and the boy smiled and took her money, then wrapped the rare book in simple twine, over each edge.

Reyan would probably be asleep by the time she got home. Well. He would wake and find it.

And this made Kasia smile. For once, she wasn't working any sort of angle. She'd just bought it and was currently nearly prancing down the street toward the palace, simply because she wanted him to have it.

When she found herself back in her rooms, Reyan was already asleep. She set the package on a dressing stool and let her dirty clothes fall to the floor right where she stood—it was too late and she was too tired to think about making a mess. Not when she planned to change the world, starting tomorrow. She slipped into bed with Reyan and tried very hard not to think of a shadow that had consumed countries, flared because of *her*, thirsting for her and her power, and snaking its fingers into her soul to consume it.

CHAPTER THIRTY-THREE

THE WORLD WAS STILL grey when Nagonia let Ri through the gate hidden in in the back corner of the grounds that bordered the forest. It was for servants, and he was with her. No one paid him any mind; hardly anyone was awake to do so. The air still held a moist chill and smelled like the dew that hung on the grass. The earth was still, waiting for daylight, and Ri could feel the quiet cold on his skin.

Nagonia drew close to him and whispered, "The queen will be there in minutes; you're late."

"I'm not late; she's early."

Nagonia pressed her lips together and her nostrils flared. "Two of the guards are sleeping—the two women closest my quarters. I offered them tea."

"Do you not think that will incriminate you, Nagonia?"

Nagonia shrugged, dark eyes sparkling. "I don't care if it does. When you flee, I will meet you. We will leave together before anyone knows what has happened."

Ri nodded, glancing up at the sky—the milk almost-blue, and that dead grey split bleeding up from the south. He didn't want to consider the damage that might have been done to Etrya while he was away making deals with Va'al to kill Jaelenian queens. Couldn't think about it—not right now. He could afford to think of nothing but the daggers at his back, his thigh, the poison that coated them that ensured the victims would, at the very least, fall into oblivion for a few hours the moment it split their skin.

He could have chosen something more deadly, he supposed, but he had no wish to murder guards, and he wasn't getting paid to take their lives. And the type of poison he chose was of little consequence when it came to the young queen. Kasia, he would stab in the heart.

Ri wiped his hands on his cloak—which was more of a dark tunic, really. He preferred to wear this kind of thing when he was doing a very particular kind of work. The kind that prompted him to keep his legs free for more places to stash a knife.

The grounds were so still this time of the morning. The silent walk across the grass was almost a meditation, which Ri found he needed today.

This felt so very different from being paid to kill someone who'd threatened a woman's son, who'd stolen enough from a family that they couldn't pay rent—someone who'd been asking for it. That had been penance.

This was murder.

And he'd seen her eyes. More than once, looked into them. They were deep and cunning and lit with laughter. He'd looked straight into them just last night, exiting the tavern. Looked at her and mumbled an apology, and felt her arms under his fingers. Her pulse in his hands.

Nausea sprung up in his gut for a painful moment, and Ri hoped he would not have to look long in her eyes before she died.

Ri took a shuddering breath and stopped thinking on it. No good could come of it. Nothing could come from thinking of her but pain. This was something he *had* to do. And gods dammit, he would do it. He shut her out and followed Nagonia through snaking back paths that wound across the grounds—paths no one frequented, that no one patrolled. There were very few patrols at all this time of morning anyway. The king generally slept in, and he was fairly lax with his subjects, from what Ri had gathered.

Then the grounds turned into the palace, and the terrifying possibility of it all came to life under Ri's skin. If he succeeded, if he failed. His country hung in the balance and his life with it. His teeth chattered and he glanced back at Nagonia.

"A few more feet," she said, "and this is where I leave you."

Nagonia's voice dropped until Ri could hardly hear it when she said, "Here," and she grabbed his hand, shrinking back against a wall in the gardens. Ri wished it was here that she came to pray. Killing a woman outside in her garden didn't feel *good*, but it didn't feel as morally reprehensible as murdering someone in a shrine.

Etrya. Etrya. Etrya. It pumped through his veins. One girl's life and he could save a nation. *His* nation. His brothers. His fathers. The boy he'd had a crush on when he was ten, the shopkeeper who'd looked the other way when he'd stolen fruit. All of them. In exchange for a single soul. He shut his eyes for a moment and breathed.

When he was a boy, he'd wanted to fight for his country. Had dreamt of being a soldier, imagined it every night—wanted it more than anything in the world. But after his mother had died in war, his family had never had a silver piece to their name, and it had been *Cling to a dream and starve* or *Risk a criminal record and live.*

He'd chosen to live. To take care of his brothers. His father. He'd done it without considering the consequences, and he would have done it just as quickly even if he had. After he'd racked up too much of a name with the authorities, the dream of soldierhood had gone up in smoke. The army didn't take boys who'd seen the inside of a jail cell as often as he had. And by then, he'd been so wrapped in the work-for-hire game that perhaps being a soldier would have tasted flat anyway. And impossible to leave such a lucrative life, when he'd spent years building a reputation.

He was on his own, and he was doing work for his country, and that was enough. He told himself it was enough. Etrya was his soul.

Nagonia said, "There's a little walkway, hidden in the shadows, from here to the first guard's station. Take his jacket; he's tall. Then you can march right up to the second guard who stands just outside the shrine and slip in the window. But hurry. You'll lose your chance once she's inside."

Ri nodded, and said, "Wait for me outside the servants' gate. Will you have horses?"

"Yes, I'll have everything. Go."

Ri licked his lips, which had suddenly gone very dry, and brushed his fingers over one of the daggers at his back, to calm his nerves. Then he stole into the little passageway that Nagonia had said would spit him out directly at one of the guards. He shrunk against the wall, trying to hide himself in the shadows that were quickly shrinking. Perhaps he *had* been a bit late.

The walkway was shorter than he expected. Because he could make out, now, the shadow of a guard.

And the path had stopped. There was nothing but vulnerable, open space between him and her. His lip ticked up in irritation. Nagonia should have told him. Dammit.

He took a steadying breath, eye on the sun, and drew the left dagger from his back. He shook his head; he didn't want to do it this way. There was too much risk. It could twist wrong in the air, or his aim could be off and he could hit a vital organ in the girl's back.

But there was no choice, and the sun was rising.

Ri wrapped his hood around his mouth and nose so they could see nothing but his eyes. And he took aim. Then released the weapon.

It sailed, completely silent, through the air, and found its mark in the woman's back. It should have missed anything important, but Ri would not be around to find out.

He ran up to the girl, who had opened her mouth to scream, and tackled her to the ground, hand over her lips, yanking the knife out of her back as she fell. He was larger than her; there would be no getting out from his grip. The poison was fast-acting; she would be asleep in under a minute.

But…dammit. Dammit, dammit. She was supposed to have been a man.

Her eyelids drooped.

She was much too short, her arms too small. Ri would hardly be able to fit the jacket across his back; there was absolutely no way he could wear the uniform convincingly.

Her eyes shut completely and he removed his hand from her mouth. Then he swore violently and tightened the wrap over his face, dragging her behind a small bush nearby. It would do nothing on close inspection but would hide her well enough at a glance.

He moved quietly through the grass, too slow. Too slow. If he'd had the uniform—but he didn't. He would have to improvise.

The second guard came into view. Right beside the little shrine, which was apparently attached to the rest of the palace. Ri crouched, channeling quiet, calm, mentally forcing his pulse to slow.

And he inched toward the guard, one shuffling step at a time.

He wiped the bloody dagger off on his tunic then stuck it on his back and pulled the other out. It would have more poison on it—it was unused.

The tall man was staring off at something in the woods, so he didn't hear Ri until it was too late. Until Ri had leapt the small distance between them and shoved his dagger in the man's leg.

The man yelled and spun, reaching for his sword, and Ri hissed. If Kasia was in there, she'd heard it.

Ri kicked the man where he'd been stabbed, and the man fell face first, Ri on top of him, knee digging into his back. He pushed the man's face into the cool, wet ground so any cries would be muffled and stabbed him again in the shoulder. The more poison in his veins, the faster it would work.

When he pulled the dagger out, little flecks of the man's blood spread out on the air and speckled his clothes.

After a minute of struggle, the guard stopped wriggling under him.

He stilled completely.

Ri slid up off the unconscious body below him, wishing he had more time. Wishing he'd brought more poison. Wishing the guard had been smaller and easier to drag to a hidden place. Wishing a million things.

But there was no time for wishing.

He swallowed down his nervousness and examined the shrine. There was a window at the back, three steps from where he was.

He took a long breath and peeked inside. Empty.

Thank the gods.

Ri slid open the glass and made himself as small as he could fold. Then hopped onto the wooden ground.

It was very small in here. Smaller than Ri had predicted, which was frustrating. It made it decidedly more difficult to hide. In the grand temples of Etrya, a person could hide in a thousand places, not that he'd ever done so for these reasons.

He'd hid in the temples more than once, listening to services where no one could see him. But he'd never done so to kill someone.

Ri shut that out and shot a look across the room. There was the little altar at the front, the candles. He couldn't very well hide in one of them. Hardly any furniture. This place wasn't even large enough for more than two people. Gods damn this.

Ri swallowed hard, panic rising in his throat. There was nowhere to go in here but the curtains. Crouching behind the curtains like a child playing shadows and light. He shook his head and ducked behind one, caressing the Andran ceremonial dagger Shev had given him. Enchanted, an ancient relic used for killing those the gods had given power. He shuddered and hoped the gods would not hold the use of this particular dark thing against him. An image flashed in his head—a queen, covered in burns, nearly stripped of skin, for daring to punish one of the gods' chosen. "Tallel, be merciful," he whispered. This was not an execution for a woman's abilities. This was for family and country. If the gods could not understand those things, then they could understand nothing. The cool feel of the blade's metal against his thigh calmed his shaking nerves.

This was his only option.

And there was no turning back.

Ri waited.

CHAPTER THIRTY-FOUR

REYAN AWOKE WITH THE sun. It had just risen in the sky, and being conscious at this hour was unusual for him. But today, they left for the south, which had had him up and down all night. He was dreaming about the grey or awake thinking about the grey and lying there, trying to force his rebellious mind into submission, and it would not listen to him.

Kasia, for her part, slept soundly. She was solid all through the night, which Reyan had been rather annoyed by. He would have liked an excuse to be up at two in the morning, losing the stress of everything in each other.

Reyan sat up, ruffling his hair, and let his legs dangle off the bed. He yawned, feeling the lack of sleep settle into his bones, then stood. Everything hurt, ached, really, as it sometimes did when sleep eluded him. He should have found a book last night. Something that would have unwound his tense muscles, allowed him to be distracted. But that probably would have failed as well.

Reyan rolled his shoulders and stood. Kasia was already gone, as she always was in the mornings. She rose so early, Reyan didn't know how it was possible. But it was her habit. He hadn't noticed her doing it to begin with, but she was apparently very dedicated to her own gods—particularly for a girl from Farowfin. His not noticing before meant very little, really. He hadn't noticed much about her before at all. Hadn't been able to see anything but the haze of her country across her face. Now, he saw her. He could hardly see anything *but* her.

Reyan crossed the room. He'd packed the night before, as had Kasia. Everything was ready. Everything was loaded on the horses now; the servants had taken it all late and gotten everything prepared. Weapons, food, clothing, water, all of it.

All that was left now was to go down there and do it.

Anticipation shuddered through Reyan, and he walked into the bathroom, of a mind to have a hot bath, clear his head while he waited for Kasia to return from her morning prayers. But something stopped him.

He frowned. There was a little item standing in the middle of the room—one he hadn't seen when he'd fallen asleep. It was a book, a thick one. One with a worn black cover and gilded print. Yes, he was sure he hadn't seen it, and Kasia didn't read. Not for pleasure, anyway.

Reyan took a step back and headed toward it. It sat on a little stool, twine folding over it in a simple show meant to convey that it was wrapped, that it was a gift. A little twine bow rested on top, under which was an ivory slip of paper.

In Kasia's unmistakably messy handwriting, it said, *For you, my boy king.*

Reyan snorted. He could see the wry tilt of her mouth when she'd written it, meaning to provoke him and entice him all at once. With her, one almost never came without the other. Warm fondness spread through his chest. He didn't know how to put a name to what he felt about his wife yet. He was enraptured by her, fascinated by her, exhausted by her...so many little things that added up into something he couldn't put words to.

It was so odd to think that now. So entirely opposite of what he ever thought he'd say. But there it was.

Reyan slipped the paper out of the twine and slid it into his back pocket, then slowly undid the rope bow and sparse, winding wrapping.

Death Takes a Thief.

Reyan blinked, knot welling in his throat when he opened the book. A first edition. This book was ancient. A story he'd read a thousand times when he'd snuck into his mother's library, before his father had burned them all. There was too much pain in living with her stories, he'd said.

But she'd found it. For him.

He flipped through the pages, smell of old books filling his nose, and smiled. Perhaps they were matched in more than their power.

He was beginning to believe that they were. And at this moment, Reyan wanted to touch her. Wanted to speak with her and figure out who she was—to take a few moments before they left to face this nameless terror that might very well kill them, kill her...

An unexpected pain ripped through him at that thought. At what point had that happened?

Reyan curled his fingers around the book, and ran his fingers through his hair to smooth his curls, and turned from the bathroom toward the door. Perhaps he would pray with his wife this morning.

Reyan pulled a decent riding shirt over his head and slid his pants up over his hips. Then he left their rooms up the steep staircase, and strode down the hall for the shrine.

CHAPTER THIRTY-FIVE

K ASIA HESITATED AT THE door. Her head was so very empty; her everything was empty. She'd slept like the dead last night, but Death had left her, and she didn't know why that hurt so deeply. He'd said he wouldn't be back today. She wagered she could kneel and burn her wrist, and he wouldn't respond to her.

The thought of facing this earth-destroying power without him whispering in her mind was terrifying. The fact remained that neither of them was sure what exactly they were doing. And the fear of the risk hollowed her bones.

Speaking with Death was what she did now. And she was leaving today. She needed to try.

She took a deep breath and opened the door to the shrine.

Kasia swallowed hard, eyes on the altar, on the candles that flickered there, always lit. "Can you hear me?" she said.

Nothing.

The wood dampened the nothing further until it was a veritable vacuum of emptiness, pulling at her mind, her heart, her skin.

"I'm leaving today," she said. "To fight *your* war."

Silence. Heavy, suffocating silence.

Kasia knelt before the altar and glanced at the flame there. He'd said more than once that he thought it ridiculous—who was she trying to talk with who would require burns? Who would ask her to hurt herself? But she did it anyway. It was habit. And more than that, perhaps it would irritate him enough that he would have to say something.

She smiled to herself—a small, hardly even turn of the lips. Then she held her wrist over the leaping orange. It stung at first. Her skin wasn't used to this anymore. The heat was too fresh, like it had been when she was a girl and it had hurt so deeply to pray.

Just when the pain had reached a crescendo, she heard a smooth voice, urgent in her mind. *Kasia.*

"Well, well—" she started.

Kasia, you're not wearing your knife. There was a rasp in his voice. Desperate worry she'd never heard. She frowned.

"I don't underst—"

He yelled all around her, *Kasia, get up!*

Kasia's eyes widened, and she jumped to her feet, then spun to find a very tall, very thin man coming at her with a dagger. Her heart squeezed, and she ducked as he slashed with his knife.

She reached for hers, the one she always kept strapped to her leg, in a dress or otherwise, and paled.

The weapons. They'd been packed. Death was right.

The man stood in a crouch, dagger shining gilded and jeweled in the morning light that poured through the windows.

It was oddly curved, the tip of the blade almost curling back on itself, shockingly ornate. Kasia wanted to laugh—and would have if her life hadn't been in danger. This wasn't a dagger meant for killing; it was a dagger meant for ceremony. What in hells?

There was no sound in the room but their breathing. Kasia backed toward the door, senses sharpened to nothing but this boy and his blade.

The first step she took backward, he lunged again, curved knife flashing for her. She side-stepped him, and she could see the top of his nose wrinkle as his wrap began to slip down his face.

"Who are you?" said Kasia, backing toward the curtains, where she assumed he'd hidden.

The man said nothing.

He moved for her again, and this time, there was nowhere to back to. His body slammed into hers with so much force it stole her breath, and tears sprang to her eyes—burning and stinging like fire. She fell, and he fell with her.

She gasped for air, and the man shifted his weight on her stomach, hand plunging toward her chest, curled around the knife. She grabbed for his wrist in a desperate move for something. Something. Her air was gone; she couldn't scream. Couldn't breathe. There was nothing in her lungs but fear.

He looked right at her. And when he did, the rest of the mask slipped down.

Fucking hells.

She knew him.

He faltered when he locked eyes with her, so her small hand was enough, for an instant, to keep his at bay. This was the man she'd seen last night in the market. The one she'd seen...

At her wedding.

Kasia's eyes widened. This was the man who'd danced with Nagonia and disappeared with her into a closet, caused a scandal at her reception. There'd been guards. The entrance to the palace was heavily guarded as well. There was no way he could have gotten in if it weren't for—no.

Nagonia.

The breath returned to Kasia in something just past agony—ripping through her lungs as though they were sandpaper. The man's arm tightened again, muscles contracting under her fingers, dagger glinting toward her heart.

"No," Kasia said in a strangled whisper, and cold spread from her hand over his wrist, leaking out over his forearm.

The man's eyes widened in surprise and he jerked back from Kasia and scrambled up, arm pale and frigid. Kasia rose quickly, back to the other side of the room from him.

"Try again," Kasia said. Her voice was still low and it hurt terribly to speak. "I'll blacken the damn thing."

"I have no choice," said the man, and it irritated Kasia how friendly his voice sounded. How sincere. How sorry.

"Pity for you," she said, and she slashed her arm through the air.

Fear darted through his eyes, scarring his face, and he leapt backward as a rain of ice stabbed down at him.

Power coursed through Kasia; she'd forgotten. She'd been surprised and resorted to helplessness, had thought herself weaponless, vulnerable, a hundred terrifying things. But she was *not*. Her heart hardened, and her mind turned to flame.

She reached into the air and pushed a gust of wind toward him, taking the eternal flames at the altar with it, leaving them in nothing but the cold half-light that came in through a single window.

"Who are you," Kasia whispered, "that you believe you can defeat me?"

"I have killed many men."

The man narrowed his eyes through the wind and frost and pulled a dagger from his back, throwing it at her leg. She jumped back, wishing she could scream. Wishing she could alert Reyan. But her voice would not comply.

"How many daggers have you got there?"

The boy said nothing, simply reached for another. So he had one fighting blade in one hand and the ceremonial blade in the other. He moved toward her, and she shot shards of ice from her fingertips, felt her blood freeze and wind skitter over her skin.

She would not die here in this shrine.

Not today.

He was six inches taller than her, but she was a *force*.

You are the wind, Death whispered in her ear, and she threw it at the boy with everything she had. He had stolen her breath, but he could not steal the air.

Kasia could not scream.

But the man screamed for her.

Her ice and wind ripped through his skin.

She nearly collapsed with sudden exhaustion at the drain. What in hells?

In the whirling torrent, the man's face contorted, and he threw his daggers. First the fighting blade from his right, which stuck in the wood at Kasia's back.

Then the ceremonial blade from his left, which stuck in her leg.

She screamed then, and it felt like shards of glass sticking through her windpipe.

But it was nothing to the searing wound in her muscle. It was too hot and too cold at once, and it all *hurt*.

And then, it hurt less. Everything hurt less. She dropped to her knees by the window, wind whipping at strands of her hair.

The man was bloody. He looked beaten. He should have been. But the seconds themselves slowed. Had he hit an artery? Did death from blood loss happen so fast—she hadn't even removed the knife.

Or did…

Or did…

She braced herself on the floor. Everything was so slow and strange.

And dim.

And dim.

And…

She breathed in and drew all the power in the world into her chest, then shot it out at the broken man who advanced on her, before she heard, *Little one. Little one*, a desperate, velvet whisper in her ear, and the world darkened.

CHAPTER THIRTY-SIX

R EYAN HEARD A MAN'S scream when he entered the hall.

And that was when he began to run.

Halfway to the door, another scream. And this one came from Kasia.

Fear clawed at his chest as he pressed forward and slammed in through the door.

Panic cut off his air supply when he found Kasia slumped over on the ground, pool of bright blood under her. The sanctuary was in shambles, the lights blown out, and there was blood everywhere. *Everywhere.* Blood—and an open window. He ran to it but could only make himself look for half an instant, because who had done this didn't matter as much as whether she was alive.

Whether she was alive. He swore for a moment his heart had stopped beating.

Reyan scanned the view from the window for less than a second before he collapsed by Kasia, and turned her over so that she faced him. Her eyes were shut, and she was pale. Loss of blood?

Oh gods. Oh gods, oh gods, oh gods.

He ran his hands down her face and yelled for help, blood soaking his pants, his shirt, running over his skin. Was it all hers? This couldn't all be hers. Not if she was...

He leaned closer to her, ear at her lips. She was breathing. Deeply.

He breathed out a sigh of relief, shoulders slumping with it, and clutched her to his chest.

"Kasia," he said in her ear, "can you hear me? It's all right, you're all right. I swear you're all right. Gods." His voice cracked, heart crashing under his ribs.

She moved once, a twitch in her sleep, and fresh blood moistened Reyan's pants. This much was hers.

He glanced down at the blade, then back at her face. He couldn't remove it without the risk of killing her; he wasn't a doctor. And where in hells were they? He screamed again. And again and again.

"Kasia, please," he said.

Her eyes shuttered open for less than a moment and she said, "Nagonia," then she fell back asleep.

The guards swarmed the shrine in a moment, and Reyan sent half of them with her, another group to look for Nagonia, and the rest to follow the trail of blood Kasia's attacker had certainly left.

He followed her to the infirmary in blood-soaked clothes and waited.

She was all right. He'd waited there, eyes ringed red and dark with exhaustion, Kasia's blood drying on his clothes, until they'd brought her back in, wound bandaged and dagger removed.

She awoke.

"Kasia," he breathed, nearly leaping to her side. His hands framed her face, and he kissed her forehead, which was salty with sweat. "I thought...I thought you..."

Kasia breathed.

"What happened?" he said.

"Did you find Nagonia?"

"Yes," said Reyan. "The guards found her waiting outside the servants' gate with horses. She claims innocence, but we have her shackled." Reyan's voice darkened. "We will see how many hours she claims her innocence when I send Lashtee to deal with her."

Kasia breathed shakily. "And the assassin?"

Reyan blinked, and the hand that wasn't touching her face, he fisted in the sheets. "No."

Kasia was quiet again.

"What happened?"

"I went to pray. And stood to find him running at me."

"Who?" said Reyan. "What did he look like?" He could hear the fury in his own voice. It was unchecked, cold and menacing and unforgiving, and he wondered how like Death himself he looked at this moment.

"Etryan," she said. "Dressed in grey to blend with the morning. Carried three daggers. He was here. At our wedding. Haru. He claimed to be an ambassador from Etrya then—"

"That could mean anything now," Reyan growled. "And there are people of Etryan descent in every damn realm; he could be from anywhere. I can't..." He swore under his breath. "I can't..."

It couldn't happen again. Another man coming after someone he loved. Another man taking a life when he should have protected her, should have been there. He was in another nightmare, walking into another room that should have been *safe* only to find a woman drenched in blood. Blood that soaked through his skin when he tried to wake her.

Not again.

Never again.

"I will kill him, Kasia. Whatever this is. I swear to you, I will find him. And when he and I find ourselves in the same room, I will not leave both of us breathing."

Kasia turned toward him, curling her body until she winced.

"Your leg?"

"Well. I did have a knife thrown through it."

"They say the curve of it did more damage than a straight one would have. Hooked in you. And it's not healing as quickly as it should. They don't know why. But you might... have a bit of trouble with that leg from now on."

Kasia set her jaw and nodded once. "This shouldn't have happened," she said.

"No," said Reyan. "It shouldn't have."

"Perhaps you'll kill him," said Kasia, "or perhaps the gods will leave him for me."

Reyan looked over her, her body outlined by the white, thin sheets, and ground his teeth against each other. If this had been Nagonia, and he intended to prove that it was, then he would get the name from her and tear her apart with his own hands.

"Sir," someone said behind him, and he whirled around with more venom than he meant.

"Proch. What?"

Proch scraped his teeth over his lower lip and nodded at the dagger that lay beside Kasia. "Is that it? The weapon?"

"Yes," said Reyan. "Why? A passing interest in archaeology does not exactly qualify you as an expert in—"

"No, not me," said Proch. He took several steps toward it and brushed his fingers over the blade. "But I know someone who is."

CHAPTER THIRTY-SEVEN

RI COULD HARDLY BREATHE. Something about the atmosphere in Jaelen had made it all worse. But he had been running for so long he couldn't track the time—his muscles shifting from burning to ripping to entirely numb. He was certain the freezing rain contributed to that. It stung his limbs, his face, his torso, everything. Because everything was shredded. He had been completely silent, and Kasia had jumped up and spun around the second before he could touch her, and none of it made any sense.

How had everything gone so fucking wrong?

Ri kept running, because he had no choice but to run, nothing to do but run, run, run until he hit the docks. Trees, back alleys, anything that would give him cover, and he ran.

She had seen his face; he was wanted. Of that much he was certain.

And he was *nearly* certain that she was alive.

He'd been so close to ending everything, a heartbeat away. Until she'd lashed out in an instant, and Ri had heard someone's footsteps pounding toward the door. Then heard the creak as the hinges began to open.

He'd leapt out the window and run.

Though the pain was so startling at first that he could hardly stand, it was collapse and find his head on a pike, or run and wish to die from the pain. He was bleeding everywhere, from weapons of ice and wind and intangible things. If he found a mirror and saw that his skin was hanging in literal shreds from his body, Ri would not be surprised.

Perhaps they would follow the trail of blood. And perhaps they would catch him, and he would bow his head for an axe. Or perhaps the ice had stayed the bleeding enough that he hadn't dripped on the ground. Perhaps his very blood was too frozen; it certainly felt that way.

It was so quiet around him. Nothing and no one but him and his failure.

At the very least, though, he had started a war. Andra would have to shift its focus from Etrya, and Va'al wouldn't be lending its support, —its "secret alliance" with Andra had certainly been fake—but perhaps it would take Andra while Andra focused on the vengeance from Jaelen. He had failed. Miserably.

But perhaps his country would survive nonetheless.

He would have to cut his losses; no doubt the Va'alian king would not be paying him for this. Which meant any financial help he'd hoped to bring back to his family, his stepfather hardly on this side of death's veil, had gone to hell. But...his country would survive. Damn everything.

Ri was exhausted. His very bones were tired. His skin was raw and frigid, and his feet felt like knives to run on.

It was a good time to finally see the docks in the distance.

Far enough away that Ri's eyes burned with frustrated tears, but close enough that he knew he could do it. He could make it this far. Perhaps Gallien was waiting there for him, even. Perhaps.

Ri summoned all the energy he had left in his gut, gritted his teeth, and forced himself to sprint.

He would not fall before he reached the docks.

A throng of voices he could not understand rose up to meet him the closer he got, and he quickened his pace. He got close enough that he could make out individual conversations, that the blur of bodies in the light of the morning gave way to separate shapes. He probably looked like a madman. Or a dead one. Perhaps he was both.

Ri slowed when he hit sandstone, relief twisting over his shoulders, rushing through his head. He wished to go back to the inn, back to his room. But there was no way in hells he was risking that—not having seen the queen as he'd come out of it just last night. That would be the first place they would search if she was alive.

His shoulders slumped, and the second he slowed, his body begged him to shut down completely. He wanted to collapse right here in the middle of the street. But he forced himself to drag forward, to fall into a tavern that was mercifully open in the morning.

"Hells," said the bartender, giving him a once-over. She was almost as tall as him, head half-shaved, very round and very skeptical. "You just come from the grave?"

Ri sank into a seat at the bar.

"Two silvers for a double shot. Throw in an extra, and I'll let you use the bath upstairs. Make it fifteen, and you can have the room."

Ri glanced up at her then. "You've a bath?"

"We do well enough," said the woman with a self-satisfied smile. "Room upstairs is fully equipped. Bath, antiseptic, bandages. Discretion." She emphasized that last word, and Ri got the impression that this was not the first time she had taken care of someone without asking why.

He wanted to cry in relief. He tossed fifteen silvers on the bar top, and the woman gave him a key without asking another question. Then he dragged himself up the steep stairs and turned the key in the lock.

As she'd said, there was a bathroom here, with a working bath. And under the sink, there were so many first aid items Ri didn't know where to look.

So, where he looked was the mirror. His skin hanging in shreds from his body hadn't been a far-off assessment. It was clotted everywhere, and the lack of blood dripping on his skin, even around the deepest cuts, indicated that it had done so nearly immediately. And perhaps the rest of the blood had blown around the room in the girl's wind.

His clothes were rags, and that was generous. Face dirt-streaked, arms and legs and torso and cheeks sliced everywhere. Gods, no wonder everyone had moved out of his way when he'd entered the town.

He turned on the water, let it run a little—not hot, hardly warm. And when he peeled his clothes off his bruised, battered body and sank inside, he fought a scream. If it had been hotter, it would have stung his wounds like a swarm of bees, and if it had been colder, it would have been razors. As it was, it was right in the middle, and it hurt like hell.

He arched his back under the water and grit his teeth, gasping for air past the stunning pain. The water opened his wounds and shifted from clear to brown to deep, dark red. Ri drained it and ran a tepid bath again, bending on his hands and knees, forehead bowed on the lip of the tub as though he was in prayer.

Maybe he would die right here.

Maybe he would sleep.

But he couldn't, with the stinging water filling the bath, opening up a hundred tiny wounds. He wondered how deep they went.

When the water finally went pink again, he slowly dipped his filthy tunic in it, scrubbing at it until the water went brown. Then he wrung them out and hung them to dry, drained the bath water, and gingerly ran a towel over himself, wincing at every fiber. It took him a half hour to clean and wrap every injury. A thousand shards of ice flying at you like glass did damage.

Though it was morning, Ri winced and carefully walked his way over to the bed. He buried himself in it.

Ri didn't wake until late that night; he'd slept through the entire day.

He was unenthused about putting his damp, ripped tunic on now, but he hadn't much choice.

He slipped it on and headed down to the bar, which was just emptying from what Ri figured had been a night of drunkenness. The woman waited for him with a pleasant expression on her face. She poured him a double-shot of something.

"Paid for this this morning and you never got it. Was a bit early for drinking anyway," she said. "But it's never a good time for wounds like that, is it? So you'll get no judgement from me."

Ri nodded at her and gulped the stinging alcohol down in a second. It burned going down, but he knew his skin would begin to numb again in a moment, as would the rest of him. She hadn't watered this down; it was real.

"You're charging too little for this," said Ri.

The woman smiled and shrugged. "Well. You're a refugee, aren't you?"

A frown flickered across Ri's face.

The woman faltered. "From Etrya? Why didn't you say anything this morning?"

"A refugee? From…oh. From the war with Andra?" he said.

The woman's face crinkled, and Ri felt for a moment that perhaps he was insane. She certainly seemed to think he was. "No, from...from what happened four days ago?"

Ri's stomach went hollow. "What happened four days ago?"

"Have you not seen the sky?"

Ri's voice was urgent now, gruff and clipped, and nausea boiled in his gut. "Of course I have; I'm not blind. What happened in Etrya four days ago?"

"Half the country's too far south, sir. It was wrecked when the grey surged."

"Etrya?" His words came out in a cracked whisper. "It's too far east. The dark hadn't even come close to reaching us—"

"Well, it has now," the woman said gently. But it felt like sandpaper on his ears. "Been a lot of damage done, son. Everywhere. We just got word hours ago. Some of the more southern countries are sending refugees here, I guess, and some are traveling up to Farowfin. 'S'why I was so confused. The war...as of now, there is no war."

"No war," he repeated, dazed.

"There's...well, there's just not much left for Andra to take."

Ri choked on a sob and said, "I'm sorry," then stood to make for the back door, grateful there was hardly anyone left here. But even they were too much. He needed to be somewhere that wasn't here. Somewhere alone. He shoved through the back door, hardly seeing anything but the dimness around his eyes and shadows he couldn't define. Maybe they were people, maybe they were buildings, nothing mattered, nothing mattered.

Sickness snaked up his throat, and he stumbled from the tavern out back, toward the chilled, dirty coast. He dropped to his knees in the rocks and lost the double shot on the ground. Then he retched for another few minutes, throwing up nothing.

Etrya was gone. Smoking. Consumed. Nothing. His family...The war was over, and Etrya had lost, and none of this had meant *anything*. He'd wanted to fight for his country, provide for his family, and instead, he'd been off having some meaningless adventure while everyone and everything he'd ever known had been laid to ruin, and he wanted to die.

Wanted Death to take him right here on this rocky beach.

The waves lapped at him, ocean moving like he hadn't just lost everything that mattered.

The pain was breathtaking. Worse than in Andra's prison, worse than after, with Adè, worse than a thousand knives of ice stabbing into his skin at once. He couldn't draw breath. How was it that his heart could beat through this?

A familiar voice behind him said, "Well, you're on time for once."

And Ri looked up at Gallien, eyes red, mouth open in silent anguish, and back toward the ocean, and he screamed.

CHAPTER THIRTY-EIGHT

G ALLIEN HAD ALMOST SAID no. She would have, if she'd been able to pry Ri away from that room above the tavern. She didn't know his business here, only that he was an absolute bloody wreck, and now his country had been taken by the grey, and she needed to go, but he was too deep in mourning to stand.

He'd snarled something about having nowhere to go back to, and what in hells was he supposed to do now, and slammed the door in her face, and that was when Gallien had gone back to her ship to wait out the storm. If he wouldn't agree to something useful by tomorrow, she'd knock him in the head and *drag* him back to Va'al.

At her ship, she'd been met with a young messenger who'd carried a summons from Proch.

It's urgent, he'd written. *I need to meet with you before you set back out. I know we never meet twice in a trip, but I am begging you to do this for me.*

It was the begging that gave her pause. Proch never begged unless one of them was naked and she was making him call her Captain.

And it was the concession he made at the end to meet in the tavern she loved, before he scrawled a hasty signature, that drove her to accept the request.

She gave the messenger girl a coin and sent her on her way, then headed across the shore into town.

She smiled when she found her way to The Knife's Edge and breathed in the smell of liquor and lies and unwashed bodies. Proch would be wildly uncomfortable in here—she could practically see him walking straight and tall, stepping light to avoid knocking into anyone and getting dirt all over his fancy clothes.

Gallien ordered a large stein of ale and waited.

He wasn't long.

To Gallien's surprise, Proch didn't dance around the clientele when he strode in. He did just that: strode. His eyes were set, skin drained of color. Gods, he looked…intimidating, almost.

He sank down into his chair across from her, bag slung across his shoulder, and signaled for the barman to give him one of whatever it was that Gallien had. It was cheap. She wondered how he would take the burn in his throat when it went down.

"Already?" said Gallien by way of greeting. "Couldn't stay away for more than a night?"

Proch shook his head. "Not that round two doesn't sound terribly enticing, Gallien, but I haven't come to try to get you into bed."

And now, he had her full attention.

She straightened and cocked her head slightly.

"There's been…" He lowered his voice and glanced around. "Is there a private room somewhere we can get?"

"Why didn't you just ask me to meet you in that private fancy establishment you always do, if you're so concerned about the rabble?"

"Would you have met me at all if I'd made a demand?"

Gallien smirked. "No."

He raised a hand in a shrug and pursed his lips.

"There's one or two private places in back, if you can pay."

Proch looked at her and she shrugged. He rolled his eyes when it became clear Gallien was not offering a single coin he'd paid her two days ago. But why should she have to pay for *his* illicit meeting?

When the barman brought him his ale, he said, "What would it cost me to rent out somewhere private? I need twenty minutes."

The barman's mouth twitched under his beard. Twenty minutes was enough time for a *lot* of things. "Ain't got rooms with beds."

Proch breathed out through his nose and said, "Don't need one. I need a room with walls."

The barman raised his eyebrows. "Back in the corner. Cost you…" He looked Proch up and down. "Eight silvers."

"That's high," Proch said, but he gave the silvers to the man without further protest. He took a long drink of the ale in his hand and choked.

Gallien's mouth quirked up and she followed him to the back room; he shut the door behind them. Only when they were this close to one another did Gallien notice the slight swell of his lip where he'd bitten it open when she'd slammed him into the door, the light feathering of a bruise at his forearm. Proch liked those things.

And he liked having to wince a bit when he sat in his chair across from her and his scratched back rubbed against the wood of the chair.

"Bit sore?" said Gallien.

Proch's lips ticked up in a quick smile, then they flattened again.

"What's going on, Proch?"

"Secrets."

"I love secrets."

"I know you do," he said. "And this is one I need you to keep. Do you understand? Swear on your life."

Gallien frowned and leaned forward, hands linked together and muscles tensed. "What is it?"

"There's been…gods, I shouldn't be telling you this. You're a damn pirate. But…there's been an attempt on the queen's life."

Gallien nearly dropped her ale. Was that…was that was Ri had been doing? Holy hells. Holy fucking hells.

"When?" she whispered.

"Early. Yesterday morning, she was attacked in her shrine. No one knows who did it or why. We don't fucking know anything except that the assassin was an Etryan man. That's it."

Gallien's hands were shaking. She had been involved in a lot of things, but never an attempted assassination of a royal. She set the drink down so she didn't truly drop it and shatter it on the ground. At this very second, she knew where the assassin was—weeping his life away and drowning in alcohol. Shitting hell, she had to *go*.

Proch took another swallow of his drink and his whole face wrinkled. "Gods, how can you drink this shit," he grumbled.

"What do you need my help for?" Gallien said.

"Identifying this," said Proch, and he set a gorgeous dagger on the table in front of her. The kind of thing that she'd have made him pay for in a hell of a lot more than gold. The kind of thing that she...that she recognized. Gods, it *was* true. She'd seen it. The weapon she'd only gotten a flash of before, that Ri had been trying so hard to hide before the grey surged. This was it. It was him.

Which meant that Va'al had sent for the death of a queen.

Her stomach twisted, and nerves ran through her harder than they had in years.

Because she was complicit.

She reached for it and ran her fingers over the hilt. Gold fell in drips over the gems inlaid in the item. It was clearly ancient but still bright. And it...no. She didn't just know this weapon from Ri. She knew it from *history.* "Hells," she said.

"What?"

Gallien's mouth hardened. The Va'alian king had sent her on a mission that could easily have implicated her in an assassination attempt. There were not many lines she would not cross, but this was one of them. This was too great a risk, and he'd done it without her consent. And she'd wanted his blood for years.

"I know this blade," she said.

Proch's voice took on a note of desperation. "And?"

"I will tell you its name, for a price."

Proch rarely looked truly frustrated with her. But there was no laughter in the hard sigh that came from his lips. "What do you want?"

"I cannot tell you. I'll give you everything I know about this item, and you give me word that you will help me in whatever I ask."

Gallien could see the thoughts whirring behind Proch's eyes.

"I can tell you who sent for the head of your queen right now, Proch. All I require is your word."

Proch locked eyes with her. His lips were thin, face drawn and nervous. And he tapped his fingers again and again, like a compulsion, on the table.

Gallien drew a small knife from her belt and held it over her palm. "I swear I will never tell a soul what you've told me. And you swear to help me."

"Va'al is a beastly place, swearing in bloo—"

"*Swear it*," she said. Suddenly, she was just as desperate as he was. Because this could be the moment. The one she'd been waiting on for a decade. The way to begin the ruination of the Va'alian king.

Proch stared at the sharp blade, then down at Gallien's hand. He said nothing. And then, he held out his own palm. "I swear it," he said.

"On my life, I swear as well," said Gallien.

She nicked her own palm, and then she nicked his, and he hissed. Then they pressed their hands together, letting the blood mingle. It was done.

"The dagger, Proch, is moinchiran."

"What?" he breathed. That fascination took over his face—the one Gallien loved so much.

"Before the great war, hundreds of years ago, when tensions had begun to rise between mortal and immortal, humans had started sneaking into the moinchire lands. They were wreaking havoc. And when the royals got involved, well, the moinchire were powerful but few and could not withstand people who could manipulate the weather. So they crafted weaponry. Surely history taught you this."

"I slept my way through history."

"Through the class, or the students in it?"

"The teachers," said Proch, eyes glittering. He was teasing. At least, she thought he was.

"Either way, you lecher, the moinchire had divined a way to craft magic that specifically interacted with the blood of those mortals blessed by the gods. To destroy them."

"Is this one of them?"

"No," she said.

His shoulders fell. Even if it meant the queen was in danger, the fascination was too great.

"Humanity caught wind of this. And Va'al was ruthless. The queen captured two moinchire and forced them to enchant her weaponry—it was such a threat to the other rulers, if she had that kind of magic at her beck and call. A weapon that could fell the choices of the gods. Who would wish to stand against it? After the moinchire fell, the remaining blades were kept in Va'al."

"So this…this is a Va'alian blade."

"Yes."

"This was manufactured by *your* king."

Gallien snarled. "You know I have no love for the Va'alian king." Proch knew a good deal more of the king's dealings with her than he should have. He did not know of her gift of fire. But he knew that she served him because she had no choice, just as she knew that Proch had once been in love with a boy whom he had not known had plotted Reyan's death. The boy had wound up executed on the end of the king's blade. They were adept at keeping one another's secrets. Something about doing dealings in the dark allowed people to be too open with who they were.

"No. No, I'm sorry. You're right. But I…why? Why would he…" Proch blinked down at the table, ran his fingers over the knife. "This is enchanted?"

"Yes."

"So Kasia could be in danger." He stood. "Gods. I have to talk with the king—"

"Wait," said Gallien. She grabbed him by the wrist. He narrowed his eyes and slowly sank back into his chair. "Now for what you owe me."

Proch said nothing. He just waited.

"If you tell a soul on earth that I asked you to do this for me—"

"You don't need to threaten me."

"I will die, Proch. He'll kill me. The king will have my head, and my blood will be on your hands."

Proch shifted, and the air around them grew thick and heavy. "What, oh what, have I agreed to?"

She drew in a deep breath. She hadn't been able to stop thinking about this since she'd realized. But she'd wanted this for ages, had been quietly wondering for years. How to destroy the king as he had destroyed her.

Perhaps this was the moment. The gods had tossed it in her lap. Vengeance.

"Reyan will not let this stand," she said.

"No."

"He will retaliate."

"Of course," said Proch.

"When he does…" She drew in a deep, unsteady breath. "When he does, I need you to do whatever you need to to convince him that the best way to get his revenge is to take Prince Adè captive."

"What in hells," Proch said, voice hardly higher than a whisper.

"It's reasonable. It makes sense. It will bait Va'al into a war against you that they cannot win."

"Why?" he said.

"My reasons are my own," she said, but of course he knew. Of course he knew that she hated the king with every fiber of her being, and there was only one way to take what he'd stolen back. To make him feel the loss she felt every day.

"If this prompts war—"

"War is inevitable either way."

"If this prompts war, you will be the first to sail with them. The first to come to our shores and fight."

"I won't come looking for *you*."

He knew exactly what she intended to do. With the Va'alian prince. He sucked on his teeth.

Gallien was desperate, and it was audible. She had never allowed Proch to hear her like this. "Your king will wage war on Va'al no matter how he starts it now. Please. *Please* let me have this. Let me have a whisper of a chance at peace in me." What she asked was too much. Too much for simple discrete identification of a weapon.

"You did not say that this was Va'al in order to fulfill a vendetta?"

"I swear on my soul, Proch. It's Va'alian. Go into your libraries, and find a book on the moinchire. I promise you, you will find these blades in the pages, and they will be listed under Va'al." Moinchire magic was taught in history, but these particular weapons were obscure. Gallien never would have known them if she hadn't been obsessed with magic and its history when she'd been blessed. If she hadn't seen these blades a hundred times in Va'al for herself. "I would not use you for my own ends, not in a lie. I can also tell you that the herb your healers need to use to counteract this particular magic is ellows' knife, and it's everywhere in the woods around your palace. It won't heal her, but it's the only thing that has a remote chance of helping. Please." She fell from her chair to her knees, and grabbed his legs. "Please."

Proch stared down at her. "I can't—gods, this is unsettling. Get up."

She did.

He stood with her and let his face rest beside her ear, then kissed her cheek. "I will give you your peace."

And he left.

CHAPTER THIRTY-NINE

KASIA WANTED HOME. IT had been three days since everything had happened and she was allowed back in her own rooms again, though under heavy guard. The blade hadn't struck an artery, thankfully, and she hadn't fallen asleep because of blood loss. It had been a sleeping draught that had coated the blade—made from edelsberry, famous for its ability to put an opponent under in minutes to seconds.

The blade had been very peculiarly carved, and extremely sharp, and the particular angle it had flown in—it had shredded her muscle and chipped her bone. She was walking on it already, with assistance, but running would be another matter entirely. If it was ever a matter for her at all. The angle it had been thrown combined with the way she'd fallen on it, first to her knees, then to the floor…the doctors had not been particularly hopeful that she would walk without a limp after this. Reyan had informed her that not only was the angle particularly wicked, but the blade had been enchanted ages ago with some kind of moinchire magic. Kasia wasn't sure she believed that moinchire magic had lasted this long on anything, but the pain that remained in her leg was slowly convincing her. It didn't matter much what she believed; the fact remained that she very well might never run. It was frustrating to consider. But it wasn't a death sentence. Thank the gods for the ellows' knife. She would live, and that was what mattered.

She wished for home at this moment. For her sweet but silly mother to sit with her and fill her head with fantasy. It made her feel very young, to wish for her mother when she was hurt. But in the end, wasn't that who dying soldiers called out for? She was allowed to wish for someone to be a comfort. To be…loyal. A friend.

She had certainly never had one in Nagonia.

Her heart hurt just thinking of it.

Reyan was there in the dungeons with Nagonia right now, listening to her confession. Trying to pull from her the name of her assassin. They'd caught her with two horses, and two of the guards who should have been watching the shrine had implicated her in giving them drinks laced with the same poison that had been on the blade the assassin had thrown into her leg.

There was no doubt.

It had been her.

And in two hours, Nagonia would be walked to a platform in the middle of town, and she would be executed. Usually, Reyan carried out these things in private. But not today. Not for this.

Kasia swallowed the sickness in her throat and slid from her bed to the floor. She was strong. She had built everything about herself on being strong and being powerful and being...everything she wasn't being right now. Because right now, all she felt was hurt.

Little One.

Kasia's shoulders sagged in sudden relief at the unexpected voice. She whispered, "You called me that in the shrine. Before I slept."

I did.

"You said you wouldn't be there."

I wasn't.

Kasia waited, looking up at the ceiling, head braced against her bed.

Until you burned your wrist.

Kasia's mouth tipped up. "Is that what it takes to get your attention, then?"

He audibly snarled. *Do not take to doing it. I was simply irritated enough by it that I needed to come stop it.*

Kasia drew in a breath that was nearly a sob. "You did stop it. You stopped everything."

Little One, he said, his voice a caress, *I warned you, yes. But I did nothing. You stopped it.*

Kasia shut her eyes and tried to imagine what Death looked like. What expression he was making somewhere a million miles away in a place she wouldn't reach for another seventy years (gods willing).

There was that laugh that rasped over her skin.

Kasia fought a pleasant shudder.

You have a difficult day ahead of you, my love.

"Yes," she said. Her voice cracked on the pain of it.

You are strong enough to withstand it.

"I know."

Death said nothing else until Kasia said, "I will not leave that assassin to Reyan's hand. I will find him myself, and I will kill him."

Yes, said Death, just this side of a hiss. *You send that boy to me.*

Kasia shivered again, this time from the chill that had descended into the room.

She opened her eyes and said nothing more. She waited until his smooth, cold presence left her, then she hobbled to the shower, washed away nothing, and dressed in black.

Kasia joined Reyan on the platform. It was stone, erected in the center of town. Reyan's father had used it with some frequency—for traitors, thieves, murderers, many things. He had rarely shown up to watch them die.

But since Reyan had ascended to the throne, he had never used it. He'd told Kasia as much when he'd come back into their rooms, dirty from the dungeons, palms wet with Nagonia's blood.

"She wouldn't talk," he said, voice rough with emotion. Nagonia had been a servant in his home for two years before Kasia had come to them. How many glasses of wine had she served him? How many times had she bowed at his feet, and how many times had he laughed at some under-the-breath comment she'd made, poking fun at some ridiculous noble at dinner? Reyan's eyes were red, and Kasia knew that it was not all from rage.

"It's all right," said Kasia.

"No, it's not all right!" he cried, sweeping the books and writing utensils and unlit candles off his nightstand in one fell swoop. "He's out there, Kasia. Again. How could this happen *again*?"

She slid her arms around him and wondered if he was seeing his mother or her behind his eyelids. It didn't so much matter which. When he opened his eyes and took a step back to look into Kasia's, she knew he was seeing only her.

"I almost lost you," he said, hands framing her face, pressing into her skin, brushing back through her hair. "I almost lost you, and I swear I would have...I would have died. I would have lost my mind."

"Over me? The Farowfin girl?"

"Miroich," he whispered into her lips when he kissed her—not in Jall. In Farowfin. *Mine.*

Kasia leaned against him, let her body melt into his and kissed him back. His hands felt very large and strong framing her face. Like he was capable of protecting her. Kasia did not often feel that she needed to be protected—or wanted to be, really. But these past three days, she had wanted to feel that it was possible.

At this moment, she did.

Reyan let her go to clean the filth from his body and Nagonia's blood from his hands. Kasia tried not to allow herself to be sick again.

The king was gone in the bathroom for some time, and when he came out, he looked like a royal in mourning—hair oiled and falling in ringlets around his stone cold face, cheekbones and jaw hard as always, dressed from his throat down to his feet in black. They matched one another well.

But now, on that stone platform, surrounded by townspeople, he did not look like a royal mourning. He looked like a royal enraged.

Kasia stood beside him, lips a thin, blood red line. Her eyes were lined and dark, her face pale. She wanted to look powerful. Wanted to look like Death.

For a moment, she felt his cool nod of approval next to her ear.

Steps sounded on the stone, and Kasia closed her eyes. She did not wish to see Nagonia. She wished to pretend that none of this had happened. That Nagonia was just her servant, this girl who was too preoccupied with the theater and suitors and some nameless Etryan ambassador to tend to her duties as well as she ought.

She opened her eyes when Nagonia was led in front of her, and passed farther by, to the center of the stone. She looked so small, in a clean, brown tunic that swallowed her. It fell below her knees, off her skinny shoulders. Kasia had never realized quite how little a person Nagonia was.

She was forced to her knees. Her face was proud, utterly impassive. Kasia's heart clenched—with what? Guilt. Pain. The horrifying ache of betrayal. It had been *her* who had orchestrated Kasia's murder, and now she was refusing to name the boy, allowing him the possibility of trying again. Kasia couldn't feel guilty for this. She shouldn't.

This was the penalty for treason.

"This woman," said Reyan, voice clear as a bell ringing over the crowd, "stands for treason against the crown."

The gathering was quiet enough, Kasia thought she could hear the ants walking beneath them.

"Three days ago, a would-be assassin was found with the queen in her private shrine,"—a small gasp rose up front the crowd at the location—"attempting to take her life. He was caught and killed on sight." The lie rolled so easily off the king's tongue that Kasia had trouble doubting it. Reyan had told her he would say this. "And this woman, Nagonia LaPrest, was found waiting with horses. One for herself, one for the assassin. She is found guilty of all charges laid against her: conspiring to murder the queen, drugging a royal officer in the line of duty, disloyalty to the state. All of these crimes amount to treason. And so on this day, Nagonia LaPrest is sentenced to death by the sword."

No one clapped, no one cheered. There hadn't been an execution this public in years; no one, Kasia figured, knew what to do.

Kasia couldn't stop shaking. A blade slicing into her neck was her worst nightmare. Now she would have to watch it. Gods, she hated this.

Nagonia looked right at Kasia, eyes shining, when she said, so low none of the crowd could possibly hear it, "I did not do this to betray you, my lady. A title you have earned. But I am not sorry."

Kasia felt that nausea again, the particular sickness of anticipation. But her face betrayed nothing.

The wind blew a little line of Nagonia's hair around her face. "I did this for my country," Nagonia said. She looked away from the queen, still managing somehow to look dignified, despite kneeling on the grey rock, each hand held out by a guard.

Reyan glanced over at Kasia, then knelt before Nagonia. There was no sadness in his eyes now, not a shred of pity. There was only cold fury. Justice.

"Do you wish to name your god?" he said.

Nagonia blinked slowly, head tilted just slightly upward. The sky was so very bright today. "Barrowin-Liu," she said. An Etryan god. Kasia hadn't even known her servant was Etryan. She shook her head. Barrowin-Liu was the god of desire. Sometimes sexual, sometimes not. Desire of all things.

Reyan stood and drew his sword from its sheath. It rang on the quiet air. "Sast k'asyanall Barrowin-Liu," he said, and he raised the weapon. Nagonia tensed.

"Wait," said Kasia.

Reyan stopped immediately, let his sword fall to his side. "What?" he said.

"Do not do this, my king."

Reyan frowned.

Kasia took a deep breath. Everything hurt. Everything felt sick. Everything was exhaust*ing* and exhaust*ed*, and she wanted to go to bed back in Farowfin and wake up to dullness. "This treason is not yours to avenge."

"Is it not?" said Reyan.

"No," said Kasia. "It is mine."

Reyan blinked, fingers twitching on his sword handle. He was itching to do it, to take this girl from the earth. And perhaps Kasia should have let him.

But if Reyan could look into the eyes of every person he'd ever sentenced to death, then Kasia could do the same.

Reyan nodded once, bright eyes burning, and Kasia crossed the platform to take his place. She knelt before Nagonia, willed her to meet her eyes. After seconds of the world waiting in silence, she did.

Kasia stood, and Reyan handed her his sword. This was dangerous, perhaps. Or it would have been. But there were dummies at the palace. And for two days, Kasia had been practicing.

She blanched. What were the words? The blessing.

Sast k'asyanall Barrowin-Liu. She felt Death shift beside her, like he was there. And for whatever inexplicable reason, it calmed her nerves. *A respectable choice for a god. One of the only respectable ones.*

"Sast k'asyanall Barrowin-Liu," said Kasia, and she looked down at Nagonia's neck and let the blade fall.

CHAPTER FORTY

R EYAN LEANED OVER THE table in the war room. Sitting on the throne
was not enough; he wanted to pace, wanted to stand, wanted to feel
something hard digging into his palm. He needed to *feel*.

"Are you all right, cousin?"

His nostrils flared. "No, Proch. I am not." He shook his head, once. "Are
you sure that blade is Va'alian?"

Proch shrugged. "My source does not lie, King." He slid a small, very old
but hardly read book toward Reyan. "Look at these drawings again and tell
me that is not a Va'alian blade."

Reyan looked again. It was. "And cursed," he said, fury licking through
him. "Specifically enchanted to interact with the blood of blessed people."

Proch blew out a breath.

"But *why*?" Reyan growled. His knuckles whitened on the table's edges.

"Power? Land?"

Reyan snorted. "Va'al? Wanted to take *Jaelen*. Please, the next time you
spot a mouse in the kitchens, remind me to warn the cat to hide."

Proch rolled his eyes. "Don't take this out on me, King."

"Watch to whom you speak."

Proch's eyes narrowed and he shut his mouth.

Guilt spread up into Reyan's chest and he blew out a breath, then just
looked at Proch. Gods, Reyan was pathetic. Helpless.

"Don't use me as your punching bag, cousin. I'm royal, too."

Reyan ran his tongue over his lower lip, and cast his gaze up at the ceiling.
"I feel *powerless*, Proch."

Proch shook his head, and took two steps toward Reyan. "You are not
powerless." He dropped to a knee and bowed, touching his fingers to his

head. "You command me, King. You command an army. The most powerful nation in the world. You are not a boy anymore." Proch looked up. "You do not have to sit by and watch your mother's killer get away. Watch Farowfin move on with no consequence—none of that has been foisted upon you. Your wife is still alive. The assailant may still be free, but you know his nation. And you think that you cannot enact vengeance upon them for this? You are the king."

Proch's face hardened into a viper's.

"That decrepit king tried to take someone you love. I say," said Proch, "that you respond in kind."

Reyan locked eyes with Proch and rested his hand on the man's shoulder. He gripped the back of his neck, and Proch rose, and Reyan drew him close and wrapped his arms around him.

Proch hugged him fiercely, and in the embrace was a promise. A promise of blood.

The war room always felt bigger to Reyan when it was filled with people. Tonight, it felt massive. Around the table sat six of his advisors, his newly appointed captain of the guard, several of her generals. People who were used to being commanded, but who also commanded themselves.

A map was laid out in the middle of the giant bloodwood table. He sat and waited, and everyone else sat in silence with him.

The door at the end of the room creaked as a servant pushed it open, and Kasia walked through it toward him, draped in deep red and favoring her left leg. Reyan's eyes darkened at her limp. He could feel his blood running suddenly hot.

He stood when she made it to his side, and when she sat, he remained upright. "Now that my queen is here, we have urgent business to discuss."

The stillness was heavy enough to feel.

"72 hours ago, your queen was praying in her shrine when she was met with an assassin. He obviously did not succeed. But nonetheless, the queen is injured, and her life was in danger. And this is something that we cannot afford to let slide by without retribution."

A muffle of noises went through the group then.

"King, do we know who was responsible for this?" his new captain said. They were small, but strong, coal black hair down to their waist and hard, assessing eyes. They had been an incredible soldier and strategist, second only to Cariq. It fell to them to be rational.

"Va'al," said Reyan.

The noise got louder then. A chorus of "What? Why? How do we know this?"

Only Proch sat silent, eyes on the king.

"We know that the weapon used was Va'alian. This was a Va'alian attack, and it must be met with justice."

A man who had been a royal advisor since Reyan's father had first taken the throne stood, trembling lightly. He had wrinkles like canyons and hair that was hardly even white anymore. It was just this side of translucent. "With all due respect, King, perhaps a weapon is only circumstantial evidence. Shaky ground on which to start a war. Without the assassin in hand..."

"Agreed," another very young man said. "To involve ourselves in another war when the queen is alive, and our resources are already spread thin—"

"Is that what you advised my father, Farien?" said Reyan, looking at the old man. "Did you tell him to sit back and do nothing when Farowfin sent assassins and *murdered my mother*? Was it you who cautioned him to wait?"

Farien stood tall and proud and said, "War was not prudent. And we did not have enough evidence to involve ourselves in one. On speculation."

Reyan clenched his teeth and looked down at the table, leaned over it. "Sit down," he said, voice slicing into the air.

The man sat.

"Proch?" said Reyan. If anyone would lend their support to this, it would be his cousin.

Proch sat for a moment and brushed a finger over his mouth. Then he stood. "The king speaks the truth. We *know* this was a Va'alian blade. Specifically created to do the most damage to our queen as possible. Our *queen*. That is reason enough to sound the drums of war. If some of you are too cowardly to wish to act, then I question why you have pledged yourself to the king's service at all."

Farien made a noise that wasn't a laugh, and when Reyan smiled, it was a thing that could cut a person.

"Since all that business with Queen Parinelle's death, when our country elected not to act, we have been seen as *weak*," Proch continued.

Farien said, "That's not—"

"It *is*, Farien. We are seen as a country with power and global reach that could fall at the whim of any other ruler. Because what consequences were wrought last time?"

"We did not act on the queen's death because it was not *prudent*," said a woman, older but not nearly so ancient as Farien. "We cannot act without solid evide—"

"I am the queen," said Kasia, and Reyan turned to look at her as she stood. "And as such, my word is law." Never had a room quieted in the presence of Kasia's authority. But it fell silent. "If Jaelen is so weak as not to press for war when an attempt on my *life* has been made, then may the gods take it in the grey."

Several gasps rose up from the table. Reyan smiled lightly.

"My queen has spoken."

Everyone who was not the king or queen sat. Reyan said, "The question is not whether we retaliate. It is how."

"Va'al is well-fortified," said Mollenne, the captain. "Their navy is a force, and their build is similar to ours. They are small, but their walls would be a miracle to breach. The only way we would have a hope of getting inside the city would be to take it from the sea, but even then, the loss would be great. The Va'alian navy is not one to play with."

"Then we do not bring this battle to them. We force them to come to us," said Reyan.

The captain frowned.

"Proch," said Reyan. "Go fetch the three soldiers you brought to my attention."

"Yes, King," he said. He bowed his head and left the table.

"What is this, your highness?" said the older woman who had spoken before.

"Retaliation," he said. "The captain is right. We cannot hope to face Va'al in a naval confrontation, and war against their walls would be foolish. We would lose more than revenge could hope to gain us. But they would be a feat to take. The trade it would open up...economically, it would be a massive success."

"The resources we would have to expend on such a small force as Va'al's would certainly be justified in what we would gain," the treasurer said in a small voice.

"And how do you plan to bait that country into marching for a war they know they will lose?" said the young man who had agreed with Farien. Cowards did lots of speaking at these sorts of things, Reyan had found.

The war room doors opened, and Proch walked in, trailed by two women and one very large man.

"What's this?" said Farien.

"Our means of bait."

Kasia said, "These soldiers are the best, the swiftest, the quietest. The captain can confirm."

"On my honor," they said. "They are."

"They will be sent down to Va'al under cover of night, and they will kidnap the Va'alian prince and bring him back here. His father will have no choice but to bring a fight to us."

"Holy gods," someone breathed.

"Does anyone object to this?"

"The kidnapping of princes," the old woman said, "is not simple business."

"Neither is deciding retaliation for the assassination of queens."

He could see it all in their eyes—none of them knew if he was talking about Kasia or his mother. But Jaelen had been weak once. It would not be weak again.

No one spoke. Perhaps they all saw the determined set of his jaw, the hardness in his eyes. He was not to be argued with.

"Dismissed. Mollenne, you and yours stay."

There was a beat of hesitation before the council disseminated. Farien was the last to leave.

"You three volunteer to do this?" he said to the soldiers.

And in unison, they responded, "Yes, sir."

"You will take my horses. They are of moinchire blood and will fly faster than you ever thought possible."

The three exchanged glances then returned to staring straight ahead at him, unreactive.

"Captain."

"King?"

"I need messages sent to our spies in Va'al. We need them setting distractions elsewhere in the city to keep the guards' attention away from the prince. Get it done, and then, I need you to begin devising strategy. War is coming."

They bowed their head and said, "Of course, my king. My queen."

"Go," he said.

They emptied the room, and Reyan reached for Kasia.

"I don't need your help just to stand, Reyan."

"I know," he said. "It is wrong that I wish to give it?"

Kasia smiled and took his hand. She stood.

"A war over me," she said. "This will delay going to fight the grey."

"Yes," said Reyan. "But the further the darkness moves, the closer it gets to Va'al. I refuse to do a thing to help them before we take care of this. If they are lost because of their own foolishness, so be it. They need to know—the world needs to know—that we are not to be played with. That they cannot take something so precious to me and stand after."

"Oh?" said Kasia. She arched an eyebrow. "Am I precious to you?"

"Kasia," Reyan breathed, touching his forehead to hers, "you are everything to me."

RI HAD TAKEN A good deal of convincing to board Gallien's ship. He'd taken a good deal of convincing to leave that room in the tavern at all, really, because what in hells was left for him now? Where was he supposed to go?

Every time he'd tried to move, he'd felt the loss like an iron pressing on his chest. *They're gone. You failed. None of it matters. They are all dead. You should have listened to your stepfather when he begged you not to leave, when he begged you to stay with the rest of them, to take care of them. That this career you had chosen would lead to your ruin. Now who is ruined?*

He was sick. And you left.

They were alone. And you left.

They are dead, and you are not, and you. Left.

He hadn't had the ability to care about the price on his head, the soldiers surely looking for him—an Etryan with a thousand injuries in Jaelen. It was not as though he blended in. And he hadn't cared at all until Gallien had come kicking his door in, hissing at him that she knew exactly who he was and what he'd done and if he stayed in that room a second longer, then that barmaid who'd given him rest would get executed right along with him.

And the thought of another iota of guilt weighing on his bones was enough to make him finally stand. They left port at night.

She hadn't pried, hadn't said another thing to him, in fact, the entire way to Va'al. The nighttime departure had slowed them. And the weather was rocky, which had slowed them further, but it didn't matter. Fucking none of it did.

He didn't know where he would even stay, where to go in Va'al. He was certain his rooms were under watch, and he was in no mood to deal with the king yet and confront his failure. Surely the man would strip him of his money, maybe even have him beaten. That wasn't standard, but Adè's father delighted in cruelty.

He often wondered how it was that Adè had escaped childhood without a scar or two—his father's anger etched into his skin. But he had. Adè was a point of pride, because he was powerful. And since royalty was not always given children with the gods' blessings, he supposed Adè must have been worth preserving to the king.

Ri hadn't a single ally in all of Va'al, and he had very little money left. So when he left Gallien's ship without a word of thanks or goodbye, he had no idea where he would go. He had fresh clothes in his bag—not shredded and blood-stained. So he could probably find himself a room in the shit section of the city without inviting questions. Fine. He'd spent enough of his life in places like that that he could take it. And the places in his price range were close to the docks anyway—populated with loud, filthy fisherman without a gold to their name.

There were a hundred around here. He would find a place and the cheapest meal and alcohol he could. And he would spend the next two days alone in the dark.

Two days, it turned out, was a lot of time to spend alone. Because really, it had been six days. Time with Gallien and her girls was almost more lonely than legitimate solitude. In a crowd with no one to speak to, silence did not feel empty; it felt oppressive.

But two days had given him time to think, time to consider. And what he considered was this: he had nowhere left to call home. Nowhere to return to. No one in the world who knew his name. Reports whispered everywhere had only confirmed what the barmaid in Jaelen had said: his home was gone. All he had left was a prince.

So he awoke in the middle of the night, which was not so unusual, since night and day became irrelevant when one spent all their time sleeping and trying to sleep. He woke. And it would take over an hour to walk to the palace, but he would.

He left his bag in his room and made his way through the silent streets. So much damn silence everywhere; even his thoughts had quieted.

When the palace came into view, Ri climbed a little side gate and hopped silently in. It was not that the palace was poorly guarded. It was that Ri was very good.

He crept across the ground to the stones beneath Ade's rooms and looked up at the balcony he'd sat on too many times. Where Adè's hand had brushed against his hip, and he'd grabbed Ade's hand once when he'd meant to take a card from it. Something in his stomach tightened. It was impossible to scale from here, which he'd known but had wanted to confirm it. Ri had a decent relationship with several guards by now, but if the king had ordered them to usher him into the throne room whenever he showed his face, there would be no escaping that unpleasant confrontation.

But it was this and risk facing the man, or go back to an empty inn and nothingness. Adè was the only hope he had. Of anything.

So he blew out a breath and stalked over to the entrance that led to the halls where Adè's rooms were.

His muscles tensed when he approached, waiting for an argument. And then he stopped cold.

Because at the entrance was silence. Dead silence. He furrowed his brow and moved forward. And when he lifted his foot, he felt something sticky clinging to it.

His stomach hollowed. And he looked down.

Blood.

Just as he laid eyes on the first guard with his throat slit, an explosion sounded behind him. Far away, fire blazing up into the dark. The docks.

What in hells?

He hardly had time to react when another rang out, and then another. Holy gods, the docks were covered in flame. There were shouts outside the palace, —on the opposite side, near the barracks—and Ri's face drained of color.

The guards had been quietly dead. Murdered. And now something far away was burning.

The docks were a distraction.

No. *No.*

He dropped all pretense of subterfuge and ran.

Adè's door was ajar. Instantly, all breath fled Ri's lungs.

He pushed inside and hissed, "Adè. Adè."

Silence.

"Tallel. If you're alive, please answer me." Desperation crept into his throat, clutching his limbs. Adè could not be dead. He would not accept it.

He ran through the prince's darkened room, nearly tripping on an over-turned nightstand, the sheets, which had been ripped off the bed. They'd gotten to him while he was asleep.

And then he noticed the trickle of blood at the window. He shook as he touched his fingers to it.

It was still warm.

There was not enough blood here for the prince to have been drained of it. No. No, perhaps he was still...

He threw open the door to the balcony and made out, in the distance, several shapes. Three horseman on some of the largest horses he'd even seen. Silent as the grave and moving too quickly to be real.

And on the back of one of them was a shape—large, tall, lolling this way and that. Tied. He would recognize that frame in the pitch dark.

Ri clutched his stomach to keep from calling out Adè's name and backed away a pace when the door to Adè's room opened. Guards.

Ri's eyes widened, and he looked down. It was too far to jump. Shit, shit, shit.

Tallel, save me.

He jumped.

He hit the ground hard, and wicked pain knifed up his leg, shooting into his hip, so his legs nearly buckled with it. This was a terrible time for a break. Fucking gods. He shrank against the wall just beneath the balcony and sucked in a breath, tears stabbing at his eyes from the horrific pain. The riders were gone. With the prince. How in hells had they gone so fast?

Perhaps there was still time. He could catch them if he could get to the stables. Gods, he could still do it. Could still save him.

He took a step to his right when the sound of the guards quieted and tripped. He could pinpoint the pain now; it was coming from his shin. Not a break. He'd had enough of those to know what they felt like, and this wasn't quite so bad. A sprain, maybe. But enough to keep him from moving quickly.

It would not keep him from moving at all. The king could send men. The king could get him his prince back.

Every step was agony as he crawled toward the entrance. He couldn't be seen anywhere near the prince's rooms, or perhaps he would be implicated in all this, and they would lose precious time sorting it all out.

Despair threatened to break into his mind, but he refused it. This was not the time for despair; it was time for action.

It was a full fifteen minutes before he reached the palace doors. The fires at the docks still glowed far behind him, and the palace was lit. People were up. Perhaps they were already mobilizing to go after the prince. Hope burst in his chest.

Ri limped up to the doors, throat raw, eyes burning, and a guard he was friendly with stopped him.

"Do not go in there, Ri."

The man put his hand on Ri's arm, short, thin fingers digging into his bicep with a purpose. Ri's throat tightened. "Why not? The prince—"

The guard, Togen, whom Ri had gambled with one or twice and drunk with more nights than that said, "The king is…severely unhappy." His words spilled out just short of panicked, which Ri found reasonable. He was on the ragged edge of coming apart himself.

Ri felt his mouth go dry. Did the king know yet? The guard glanced at the woman next to him, who jerked her head toward the door.

"I have a few minutes," said Togen. Ri followed him outside.

It was deathly quiet out here—nothing but the occasional shuffling of feet and call of a nightjay. The musical buzz of insects that hid in the grasses. The quiet was maddening when the prince was moving farther away every instant.

Togen crossed his arms over his massive barrel chest and shook his head once. "The king knows about your failure, Ri."

"I don't care about my failure! The prince—"

"Has been taken by Jaelen. They set the fires to distract us."

"Jaelen?" That did give him pause. "But...why did they come *here*? They should have made for—" Ri froze. "No," he said under his breath. "The dagger. And...no. No, no, no, no, no." His hand leapt to his head, fingers digging into his scalp. Could it have been that the dagger...no. Shit. No. He'd been so exhausted, dehydrated, in pain after the Andran dungeons that he'd assumed the hands reaching out to help him from that prison had been friendly ones.

But perhaps...

Togen lowered his voice. "The king knows it was you, Ri. That whatever you did, the Jaelenian queen is still alive, and Va'al has been implicated. That looks very, very bad for you."

Ri blew out a breath and looked out across the dark horizon. "He wants me in irons?"

Togen laughed without humor. "Irons? He wants you dead." Togen shrunk up against the wall with Ri. "He hasn't issued an order yet, or you would have been caught already. But I heard him. He is ravenous for your blood."

"Because of the prince."

"Yes."

Ri's voice was rising, and he didn't know how to stop it. "The fires are still burning! Why has the king not dispatched a hundred men to get him back? I *saw them*, Togen! We can catch them; I know it. Fuck what he thinks of me. We have to—"

"He thinks the risk of leaving the city so vulnerable is too gre—"

Ri choked out a laugh. "It's his son. Adè is his *son*."

"Which is why he will very soon be calling for your head."

"I don't care about my head; I care about the prince's, and how in hells can his father care more for vengeance upon me than rescuing him? Gods. I can't stay here a moment longer. I have to go. If I left now, perhaps I could—"

"They're using some kind of travelling magic, Ri. Or...I don't know. Something. They were here, and now they are gone."

Travelling magic. That was utter bullshit. An excuse. Ri snarled and curled his hand into a fist at his side.

"I swear to you, I *saw it*. I saw them."

"Ri."

"I have to go," said Ri.

"I would say that is wise."

"To Jaelen."

"I would say that is...less wise."

"Thank you," said Ri, gripping the man's hand and pulling him in for a quick embrace.

Togen nodded once, then turned back to the place to slip inside.

Ri didn't think, didn't consider, didn't wonder about Adè or his leg or the risk at all until he'd gone from the palace to his rooms to the stables, much too slowly, and loaded two horses with supplies. Didn't consider a thing but what he had to do and how he had to do it, until he and his horse and the prince's massive one, were riding away from Va'al. He kept Adè's horse linked to his. When he reached Adè to free him, —and he *would*—he would wish for a second horse.

The night darkened, and Ri was riding on such adrenaline that he couldn't feel tired. Could hardly feel the screaming wound in his leg. Couldn't feel the exhaustion that had taken up residence in his muscles ever since he'd first made the deal with the Va'alian king. No, he was fueled on by that adrenaline and rage.

When he was all alone, far enough away that he could no longer see the red orange flames flickering in the city, far enough away that not a soul was near him in the plains, he let himself think. The pain of his country and his family was present, breathtaking still. He thought it would always be.

But the pain of Adè was fresh.

He was gone. While Ri was out trying to kill someone for a king who cared about no one and a country that didn't exist anymore. Adè was gone. And they had him, and who knew what they would do to him. They could let him rot in a cell like Ri had. He was so much slower than them—he injured, and they on horses so gigantic and fast he would not have believed it if he hadn't seen it with his own eyes. They wouldn't kill the prince; at least, Ri didn't think they would. Reyan was not known for brutality. And it would be a stupid political maneuver. No, he would survive.

He had to.

Ri urged his horse on faster, and Adè's galloped to keep up. Adè's father was a violent sociopath. He'd known they'd left with him and not gotten a horse himself to bring his son back.

Ri had always hated the Va'alian king, but now, his own heart cried for that man's blood the way the king cried for his. He would ride to Adè, and when the king marched his army on Jaelen, Ri would find the prince.

And later, he would find the king alone and plunge his blade into the man's stomach. For him, for Adè. A man who cared more for his political alliances than what his son wanted, who cared more for war and himself than for going after Adè the moment he was taken.

No. The Va'alian king's blood would be red on Ri's hands that he would not feel guilty for.

That list was small, but it was growing. The king's name was on it, as was the Andran fuck. He hadn't been able to process it at first, had only been able to taste the very edges of it—of what had surely happened. Shev had offered him salvation, and they'd set him up. Promised an Andran blade and given him a Va'alian one. Probably the one they'd brokered the false truce with. Some nobody servant had baited him with safety and used a dying man to start their own war. He didn't know why. But it didn't matter.

Because now, Adè was suffering.

Fury replaced his blood.

When he found *them*, he wouldn't kill them with a knife. He would kill Shev with his bare hands.

He hardened his jaw and pushed his horse forward. And they rode like ghosts across the heather fields.

CHAPTER FORTY-TWO

GALLIEN WOKE TO CHAOS.

She'd been holed up in her room on the palace grounds for a couple of days—getting her feet under her, ferociously ignoring the hollow drain in her blood, in her spirit, gritting her teeth against what that could mean long-term, waiting to see if Proch would keep his word. And she woke to a furious pounding on her door and a red-faced guard shouting at her to please make way to the throne room.

She pulled on clothing and marched out into the night to find a fire that blazed behind her on the dock, smoke pluming up black into the sky, obscuring the stars. There was a promise that hung in the air—something Gallien knew better than she wanted to. It whispered of war. It felt like waiting, like blood; it felt like steel.

Gallien made her way to the throne room to deal with the rotten old man who had the crown. He was so desperately bitter, so tired and angry and so much a person that his son was not. That thought slowed her for a moment, guilt washing over her at what she desperately hoped Proch had done for her. But it was not enough to make her stop.

The king deserved to be destroyed, even if that meant sacrificing someone who did not deserve it. He had enough exhausting traits rolled into one that it was a wonder the gods had blessed him at all. Gallien thought it might have come by default. The king of Va'al had had the right name, the right blood, so he'd been granted a little power over the rocks.

Did the gods make mistakes?

It was a question that haunted her. Even now, as she pressed forward, fire begging to rise to the surface of her hands. Had they made a mistake when they'd given her fire while her spirit longed for the water? Had they made one by blessing her at all? She scoffed silently. This power was not a blessing; it was a curse.

A curse that was draining from her each time she fucking *used* it.

Which proved it: sometimes the gods were wrong.

They had been wrong about this man.

"What has happened?" said Gallien to the guard who had disturbed her.

"They've attacked," he said. "Sent a small squad down here, looks like."

"Who?" It had to have been Jaelen. Please, dear gods, let it have been Jaelen.

"Jaelen."

She tried not to let the elation show on her face.

The guards opened the doors for her when she reached them and beelined for the throne room. And another set of guards opened those. She was practically shaking with nervous energy. Gallien approached the old king, who sat, quiet and serious and looking so very, shockingly frail.

She dropped to a knee before him.

"Gallien," he said, voice cracking everywhere, "rise."

She did. Forced herself not to shake, to set her jaw so he could not see the worry and the thrill there.

"Jaelen has come to us. Right in the middle of the damned breaking of the world, they've..." He drew in a deep breath, and when he looked directly at her eyes, his were milky—tired, angry, sad, she couldn't tell. "They've taken something...very important to me. Trying to bait us into coming to them."

"Yes, my lord," said Gallien. "What, might I ask, have they taken?"

She did not expect him to answer. But she needed him to. Needed to hear it from his lips.

"My son."

Every part of her became a rush of adrenaline. Proch had done it. He had risked it for her. Gods. She would kiss him on the mouth when she saw him next and give him whatever he wished. Perhaps she wouldn't even make him call her Captain.

Gallien had rarely had use for tears, but there was just *too much* everywhere. Too much emotion. Too much energy. Too much everything. She felts tears pricking at her eyes. This, perhaps, was what vindication felt like.

"We have allied with Andra. Jaelen has baited us. We are coming."

"Yes, my lord," said Gallien again, though her voice shook in her chest.

"I will need you and yours at my front lines," said the king.

"And you have us. As always," she said. She dropped to a knee.

CHAPTER FORTY-THREE

I T WAS UNNATURALLY QUIET. The night was so very calm and the stars so bright against the black. Kasia simply stood at the open window and stared, let the stillness sink into her skin.

It had been over a week since they had made the decision to incite war. And she needed the quiet.

"Why is it open?" said Reyan, slipping his arms around her waist and resting his chin on her back.

"Because then the sky can seep into the room, and I can breathe."

"Are you having trouble breathing?" Reyan murmured against her shoulder.

"Sometimes."

He pressed his fingers into her hips, turning her to face him. Her thighs rested against the windowsill, her back open to the air. "Why?"

"Because the Va'alian prince rests in the palace in chains. And the darkness—can you not *feel* that it's only waiting? That this crack, this oppression in the air, the surge, is nothing but a preamble? Gods, I can feel it in my marrow, Reyan. This is not a finale with the grey; it's the beginning. It's shifting. Changing. The reports...and it creeps forward—"

"It hasn't moved in weeks—"

"—and because war is coming."

"With Va'al," said Reyan.

"What do the scouts say?"

"That they are coming. But their numbers are half of ours, Kasia. They will march on us tomorrow and fall."

"Tomorrow," said Kasia. "Hells, that feels soon. You and I will fight with them."

Reyan nodded once. "They will launch their first attack from the sea. You and I will need to be there."

"Damn. Here I had prepared a rousing battle speech to spur you into action. What a waste."

"Shall I argue so you can give it?"

Kasia shook her head. "The moment is over. Curse you for choosing bravery."

Reyan swallowed, trailing his finger absently down her back. "I want to tell you something, Kasia."

Kasia's pulse spiked when he trained his dark eyes on her. "I thought you weren't scared."

"I'm not."

His biceps tightened around her, drawing her into him, and her blood ran hot in a hundred places. "Then why do you choose this moment to confess a thing, if you are not afraid of death?"

"I choose this moment because it is the first moment I am certain."

Kasia locked eyes with him, and the world stilled.

He ran his fingers down the side of her face, brushing her ear. "I did not think you would be a thing to me but a signature and a hollow pronouncement from the gods. I thought to hate you. And to sleep side-by-side in this bed until I died, and that would be the end of it. But you..." He bowed his head and touched his fingers to his chest. "You, my queen, have destroyed me utterly. I am more"—his voice cracked—"more in love with you than I believed possible, Kasia Vane."

She stilled.

Quick concern flitted over Reyna's face, a flash of vulnerability no one ever got to see in him but her.

Then, she said, "And I wanted only your power. But here I find myself in love with a king."

Reyan smiled, relief washing over it like rain, and pulled his shirt over his head, wind blowing around Kasia to lift the hairs on his head, moon lighting up the hard planes of his chest.

The odds favored them tomorrow.

But what if...

Reyan caught her wrists in front of her, pulling her attention back to him, and whispered into her mouth, a breath of cold, "For you, kings would kneel."

He dropped to his knees, teeth at her thighs, hands digging into her hips.

She shifted so that she wasn't up against an open window, and Reyan growled, holding her there, in place. He pressed her back against the wall, and her knee brushed his shoulder. He nipped higher on her thigh, and Kasia yelped, slender fingers pressed into his shoulders, the others curled in his hair.

His tongue trailed up higher, and he bit down on the bone at her hip. Kasia cried out and tightened her fingers in the curls of his hair. He fluttered his tongue over her and ran his thumb over her hip, and Kasia drew a sharp breath in. She rose up on her toes and he tightened his grip on her skin. She gasped, "Reyan!" and he kissed her again, tongue slipping over her exactly where she needed it and fingers playing on her skin, tightening every muscle in her body. She couldn't speak at all, could do nothing but try to breathe. Everything pulled down into this single pinprick of focus as his tongue moved and heat spread out between her legs to every other surface of her body. The world went blank, and everything coiled and coiled until she screamed his name and collapsed to her knees against the wall.

"Would you have me dead? The night before the war?" she said, flushed, skin damp with sweat.

"I would have you remember this. Remember me. Tonight."

He framed her face with his hands, grip hard and desperate and unforgiving, and kissed her below her ear.

"Don't say that. As though there will be a reason for me to have to remember you."

"There won't," said Reyan, and his voice was fierce. "There won't; I'm sorry."

Kasia grabbed him by the shoulders and pushed him back against the bed frame, sliding from the floor onto his lap. She kissed his chest, bit his shoulder, and he hissed, back arching. She worked his pants down off his hips and discarded them on the floor, then moved back to his lap.

"Do you know," said Kasia, "I don't know if I'm glad or not that your god cheated. That he engineered the circumstances to bring us together."

Reyan worked his fingers through her hair, meeting her eyes.

"That's terrible to say," said Kasia. "It's horrible. For all of those people caught in this dead nightmare, everyone who has lost someone. And I'm certain that were I staring down the grey myself, whenever I *do*, I will have a different answer. But if you asked me, in this moment, to take it all back..."

Kasia did not have to finish her sentence. Reyan simply said, voice rough, "I know," and he kissed her, jaw hard—taking control of her mouth. Kasia yielded to it. To his lips and his tongue and his hands that were slowly driving her mad.

They fucked each other into silent oblivion on the bed.

And after she'd come back to herself, he rolled her over, and they fucked on the floor.

The hard ground bit at her bones, but none of it mattered. All that mattered was her and Reyan and the certainty that tomorrow, blood would be spilled.

But it would not be hers.

It would not be his.

They had this perfect, passionate moment—struggle for power, and fire, claiming control and losing it again. Warring in this exquisite blend of agony and bliss, love and violence. That was what passion was, really. At least it always had been for them. And they would have it tonight, and it would not be the last time.

They waited several minutes in quiet, lying side by side on the ground. Kasia could hardly hear past the hard pounding of her pulse in her ears, couldn't think much beyond the slow circles Reyan's thumb trailed on her wrist.

"Kasia," he said.

It had been long enough since either of them had spoken that the sound of his voice made her jump.

"Sorry," he said, laughing.

"What?" she rolled over, leaning on her hand.

"I wanted to know if you would do something for me?"

"Gods, already?" she said, glancing down his body.

"You are wicked," said Reyan, grinning. "No. I wanted to know...a long time ago, I walked into these rooms and I heard you playing your violin."

Heat rushed to Kasia's face for some reason, as though the mention of his hearing her play was somehow more personal than what they'd just done. "Yes," she said.

"I wondered if you would play for me."

Kasia met his eyes. "You have such a fondness for the violin."

"Yes," he said.

"Do you play?"

"Oh gods, no." Reyan started laughing, shaking as he did. "My mother insisted I learn when I was a boy, much to the chagrin of my father, and she found herself sorely disappointed in my musical prowess."

"Perhaps you just didn't find the right instrument."

"No," said Reyan. "We tried a *great* many. Every last one I could get my hands on. My rhythm leaves something to be desir—"

"Your rhythm is perfectly adequate. You danced beautifully at our wedding."

Reyan said, "Well that rhythmic skill does not extend to my fingers."

"I beg to differ," said Kasia, smirking, and Reyan pushed her shoulder lightly.

"I also have no ear for tone."

"Really?"

"Ask me to sing something for you, and you'll believe me."

Kasia laughed, then rolled over onto her back. She reached for one of Reyan's shirts, which lay crumpled on the floor, and sat up to pull it over her head.

"What are you doing?"

"I'm not going to play for you naked," Kasia said.

Reyan laughed and sat up, pulling a sheet over his hips and leaning back against the wall. "So you will play for me."

Kasia walked to the closet and pulled the violin down, cradled it to her. She plucked each string and left the closet with it. She sat on the floor, refusing to look at Reyan, and plucked, turning the tuning knobs so the noises shifted from dissonant to lovely. Then she brought it to her chin and drew out her bow, and began to play.

She chose a song of the winter—it had always sounded like snowfall to her when she was a girl, and perhaps part of that was that she had learned it in the dead of the cold season. But there was something magical about this particular song—quick in the beginning, then slow and languid as the chill set in, and the rivers froze. It was little flakes of ice falling quietly to the earth, changing it speck by speck. It was winter. It was Reyan.

She looked up as it ended and saw him, head leaned against the wall, eyes closed. "Thank you," he whispered.

She set the violin to the side and crawled over to him, then lay her head against his chest before they both slid into bed.

Kasia spent most of the night in the quiet, listening to Reyan turn pages in the book she'd found for him in the market. And when the pages stopped turning and she thought he'd fallen asleep, she lay awake wondering, wondering, thoughts tearing too quickly through her head. She was worried for tomorrow, for her, for Reyan, for too many things to count.

Reyan whispered to her, in the middle of the night, "Kasia."

She said, "Yes?"

He said, "Have your gods ever spoken to you?"

Kasia's pulse spiked. As though she owed him her relationship with Death. She said, and it was not exactly a lie, "No."

Reyan ran his fingers over the scars that peppered his skin. He said, "I haven't—"

"What?"

"Nothing. Forget I said it. I'm just...tired."

"No," said Kasia. "I've been bored for hours, and I'm desperate for conversation."

"I haven't spoken to Thakros in weeks. Since..."

"You haven't spoken to him, or he hasn't spoken to you?"

Reyan did not answer.

Kasia stared at the split in the sky and wondered.

Wondered if Reyan's god ignored him for what they'd done, what they'd been *set up* to do, or if he ignored him because of what had happened with the sky.

It was not until dawn broke the sky that a familiar soothing, cool voice began to whisper words of reassurance in her ear. *Sleep, darling girl. You are safe. Sleep. I swear to you that the world will turn if you do. I am here.*

It was not an answer to the question she'd been whispering over and over. But it didn't need to be. Not yet. She clung to the most powerful presence in this world and the next, and the solid surety with which he whispered to her. And she fell asleep in the grey light to the soothing caress of the power and certainty in his voice.

CHAPTER FORTY-FOUR

G ALLIEN DID NOT FEEL the fire of battle pumping through her veins. She hardly felt the fire at all.

All she felt was emptiness and nerves. Her body did it whether or not she wished it to. She shut her eyes as the fleet moved forward, salt wind over the sea caressing her skin, propelling her on. The *Horizon's Promise* was surrounded by war ships, so many of them Gallien couldn't count.

The official plan was not overly complicated—in fact, it was downright simple, a rare moment of quick black and white in a war. They would storm Jaelen's port. And Jaelen, of course, would be waiting. They knew Va'al had a decent sized navy. They had no idea just how large, of course, which would work to their advantage. And they further did not know that Andra had forces *everywhere* that they had called upon. That Va'al was an afterthought in this battle. The Jaelenian king and queen would assume the battle to be impulsive, terribly planned and executed, the whim of a hurt royal.

They could not know that this was something Andra had apparently been planning intricately for years. The Va'alian king, of course, knew, and had been more than happy to be the vehicle.

Not that the bastard was here. Even on a mission to rescue his son, the damned old coward preferred to remain safely curled away in his throne room, tucked in the comfortable dark. Let the armies get him. That wasn't a king's job. Gallien's lip curled.

If he had not deigned to protect him personally, —and she had known he wouldn't—then she would take care of the prince for him.

A small hand slid over hers as she stared out over the endless ocean that suddenly seemed so confined—there was a port at the end of it, after all. And she and hers would have to storm it. Gallien was so very good at war. And she hated it so very much.

Leylya's hand surprised her. She had thought the girl would be with Nazalie. Probably, she would go to her after they were done talking. Gallien tried not to let it hurt.

"Are you ready?" Gods, Leylya's voice was so soft and lilting. She almost shivered at hearing it so close. But she didn't. Her face remained carefully unchanged.

"Of course," said Gallien. "Are you?" She slid a glance over at the girl who could easily bring her to her knees.

Leylya said, "I always am."

They locked eyes, and Gallien found herself saying, "Leylya," through traitorous lungs.

Leylya cocked her head, playful challenge in the raise of her eyebrow.

Gallien opened her mouth to say something, and the words died in her throat. So she said instead, "It will be you and me out there, at the gates."

Leylya blinked. "Y—yes," she said. She slid her hand away, and Gallien's skin noticed its absence.

"Stay close to me during the fight. When we break off and cut our way through the city to those gates, I don't want to lose you." *I don't want to lose you.*

Leylya swallowed and nodded. "Of course, Captain. Nor I, you."

"If I lose you, those gates will be awfully difficult to raise by myself. And then we'll be responsible for the loss of a war."

"Yes," said Leylya, with a little nod. And she left.

Gallien curled her fingers over the wood rail of the ship and waited for the horizon to come into view. They were all armored, and they outnumbered the Jaelenian force significantly. This would be all right; *they* would all be all right.

She would begin her vengeance today.

And they would be all right.

Gods, she needed a drink.

She waited, watching, fingers jumping between the rail and her sword, until the waters lightened, and a distant shore came into view.

The *Horizon's Promise* was nestled safely in the middle of the fleet of Va'al's ships. It needed to be if it was to break off from the fighting and she and hers were to carve their way through the capital city, to let those waiting outside the gates inside. But simply being surrounded did not mean they were safe.

And when they got closer to the shore, a deep, wicked cold lit her bones. Fear.

Something stirred in her gut—a warning. Something about the sea whispered to her to turn back.

"Yaloi," Gallien started, looking back over her shoulder, and then the first wave hit.

The boat rocked violently, tipping for a moment, frigid spray licking over the edge. Gallien nearly fell. "What in hells?"

"Captain," someone cried, and Gallien couldn't figure who, because the ocean was suddenly roaring.

A deep frown lined her brow and she peered out over the sea, which was now dark. Violently dark.

"What is happ—"

Another wave. This time larger, soaking the floor completely. Gallien slipped on the wet wood below her, and braced herself.

She stood, then, deepest fear settling in her muscles, wrapping up to claw its way around her throat.

The temperature dropped around them, and she peered out into the dark. A rushing filled her ears. Then, a low, mournful noise, as if the sea itself was groaning.

"Leylya!" Gallien called, as though could do anything. As though if Leylya were close, Gallien could protect her.

The girl, of course, couldn't hear her.

There was a beat of silence, of utter, still dark.

And then a cyclone burst out of the water with a noise loud enough to shatter a person's eardrums, or at least, Gallien wondered if it had shattered hers.

It popped up at the front of the fleet, splintering ships and sending men hurtling into the frigid, dark sea.

Gallien leapt back as the hurricane grew and screamed, "Avoid it, avoid it! We cannot get caught in this storm or the whole battle is lost! Shit!"

Her feet scrambled for purchase as the moaning wind grew around them, and the sky lightened—from black to a stormy grey. And suddenly Leylya was at her side again. She was soaked, dripping, rare panic in her eyes.

"What in hells is going on?" she shrieked over the sound of the storm.

"I don't—" Gallien froze. "Wait. Look," she said, and she inclined her head toward the shore, which was coming clearly into view now. Leylya followed her gaze.

Far back on the beach, two tall people were moving their arms with the storm, ice and water and wind flowing out from their fingers.

The king and queen of Jaelen were here. And they had come for a fight.

CHAPTER FORTY-FIVE

HOLY GODS, VA'AL'S NAVAL fleet was massive. Much larger than Reyan had ever imagined. It wasn't unbeatable, but they hadn't prepared for this.

Shit.

Shit.

"Kasia," he said. His voice sounded exactly as worried as he felt, which he was not accustomed to.

"I know," she said.

The ships got closer, and Reyan wrested the ocean into his grasp. He willed mist to rise from the surface of the sea, a heavy fog billowing out to coat the ships and muddy the visions of the rocks at shore. The cyclone was whirling on its own now, so he and Kasia could focus their energies elsewhere, and Kasia was pushing hers toward that thick blanket of fog.

Sweat beaded up on both of them; the entire surface of Reyan's skin was damp. Fear tore at his throat. Those ships could *not* break the beach. Their naval forces absolutely could not press past the docks into the city. Jaelen's strength was in its walls, and the archers lining it were easily decimating the soldiers who approached from the fields. They were more numerous than Reyan had accounted for as well, but beatable.

If they could hold this damn beach.

Their own sea forces were being picked off, ship by ship, and anxiety welled up in his chest like a monster. Hells, when the scout had returned early this morning, Reyan had panicked and enlisted merchant ships to fight. Half the people on that water weren't even soldiers. They were bodies to fight through. And the cyclone could just as easily rip through them as the enemy.

"Archers!" Reyan cried, voice roaring into the chaos of the sea battle. "Draw!"

His muscles were shaking. They burned with the exertion of the fog. Kasia had dropped to her knees. But her arms held.

The line of archers that shielded them dipped their cloth-wrapped arrows in oil then lit them. They raised their arrows to fire them at nothing but freezing fog.

How many of their own ships would burn?

Reyan swallowed the terror, the sudden, choking guilt. "Fire!" he called, and the fog thickened when he dropped to the ground, arms raised over his head.

A chorus of screams rose up from the sea. Splashes everywhere.

Kasia nodded at Reyan and dropped her arms, as did he, so the fog receded. The cyclone had quieted, fading back into the sea. And on the water, ships were burning.

Black smoked plumed into the sky, and too many ships drew closer. They were a mess, and what had been hundreds of small boats was now fifty, but fifty was too many; it was too many.

And where in hells was Farowfin? They should have been here by now. Unless something had gone wrong. Perhaps they'd gone back on their promise, or perhaps Andra had forces stationed everywhere, places he didn't know about, and they'd cut the army off. They wouldn't have held back because he'd cut funds for their damned celebration. No. They wouldn't...Dammit. Gods dammit.

Was this what Va'al had wanted? Was this why they had sent someone to assassinate Kasia in the first place? To bait him into a war he knew he'd win, then trap him once he was already so far in it that he couldn't escape?

"Again!" Reyan roared.

They were too close to shore now. If he and Kasia raised another cyclone, it could spin out of control and jump up onto land. Rip through their soldiers.

Kasia steered the wind so the boats heading for them moved haphazardly. But they were coming.

Reyan drew a ragged breath, glancing down at the water, then froze.

Hells. He could do this. He could do it.

He inched toward the shore and Kasia screamed, "Reyan, what are you doing? You're unprotected! Reyan!"

But her voice faded into the din when he dipped his hand in the water. And it froze around his fingers.

He ripped his hand away once the process had begun and ran back to the cover of the men, just as an arrow from the sea flew over his shoulder, and another, on fire, singed the hair that hung over his ears. He ducked behind a large rock with Kasia, smell of burnt hair rising between them. Then he popped his head over, slick with sweat that stung his eyes, and whipped his burning arms toward the water. Slowly, too slowly, it began to freeze.

Ice seeped out where there should have been water, and little by little, feet out from the shore, the sea froze.

"Holy hells," Kasia breathed. She grinned at him for a half-second. "You're welcome," she said. His power would never have approached the strength to freeze the sea without her.

Reyan laughed once. Loud and clear as a bell.

Then he turned his focus back to the ocean and willed the freeze the spread faster.

But quicker than he should have, he felt himself reaching for the dregs of his power. He furrowed his brow and stumbled.

He was exhausted.

Suddenly, not just tired, not simply worn, utterly gone into his bones. He blinked and closed his fingers into a fist. Let the waters do as they would.

He would—he would wait.

Kasia worked the wind, tried to push them back, and several small boats caught it the wrong way, gusting east with the breeze. One crashed into the ice and splintered. And twenty men came pouring out of it, slipping and falling everywhere on the wet, slick surface.

Reyan almost felt a heartbeat of pity when every one of them was met with an arrow to the chest, the leg, the eye. It didn't matter where they were hit; they all fell. And the moment they did, Kasia shifted her attention from the wind to the water, opening the seas under them, then refreezing it. The ones who weren't dead already would drown.

Reyan swallowed hard and stared down at his wife. But she was already working the winds again, directing a hundred sailors to death on, and then beneath, the ice.

Gods, that fleet.

There weren't enough soldiers on this beach, and Reyan's lungs felt like they were filled with shards of rock and ice. Like if he made another move, he would be crushed from the inside.

"Kasia," he said.

She nodded once. "I know." Her voice was exhausted, and she was pale. "I know," she choked out, and she swept her hand out in another grand arc before she collapsed to the sand.

CHAPTER FORTY-SIX

"U SE IT!" LEYLYA SHRIEKED. "Gallien, you have to!"

Jaelen did not have an impressive navy, but the few ships it had left were closing in on them. Gallien and her warriors wore blood red armor, and she herself was a foot taller than most women should have been. People had heard her name. They knew that she and her warriors were women to *fear*.

So here they were, these foolish men, closing in.

"Gallien! Gods!"

Gallien gritted her teeth, rage welling up in her chest. She shouldn't have to do this, shouldn't have to do this for the king just for the right to fucking sail.

She did not think about the fact that her magic was draining every time she used it.

She did not think about the punishment she might receive for having hid this for a decade. Leylya's face flashed in her mind. And then Proch's. No. She could not think about them, and whether they would suffer for it. There was *no time*.

Fire licked up her arm as she drew it across her body, and she lashed out, lighting three Jaelenian boats. The blaze was haphazard, and not as high as she would have liked, but it did enough. The screams and the sudden smell of burning flesh turned her stomach.

"We can't get straight to that port, Yaloi. The damned king has frozen the whole thing to ice."

"What do we do?" she said. "Land on the rocks?"

Gallien looked over at the rocks that jutted up just to the side of the ice.

"Better than landing right in the ice and getting closed into it by that witch queen; go!"

The ship veered right.

Va'alian forces were beginning to land, and though many of them were being trapped, crushed and suffocated beneath the ice, several had made it to the beach. There were simply too many ships for one pair of royals to hold them all off, no matter how inhumanly powerful they were. And the ice didn't look as though it was melting beneath the feet of the soldiers anymore.

Perhaps they were drained.

"We have to get there now!" Gallien cried. The rocks approached. "Gods," Gallien whispered. "Please do not take my ship."

They slammed into a submerged rock with much more force than Gallien had thought they would, and she felt the ship crack in her bones. It would be fine, it would be fine, it had to be fine.

She could feel it scrape the sand, and then it stopped.

Gallien breathed deep and sprinted to the bow of the ship, where her warriors were gathering to leave.

She stood steady, legs wide and solid, and pumped her fist in the air. "Sha'aran kasaleem!" *Life and death.*

They shouted back, "Anoha-iri travell!" *In our steel.*

"Kha-den vo iri isen!" *And the sea goes red.*

In one voice, "Vik mara zhalen." *With the blood of men.*

They poured out into the knee-deep water.

Gallien and Leylya came last, and the stunning cold of the water stabbed into Gallien's calves like shards of ice so sharp they should have had hilts.

Her breath froze in her lungs.

But Leylya moved forward, and so Gallien drew a ragged breath and moved forward with her.

They had landed on the side farthest from the king and queen, thank the gods. Several soldiers had already stormed the beach, and many lay dead on the melting ice or the sand that was darkening with their blood. But several of Jaelen's archers lay dead as well, and their forces were dwindling already. Archers had begun firing from the boats to the beach, and some of their arrows were landing.

Gallien filled her lungs and exhaled slowly to steady herself. Then she lit the beach on fire.

The panic was instant.

Several of her girls were able to scramble up past the line of archers just from the shock and the smoke. Gallien sprinted up to them before the royals on the far side of the dock had the chance to notice and douse her fire, and she cleaved one man's head from his shoulders. It landed on the ground with a sickening thump, and blood sprayed across her face. Leylya was just ahead of her, stabbing a burning woman in the back.

She and Leylya carved their way through the beach together, like one person in two places; they had always fought like this. And after the fifth or sixth man fell, Gallien began to feel that familiar adrenaline, the heady rush of battle that always shamed her later and fueled her now.

In this moment, Gallien was not just a warrior; she was an artist, and her medium was blood.

The city appeared as they crested the beach. It hadn't gone as smoothly as they'd planned, but nothing ever did. The assault was supposed to have been quick and overwhelming, and Gallien and her battalion were supposed to have split off from the massive fleet right away, and snuck quickly through the city, as close to undetected as possible.

Of course, as the gods and fate had had it, they'd had to cut a line right through the middle of everyone, and Gallien chose not to think about the soldiers of hers who might have been lying dead in the streets, or were dying still.

She couldn't think about it. All she could think about was sprinting through this city and raising the gate.

"Gallien!" she heard, a desperate yell from up ahead. She quickened her pace, every muscle already burning, head filled with the push to move, to keep moving. The gate, the gate, the gate.

It was Leylya. Of course it was.

"Oh, thank the gods," Leylya said, nearly gasping when she tried to breathe. "I saw someone fall back there, and I thought it was…and then Yaloi—"

Gallien gripped Leylya's face, hands like vices. "Do not think of Yaloi," she said. Leylya's eyes shone with fear and the fierce passion and bloodlust of war. Someone's blood had splattered her and rested in an angry line in the scar that split her face. "If I fall, you do not think of me either. You think of that gate, Leylya. All that matters is raising that gate. Do you understand?"

Leylya shut her eyes for an instant, allowed herself a single steadying breath. Then she said, "Yes, Captain," and they moved together through a panicked ruin of a city.

Jaelen relied mostly on its walls, but inside, its city was heavily guarded as well because of the port. Guards were stationed everywhere, and Gallien and Leylya and the rest of them, wherever they were, were not inconspicuous. Scarlet armor and women soaked in blood did not blend easily into a crowd.

Further, the only people outside their homes were dead or soldiers. No civilians had chosen this moment to go shopping at the market.

So they ran through the streets, and every guard not stationed at the wall or the beach knew that they were enemies.

But Gallien was no ordinary enemy. Dammit, she was a legend.

She did not cower when men came at her with their swords drawn and their faces contorted in a battle-provoked rage. She only ran faster, slicing through their torsos and necks like they were nothing.

After they'd been running long enough that they'd covered half the city, Gallien shrunk back against the wall with Leylya, just for a second to breathe.

"You're drenched," she said.

Leylya laughed. "In blood or sweat?"

"Both, I imagine." Gallien looked up at the sky. "Do you think any of them has made it there yet? Do you think they've raised the gates?"

Leylya shook her head. "If they had, this city would be swarmed already. And those royals would have fled it."

Gallien breathed. "Gods. I'm so tired already."

"We will *do this*," said Leylya. "You and I. Captain."

She stared at the stone on the ground then locked eyes with Leylya. A heartbeat of quiet.

"Let's go."

They burned their way through the rest of the city. It didn't matter who saw her wield her flame now. She'd done it enough, the world would know soon. And it didn't matter. She would never bow to them simply because of what she *could* do. She would do what she wished and set the world on fire if they tried to get in her way.

As she did with Jaelen.

The walls came into view, and so many women she'd sailed with were already there, hacking their way through the guards. There were bodies on the ground, but Gallien didn't look at them. She couldn't—couldn't see a member of her crew lying there if she wanted to get this done. The time for mourning was later.

This was the time for war.

The archers on the wall who, Gallien assumed, had been stationed there to attack the soldiers outside had turned inward. One or two of them had been shot in the back by the few archers who waited outside the walls on the plains, but a good number of them were firing on her and her soldiers.

Gallien curled her fingers into a fist, every muscle in her body tightening, then she whipped her hands in the air and released, fire shooting in a blaze from her fingers. They were high—too high. But her flames reached their feet, and that was enough.

Shrieks rose up from the walls, and in the confusion, Gallien broke away to the gate. There were guards stationed there, of course, but most of her soldiers had been fighting here already, and none of the guards could spare an instant to turn toward Gallien and Leylya when they were worried about the steel flashing toward them from all sides.

Gallien took hold of the lever and pulled, and Leylya pulled with her. Sweat beaded up on her brow, on her arms and shoulders, soaked her beneath the armor, and Leylya's face reddened with the exertion. But the gate rose.

And by the time the guards turned to focus on them, the gates were too high, and soldiers from the outside were pouring through.

Gallien looked up to see a flash of terror in an archer's eyes when she broke the lever altogether, sticking the gate where it was.

They hadn't known. Of course they hadn't. Jaelen's army was fighting outside the gates and lining the walls and working the beach. Their forces were admirable. But they could not have known that they would be facing Andra and Andra's small armies from every side, Va'al's navy, and thousands of soldiers all at once.

In the archer's eyes, Gallien saw the fear of a man who had thought he would go home tonight after a swift battle and eat dinner with his family. And who now knew that his world was going to burn.

Gallien shut her eyes for a moment, then steeled herself against the city wall, Leylya leaning beside her.

Gallien nodded at the girl, and they poured into the city with the rest of them.

CHAPTER FORTY-SEVEN

R I WAITED UNTIL THE gates were open. He had his horses tied and waiting far outside the city walls, hidden in the shadows. They snorted and hoofed at the ground, kicking up dust and breaking the sharp silence around him.

The quiet was contained only to the several feet around him, stillness in the trees. Outside the wood, there were men. Hundreds, perhaps thousands. Ri hadn't stayed there long enough to find out the battle plans. But those didn't matter.

He was certain the king wasn't marching. He was certain he'd sent someone else to find his son, and those someone elses would not be able to get to Adè until they'd broken through Jaelen's walls and the entire battle was over. Then they would look for him in the smoking remains. The Va'alian soldiers were not known for their stealth.

Ri swallowed hard and rolled his shoulders.

If you don't come back, Adè had said, *I will cross the sea to find you.*

Well, Ri had crossed the plains. And he would not leave without his prince.

He wore black leather—hot, particularly in the crushing humidity, but tough enough to stop a blade if it needed.

And when the gates rose and the army poured in, Ri waited several minutes—long enough that most of the din had moved away from the entrance, but not so long that he risked getting lost in the next wave that was coming.

He slipped into the city without a sound, and slid in and out of empty alleyways for the castle.

He'd been there enough times that he could get there without much issue. And as he was in nothing but leather, clearly not a soldier, and an Etryan, no soldiers on either side gave him much trouble. That was fortunate, as his shin was on fire. The pain had dulled the longer he'd ridden, but it was still there, pulsing with every step. He was slower than he would have liked.

He disappeared into the forest that bordered the castle, where he was supposed to have escaped with Nagonia after his failed attempt at assassinating the Jaelenian queen, and snuck quietly in through the servants' entrance.

"Go!" he heard as she shrunk back into the shadows. "We have to defend the city; the damn prince doesn't matter. Holy gods, they're going to take it. They're going to take it."

A few soldiers ran past him, coming within feet of where he hid in the leaves, and Ri was silent.

In minutes, the palace grounds were empty. Empty and eerily quiet. It was too simple. Ri feared, as he slunk across the grounds to the little building set far enough away from the palace that it must have been the dungeon, that perhaps the sky itself would open up to resist him.

Something had to.

But perhaps he would reach Adè's cell before it did.

The walk felt long. An absolute eternity waited between him and his destination. But there was no one there. And there was no one to stop him heading straight down into the dungeons.

They were damp and dark and made of stone, like most dungeons, he figured, but larger than those of Andra.

"Adè?" he said. Several catcalls from prisoners he was certain couldn't even see him. Swears, and several words he couldn't make out.

He wound through the cells, digging deeper and deeper, and the darkness blackening, until he was lower in the earth than he'd ever been. The air was both cool and crushing, and every time he breathed, particles of dirt invaded his lungs.

"Adè?" he said. A bit farther. "Adè?"

He stilled. If the prince was here and conscious, he would answer.

Just when panic had begun to wrap its fingers around his heart, he heard it: "Hello?" That smooth baritone that quickened his pulse and warmed his blood. Adrenaline coursed through him. Adè was here.

He followed the echo through the dripping hall to the last cell in the whole block. And dropped to his knees at the bars. "Adè. Gods, you're alive. You're alive."

Seeing him like this, clammy, wrists shackled to the wall, breathing ragged, blood dried on his face, Ri was seized with panic. For a moment, he was back in there, back in Andra's prison. He couldn't think past the pain of hunger, the desperate want for water, the sharp pain that cut through his back and wrists every time he moved.

"Ri?" said Adè, and Ri blinked, back to the present. The darkness crushed in on his lungs, but more than that, destroying him was this picture of the prince. Ri grabbed the bars and tried to breathe without sobbing from the pain at seeing him here, and the immense relief.

"Yes," he said. "I'm here. I've come for you."

Adè stared up at him, and Ri could hardly make out his face in the dark. But he could see the anguished lines, the regretful light in his eyes. *I should have come for you as well*, they said. But it didn't matter; none of it mattered.

"I have to get you out of here," said Ri. "Where do they keep the keys? Do you know?"

Adè shook his head. "I didn't see, but—the king. He came down here personally. More than once. And each time it's been him with the key, and he puts it back in his pocket and takes it with him. The guards had to go find him whenever they needed it. I think he must keep it with him. But if he's fighting...in his rooms, maybe?"

Ri groaned. The king's rooms were all the way across the grounds. "This is very inconvenient, Prince," he said. "Perhaps I'll leave you here."

Adè smiled and leaned his head up against the wall, broad chest rising and falling, rising and falling. Too slowly. But it was enough. "I'll reward you handsomely if you don't," said the prince.

Ri's pulse quickened, and he grinned. "I'll be back," he said, and he left, winding his way through the labyrinth that was these dungeons. Some kind of grime on the walls coated his arms when he got too close to them, and he scowled. Always something; gods, it was always something.

The king's rooms were far, but they didn't look so impossible to reach, not without guards swarming all over the grasses. Ri's leg hurt. And he was tired.

But tiredness was nothing. Not next to the energy that flowed through him, crackling like lightning, at the promise of Adè and riding with him away from all this shit.

He jumped into the open window of the shrine, a deep sense of wrongness, of foreboding, washing over him, just being here. He never had felt good about having attempted a murder in here, in front of the gods. And perhaps they were unhappy about it, too. Or at least one of them was.

Ri rushed from the room as quickly as he could. Then he ran up the long, dark hall and forced himself up some of the steepest stairs he'd ever seen in his life. Holy hells, did the king and queen descend these every day?

His muscles were being torn apart by the time he reached the top.

Ri pushed open the door to the king's rooms. And froze.

He was not alone.

CHAPTER FORTY-EIGHT

I T BECAME VERY CLEAR, very quickly, that they were going to lose. Kasia had never seen such a fleet on the sea, and she had never heard such a roar as she heard the moment Va'al broke through the gates. And she was quite certain she had never, ever seen a look in Reyan's eyes as sick with fear as she saw now.

They had fled the rock at the beach long ago, and were now holed up near the palace, in a small inn that the Va'alian soldiers had yet to raid.

Reyan peered out the window. "It's not just Va'al; it can't be. Their whole damn country couldn't hold this many people, let alone house this kind of army."

"Those colors are Andran, Reyan."

Reyan swore. "I had no idea they even had a treaty, or I never...dammit. Gods dammit. There's—Kasia." He turned to her and grabbed her arms. "There's nothing we can do. I can't—I can't use any more magic. It's like every time I do, it leaves. I'm fucking exhausted. And they just keep coming. Our scouts didn't see because they come in waves. The second and third were so far off, they didn't even know they were on their way. And did you see the pirate lord? Did you see her spitting *fire* from her fingers? None of the stories ever...I don't know where in hells Farowfin is—probably an army of theirs is destroyed somewhere in the north."

He paused, and Kasia just looked at him. She had the grace not to say, *I warned you not to rescind your funds. I warned you.*

He coughed and continued, "Andra and Va'al have breached the gates, and half our forces are stationed elsewhere, because I thought—shit. I thought it was just them. I've ruined everything." He sucked in a breath. "I've destroyed our whole country, Kasia. How in the hells..."

Kasia pulled free of his hands to frame his face in her own. "No. This is war, King. The greatest men are felled by steel, and you will not take this upon yourself. And none of that matters now. What matter is what we do here, in this instant."

"We have to flee," he said. His voice broke on the word. He was devastated. Disgusted at the thought. But he was right. There was no sense in going down with the ship. It did nothing but add another body to the water. "We're royals, not soldiers. If they catch us, they will execute us in a public square. And then there's no hope for Jaelen at all, and you and I are dead."

"You're right," she said.

"Don't do that," said Reyan.

Kasia furrowed her brow. "Do what?"

"Agree with me. It's unsettling." Reyan's lips turned wryly for a moment, and Kasia hit him in the chest, then pulled her hand to herself with a sharp cry. Punching armor was a terrible idea.

"Where shall we go? The forest?"

Reyan looked out the window again. "Forces are beginning to gather outside the palace. If we go now, I think we can make it there before—shit."

"What?"

"Proch. He'll be with the guard, defending there. I have to find him. He's my cousin, and the only person in this world apart from you that I—"

"Go," said Kasia. "Get Proch. I will meet you at the grove. The one—"

"I know the one," said Reyan.

Kasia nodded and took a deep breath. Then she reached for the door, but before her fingers brushed the handle, Reyan grabbed her arm and twisted her into him. His lips crushed into hers, stealing her breath, tongue tasting every surface of her mouth. She reached for Reyan's hair, fingers fisting in the curls, and his strong hands pressed her into him.

"I love you," he whispered, and she could feel the feathering of his breath over her lips.

"As I love you," Kasia said, "boy king."

"Holy gods," was the last thing she heard him say before she stole out onto the city streets.

Her armor was safely secured around her, and it allowed her to move like water, which was comforting as the streets were lined with madness. The city was burning, and blood colored the grey stones on the ground. Everywhere she looked, swords clanged and crashed, and she couldn't move without hearing another scream. Men, women, they came from everywhere. Shame strangled her at the thought of abandoning this city, *her* city, her country, like this. But what choice did she have?

She looked up at the palace grounds, which were so quiet and empty, particularly given the lunacy just outside the gates. She couldn't cut her way through that throng; she was too drained already, and her bad leg was giving her more than a trivial amount of trouble. But she could take the back entrance.

The servants' entrance. There were two, one on either side of the grounds. She needed to cross the palace lands entirely to get to the clearing where she was to meet Reyan, but on this side of the grounds, she could slip into the dense trees and at least get inside the fences.

She limped back from the storefront into the cover of the wood, away from the din and mess of blood, and struggled to climb over the servants' gate, then slid down the other side to fall to the ground. Her bones rattled from it, and she hissed and grabbed at her leg. But she was inside. All she needed to do was get across the grounds, and she would be safe. Or as close to it as was possible.

But then, she looked over outside the front gate—yards and yards away. And all the fighting wormed into her ears. Proch's face, Reyan, desperate and exhausted, and mad with love for her. And she...she couldn't. She couldn't just run away. Couldn't disappear into the trees. Slip away like a ghost and wait for him, praying that he would come to her.

She let her gaze slide up to her room. It was the tallest tower in the city, or one of them, anyway. An incredible vantage point. How many times had she cursed it while climbing the stairs every night and descending them every morning? From there, she could see everything. She could wreak havoc on the world.

Her heart steeled.

She would make for her rooms.

Even though she was just this side of drained, so exhausted she could hardly stand, fear and a strange sense of valor washed over her. She limped the whole way there, and her leg screamed in pain with every step she took. Damn that Etryan assassin; it would take her twice as long as it should have to get there.

Kasia inched across the field, and the tower rose taller and taller in front of her. Yes. She could do this. Perhaps she could even turn the tide from up there.

Perhaps she would not flee at all.

Kasia went straight through the little passage that was known only to she and Reyan—the one that went directly to her rooms. She had no time for anything else. And she limped up the steep stairs, breathing ragged. She could do this, she could do this. She could save Proch. She could save Reyan. She could save them all.

Her rooms were empty and still and filled from wall to wall with memories. Gods, no, she couldn't think that way. She had no use for memories. This wasn't over.

Kasia hobbled over to the floor-to-ceiling window, which she'd left open from the previous night. A smirk turned her lips.

Then she looked down. Bodies and steel and flashes of grey and silver and chilling red. Reyan was down there somewhere. Fortunately, he was in charcoal grey armor, while Va'alians wore blue. Andrans wore gold. And there was the occasional burst of blood red that she assumed came from the only real legends Va'al had to its name—Gallien and her warriors. A shudder went down her spine at every flash of scarlet she saw.

And that fear was enough to propel the ice and wind from her bones to the air.

From this distance, directing it was difficult, but she could try.

She put every bit of energy she had into summoning water from the ground to freeze the boots of the men wearing the wrong colors, give the Jaelenian soldiers enough time to cut them down.

Kasia itched to slice through the air with a knife of wind, but it was too risky. Too much power to risk cutting through her own people.

So she stuck to the ice. It roared through them, rippling men and raining panic down like water, and Kasia felt power surging through her veins. She was so exhausted, the force of it so heady, that she nearly laughed.

When she reared back to hit them with another blast, the door to her rooms slammed open.

Kasia, she heard, a frantic yell in her ear.

She whirled around, back to the open air, and her heart stopped.

The Etryan boy.

They locked eyes for one silent, charged moment, and a pain shot up through her right leg, so suddenly weak she could hardly stand on it.

Before she could remember to breathe, the boy had a dagger in his hand, and then it was flying through the air.

It embedded itself in her left leg, and she stumbled back. Her right refused to support her, and when she moved, she could feel the sharp windowsill dig into her already weakened, screaming thighs.

Her balance failed her.

There was nothing to catch her but the sky.

She fell.

CHAPTER FORTY-NINE

REYAN WATCHED FROM THE battle as his wife appeared in the window and wreaked havoc from the sky.

He watched her freeze the feet of the soldiers so he could hack them apart, and Proch joined him, drawing his sword from its sheath and stabbing with his arrows into the eyes of those close enough to meet an unfortunate fate at the tip of his steel.

He watched as the army slowly recognized the source of the elemental chaos and cursed her for not listening and fleeing immediately to the grove in the wood.

He watched a shadow appear in the doorway, and he watched her as she fell. And then, Reyan watched as a living myth, six feet tall and clad in scarlet armor, lit the ground on fire before Kasia hit it. If it had been unlikely anyone could have survived that fall, living through a drop into flames that high was impossible.

He fell to his knees. He couldn't breathe. No. *No.*

"Get up!" Proch screamed in his ear.

"Proch, she's—"

"I don't care! I don't care; get up!"

Proch sliced the throat of a soldier who had come for Reyan, and warm blood soaked Reyan's face. He stood, face contorted in rage. "Get down," Reyan said to Proch, voice low and dangerous, and Proch rolled to the ground.

Reyan let rage and pain burst out of his chest in a single explosion of ice and wind and rain, and the battleground was suddenly silent, apart from Reyan's violent scream.

His power was gone.

Everyone was frozen—each member of this little skirmish. All but Proch, who had been low enough to the ground to avoid it.

Reyan wondered absently if they would die. If the ice would hold long enough to suffocate every damn last one of them.

"Reyan, we have to go."

Reyan opened his mouth to protest. He wanted to cut down every soldier not in charcoal right then and there.

"We don't have *time*, King. We have to leave now!"

"But Kasia—"

"Is DEAD. I'm sorry, but she is dead, and you and I will be dead soon if we do not *go*."

Hot anger and anguish and a thousand unnameable things coiled up in Reyan until he was choking on all of it. He turned toward the tall, dark-skinned woman in the red armor and made for her. The ice had barely touched her, —she was too far away—but it would hold for another thirty seconds. Proch jerked him back by the armor at his neck.

"No," he screamed. His voice was utterly desperate. "We make for the stables, and we go. You can take your vengeance another day. These soldiers will thaw any minute. And the rest of the armies are coming. Come *on*."

Reyan swallowed, and his fists uncoiled. Though everything in his body begged him to leap right into that fire with Kasia and pull her from it and to rip Gallien's head from her body, he let Proch drag him away.

And he ran with his cousin for the stables.

They saddled all three moinchire horses in a panic, and the horses themselves seemed to sense it, anxious, and agitated, snorting and hoofing the ground.

They both mounted the animals and drug a third along, Reyan actively pushing thoughts of anything away, anything but getting out of here, getting far, far, far away.

The horses galloped, and his thighs bruised on the saddle. He was keeping up with Proch, but just barely, and they plunged deep and dark into the forest—the forest no one who wasn't mad would venture into, not past its edges. Far enough that the grove was long-gone, and it didn't matter because his wife would not meet him there.

Far and long enough that the freezing cold set in as day gave way to night, and they were so surrounded by trees there was hardly air to break them up.

Reyan had never been this far into the wood. People were suspicious of it, thought it haunted by spirits and moinchire. The moinchire were long, long dead, but that didn't stop people from inventing stories of their ghosts. And Reyan was not afraid of a tale.

What he was afraid of was the moment the horses nearly collapsed from exhaustion beneath them, and the cold of nighttime whispered into their bones, and they had to stop.

Eventually, they did.

Reyan fell to his knees on the black earth next to Proch. And he allowed himself to grieve over his legacy, over his kingdom and all the people in it. Of those people who hadn't escaped, who had lost everything because of his shortsightedness. Of the blood-soaked guilt that spread in his chest, and of silly things. Silly things like his books. And in particular, the one Kasia had given him.

When he let her name enter his mind, his throat closed up, lungs nearly caving in. Gods, holy gods, holy gods.

He didn't say a word to Proch when he ripped away from the little clearing and lost himself in the suffocating black wood. Proch didn't try to stop him, and even if he had, Reyan wouldn't have heard it.

She was dead.

Dead.

He had seen her fall, and her body was now ash. Everything in Reyan hardened, until every curve, every bit of softness in his soul was replaced by edges. Knives of pain and fury that sliced through his skin and burst him open. He tried to breathe and choked on the anger and grief, so quick and sharp that it was startling.

He'd had her. He'd *had her*, and now she was gone.

He roared into the still black of the forest, and the last bits of ice and wind left in the furthest recesses of his bloodstream roared out with him, carrying his rage on gusts and snowfall. Until the darkness was lit up with his power, until the very air feared him. He would burn the world to the ground.

Minutes, it raged. And raged and raged until Reyan was so spent that he couldn't keep it going. Couldn't even stand.

He heard Proch's voice, murmuring something he couldn't understand.

When he fell, his cousin sank to the ground with him and wrapped his arms around him while he wept himself raw. The exiled royals would form a plan tomorrow. Tomorrow they would think. And they would decide where in hells to ride and how to take revenge. But tonight, Reyan cried. And he fell into a fitful sleep against the chest of the one thing that had not, in an instant, been taken from him.

CHAPTER FIFTY

THE BLADE LANDED.

Kasia bled.

And she fell.

Ri blinked at the emptiness, at the sudden vacancy where the queen of a nation had once stood. It had been over so quickly that Ri had hardly had a chance to process what had just happened.

He had seen her, and instinct that screamed to kill or be killed had taken over.

He swallowed hard. She was dead. She was dead, and he was alive, and he was going to get Adè back. Right all of his wrongs.

Perhaps he should have felt guilt, but all he felt was a cold that wound with elation and popped in his chest. Ri clenched his teeth. He couldn't think about killing queens. He needed Reyan's key.

He tore the room apart. Books stacked everywhere, rumpled sheets, clothes, a violin in the middle of the floor that he stepped on before he saw it. It splintered under his feet.

Gods, where was it?

The army was close to breaking through into the palace. He needed it. He tore through every bottle, every glass in the bathroom, shattering oils and perfumes and soaps so sweet his stomach turned.

Gods, gods, gods. There wasn't time.

He overturned drawers and flipped books, then his leg lit with sudden agony, and he tripped into the king's nightstand. It fell.

When he could breathe past his screaming bone, he looked at the destroyed room around him. It wasn't here. Maybe a Jaelenian soldier would get to Adè, a final act of revenge. Or maybe Adè's father's soldiers would reach him first, and Ri could not decide which was worse.

He turned to leave, chest heavy with solid fear.

But as the items fell from the king's night table, out of the middle of what looked like a *very* old book, tumbled a key.

Ri froze, then reached for it.

This was it. It had to be, or Adè would go back to his father. His rotten father who'd never cared about anyone but himself, his power. Had never cared about Gallien, and certainly never about Ri, and never about his son. He had never loved Adè, or else he would have *been here*.

Ri was here.

He pocketed the key and barreled down the stairs, coming out by the shrine and sprinting as quickly as his long legs would carry him.

It was silent.

Ri frowned. What in all hells?

He slowly turned to find a group of soldiers, frozen. Several had breathed enough heat to have melted the ice around their noses and mouths, but there they were. Ri found himself standing there, mouth hanging open, frozen as all of them for a moment, before he decided that it didn't matter. It couldn't.

This was nothing but a strange opportunity from the gods. If this was the state of this army, and the rest of them had yet to arrive, then this was his only chance to grab Adè and flee. He shook his head and ran.

Ri pounded his way underground, leg zinging with pain every step of the way, back to the deep dark of the dungeon, until he hit Adè's cell.

"You're here," Adè breathed, voice thick with relief.

Ri cocked his head and smirked. "Of course I am."

He unlocked the door and strode in. His muscles didn't hurt, his bones didn't hurt; nothing did. He was fueled entirely by nervous excitement. For the first time in months, something was going to *work*.

Ri turned the key in the shackles at Adè's wrists, and they unfastened.

"Are you all right?" Ri said, taking a step back. Giving him space to breathe.

"Yes," said Adè. His lips were cracked, and his voice was hoarse, wrists rubbed pale and peeling. Ri cursed himself for not bringing water or salve or anything useful inside the gates. "There is war," said the prince.

Ri choked out, "Yes," as Adè stood on shaky legs and stretched his massive arms.

"Has my father come for me?"

Ri did not answer. The presence of someone else in the dungeons stole the silence from the room.

CHAPTER FIFTY-ONE

WHEN THE BATTLE AT the palace died down, Gallien was only mildly worse for the wear. She'd feared frostbite from the king's damned ice, but it hadn't come. She'd summoned fire, and the heat of her skin had melted through the ice in less than two minutes. Leylya was back with the rest of them at the gates, cheering victory.

They had taken the city.

Four of Gallien's girls lay dead, Yaloi included, and that cut her to her core. She would burn them all tonight and say a prayer to their gods as their bodies lit the black.

But at this moment, she had no time for grief.

She sprinted, soaking wet, to the dungeons.

While she'd been frozen, she'd seen Ri running for them, and something about that made a sick feeling well in her gut. What was he doing there? Gods, if he had his hands on Adè...but no, that didn't make sense.

She ran.

The dungeons were not far off, and no one was guarding them. The king's men could come at any second and wrench this from her, and she would be damned if she let them.

She was faster than any of them.

The dungeons rose up to meet her and she practically tumbled down the stairs, drawing her sword. Not that that was necessary; the prince was certainly chained behind bars, and she had no key. She would stop at the cell and light the boy on fire, even if it took every last bit of the magic in her bones.

And the king would know what it was to weep.

Her footsteps echoed in the stillness as she ran deeper, eyes searching every cell she passed. And she stopped just as she reached the bottom.

To find Ri, standing with the Va'alian prince, loosing him of his shackles.

"What in hells?" she said.

CHAPTER FIFTY-TWO

"**G**ALLIEN?" HE SAID.

She just stood there and blinked. "Ri. Stand aside."

Ri furrowed his brow and straightened. "I cannot."

"What are you *doing*?"

Ri let go of Adè's wrist and left the cell to face the pirate captain. "Gallien, what is this?"

"Are you rescuing him? You're *loyal* to the king?" Betrayal laced her voice. As though he owed her something. As though they were more than client and a woman who had provided a service.

Ri's voice turned dangerous. "I have no love for that man, and it seems neither do you."

"Good," she said. "Then stand aside."

She moved to cross him, and Ri stepped to the side, blocking her. "Why?"

"The prince is *mine*."

Ri's eyes widened. "You mean to...you mean to murder Adè?"

Gallien looked between them, and something like understanding washed over her eyes. "We don't have time for this; stand aside!" Her voice was hoarse. Exhaustion, bloodlust, want, so many things that combined into forcing Ri to draw his knives.

"If you want to leave, you will leave whatever this is, Gallien. I told you I was not someone to fight."

"And I told you. Neither am I." She came at him with her sword, and Ri's stomach knotted.

He spun out of the way of her blade and lashed out at Gallien's side with a dagger, but she had armor everywhere. And there was no way he was getting a shot at her face; she was too tall.

She slammed her sword toward him again, and Ri rolled. His leg felt like a thousand knives were puncturing it at once. He screamed and stumbled. He was shaking everywhere when she brought her sword down, a wicked blow intending to split him in half, and Ri rolled again, so it glinted off the stone. Then he slashed at her wrist. Blood poured from the wound, and Gallien yelled.

But it didn't stop her.

He was going to die. He was an assassin, but he'd brought a knife to a swordfight, and she was a damn living legend. He would die. Like this. In a wet hole in the ground.

She slashed again, and Ri's leg refused to budge.

"Tallel!" he cried. He couldn't roll.

And then Gallien fell. Her body lit on fire all at once, and Ri used his arms to pull himself backward across the stone, eyes wide and terrified.

She screamed and crashed to the floor, burning.

Adè stood behind her, fingers smoking. His eyes were hotter than the flames.

Adè stepped over her body and pulled Ri up by his arms, and Ri limped out of the dungeon, leaning on a man who he couldn't believe had the strength to support his weight.

"Are you all right?" said Adè when they hit the dungeon's mouth.

"Yes," said Ri. "Yes. Thank you; holy gods. I'm all right. It's only my leg." He could stand now, if he put next to no weight on the leg. He moved his arm off Adè's shoulder. He was all right. They had saved each other.

"Good. Then I need to know. Did my father come?"

Ri looked out over the palace grounds. "Your father has sent his warriors for you."

Adè's jaw locked. "That is not the same," he said. And Ri had not realized until this moment how perfect the man's accent was. That high Va'alian way of speaking that made everything he said sound as though it was a matter of importance. As if every word was a piece of a poem. "If I go with you," Adè said, "do you plan to return to Va'al?"

Ri steeled himself and stood very straight, his mouth a hard line. "No," he said.

Adè nodded, and Ri could see the strength beginning to return to him, just from being allowed to stand. Being given a choice.

"Where do we go?" said Adè, and through the ache in every bone and muscle in his body, Ri grinned.

It was not as difficult as it should have been to leave. Probably because by the time he and Ri had left, the soldiers were just beginning to thaw, and no one was in the condition to run after them or to recognize them at all—if they could even see them. The prince and the assassin were well-hidden, far enough off that no one could find them, and very soon, they were exiting through the servants' quarters into the forest that some believed was haunted.

They followed it, more slowly than Ri would have liked, until they reached the plains just outside the gates. It was empty, and the sounds of battle inside the city even seemed to be dying down. The city was quieting with its dead.

They crossed the plains swiftly, in the eerie quiet, both hobbling messes, and Ri nearly collapsed when they reached the trees. The horses were still there, thank the gods, and Adè drained the first water skin in seconds.

He said, "Gods. I'd forgotten how good water tasted."

"There's a cave just north of here," said Ri. "Far enough away and deep enough in this tangled mess of a forest that they won't come looking for us. But close enough that neither of us will tumble off our horses and die before we get there. We should go and camp for the night. Bandage your wounds. We'll lay a more concrete plan in the morning."

Adè said, "I cannot believe you got here this quickly. And you brought my horse."

Ri swallowed hard and mounted his horse, then waited for Adè to mount his.

"You once told me you would cross an ocean to find me," said Ri, and both men let the sentence hang in the quiet.

They rode north. Or what Ri supposed passed for riding. The horses hardly fit anywhere in this damned bramble of a landscape.

The cave was only as difficult to find as quite literally everything else in this forest. The trees were tangled and twisted, and it was no wonder people thought it was haunted. Ri wagered that many a person had ventured in here and gotten themselves lost. It would have been next to impossible to find a body in this wicked, thick dark. So the myths went that they had been spirited away by magical creatures. Ri did not think he believed in them.

But he did believe in the ability to get lost. And he was a very devout believer in death.

He began to worry when darkness fell, began to be concerned that perhaps he had not scouted as well as he should have, when Adè said, "Look," and pointed just to the east.

Ri's shoulders drooped in relief. There was the little cave.

It secured one thought in his mind at least: if he had had this difficult of a time finding the cave when he knew exactly what he was looking for, there was no way the Va'alian forces would.

Ri guided his horse toward the little opening in the rocks, muscles crying for it as though it was a palace. It may as well have been. He slid off his horse, and Adè did the same, though with considerably more groaning. Ri felt a pang of empathy. He knew, quite intimately, what that felt like. It was like death, or something worse.

They tied their horses to trees, and Ri gave them a bit of water, some grain he'd stolen. Then he took another skin and some dried fruit and meat from the saddlebags. "There's salve and ointment in yours," said Ri.

He nearly asked for some himself, but then realized Gallien hadn't actually cut him. Thanks to the prince.

They entered the cave, and Ri dropped their supplies off, then went about limping in the dark for several minutes, collecting things that looked like easy kindling. In the night, by himself, he stripped out of his leather and into a loose tunic. Something he could breathe in while he slept.

He dropped the kindling on the stone floor of the cave, and Adè waved his fingers to light it. In minutes, they were warm, and Ri looked up from the flames to find Adè with his shirt off, clean lines of his body bent so he could reach the cuts that stole across his torso and chest. He'd managed to bandage himself quite well and was securing the final wrap.

"Water?" he said, and Ri blinked down at the stone, then rolled the water skin to Adè, who took a long drink of it. He ate a handful of berries, several strips of dried meat. Tore into them, really. He was probably starving. Ri followed suit, if only to have something to do with his mouth.

Gods, this forest was quiet. There was nothing, save for the crackling fire and a few bugs and the sound of their breathing.

Adè leaned back against a wall in the cave's mouth, faint smile on his lips as he chewed on a mint leaf.

"Why did you come for me, Ri?"

Ri looked up, suddenly very nervous. Very tired, but also perhaps very, extremely, not-tired. "Because…"

Adè waited, but Ri wasn't sure what to say. How best to finish that sentence.

Adè said, "You knew the army was coming. That they would save me." He inched closer, and Ri swore he wouldn't be able to breathe. Perhaps it was the smoke. It was the smoke clouding his lungs; that was all. "So why did you risk your life?"

"Adè."

"Ri."

Ri scraped his teeth across his lip and spit out the flower he'd been chewing on for the last three minutes, entirely out of nervous anxiety. "Because I wanted—I wanted to give you a choice." He met Adè's eyes then, and set his jaw. A choice was something neither of them had ever had much of. The prince in particular. Ri was allowed to want that for Adè.

He was allowed to *want*.

Adè's eyes darkened. "Then I would like to return the favor."

Ri raised an eyebrow. "I'm afraid it's a bit late. I've already been to prison and out of it. And you did save my life in a cell, besides."

"No, you ass. A choice. I'd like to give one to you."

Ri crisscrossed his legs and leaned forward. "I'm listening."

"You can kiss me," said Adè, "or not."

Ri choked.

Adè did not move.

There was a heartbeat of quiet before Ri grabbed the back of Adè's neck and kissed him. Adè slid his hand down Ri's back, cupped the back of his head with the other, fingers tangling in his hair, and bit his lip. Ri sucked in and let Adè move over him, back pressed to the cave wall. Maybe he still couldn't quite breathe, but maybe he didn't want to. Maybe he didn't want anything but his own fingers sliding over this prince's chest and bandages, moving softly over the places Ri knew he was bruised.

Maybe he wanted a moment where he didn't have to think about who he'd killed, and who he needed to kill next, and the look on Kasia Vane' face before she'd fallen from that tower, the sickening give in her leg when he'd thrown that knife.

Maybe all he wanted was to be thoughtless with this man he'd wanted since the moment he'd seen him. This man who had tortured him with a smile when he'd wished to hate him, or better yet, to feel nothing for him. Whom Ri had stayed up late with gambling and drinking far too many nights in the Va'alian palace. Ri wanted to enjoy something. Nothing else. Just to enjoy a single stolen moment for himself.

They were fugitives now, or he certainly was. And they would decide where to go tomorrow. But tonight, all that mattered was that he had found Adè. And not just to hand over to someone else. He'd made a choice. And Adè had chosen *him*.

Adè moved between his thighs, reached for him, and Ri said, "Is your wrist not sore?"

"I wasn't in those dungeons long," Adè growled, and he slipped his hand up under Ri's tunic, fingers brushing over Ri's dagger, and then over something else altogether.

Ri hissed, and Adè kissed him and touched him until his back was arched, and the world nearly went black. "Fucking gods," said Ri, digging his fingers into Adè's shoulders.

"Not a god," said Adè. "Just a prince."

Ri choked out a laugh. "Fucking prince."

"That is the idea."

Adè kissed him again, so deeply Ri felt like he was literally breathing him in. And he lost himself completely.

CHAPTER FIFTY-THREE

G ALLIEN HAD NEVER KNOW what real pain felt like.

She was sure of that as the fire burned over her skin. She'd felt the searing heat on her back and known. Of course he had done that. There had been no mistaking what was between the assassin and the prince when Ri had said, "You mean to murder Adè?" His name had sounded like Leylya's when it was on her own lips. She was a fool. Of course Adè would save him.

Of course.

Seconds after the fire had lit her, she pushed it away with flames of her own that had sprung from her skin, coating her in a strange barrier. But everything hurt. Everything burned. Her wrist was weeping blood, and she was burned everywhere. Probably minor; she had gotten her own flames up quickly enough that it only stung. It didn't cripple her. But she hardly had the energy to get up off this floor.

They had won.

They had won, and she would never have her vengeance on the king now. Because they were gone.

Gallien choked on a sob.

And it was in that state that Leylya found her—bleeding and burned and next to death on a dungeon floor.

"Captain!" she'd screamed. Gallien did not think she had ever heard the girl scream like that.

She dropped to her knees. "Oh gods, oh gods."

"I'm all right," Gallien choked. "I'm all right."

"No. You're bleeding out. You're pale. Oh gods. Fuck. Your wrist. Are you burned?"

"It's all—"

"It's not all right," she said, and she screamed, "Nazalie! Nazalie!"

The other girl came running and choked when she saw Gallien. Perhaps the captain looked as bad as she felt. She hated that.

"We're getting you back to the ship," said Leylya. "Our medic survived the slaughter, and she needs to tend to you *now*. Then we'll sail off and—"

"Fine," said Gallien. "Fine," and she began to drift into unconsciousness.

The dragged her up the stairs with considerable effort, and Gallien looked at the ground. Someone else had dragged himself the opposite way. Toward the forest. She could see it as clearly as she could see the sky.

Perhaps this was not over.

No.

As her vision faded in and out, she clung to it.

She would allow herself to be tended. And the instant she had enough blood left in her to move, she would leave her ship under Leylya's command. And she would take a trip to the forest. And claim her vengeance.

CHAPTER FIFTY-FOUR

KASIA WOKE WONDERING IF she was dead.

She decided very quickly that that could not be the case; she hurt too much to be dead.

Everything ranged from sore to excruciating, and her mouth tasted like blood. But she was lying down, and it was not on the flaming earth. She was certain her bones were not broken, and her skin was not charred.

She was on a massive bed, on soft cream sheets that caressed her body and made her not so terribly sorry to have fallen from that tower.

Massive, ornately carved posts jutted up from each corner of the bed, nearly touching the ceiling. The blanket she'd been tucked under felt like a cloud.

The room was bright—creams and silvers and sparkling lights that wrapped across the ceiling. Kasia breathed.

There was wine in a very simple clay goblet by her bed, and she wasn't in much of a place to consider the dangers of drinking it before she did. It slid down her throat—smooth, sweet, and dark, like berries and honey and nightfall.

Where in hells was she? Someone had washed her hair, cleaned her wounds, dressed her in something that wasn't armor.

"Hello?" she said to no one. She slipped out of the bed, wincing when she did, and padded toward the window in a silk shift that fell just to her thighs. It hurt to move, but it didn't hurt as badly as it should have. "Hello?" she said again. "Gods, I wish someone would talk with me."

She didn't hear the door open and shut behind her, and nor did she hear the person approach, as much as she *felt* it.

"I'll talk with you," he said, in that familiar silk and smoke voice.

Kasia stilled, hand on the closed silver curtains. And she turned to see him.

He stood in her doorway in a bright white suit, tall and lithe. Kasia was certain that the lines underneath his clothes were just as hard and crisp and the ones in the fabric. She let her gaze trail too slowly up—to his pale skin, his long, straight, black hair that hung just past his chin, his angular eyes. His jaw was hard, cheekbones high and prominent. He looked Etryan.

"What?" she said. He was…breathtaking. In the way he looked, the way he stood, the power that silently effervesced off him.

"I will talk with you."

"Am I dead?" she said.

"No." He didn't move toward her, didn't back away.

Her heartbeat quickened, pulsing so fast under her skin she feared she would pass out. Just faint right here on his floor. "Am I alive?"

A flicker of something in his eyes, then. Something unreadable. Then it was gone. "Not entirely."

Kasia blinked down at the ivory carpet. "Where am I?"

"You're with me," he said, and Kasia laughed.

"Well. No shit."

Death's lips quirked up. "It only took you thirty seconds in the presence of Death himself to start swearing. There really is no reverence in you."

And Kasia felt something in her relax. She laughed again and took a step toward him.

He stiffened minutely, as though he were holding his breath. Then he breathed normally, relaxed again. All of his movements were so very small. But they took up all the space in the room.

"Did you—save my life?"

Death ran his teeth gently over his bottom lip. "Yes."

"Why?"

His throat bobbed when he swallowed. It was so strange to see him like this—human. So strange to see him at all.

"The world—was not ready to lose you yet, Kasia." He looked straight at her, and his eyes were so intense it almost hurt to look at them. "And I was not prepared to take you."

A chill came over her skin at that. *Take you.* She fought a shudder.

"I won't hurt you," he said, and his voice settled over her gently. Like a touch.

"I know," said Kasia. She hesitated. "Do I stay with you? Or do I...go back?"

"I don't know," he said.

It was the first time she'd ever heard him wonder.

"It's wildly uncomfortable, I'll have you know," he said. "I'm unused to being unsure. But the fact remains. I do not know."

Kasia rubbed her hands over each other, and only then did she remember what she wore. She felt her cheeks heat.

"Why are you blushing?" Death said with a faint smile.

"You can't hear it?"

"Not here. Here, I do not know what you are thinking unless you choose to tell me."

Kasia considered. "I'm wearing...little," she said.

Death laughed, and it was so pleasant she wanted to fall into it.

"I can avert my eyes if you wish it."

"No," said Kasia. "I suppose it doesn't matter. Not in the scope of things."

"There will be consequences," he said. "To...this. I make the rules, Kasia. It was I who cut the gods off from the world when you broke it and I who gave them permission to play the game in the first place."

Kasia's mouth fell open, and she moved to interrupt. Of course she did not—not when Death continued to speak.

"But," he said, "there will be someone to pay, and I don't know what or to whom." His hand jumped to the back of his neck. "I suppose I broke a rule. Which I didn't know was even possible; I've not broken one in all of my existence."

Kasia felt a delicious flare of power trickle up her spine.

"Don't be so satisfied," he said.

"I thought you couldn't read my mind."

"No, but I can read your body."

Kasia blushed again, and this time, Death did not ask why.

He took several steps toward her, languid in every movement. He held out his hand. "For the moment, you are here. With me. And I do not know the way things will go. But you may as well come with me."

Kasia waited, breathed in the air that smelled like ice and wine, felt the truth of everything settle over her skin. She slid her gaze up his arms, his long fingers, the veins that stood out against his forearm where his suit sleeve had fallen back. He looked so human. And she was terrified to touch him.

"As I said," he continued, arm still outstretched, "I won't hurt you."

She met his eyes, and said, "I know."

He smiled and waited and she stepped toward him.

Kasia took Death's hand.

ACKNOWLEDGEMENTS

A quest would not meet its end without a party, and neither would a book. Far be it from me to let my companions on one as long as the Gods and Kings series' journey go unacknowledged.

Thank you, first of all, to my critique partners on this series: Rae Loverde, blessedly brainstorming with me at all (AND I MEAN ALL) hours, when I asked questions like, "Hey, so, like, what do kings do?" and helping me through the thickest plot tangles with astounding brilliance.

Tabitha Martin, who has been my friend since we were only beta-testing versions of the people we became, and who was my first critique partner. Constantly encouraging and happy to brainstorm over Zoom, silently or with loudly interrupting dogs, you have been instrumental in bringing this story, and so many of my other stories, to life.

Colleen Oakes, my witty, magic-imbued compatriot, for making it through a very early version of this book, giving me a beautiful blurb, and being an absolute ride-or-die no matter where in the country the winds take us.

Ephraim Stone, you may not have been my critique partner yet when this book was written, but you are a hell of one now, and were a hell of one when I started the laborious work of editing. Platonic husband. Fantasy extraordinaire. Whiskey and Bridgerton companion, who allows me to fall asleep on a Zoom camera and not make fun of me too much about it later. Sorry I crashed you into a semi-truck.

Ross Birdsall, constant shining light of support, family because blood doesn't matter, and ever-tolerant when I stopped you once again from reading YET ANOTHER version of this book with a, "WAIT THE PLOT CHANGED AGAIN. HOLD ON." You can read this version.

To my agent, Becca Podos. for being witty, sharp, and insightful, utterly baller on edits, and a fearless champion for me, this book, and other things in the world that *matter.* I am so fortunate to get to call you agent and friend.

To my grandparents, for giving me a love of words in the first place.

To my parents, Mom, Dad, and Alan, for always supporting my love of writing, even if it meant being late on rent and calling asking for help AGAIN, and for being guides in my life.

To my siblings. You are the reason I WRITE siblings (though I suppose there aren't any in this book). Chase, Makenzie, Taylor, you mean more to me than you know. That may not be true, as we all mean that to each other. Thank you for loving me, always being down to listen and brainstorm, for loving stories, and for giving me so many to tell. (Even if a bunch of them involve things like Chase and I dying each other's hair without the other's permission, Makenzie running down the street while I ran after her with a sauce-covered pizza knife, and Taylor giving everyone heart attacks when she decided to swing a snake like a lasso over her head at four years old for fun.)

To my cousin Kayla. I think you may own more of my stories than I do. No one has EVER had a more supportive cousin or friend.

To my kids for always understanding when I ranted about magic and people I'd only met in my head, for inspiring me every single day, and for giving me the best reason to wake up in the morning and create a world where stories live.

To Patrick, for not only creating an incredible map from nothing but words on a page and my vague blob-shaped geographical ideas, but for being the love of my life, my constant support, companion in this journey and every journey. I will never forget watching you stay up every night to read this story by lamplight. Sometimes, I think that maybe I wrote you into existence. If I didn't, I'm glad someone did. I cannot wait to marry you.

And to you. Gentle reader. You are the reason that we tell stories. The reason they don't disappear on the wind. Thank you. What a thing you do just by existing.

See you all in the next several hundred pages.

ABOUT THE AUTHOR

Brianna R. Whitrock is a fantasy and romance author whose work has been translated into multiple languages across two continents. She is queer and Jewish and rebelliously lives in the Bible Belt with her fiancé and gaggle of kids and animals and chaos. She loves all things villainous, magical, and strange, and when she's not writing, you can find her listening to horror audiobooks in the pool or sawing away at her fiddle. She also writes as Brianna Shrum, under which she has had many YA titles published along with several shorts and interactive novels.

http://briannashrum.com

Twitter: @briannashrum

TikTok: @hungry4appl3s

Instagram: @bchrumby